MW01697661

On the Wings of a Whisper

Lynnette BONNER

Jn. 12:24

Lynnette

Pacific Lights

On the Wings of a Whisper

Cover design by Lynnette Bonner of Indie Cover Design
images ©

www.istock.com, File: #000009303865Medium
www.istock.com, File: #000010626067XLarge
www.bigstock.com, File: #41454838, Zebras at Sunset
www.bigstock.com, File: #26740817, Old Map of Equatorial Africa

ISBN: 978-1-942982-06-7

Printed in the U.S.A.

On the Wings of a Whisper

Psalm 10

1 Why, Lord, do you stand far off?
Why do you hide yourself in times of trouble?

2 In his arrogance the wicked man hunts down the weak,
who are caught in the schemes he devises.
3 He boasts about the cravings of his heart;
he blesses the greedy and reviles the LORD.
4 In his pride the wicked man does not seek him;
in all his thoughts there is no room for God.
5 His ways are always prosperous;
your laws are rejected by him;
he sneers at all his enemies.
6 He says to himself, "Nothing will ever shake me."
He swears, "No one will ever do me harm."

7 His mouth is full of lies and threats;
trouble and evil are under his tongue.
8 He lies in wait near the villages;
from ambush he murders the innocent.
His eyes watch in secret for his victims;
9 like a lion in cover he lies in wait.
He lies in wait to catch the helpless;
he catches the helpless and drags them off in his net.
10 His victims are crushed, they collapse;
they fall under his strength.
11 He says to himself, "God will never notice;
he covers his face and never sees."

12 Arise, Lord! Lift up your hand, O God.
Do not forget the helpless.
13 Why does the wicked man revile God?
Why does he say to himself,
"He won't call me to account"?
14 But you, God, see the trouble of the afflicted;
you consider their grief and take it in hand.
The victims commit themselves to you;
you are the helper of the fatherless.
15 Break the arm of the wicked man;
call the evildoer to account for his wickedness
that would not otherwise be found out.

16 The Lord is King for ever and ever;
the nations will perish from his land.
17 You, LORD, hear the desire of the afflicted;
you encourage them, and you listen to their cry,
18 defending the fatherless and the oppressed,
so that mere earthly mortals
will never again strike terror.

Chapter 1

On the Wings of a Whisper

Stone Town, Zanzibar
March 1866

Captain Trent Dawson tucked his tricorn beneath his arm and ducked his head as he entered the stifling heat and noise of Azim's Ale House.

He'd sailed into port only this morning. What could the good English commodore Llewellyn Cornwall want with him?

He allowed a moment for his eyes to adjust to the dim interior and then began to search the faces of those gathered. Removing his riding gloves one finger at a time, he methodically scanned each table. He had begun to think Llewellyn had not yet arrived, when he spotted him at a cramped little table in the far corner.

The scent of stale beer, frying chapatis, and spicy samosas mingled with the sickly sweet spirals of smoke wafting from the incense that was burning before the potbellied god he passed as he crossed the room. "Is there a darker or danker pub on all the island?" He lifted one corner of his mouth in greeting.

Llewellyn grimaced. "Hardly." He raised a glass half filled with amber liquid. "But drink enough of whatever this is, and the place starts to look downright cheery."

Trent eased himself onto the chair across from his friend and waved away the drink an Arab girl, with invitation in her kohl-darkened eyes, tried to place in front of him. "What can I do for you, Lew?"

A thin smile tugged at Lew's lips. "Straight to the point, is it? You colonials are always dashing about in such haste."

Folding his arms, Trent waited, knowing that pushing for the information wouldn't extract it from the commodore a moment before he was ready to reveal it.

Lew rolled the base of his glass around on the table, his scrutiny calculated. Finally he spoke. "I've an employment opportunity to discuss."

Trent's eyes dropped closed. "I just got into port after six months at sea. I'd something more along the lines of rest and relaxation in mind."

Lew only looked at him blandly. "This, dear fellow, is an opportunity to do something about an issue that lies close to your heart."

Trent sat a little straighter. "Smuggling? Slaves." The last word was not a question but a statement of confident realization. Commodore Llewellyn Cornwall had been tasked with putting an end to the illegal smuggling of slaves across the Indian Ocean.

Llewellyn leaned across the table to speak in an urgent whisper. "I have authority from Her Majesty herself to hire you for six months of your time. And a bonus if we complete the job to her satisfaction." He tugged a paper from his pocket, consulted it, and then slid it across the table with one blunt finger.

Trent blinked at the figure written there. The amount was more than he made in three years of hard sailing. It would allow him to purchase the first of his father's fleet. Still, why would Lew be coming to him for help with this? He voiced the question. "So why do you need my help? You have the whole British navy at your disposal."

Lew blew like a horse. "We are only allowed to stop ships which are not flying the Sultan's flag. I've been following an Arab named Ali Khalifa."

"Commodore of Harcourt Shipping?"

Lew nodded but then brushed the man's name aside with a swipe of his hand. "He's just a trained dog. I want the man at the top."

"Who?"

"I wish I knew." Lew slurped rather unsteadily from his glass. "I know you've received an invitation to the Harcourts' Annual Ball, Friday next. Ali Khalifa will also be there. I've noticed him in several rather"—he rolled a hand through the air, searching for the right term—"clandestine meetings with the Harcourt heir, Brayden."

Trent's eyebrow winged upward at that. Brayden Harcourt was young. A score, at best. But his father owned one of the most successful indigo plantations on the island. And to say they lacked for naught would be an understatement.

Would young Harcourt risk it all to smuggle slaves? Perhaps he was simply naïve and unaware of Khalifa's actions? Trent rubbed his upper lip slowly. No. Brayden was a lot of things, but naïve and unaware were not among them.

Could Lew be mistaken about Khalifa? He studied the man, who lifted an unsteady finger and gestured for a refill of his drink. He hadn't been the same since he'd lost his wife last year. But he'd always been solid. And he never bandied names about unless he could back up his accusations.

Trent had no doubt that if Lew was certain enough to offer Khalifa's name, he had some fairly compelling evidence against the man. "Why do you suspect Khalifa of smuggling?"

Lew gave the serving girl a coin, picked up his refilled glass, and then met Trent's gaze with a rheumy one of his own. "Khalifa supposedly sails to England twice a year with Harcourt indigo. However, not long ago I was sailing south from the coast of India when on the horizon, I saw a ship I swear was Khalifa's *Indigo Waves*—and at a time he is sworn to have been in England! They unfurled every sheet and lost us in the chase, so I never came close enough for confirmation. But…" He shrugged and took a noisy slurp. "Proof is what I seek." Lew pinned him with a look. "Khalifa is set to make a trading run to the Interior. To the shores of Lake Nyasa, he says."

Trent rubbed his neck. "I can't just follow him. You know how quickly word spreads of white traders in that region. He'd know I was on his trail, and we'd never get anything on him."

Lew held up a palm. "That's the beauty of it! I believe you know a Dr. Ryan Hunter?"

"Yes. The man has been after me for months to guide him into the Interior…" Understanding dawned, and he let the words trail away.

A touch of humor leapt into Lew's expression, and he nodded. "Just so. I assured Her Majesty of your qualifications for this very reason! Agree to help the good doctor. And"—a full-out smile lifted his lips—"maybe you'll even get to spend some time with one of his pretty daughters before you leave, eh? I hear tell Hunter's youngest, Miss RyAnne, has been seen about with Brayden Harcourt. Perhaps she will be able to offer some information on the man."

RyAnne Hunter seen with Harcourt?

Trent didn't dare respond to that. Truth be told, the last thing he wanted was to give the doctor the impression that he was interested in one of his daughters. RyAnne in particular was nothing but trouble—or at least she had been the last time he was in port—but the thought of her and Harcourt…well, that simply didn't sit right.

He held out a hand to his friend. "I'll see what I can find out for you."

Stone Town, Zanzibar
The Day of the Ball

RyAnne Hunter pushed her worries about the evening ahead from her mind and tried not to grimace, even as the crowd around her cheered with a wild frenzy for their favorite of the two roosters pecking, flapping, and gouging each other with long talons. Dust and feathers flew as the red cock momentarily pinned the black.

She winced. She'd never seen the joy in watching two of God's creatures, miserable mean fowl though they might be, fight to the death. In fact, she felt rather a great amount of sympathy for the poor little beasts.

But this was where Halamme had insisted they come.

Beside her, Princess Halamme, twelfth daughter of Sultan Majid's brother Bargash, chatted animatedly with Valah, her half sister. Valah was the host of this evening's entertainment. The dusty courtyard, boxed in by the two-story stone walls of Valah's quarters, was too small for the throng of people currently clustered around the cockfight, and the late-afternoon sun beat down mercilessly, radiating off every surface in the oven full of wriggling humanity. RyAnne flipped open her fan and flapped it aggressively, more to ward off the stench of the close-packed bodies than for the tepid air flow.

The man in front of her leapt back, tromping on her foot, and RyAnne squeaked in pain.

"You there! Watch yourself!" Halamme's eunuch, Ahmed, a hulking giant with a scimitar slung at his side, stepped forward and shoved the man back into the fray, then turned and scanned RyAnne with concern, his dark skin glistening with sweat. "*Umzima*?"

RyAnne smiled her thanks. "I'm fine, Ahmed. Thank you."

Ahmed had just cleared a path between her and the cocks, and she saw her chance. On the pretense of moving her parasol from one shoulder to the other, she swung it wide and knocked over one section of the portable fence penning the poor creatures in.

A loud outcry arose, and several men rushed to right the wood and wire section.

So much for freeing the poor little things. The roosters were once more caged in with only each other and their disproportionate desire to destroy.

Several of Valah's guests turned to glare at her.

Murmuring an apology for her clumsiness, she returned to her pretended interest in the fight. That's when her gaze settled on the man across the way. Her fan stilled of its own accord as her heart stuttered in her chest.

Arms folded, feet planted wide, and his gray-green gaze fixed directly on her, he stood like a pillar, seemingly unaffected by the milling mass surging and bumping around him. A glint of humor in his eyes, and the uptick of one corner of his mouth, said he hadn't been fooled by her little charade. He looked quite out of place dressed in ballroom finery amidst the crowd full of people wearing hijabs, kufis, and kangas. Yet despite his burgundy brocade waistcoat, lace cravat, and black long-tailed coat, not a drop of sweat glistened on his forehead. His eyes narrowed, and he dipped his chin, tipping his head to indicate he would meet her by the tall palm near the fountain to her left. He began to shoulder his way through the throng.

The son of an American merchantman who had sailed frequently to Zanzibar since RyAnne was a girl, Captain Trent Dawson was most recently of his ship, *The Wasp*. And he was part of the reason so much weighed on her right now. If he hadn't agreed to guide Papa into the interior of the African continent, her world wouldn't be falling apart on the morrow!

Yet his sudden desire to rendezvous by the tall palm in all certainty had nothing to do with the fact that his ship was leaving port on the morning's tide. Her eyes narrowed.

Longtime family friend and constant thorn in her side, he'd no doubt been sent here by Mother to fetch her home. Like a servant sent after a straying dog.

Earlier this week, Mother had promised Lady Harcourt that RyAnne would play her violin at the Harcourts' Annual Ball this evening. Mother was surely beside herself that RyAnne had snuck away just after luncheon.

Well, Captain Dawson would just have to go back to Mother empty handed tonight. She must attend the ball, because tonight would be her last opportunity to cajole Papa into staying on island. However, she didn't plan to arrive until well after the time she was expected to entertain the masses. Playing her music in front of a crowd had always terrified her. It was like offering her heart on a platter to virtual strangers—much too vulnerable.

Brayden Harcourt was the only one she'd ever played for without terror. Brayden would undoubtedly be at the ball hosted by his parents. She'd been looking forward to seeing her childhood friend again. Maybe if she concentrated solely on him, it wouldn't be so horrendous to play. How long had it been since they'd last spoken? Six months, at the least. So maybe… *No.* She gave herself a little shake. She could catch Brayden late into the ball and coax him into the garden for a moonlit stroll.

But for the time being, she needed to keep herself hidden. She glanced around. How to make her escape from Captain Dawson—that was the question. Panic nipped at her pulse.

At that moment the black-and-white rooster collapsed to the ground, and a great shout of exultation rose from those who had just won bets. Captain Dawson's pinched-lip expression disappeared behind the bobbing white turban of a wizened Arab with a monkey on his shoulder.

Seizing the moment without delay, RyAnne snapped her parasol shut and tucked it under one arm. Nothing like a parasol sailing above everyone's heads to give away her position.

"Halamme, dear." RyAnne laid one gloved hand on her friend's arm. "I've had quite enough of blood and feathers for one evening. But we really ought to do this again sometime." She air-kissed the space next to each of Halamme's cheeks.

Halamme chuckled and adjusted her veil as her gaze settled on something over RyAnne's shoulder. "Best hurry. Your mother's leopard prowls this way."

RyAnne smirked. Wouldn't Captain Dawson be thrilled to know the girls thought of him as Mother's pet!

Valah followed Halamme's gaze. "That one? Oh, but he's so handsome! That is a cat I wouldn't mind cuddling with!" She tittered behind the gauzy blue silk that hid all but her dark kohl-lined eyes from view.

RyAnne grimaced, brushing past them with a glance over her shoulder. "That leopard is all beautiful pelt and snapping jaws, dear ones. Inside, he's nothing but sour sentiments and harsh reprimands. Trust me, that cat has no purr."

Captain Dawson, apparently having noticed she wasn't heading for the palm, worked his way purposefully toward her, elbowing celebrants aside.

"Stall him for me if you can," she pleaded. Ducking down, she pushed and shoved her way through the crowd, only caring that it was in the opposite direction from him and that she knew Valah had a side exit to an alleyway that led to Malindi Street. Mother's friends would just have to conquer their disappointment at not getting to hear her play.

"Next time bring your brother!" Valah called after her, and RyAnne rolled her eyes as she dodged between two turbaned men haggling over a handful of coins. A week ago RyAnne, along with her mother and father, and siblings, Jasmine and Rory, had made the trip into town from their indigo plantation on the other side of the island. RyAnne had been doing her level best to keep Rory *away* from Valah ever since.

A breezeway opened to her right, and she hurried into it. The arched door to the alley lay just ahead. She lifted her skirts and ran. The captain would not be far behind, for she knew he would simply brush by the princesses no matter their delay tactics, and there was nowhere to hide here. All she had to do was make it to the road outside the walls, and hopefully she'd be able to escape him in the jostle of rickshaws, wagons, and market vendors.

She laid one hand on the doorknob and tossed another glance behind her.

Captain Dawson wasn't rushing after her down the cobbled breezeway. Relief eased the tension in her shoulders, and she waited a moment, watching. After several seconds, he still hadn't darted around the corner in hot pursuit. Her brows rose in surprise. Maybe the princesses had been able to distract him after all.

RyAnne smiled and twisted the handle. "Maybe," she murmured as she faced forward and yanked open the door, "the man is going SOFT!" The last word became a shriek as she crashed into an immovable wall of solid flesh.

"Or maybe"—Captain Dawson wrapped firm hands around her upper arms, the only thing that kept her from falling backward in surprise—"he's developed the astute ability to outthink you."

Despite the calmness in his tone, his breaths came in rapid puffs. The dratted man had gone through the front door and beat her to the alley!

RyAnne stamped one foot, feeling the hard rod of her parasol bruising the inside of her arm. "Unhand me at once!"

The captain cocked his head and only looked amused. "I wouldn't need to manhandle you at all if you would just obey your mother like a devout daughter should. But then…" He leaned in, all amusement hardening into a mask of seriousness as his gaze drilled into her severely. "You've never had a problem with being devout, now have you?"

She would have slapped him if she could have moved her arms!

What did he know of the nightmare that was her life? Of a sister and brother who could do no wrong in anyone's sight? Of a mother who despised her because she wasn't her own flesh, yet dared not allow anyone, let alone her society friends, know?

Not even Captain Trent Dawson knew *that* little Hunter secret.

But she knew him well enough to know that anger and demands would get her nowhere. So after a fortifying breath, she changed her tactic and softened her stance.

"C-couldn't you pretend you didn't find me? Just this once?" Sidling a step closer and tipping her head to one side, she angled him a look that surely would beguile him to her plight.

She was so close she could feel the warmth of his breath wafting across her forehead, see the flecks of green granite in his gray eyes. A small white scar puckered his jawline, preventing the day's worth of stubble shadowing his face from growing there. His lips were pressed into thin aggravation, and her fingers itched to smooth the grooves of irritation from them.

She swallowed and fisted her hand, reminding herself this was just a ruse as she forced words through her tight throat. "Halamme has invited me to her quarters tonight to celebrate her brother's return from Oman. And Mother's going to force me to play in front of the entire crowd at the ball." An involuntary shudder quaked through her even as she laid her fan gently against one muscular shoulder and pushed her lips into a soft pout, blinking up at him. "You know how much I hate doing that."

The captain's throat worked, and his eyebrows rose slightly. His mouth dropped open. His focus shifted from her eyes, to her hair, to her lips. One hand loosed her arm and slid behind her waist as he tilted a little closer. His hungry scrutiny sent a tremor through her, eliciting the errant thought that she might have wandered a little farther into the leopard's lair than safety prescribed.

Yet satisfaction squeezed her heart. Her wile was working! She angled her face up and clasped her hands behind his neck, waiting for the kiss he'd be giving her any moment.

He eased closer, his face only a hand-breadth away, and then he stilled and his eyes hardened.

Confusion plucked at her brow.

A bark of laughter escaped him, and once more he had her in a firm grip. He spoke softly, his lips hovering just above hers. "Don't believe for a moment that all men are so easy, Miss Hunter. Save your pretty pout and big green eyes for the likes of Brayden Harcourt. Now"—he took a step back and assessed her with the arch of one eyebrow—"are you coming willingly? Or should I throw you over my shoulder like a sack of cloves?"

Anger clenched her teeth so tight she was barely able to squeeze out, "You wouldn't dare!"

He snorted and leaned his shoulder toward her, set to plant it into her midriff.

"Oh!" She leapt back and smacked his head with her fan. "You beastly scoundrel! I'll come!"

Straightening, he folded his arms with a self-satisfied smile. "Good. I have a feeling you'd be some heavier than a sack of cloves. I wasn't looking forward to packing you all the way across town. The day is warm enough without adding such strain to it."

The audacity of the man knew no bounds!

Trent Dawson resisted a chuckle as Miss Hunter lifted her nose into the air and thrust her parasol open. He held out his arm, and she slipped her gloved fingers into the crook with narrowed green eyes and a short huff of impatience. Pity the man Ryan Hunter entrapped with this little lioness. She was bound to cause a husband nothing but trouble.

Trent had only been back on island two weeks, and this was already the fourth time Anne Hunter had summoned him to request he track down her daughter "just once more."

Lucky for him, they'd loaded the last of Hunter's supplies onto *The Wasp* earlier this afternoon. He and her father would be leaving for the African continent in the morning, and then Mrs. Hunter would have to find another lackey to keep track of her troublesome daughter. With any luck, the next time he met Miss RyAnne Hunter, some man would have her firmly in hand.

He gritted his teeth and refused to analyze the tightening in his chest that thought brought about. He had too much riding on this trip to the Interior to take time for a dalliance right now. *Still…* He stifled a grin at the thought of her little charade moments earlier. *Only the intractable Miss Hunter.* He should have kissed her and *then* made her go back home. At the thought, the grin broke free to tug at the corner of his mouth.

He settled one hand over hers where it rested against his arm, for all appearances enjoying a simple afternoon stroll with Dr. Ryan Hunter's pretty youngest daughter. In reality, he wanted to be able to grasp her quickly if she tried to dart down some narrow alley in the middle of Stone Town.

Stepping around a slave polishing the brass-work on an elaborately spiked door, he tried to shake off the claustrophobia being in Stone Town always brought on. Streets so narrow he could easily stretch out his arms and touch the buildings on either side, felt even more constricting due to the towering arches of bronze-studded doors and the stone balconies looming overhead. Give him open seas with the snapping of sails and the wind in his face any day over these cheek-by-jowl conditions. Only a few more streets and he'd be able to breathe again when they stepped into the more open courtyard of the doctor's town residence.

That didn't lessen the feel of his collar cutting off all breath. He needed a distraction. "You'll be happy to learn that your father's supplies have all been loaded."

She huffed. "Off to the Continent to find your fortune in ivory, are you?"

Trent gritted his teeth. It had seemed like as good a cover as any for the reason he'd so suddenly agreed to guide Dr. Hunter to the location in the Interior where the man planned to build a mission station. But he didn't like the way the question rolled off Miss Hunter's tongue like an accusation.

Some of the wind seemed to leave her sails. "When will you be heading off then?"

"First thing in the morning."

Her hand tensed beneath his. "So it is final? Then tonight really is the last—"

She broke off with a small sound in her throat, but when he glanced down, she seemed to have shuttered her emotions. Whatever she'd been feeling was hidden beneath a stoic facade.

"How long does Papa plan to be gone this time?" She nibbled the inside of her lower lip, and her gaze flickered to his. Was that a twinge of sadness he noted? Could the ever-troublesome, flighty, living-only-for-herself Miss Hunter actually know what her father's real plan was?

He swallowed and focused on the cobblestones of the narrow street ahead. "He packed provisions for six months."

"I see."

Her tone was so plaintive he could almost feel sorry for her if he hadn't spent the majority of the last couple weeks fetching her from one sector of the city or another—the price he paid for being easily accessible at the guesthouse next door to her home while he was in port. Today the cockfight. Yesterday he'd found her without a chaperone in the slave market, of all places, her father's medical bag clutched firmly in one hand. Truth be told, he'd leave her to her own devices if he didn't fear for her safety. The girl had no sense or notion of the danger she put herself in when she wandered the island alone.

As they stepped from the mouth of the narrow street and the doctor's residence stood ahead across a small lawn, he pulled in a long breath of relief.

The spongy grass beneath his boots was a welcome contrast to the hard stones of the cobbled streets. He opened her front door and ushered her inside.

Mrs. Anne Hunter glided into the front hall. Her lips

pinched into a disapproving glower as she raked her daughter from head to toe. "Gather your things. The doctor has engaged Captain Dawson to escort us to the Harcourts' estate since he and Rory have already hastened there with hopes to speak with Dr. Livingstone. Jasmine and I are ready to go. Your gallivanting has made us dreadfully late."

RyAnne's hand slid off his arm, and her shoulders drooped as she slowly took the stairs to her room without a word of reply. The only time the fight drained out of her was in the face of her mother's scorn. Why the woman couldn't see the damage she was inflicting, he didn't know, but it wasn't his place to comment. He only said, "I'll make sure your driver has readied the carriage and have it waiting out front."

Anne Hunter gave him a genuine smile. "We're most indebted to you, Captain Dawson, for fetching her back and for escorting us over."

Sketching a bow, he managed, "Think nothing of it," then made his escape.

Chapter 2
On the Wings of a Whisper

Dressing quickly with the help of her maid's deft fingers, RyAnne stopped in front of the mirror to clasp an amethyst necklace around her throat. Tiny lavender earrings of the same precious stone graced her ears. As she eyed her complexion, a small smile traced her mouth. Brayden was sure to like what he saw this evening, even if the charms she'd aimed at Captain Dawson had all the effect of a dried pea against a Zulu shield.

Turning her head to the side, she patted the upsweep of dark hair at the back of her neck, making sure every curl was in place. Ringlets hung down by her ears and bobbed up and down with every shake of her head. Her sister, Jasmine, had often coveted RyAnne's mass of curls. But as RyAnne tucked several more curls into place, she couldn't help but wish she had her sister's lovely straight locks that always seemed to fall into place so easily.

Her fitted bodice, a *V* of creamy lace, ran from her neckline down to a point just below her waist. Lace of the same color graced the hem of her sleeves, draping softly over the back of her hands. The full pale-pink silk skirt and puffed sleeves accentuated her small waist. The hem of the skirt was pulled up in several scallops, revealing lace of the same creamy color as the bodice. Sarah bent and straightened the cream bows that graced the points between each scallop.

She loved this dress. It was one of her favorites, but not even the joy of such beauty could erase her dread of the night ahead. The performance on her violin. The talk where she would once again beg Papa to stay home and he would pat her on the shoulder like she was a child of six who had no idea why he was hieing off to the Continent. Her teeth pressed together so hard her jaw ached. She must not fail to convince him this time. She *would not* fail.

With a sigh of resignation, RyAnne shrugged her shoulders,

squinting at the image in the mirror. There was no need to pinch color into her cheeks, as they were flushed. Her eyes looked rather glassy, but she hoped in the bustle of the ballroom no one would notice. She snagged a wrap from the bureau to ward of the chill that suddenly soaked through her, praying the chill and flush weren't what she feared they were.

She turned and smiled fondly at her maid, Sarah, who arched one brow and nodded in the direction of the violin case sitting in the corner.

RyAnne's stomach knotted. Maybe Mother wouldn't notice if… She shook her head. "I'll just leave it here this time."

The maid gave a despairing sigh but nodded her head slightly, reaching out a hand to adjust the lace at the neckline of RyAnne's dress and flick imaginary lint from the puffed sleeves. RyAnne gave her a smile of thanks, and then picking up her full skirt, made her way downstairs to the waiting carriage, her petticoats rustling with each step.

But the moment she stepped onto the curved drive with only her parasol and reticule, Mother let out an exasperated sigh.

"I declare, child, you haven't the brains the good Lord gave a centipede. Where is your violin? I promised the Harcourts you'd play at least two numbers this evening."

From his position on the seat across from Mother and Jasmine, Captain Dawson shifted uneasily, but his gaze remained fixed on the floorboards at his feet.

RyAnne hated the fact that even after all these years Mother still had the power to hurt her, even if it was only to humiliate her in front of others. She chewed the inside of her lip, debating the merits of telling Mother she had no intention of playing before everyone at the Harcourts' ball. But one more glance at Captain Dawson, who was now watching her with a touch of something indefinable in his expression, and the fight suddenly drained out of her.

Resigned, she turned back to fetch her instrument. Sarah met her just inside the door and held out the case with an arch of her brows. RyAnne took it without a word, then returned to the carriage and allowed Captain Dawson to help her up to the seat next to him.

The coachman clucked to the horses, and with a gentle lurch they were off.

The moment the coach pulled to a stop under the portico at the Harcourts' mansion, Mother's attention turned to socializing, and RyAnne went looking for Papa. But between the scurry of attendees and servants, the people who kept impinging on her search with their enthusiastic greetings, and the sheer size of the Harcourt mansion, she couldn't seem to find him. Finally the stifling heat made her give up and escape into the back garden.

The night was young, yet she fretted. What would she do if she couldn't convince Papa to stay? Papa's health and her happiness demanded that she not fail her self-appointed task. For a moment she gave up worrying to enjoy the beauty of the mansion's thickly walled gardens.

The sun had made its daily descent into the ocean, but a warm breeze still blew gently. She let the silk shawl slide off her shoulders but kept it wrapped around her. Gathering the corners in front of her, she let the fringe run through her fingers as she sauntered through the fragrant foliage, studying the diamond-bright stars against the inky velvet sky. The rhythmic song of the cicadas filled the night air, and the gentle lapping of the ocean waves just outside the plantation walls soothed her frayed nerves.

Off to her left the golden glow of soft light poured from the windows of the big plantation house and reflected on the swaying leaves of gardenia bushes, causing them to stand out in stark contrast to the black earth below. The fragrance from the flowers was strong and heady in the cool evening air, and RyAnne drew in a deep breath of the scent. Reaching one hand to rub the muscles of her shoulders, she tried to relax as she walked, rolling her head from side to side.

Captain Dawson had said Papa planned to be gone for six

months… She swallowed. In his condition he would be lucky to last a month, much less six! He thought she didn't know…but she hadn't trained with him for so many years and not learned a thing or two.

She glanced toward the house. Behind the rounded columns of the back portico, the gilded light accentuated the large ballroom windows. Papa was in there somewhere, right now. Conversing with everyone as though he hadn't a care in the world. And tomorrow, unless she could yet change his mind, he would sail away to the heart of the African continent, where he would die.

She would never see him again, and they were spending their last hours separated by social frivolity. But the Hunters were nothing if not carefully attuned to how they were viewed by society.

On the small island of Zanzibar, there were not many social occasions. So when the opportunity arose for a social gathering, anyone from near or far earnestly made the effort to be present. Tonight's ball would overflow with the upper crust of the island and anyone wishing to make a name for himself. Mother and Papa wouldn't have missed the occasion for the world.

The scent of honeysuckle drew her attention and brought with it a memory, and the reluctant admission that, despite her frustration with the festivities, she was looking forward to seeing one certain young plantation heir herself.

A slight smile flitted across her face. The last time she had walked in this garden, Brayden had dropped to one knee for his annual proposal, and RyAnne had, again, said no, when suddenly the sky had let go buckets of torrential rain. Laughing, they had raced for the shelter of the patio, hand in hand.

RyAnne would be the first to admit that she and Brayden didn't have what most would call a conventional relationship. Friends since before both could remember, they shared an easy camaraderie. He had been fifteen, she fourteen, the first time he had told her he was going to marry her. She had arched a slender brow and haughtily told him that perhaps she wouldn't have him.

He had responded confidently that she would be begging him to become her husband before they were wed. He had not missed an opportunity to propose since.

Anticipation at seeing him again lifted the corners of her mouth. It had been months. Would their relationship still be the same? Would it be as easy to talk to him as always?

As she walked past a flaming torch set in a green metal sconce next to the garden path, she rubbed at the slight chill along her arms. A wooden framed trellis, buried underneath the abundant fuchsia blossoms of a bougainvillea vine, arched over the path. Shadows thrown by the flames danced over the blooms, causing their color to darken and brighten at the whim of the breeze wafting over the wall. The zephyr brought with it the unpleasant smell of the town of Zanzibar and increased her chill.

She pulled the shawl back up over her shoulders and clenched her eyes in dread. She was running a fever—again. They always came on so suddenly. She'd felt fine earlier this afternoon at the cockfight. Perhaps her encounter with Captain Dawson had brought it on. She smirked…then sighed, her wandering thoughts coming full circle.

Papa was leaving for the Continent tomorrow, and she had to stay well long enough to stop him.

If I let him go, I'll never…

The thought of never seeing Papa's loving face again was simply unbearable. Not to mention, she wouldn't be able to stand Mother—not even for the claimed six months—without Papa's softening influence. Papa simply had to stay here, but she'd tried to talk him out of the trip many times already, and he'd always been adamant.

She pushed aside what she knew of his condition and focused instead on her plan. She would give one last valiant effort at convincing him. But if that failed, what then? She considered, and tossed aside, several options. There was nothing for it but to make him see reason. She took her resolve firmly in hand. She was going to find Papa and convince him how dangerous and downright selfish it was of him to run off to the Continent at a time like this.

Around a corner in the garden path, she saw a wooden bench surrounded by several large bushes. Her renewed resolve sapped some of her strength, and the fragrant blossoms of an orange tree dripped from overhead, whispering a breezy invitation to sit awhile. She sank down with a sigh and, leaning her head back, closed her fevered eyes. Folding her arms in front of her, she sat still, listening to the evening sounds around her.

She had been there only a few moments when she heard voices, and her eyes opened with a start. They were coming from somewhere toward the back of the garden, near the wall that separated the house from the beach beyond.

She sat up, hunched her shoulders against her shivering, and strained to hear. Something in the conversation arrested her attention. It was not any word she had heard, because from this distance she could not make out exactly *what* was being said, but it was the tone in which the words were spoken. There was a sense of urgency to them, even perhaps anger.

Then suddenly the wind stilled. The hushed conversation came to RyAnne as clearly as if she had been one of the participants.

"...could ruin everything." A man's agitated growl.

"I tell you, nothing will go wrong as long as you keep your head about you," said a second voice, more commanding than the first.

"He is heading right to the same region! I heard them talking in there!" The rasped words sounded like a yell in the silence of the garden.

"Stop worrying. The Continent is a vast place. You will not run into him, and even if you do, you will say that you are there to trade. A perfectly legitimate business."

"So *you* say. It will not be *your* neck on the line if *I* am the one to get caught."

"It had better *not* be." The second person's tone had turned decidedly menacing. "You have to return here anyway. If someone questions or follows you, we will just sell them all here. There is nothing illegal in that. We won't get the best price, but we may have to…"

The wind came up again, and RyAnne could hear no more of the conversation, but she suddenly didn't feel so at ease in the garden. Goose bumps pebbled her arms and not because of the fever. She rose quickly, tossed a glance toward the far wall, and then made her way back in the direction she had come, forgetting for the moment anything but getting back inside. As she hurried along the garden path, the shadows were no longer friendly. The night sounds were no longer soothing but instead caused tremors to race up her spine.

However, it wasn't until she realized she was running from two people she'd probably known all her life that she gave a little gasp. The import of the thought slowed her steps as it made its way into her fever-numbed brain. She halted at the base of the steps leading up to the long portico that stretched the length of the Harcourts' ballroom. She glanced over her shoulder into the darkness.

Indeed, almost all attending the ball tonight were people RyAnne had known since she was just a child. The island of Zanzibar was like a small town. Everyone knew everyone else's business. So who could possibly have been talking in the garden? And what was it that they didn't want someone to know about? *And* who was that someone the first man in the conversation so dreaded meeting on the Continent?

Her curiosity got the better of her. She turned and took a step back down the path, intending to discover who was out there. Behind her one of the French doors banged open. "There you are! RyAnne, Mother is looking franti—"

RyAnne squeaked and spun around, the blood draining from her head in a knee-weakening rush. "Jasmine!"

"Whatever is the matter?" Jasmine eyed her questioningly.

RyAnne pressed one hand to her chest as if by so doing she could calm the pounding of her heart.

Mother bustled up behind Jasmine. "RyAnne! I've been looking everywhere for you! You're supposed to be playing in less than five minutes, and you don't even have your violin in hand. Where is it?"

"I-I'm sorry, Mother. I went for a walk in the garden and lost track of the time. I'll only be a min—"

"See to it then." Mother cut her off with an impatient dismissal of her hand as she disappeared back inside.

Jasmine tossed her a sympathetic glance before following Mother into the flurry of the ballroom.

RyAnne wrapped her arms around herself and dropped her head back. A falling star blazed across the inky blackness and faded to nothing at the edge of the horizon. Would that she could disappear as easily.

"You'll do fine."

She spun toward the voice.

Captain Dawson stood in the shadows between the two farthest windows, one shoulder resting against the plaster of the house, arms folded over his chest. "I've heard none better than you on a fiddle, and I've traveled a fair bit these past years."

She swallowed away her pleasure at the compliment and lifted her chin. "It's a violin." She cringed inwardly. The statement had emerged with much more condescension than she'd intended.

The corner of his mouth ticked up, but he nodded acquiescence to her correction and sauntered toward her. "Where is your favorite place to play?" He stopped at her side and turned his attention to the night sky.

"I don't play often when we are at our Stone Town residence. But back home at our plantation I go out into the indigo fields." Why was she even engaging in conversation with this boor after the way he'd treated her earlier?

He moved so they stood face to face and looked down at her. "When you are playing tonight then, close your eyes and imagine yourself there."

She eyed him quizzically.

"Imagine fields awash in blue blooms. The scent of the indigo swirling all around you. The brush of the wind against your face." He stroked her cheek with the back of one finger, as softly as the caress of a butterfly wing.

Her eyes widened, and she held her breath. Like a zebra colt in sunshine, her heart seemed to kick up its heels. Where had this tender side of the man been hiding all the years she'd known him?

As though the gesture had surprised him, he stepped back and thrust his fists into the pits of his arms, returning his attention once more to the spangle of stars overhead.

Imagine she was elsewhere? Why had she never thought of that? Still… She huffed. "The saying of such is a great deal easier than the undertaking."

He dropped his chin, indicating his disagreement, but he only said, "Maybe so." He shrugged then, tilting her a cocksure smirk, a glint of mischief in his eyes. "The only solution in that case, I suppose, is for you to put as much effort into wooing the crowd as you did into seducing me this afternoon."

"Seduce—" Her jaw dropped. "Of all the—" With an unladylike growl, she hoisted her skirts and stormed away from the man, his laughter nipping at her heels.

Suppressing a grin, Trent followed at a safe distance, imagining a trail of smoke and sparks wafting in her wake.

Her anger carried her straight to her case, and she clenched her jaw as she swiped dark curls away from her face, tucked the violin beneath her chin, and tested the tuning. Two slight adjustments and she was apparently ready.

The bandmaster, Bishop Tozer, gestured her over even as he continued to direct the current song. Tozer motioned her into a seat at the front of the musicians.

Her green eyes were as wide as the bush baby that had howled in the tree outside Trent's room the night before when he'd surprised it with the lantern light. And she looked just as ready to flee.

Her mother and sister had settled in amidst the local ladies,

Mrs. Hunter pretending she had no idea RyAnne was about to perform. Pretty soon she would titter and fan herself and then revel in the compliments her friends would give her over RyAnne's performance. Like the proud owner of a performing monkey.

He drew a slow, steady breath. Was it any wonder the girl was constantly running off in rebellion?

He skimmed the rest of the room, reminding himself he was not here because of Miss Hunter. With interest, he took in Ali Khalifa speaking solemnly to Ryan Hunter across the room. Frustration coursed through him. He'd been following Khalifa in the garden earlier, but when he'd noticed Miss Hunter once again alone with no idea that danger lurked nearby, he'd been forced to stay close to assure her safety. Who had the man been meeting? And why had they needed to meet in the dark seclusion of the garden?

A glint of light at the front of the room drew his attention. Brayden Harcourt stepped through the front door and shook hands with several near him, but his gaze caught on Miss Hunter and stuck fast, like a ship on a sandbar. Trent's eyes narrowed. He'd seen the man the evening before at Azim's Ale House, and the woman by his side had not merely been serving him drinks, and yet now he wasn't even trying to disguise his interest in RyAnne.

She sat quietly waiting for the current song to end, but the moment she noticed Harcourt, the smallest hint of a smile graced her lips. Harcourt nodded at her with a bold wink. Her face flushed and she fidgeted, studying the folds of her skirts.

Trent clasped his hands behind him and shifted slightly. The girl once again toyed with fire. Harcourt was not—

Confound it! He rubbed the back of his neck. What concern was it of his who she fancied? He'd be gone on the morrow anyhow, most likely never to see the troublesome lass again, thanks be to God.

The ballroom began to quiet now, as those assembled realized Miss Hunter sat in preparation to entertain them.

She raised her bow ready to draw the first note. Her gaze flicked to his, and in it he read all her insecurities. Despite her gallivanting rebellion, the girl truly wanted to please her mother. Yet for some reason, the matron would never be pleased.

He'd meant what he told RyAnne earlier. She had a talent on the instrument like none he'd ever heard. She just needed to scuttle her fears, and she would do fine. He arched his brows and offered what he hoped was a reassuring dip of his chin.

She stiffened but then tucked the violin close and drew her bow across the strings. As the first note rang out strong and clear, she dropped her eyes closed, and he knew she was taking his advice. He couldn't resist the tug of a smile. She would do fine.

Across the room Harcourt shifted and folded his arms. Trent offered him a gentlemanly bow of greeting that Brayden returned, but the glint of assessment in his eyes did not bode anything but challenge.

Chapter 3

On the Wings of a Whisper

RyAnne could not swallow down her terror despite Brayden's sudden appearance. With a glance at Captain Dawson, she decided taking his advice couldn't hurt and closed her eyes, imagining the indigo fields of home as she launched into the first notes of Franz Schubert's "Serenade." And when the sweet strains of the last note trilled from her strings and she opened her eyes to the applause filling the ballroom, she was surprised how quickly the time had passed.

Mother adjusted her gloves, looking inordinately pleased but trying not to show it. Brayden gave a great whoop and raised a clap high above his head in a salute of appreciation. With a nod, he offered a big grin that she returned. Relief eased through her. She'd made it through one. One more to go.

As she dropped a deep curtsy to the crowd, her gaze traveled to the back of the room of its own volition. Captain Dawson, one shoulder leaning against a support pillar and chin cupped in one hand, had a light shining in his eyes that she didn't recall seeing before. He didn't clap or whoop, but tipped his head as though to say he'd known she'd do well.

And heaven's mercy if her face didn't heat up right here in front of the good Lord and everyone. She jerked upright and turned her gaze to the concert master, indicating she was ready.

Mother's brows lifted in disapproval, and she looked from RyAnne toward the back of the room in an obvious attempt to see who she'd been looking at.

RyAnne gritted her teeth. Why was it a slight nod from the captain elicited more emotion than Brayden's obvious and exuberant approval?

She clenched her teeth and shook off the thought as she tucked the chin rest against her jaw and held her bow at the ready. The next piece they would play, a portion from Beethoven's Violin Concerto in D Major, was longer and would require all of her attention.

This time she refused to cower in pretense of being in the fields back home. Instead, she studied the room as she played.

Large crystal chandeliers hung from the ceiling, the flickering light of the candles, multiplied by their many facets. A huge gilt-framed portrait of Queen Victoria herself graced the wall opposite, while tapestries, paintings, and mirrors gave the large room the feeling of comfort and elegance. In several locations, in corners and along the walls, small groups of red, velvet-covered, high-backed chairs were arranged to allow quiet conversation among friends and family. Across the room she could see the large square opening, draped on either side by long red velvet curtains tied back by golden cords, that led to the billiards room. And through the opening, she could see the balding figure of her father, Ryan Hunter, in conversation with another man who stood just out of view.

Relief flooded her. Finally she would get her chance to plead with Papa. She would go to him as soon as she was finished playing.

Rory had suddenly appeared by Captain Dawson's side at the back of the room, and the two leaned close together as they spoke, as though they didn't want their conversation to be heard by anyone close by. What business could her brother have with the captain?

Couples began to fill the dance floor now, and the knowledge that they would be paying more attention to each other than to the music allowed the notes to flow more freely—until Brayden pulled Mercy Carrigan, Jasmine's best friend, onto the dance floor and tucked her so close no light could be seen between them.

RyAnne's bow squawked like a baboon, and Bishop Tozer frowned at her over his baton.

She cringed an apology.

By the time she'd recovered the timbre of her music and could find the couple in the milling crowd again, there was a proper amount of space between them, but Mercy was not smiling. As they twirled near Rory and Captain Dawson, Rory stepped forward and tapped Brayden on the shoulder to cut in. Mercy looked relieved but didn't meet Rory's gaze as he studied her. RyAnne's curiosity piqued. *Rory, darling brother, what have you been up to?*

Her focus returned to Brayden, who stalked along the far end of the ballroom and pushed through a set of double doors onto the veranda.

Interestingly enough Captain Dawson casually sauntered in the same direction. He paused sporadically to respond to conversations directed his way, but his obvious intent remained on the doors where Brayden had disappeared. And as he finally moved out into the darkness outside, she swallowed. Would that be the last time she saw him for six months? It would be if all went according to plan this evening, and a trace of heaviness weighted her down at the thought.

She gave herself a mental shake. And what if it was the last time she ever saw the annoying rogue? It made no difference to her. She had more important things to worry about tonight. A quick glance revealed Papa still in conversation just inside the billiards room.

The song wound down, and after giving the proper curtsies in acknowledgement of the applause directed her way, RyAnne hurried through the entry into the adjacent room, where she stopped quietly by her father.

Please, God of mercy, don't let Papa notice my fever, and grant me favor to change his mind.

Papa turned to her with a smile. "RyAnne! Lovely playing, as usual. How are you dear?" But he didn't give her a chance to respond, because he gestured to the man with whom he was speaking. "Ali Khalifa, may I present to you my youngest daughter, RyAnne. RyAnne, Ali Khalifa. Mr. Khalifa is commodore of the Harcourt fleet."

She curtsied deep, bowing her head slightly. "Pleased to meet you, Mr. Khalifa."

"I assure you, madam, the pleasure is all mine." Khalifa

pressed the fist of one too-large hand into the palm of the other and bent forward at the waist, his head slightly inclined toward her. He was not a handsome man by any stretch of the imagination. He had overly large ears that stuck out from the sides of his head, and although his jet-black hair was combed neatly where it showed beneath his kofia, it did nothing to detract from his sharp, pointed nose. His lips, too pale for his dark face, were thin, and his black, beady eyes were too free in roaming from her head to her toes and back again.

The room was suddenly overly warm, and RyAnne rubbed her palms together as Papa cleared his throat in obvious irritation.

Now was her time to get her father alone on the dance floor. "Papa, will you dance with me?"

Papa smiled affectionately. "RyAnne—"

"Dr. Hunter!" A movement to their left drew his attention. "How good to see you!" Brayden's father approached. "So sorry that I wasn't here to welcome you when you arrived this afternoon. There was a problem out at one of the vats that had to be looked into right away." William Harcourt extended his hand to Papa, then continued, "Miss Hunter. Nice to see you again. You will forgive me if I take your father away for a few minutes? David Livingstone has just arrived, and I know Ryan will want to meet him straight away. Khalifa." He nodded at Ali, and then taking Papa by the arm, left RyAnne and Ali standing next to each other in awkward silence.

Papa glanced back with an apologetic smile but could do nothing to escape the firm grip Mr. Harcourt had on his arm.

RyAnne despaired the critical loss of time alone with Papa.

After a brief pause, Ali ventured, "You play quite beautifully."

Her smile felt stiffer than a week-old chapati left lying in the equatorial sun. "Thank you." She thought quickly. "If you'll excuse me, I need to go find my mother and my sister."

Khalifa pointed toward the dance floor, and RyAnne turned to look. Jasmine swept by on the arm of Captain Dawson's first mate, Garrett Holloman. And Mother stood chatting with Mrs. Ropes, the wife of the American consul to Zanzibar.

When was the last time she'd felt relief at seeing Mother?

"Oh, there she is! I'll just go join her, if you'll excuse me?" She had turned to walk away, when she heard Ali shuffle forward and speak.

"May I have the honor of this dance, madam?"

Her back still to the man, she closed her eyes in dread. If she refused him without just cause—something much more just in cause than the free-roaming of his gaze—the tale would surely wend its way to Mother's parlor. And the tongue lashing Mother would render for the offense to one in the employ of the Harcourts, and under their own roof nonetheless, would be the likes of which just might cause a burn.

So, turning back to face the man, she forced a smile and nodded her head.

Khalifa's hand felt clammy as he led her onto the floor.

Or was that *her* hand? RyAnne's eyes stung from the fever, but she forced herself forward and prayed her strength would hold out. They had only made two turns of the reel, however, when the dizziness washed over her. Her foot twisted and gave way. She caught herself on Khalifa's arm.

"Miss Hunter, are you all right?" Polite alarm rang through Khalifa's voice.

"Yes." RyAnne shut her burning eyes tightly for a moment.

"I think you could use some fresh air."

Trepidation of going into the garden with this man swept through her, but both Brayden and Captain Dawson were out there somewhere, and if she didn't cool herself with a bit of a breeze, Papa was sure to notice her fever-flushed skin and insist on taking her home to rest.

Besides, the man was commodore of the Harcourt fleet. Surely Harcourt wouldn't have hired anyone overtly unsavory, even if he did have wandering eyes.

Quit being a ninny. Papa wouldn't have introduced her to the man if he was someone to be avoided. Of course he could be trusted.

She nodded acquiescence.

Khalifa took her arm gently and led her through the French doors and out onto the patio. And, just as she'd assured herself, he was nothing but a gentleman as they walked through the fragrant foliage in the Harcourt's back garden.

RyAnne released the remains of her unease.

He took her elbow only when they came to a rough place in the trail and then, as soon as he saw her footing was sure, let go again. He chatted easily about different plants along the path, every now and then asking if she felt any better.

They passed the great domed building that housed the Persian baths of the plantation. And although her eyes still burned, she was not at the moment experiencing the chills, hot flashes, or dizziness that came with the fever. The cool breeze must be doing its work.

They walked up the steps of a white octagonal gazebo, overgrown with dark shadows of ivy. Benches ran all the way around the inside of the octagon, and the rail around the perimeter held several potted plants that added pale moonlit splashes of color to the tranquil setting.

She turned to look back at the plantation house and, with a jolt, realized they had come far enough that not even a glimmer of light from its windows could be seen through the garden's vegetation.

Her unease sprang to life anew. "Sir, I really feel much refreshed and would like to return now." Proud of the fact that her voice only trembled slightly, she lifted her skirts and started back down the stairs.

Ali caught her elbow and stilled her retreat.

She darted him a look. Her heart threatened to clamber right out of her chest.

He smiled, but it was not a comforting smile. He took her hand, gently at first, but when she tried to pull away, he would not let go. "Stay with me for just a few minutes more, madam. Your skin is so enchanting in the moonlight."

His fingers grazed over RyAnne's cheek, and a shiver of revulsion slithered down her spine. She jerked back only to find the benches of the gazebo grinding into her knees.

He stepped closer.

She tried to push him away, but he possessed strength much greater than hers. He grabbed her waist, pressing closer.

"Sir, I must protest!" She shoved him as hard as she could and lurched to one side. *Father in heaven!* Her elbow knocked one of the potted plants to the ground with a crash. *The pots!*

"Just a moment more, madam. I won't hurt you."

But still, the man held her and leaned even closer.

"Your actions belie your words, sir!" She scrabbled her fingers along the rail until she contacted another pot. Snatching it up, she swung it hard at his head. A satisfying *thunk* preceded the tinkling shards of clay falling at their feet.

Khalifa cursed loudly. His large, bony hands clutched at the side of his head, and he staggered backward.

RyAnne didn't lose a moment. She lifted her skirts and fled down the steps of the gazebo and up the path.

She dashed past the Persian baths. One of the ornate double doors was open a crack! Even as she skidded to a stop, thinking to hide inside, she caught a flash of movement and then felt strong hands around her waist. One solid arm yanked her back against a solid wall of chest, while a hand slammed over her mouth and cut off her frightened shriek.

This wasn't Khalifa! She could still hear him muttering and stumbling about on the planks of the gazebo. Who had her then?

Her eyes widened as the new assailant pulled her through the doors into the dank, dark interior of the building. He nudged the heavy wooden doors shut with his foot and dragged her further into the darkness. Her heart pounded in agony, and she tried to pry loose the hand blocking her screams, but to no avail.

The man whispered something, but the blood rushing through her ears kept her from understanding what he said.

The interior of the baths smelled of wet stone, reminding RyAnne of a damp cave, and the floor under her feet was slimy and slick, preventing her from catching her balance. As she tried to gain her footing, the man pulled her back into the blackness of a side chamber, and a cloying terror enveloped her. She clawed at the hand covering her mouth and brought one small boot down on the man's foot, but it was all without effect. She was firmly held in the strong arms of her captor.

Trent held her against him as gently as he could without letting her get away. If he didn't want to avoid having Ali know he'd been following, he'd let her scream and give the man a good thrashing when he showed up.

Alarm shot through him as he realized how warm she felt. Her skin was hot and dry to the touch, and although the little she-cat did her best to get away, he could feel her trembling all over.

"Miss Hunter, 'tis I," he whispered in her ear again. Pain shot up his arm as her teeth sunk deeply into the heel of his hand. The throbbing filled the back of his throat with a growl, and he snatched his hand away for a split second. But before she could scream, his palm was back over her mouth, more firmly this time, so she could not bite him again. "Miss Hunter! Be still! It's Trent—Captain Dawson." He gave her a small shake for emphasis. "Quiet now, or Ali will find us. And," he added dryly, "I will be forced to get dirty teaching him a lesson."

The reality of who he was must have finally penetrated, because she went still in his arms.

"I will take my hand away now, but you must not speak." When she made no response, he prodded, "Understand?"

She nodded slightly against his chest.

Easing his hand down, he rubbed the throb that still pulsed in the heel of it against his trousers. Keeping her against him, he shuffled them deeper into the shadows of the baths.

The doors burst open with a bang, sending a long rectangle of moonlight onto the floor.

RyAnne flinched perceptively, and the sudden urge to forget about being covert, step out of the shadows, and teach the man a lesson on the finer points of being a gentleman was nearly more than Trent could suppress. Instead he wrapped his hand around the comforting feel of the pistol tucked into the waistband under his coat.

"Are you in here, madam?" Ali's voice rang with deceptive calmness. "I am sorry, Miss Hunter. Your beauty overcame me. Come out, and I will take you back into the ball." When he received no response, his patient demeanor vanished. "Come now, Miss Hunter. Let us be done with these games. We will go back to the ball and pretend this never happened. You have my sincerest apologies."

A tremor vibrated through RyAnne, and Trent squeezed her arm gently, a reminder to keep quiet.

After glancing around the interior of the baths one more time, Ali was apparently satisfied no one was present, save himself. Grumbling, cursing, and rubbing the back of his head, he stomped from the building, leaving the door half open.

RyAnne didn't move, other than to drop her head back against his shoulder in relief.

Trent kept her in the shadows for several minutes. He listened carefully to the sounds coming from outside. But the longer he stood there, the higher the flames of his anger grew. If he hadn't come along when he had…

Another tremor coursed through her.

Good! Hopefully she was, at this very moment, realizing how lucky she was!

He swallowed.

Once satisfied that Ali had indeed left, he loosened his grip on RyAnne's arm and moved around in front of her. He led her to a step near the milky rectangle of moonlight spilling through the doorway, and motioned for her to sit before her legs gave out.

She complied and then pressed her face into her palms as though to block out the memory of the last moments.

Squatting down on the balls of his feet, he glowered at her. But he couldn't ignore a twinge of concern. "Are you well?"

Her fingers shook as she smoothed them across her brows,

but she nodded. "Thank you."

The anger he'd been doing his best to keep at bay rushed out like a flood. "Are you a half-wit?! Going out into the dark quiet of a garden alone with the likes of Ali Khalifa?!"

Moisture glistened on her lower lids, and she didn't bite back with a retaliatory comment as he'd expected her to. Her words were distant and resigned. "We'd had a proper introduction from Papa. And I needed some fresh air."

The anger drained from him and regret took its place. He reached out a finger to tilt her chin up. "Forgive me. This was not your fault. Did he…" He couldn't bring himself to voice the horrible question.

"No." She looked away, rubbing her upper arms with her palms. "Intention was as far as he got."

Relief washed over him. He spoke again. "You need to tell someone you are sick."

"I can't." She glanced up at him with a shrug.

He opened his mouth to protest, but she lifted a hand to silence him. "Mother has looked forward to this ball for weeks. Let's not ruin it for her by making a scene over a silly fever. If I'm not feeling better in the morning, I'll make a visit to Dr. Kirk, who is in town with the Livingstone expedition."

"And yet only this morning you were willing to ruin it for her by hiding out with your friends at Valah's little cockfight." He did nothing to disguise his disbelief of her magnanimity.

She blinked. Then shrugged as though she couldn't bring herself to care if he believed her or not. "Think what you want, Captain."

He tilted his head. "Oh, I do, Miss Hunter. And right now I'm thinking I wish I knew what connivings were rolling around in that head of yours."

Perhaps for the first time since he'd known her, the lady remained silent in the face of his taunting. That, and perhaps the touch of pleading in her gaze tugged at his heart, and before he realized it, he nodded agreement. "Very well. I will keep your confidence in this matter." However, he couldn't help but feel she had an ulterior motive hidden in the request somewhere. "I will see if our way is clear."

He stepped to the door and eased it open, peering out into the moon-washed garden to give her another moment to collect herself.

He pondered the past several weeks and considered the job he'd been given to do. Was the Harcourt fleet really being used to smuggle slaves to India and beyond?

After he'd left the ballroom earlier, he'd followed Brayden to the stables, where he'd saddled a horse and then ridden out of the gates. Trent had returned to the ballroom just as Ali had led RyAnne out onto the patio. But as he'd made to follow, a rather plump dowager, to whom he had been introduced earlier in the evening, had approached him and smiled coyly. Trent could not get away politely without engaging her in a few words of conversation. He had made his escape as soon as propriety allowed, and had come around the corner of the baths just in time to see RyAnne smash the clay pot over Ali's head.

Trent gritted his teeth. He should have excused himself the moment he'd seen Ali lead her outside. Maybe he could have spared her some emotional distress.

He watched as she rubbed her temples in a circular motion, and reached out to touch her elbow. "If you think you are ready, we should head back inside now."

RyAnne nodded, lifted her skirts, and followed him out of the baths. He led her down the path, but he paused when they came to the steps leading up to the main patio outside the ballroom. He folded his arms and looked down at her. "You should rest."

Her chin tipped up. "I will be fine. Thank you for your concern." Her tone indicated many things, but gratitude was not among them.

One brow arched, and he studied her determined face in the light emanating from the dance floor. He wanted to remind her that if he had not followed her outside… But he couldn't finish the thought. His fists clenched merely considering what could have happened to her. Instead he turned and preceded her up the steps, then took her elbow as they entered the room through the French doors.

As they stepped into the hustle and bright lights of the ballroom, RyAnne's eyes burned, and she wished to do nothing more than follow the captain's advice and find a quiet dark room to rest in. But she still hadn't gotten her chance to speak to Papa. And there was only an hour or so left in the evening to accomplish her task. Her time to change his mind was rapidly disappearing.

"RyAnne!"

She turned toward the call.

Brayden hurried toward her, turning this way and that to dodge clusters of people.

Beside her, Captain Dawson stiffened and folded his arms.

She glanced at him and noted that instead of the irritation she'd expected, his face held a puzzled curiosity. He looked as though he was surprised to find Brayden here, but that couldn't be right, because he'd followed him out into the garden only an hour ago.

She pulled her assessment from the captain and turned to watch Brayden striding confidently the last few steps toward her. He had straight blond hair, parted in the middle. His rounded, handsome face, blessed with a generous mouth, broke into a smile as he approached.

"RyAnne!" He took her hand in his own, placed a featherlight kiss on her knuckles, and with his pale-blue eyes twinkling up at her, said, "I am so pleased to have found you at last. I've been looking for you ever since I heard your entertainment obligations had been fulfilled. Come dance with me." He started to lead her toward the dance floor, but no matter her constant irritation with the captain, she couldn't just snub him without a parting word.

She held her ground. "Brayden, you know Captain Trent Dawson, I presume? He leaves on the morrow to escort Papa to the Interior and seek his fortune in ivory." She couldn't resist that last jab. The captain always seemed a tad uncomfortable with her mentioning his desire to get rich on ivory.

Brayden seemed to notice the captain for the first time. A hardness crept into his jawline, but he stretched his hand toward the man. "Dawson. Good to see you again. Look me up when you get back with your haul. Maybe we can cut a deal for your ivory. Harcourt Shipping is always looking for goods to supplement our shipments of indigo to England."

The captain's gray-green eyes glinted, as if maybe he had read something subtly hidden in Brayden's words, but he only said, "Thank you." He shook Brayden's hand, then turned toward RyAnne and inclined his head. "Miss Hunter, it has been a pleasure." Leaning close to her ear, he spoke low. "You should rest."

RyAnne merely raised her eyebrows and looked at him. The man was persistent, she'd give him that, but he was not to have his way in this matter. *Could not*, for her very future depended on it.

Brayden glanced from them to the open veranda doors just behind them. "Have you just come in?" Slight suspicion edged his voice as he glanced back and forth between them.

"Captain Dawson—" RyAnne started with a gesture of her hand toward the garden but then found she couldn't finish. Her throat constricted in embarrassed silence, and she looked at the man for help.

The captain leaned toward Brayden as though he was about to offer something in great confidence. "Miss Hunter and I have been out strolling in the garden." A hint of a smile curved his mouth, and with a sketch of a bow in RyAnne's direction, he turned and walked away.

Oh, that irritating man! He had made it sound as though they had been out for a moonlit tryst!

Brayden's eyes narrowed.

She lifted her chin. "He found me in need of an escort and walked me back to the house. And that was all."

Brayden folded his arms, not looking convinced.

With a dart of apprehension, she turned from his questioning perusal. Why were her feelings all a muddle, of late?

Across the room, Captain Dawson approached Alicia Harcourt, Brayden's beautiful golden-haired sister, and asked her to dance. Alicia agreed with a stunning smile, and he led her onto the floor and pulled her into his arms.

RyAnne wondered at the wave of distress that coursed through her. She should engage Brayden in conversation, but no topic would come to mind.

Awkward silence stretched for the space of several seconds as Brayden watched Captain Dawson and Alicia with a look of speculation.

RyAnne cleared her throat and forced her attention to fix on Brayden. She'd been looking forward to seeing him all day, after all. "It's good to see you again, Brayden. How have you been since I saw you last? When was it…Christmas past?"

Brayden seemed to shake himself from his reverie. "Yes. Over half a year. Too long." He brought his gaze back to her face. "You look very lovely this evening, RyAnne." He took her hand once more and led her onto the dance floor. They danced for several minutes before he spoke again, looking deep into her eyes. "When are you going to accept my proposal?" Somehow there was more seriousness in his question this time than in times past.

She swallowed away the trepidation that thought raised and grinned at him. "A proposal is it? And earlier with Mercy Carrigan… What was that? Anything a girl with a beau interested in marriage should be concerned about?"

He chuckled. "Mercy is…well, she's like a sister to me! You know that."

In a pig's eye! But all she allowed herself to say was, "I am only eighteen, Brayden. I don't want to get married yet."

"Judith Tanner is fifteen, and she is getting married next month."

RyAnne thought about Judith for a few moments and then answered, "Yes, and I feel sorry for her."

"But I am not George Crowley." Brayden's devilish smile

revealed even, white teeth just before he spun her into a twirl.

RyAnne sighed again and tried not to offer too much encouragement. Indeed, Brayden was nothing like the elderly, hunched Mr. Crowley. *Mr. Crowley will probably be faithful to poor Judith Tanner.*

Oh stop! No formal commitment existed between them. Brayden owed her no fidelity.

"So?" he prompted. "What say you?"

She pressed her lips together.

The captain and Alicia twirled by, Alicia tittering in a shrill flirtatious way that set RyAnne's teeth together.

She forced her thoughts back to Brayden. Was she ready for matrimony? It would mean leaving her friendships with the princesses behind because Brayden always grew stiff and recalcitrant whenever she spoke of them. That thought seemed unbearable.

She tried to envision herself running Brayden's household, and somehow she just couldn't picture it. At least not yet.

So how did she once more decline his request without arousing rancor? She swept the tip of her tongue over her dry lips. "I just don't feel ready to make such a commitment yet, Brayden." Besides, she didn't think Papa would give his consent to the union. She'd heard him voice displeasure over Brayden's behavior on more than one occasion in the parlor back home.

And if she couldn't convince Papa to stay and they lost him forever? That would leave Mother in control of her future, and that thought was even more unbearable than having to cajole Papa into agreeing to let her marry Brayden.

"I have a lot weighing on my mind just now. Maybe after a few days I will feel differently than I do now. I promise to consider your proposal in earnest this time."

She thought a flicker of impatience touched Brayden's expression, but in a blink he was smiling down at her. She must have imagined it.

Still…she was suddenly most relieved that she'd been able to put him off once again.

Chapter 4
On the Wings of a Whisper

Trent quite happily bowed a good-bye to Alicia Harcourt at the end of only one dance. The woman could have talked a starving dog away from a meaty bone using fewer words than she'd plied him with during that dance. But he'd learned a few things about the way Harcourt indigo was shipped.

He cast a glance to where Brayden was leading RyAnne into a second set. Couldn't the man see she was limp on her feet?

He started toward them, then froze. With a shake of his head, he chuckled in self-deprecation and forced himself to reverse course and saunter toward the billiards room. He'd obviously been sent on one too many trips to rescue the damsel. He'd tried to tell her to rest, and by her own account she was a full-grown woman and didn't need him nannying her.

Ryan Hunter, Ali Khalifa, Dr. David Livingstone, and a small group of other men stood in a cluster deep in discussion. Although the talk seemed casual, he could tell by the tension on the faces of most of the men that this was a subject all of them felt strongly about.

He leaned one shoulder into the wall and crossed his arms over his chest. With his ankles crossed and the toe of one boot resting on the floor, he scanned the room lazily. It wouldn't do to appear too interested in Khalifa's comings and goings. He'd stuck pretty close to the man all evening. Although, he'd been careful.

"It will never happen, Livingstone," a short, pudgy, balding man named Ludlow said. "The slave market on Zanzibar will be here for years to come."

"Indeed, sir," returned David Livingstone sadly, "I believe you may be right. I cannot, however, allow my conscience to ignore the continuing evil that pervades in the form of slavery. Man's greed, even at the expense of other human beings, has shown itself to be insatiable. I must do all that I can to prevent the continuance of such an evil and firmly believe that were all men to respect the laws of the Scripture as they should, the exploitation of the natives would have ended long ago."

Ryan Hunter stepped into the discussion. "I for one do believe that the slave market will be shut down, and soon. Majid will not be able to stand the political pressure for much longer."

Trent rubbed at an invisible spot on the floor with the toe of his boot. Hunter may be right on that count. The reigning sultan of Zanzibar had made clear his intentions to keep Britain happy on more than one occasion.

"The Scriptures, sir?" Ali addressed Livingstone. "You go to the Bible to support your campaign against slavery? The Bible has nothing to say against slavery. In fact, in many areas the Scriptures admonish slaves to be subject to their masters in obedience of service. The Old Testament itself has many laws telling masters how to treat their slaves. As does the Qur'an."

Livingstone exhaled a tired sigh that made it evident he had heard this argument before. "Let us set aside the Muslim holy book and speak only of the Bible. Why, sir, do you think that there were ordinances about slavery in the books of the law?" He continued without pause, answering his own question. "Because of the hardness of men's hearts. Did not Christ himself make this argument before the Pharisees when they asked him why Moses commanded that a man give his wife a certificate of divorce? God in his omniscience understood that men would divorce, so he set forth laws to ensure that the evil therein would not be so great. It was the same with the laws of slavery. They are not there because God condones evils done to one's fellow man, but to ensure that even in the hardness of man's heart, evil should have some limitations."

"I do not see these evils that you proclaim exist, Mr. Livingstone," Ludlow said.

Ryan Hunter's voice was barely controlled as he said, "You don't see the evils, Ludlow? How can you miss them? In the harbor, as we speak"—he gestured toward the outside of the mansion—"there float the corpses of captured *people* who were thought to be too sick to live. Instead of bringing them onto the island where medical attention could be obtained for them, the slavers, in their greed, not wanting to pay duty on property that might not prove its worth, simply threw them overboard. You don't call *murder* an evil, Ludlow?" His voice had crescendoed until at the end of his statement, the whole room had fallen quiet as everyone turned to listen.

Trent watched in amusement as Ludlow sputtered, trying to think of a coherent reply.

Ali was the first one to speak. He waved his hand in a careless arc. "You own slaves yourself, Mr. Hunter. There are few slave traders who practice such things. You propel the evil actions of the few onto the good intentions of the many, Mr. Hunter."

"Good intentions, Mr. Khalifa?"

Trent jolted upright and turned toward the entry.

RyAnne Hunter stepped fully into the room and stood next to her father. Her head didn't even reach his shoulder, but her tiny frame vibrated with a fury that lent menace to what she lacked in stature. Her mother, who had come in behind her, plucked at RyAnne's sleeve in an obvious attempt to remind her it was improper for young ladies to enter into such discussions, but RyAnne ignored her and continued, "What are these good intentions you speak of with such candor, sir?" Only Trent and Ali knew she spoke of more than the issue of slavery.

Khalifa turned to her with the air of a perfect gentleman, as if the incident in the garden had never taken place. Although a spark of anger lit his eyes, he said calmly, "Why, madam, will you not agree that the natives are heathens, bent toward evil practices of all kinds? We would never be able to civilize them if we left them in amongst the wicked influences of their society."

"'Civilized' seems to be a relative term, sir."

Trent smirked. Ali's face turned a shade paler. But the rest of the room didn't seem to notice the undertones.

Ludlow said, "I have to concur with Khalifa. No native is going to understand the way of Christianity if left on the Dark Continent among so many infidels. We must bring them out of the darkness so they can see the light of the truth."

Dr. Livingstone stiffened and brought a hand up to trace his mustache slowly, but he did not speak. Trent had heard the man tell of several natives who had confessed Christ during his time on the Continent.

RyAnne threw back her shoulders and pinned Khalifa with a look that made the man take half a step back. Any other woman might have cowered before a man who'd assaulted her, but not Miss Hunter. Trent allowed himself a moment to appreciate the woman's strength and tenacity…the spark that lit her green eyes…the way passion had clenched her tiny hands into fists—

He forced his gaze back to the spot on the floor at his feet. Tomorrow he would leave for the Interior for months. Best he remember that.

Miss Hunter turned the force of her ire toward Ludlow but included Khalifa in her glare as well. "So you say you are *stealing* these people from their homes with the pure intention of converting them?" Her voice rang with incredulity. Even Brayden, who had come to stand by her, now pulled on the sleeve of her dress, but she continued undeterred. "Slavers commit a crime against humanity—going so far as to steal natives from their very homes—in order to…*preach the gospel?* I think not!"

Ali stiffened. "I have never stolen any one from their home, madam, nor do I ever have the intention of doing so. Prisoners of war are captured in the heat of battle between two or more tribes. I merely come along and relieve those captives from their terrible fate and offer them a chance at a wonderful life serving somewhere that is not so backward as the Dark Continent." Ali's words were spoken placatingly, yet there was an undertone of hostility as he obviously attempted to control his temper.

"RyAnne"—Anne Hunter's voice held a ribbon of reproach—"we really should be bidding everyone good-night."

Dr. Hunter added, "Yes, RyAnne, you really *should* say good-night." His tone left no room for his daughter to argue.

RyAnne opened her mouth as if to protest, but then she folded her hands and bowed her head with a nod. "Papa, come dance with me?"

Ryan nodded. "Just wait for me in the other room, dearest. I'll be right along."

Brayden offered his arm to RyAnne, but before they walked away, he gave a parting word to Ali. "Maybe you have never been part of an actual slave raid, Mr. Khalifa, but no doubt you have funded them, and that is just as bad, if not worse. And," he continued, not allowing Ali to interrupt, "if we weren't so ready to purchase prisoners of war, perhaps the natives would not be so ready to raid and plunder one another. In any case, the Harcourts are glad you've given up your slave-running days and put your skill as a captain to use for our fleet." He paused, looking Khalifa directly in the eye. "But perhaps in the future you could temper the vocalization of your views at social gatherings to avoid putting us in a bad light, hmmm?"

Ali and Brayden looked at one another for a moment, and Trent caught something in the exchange that gave him pause.

The moment was broken when Brayden turned and led RyAnne back into the ballroom.

Khalifa and Ludlow snorted in disgust at their retreating backs. "It's not like we are breaking the law," whined Ludlow to the men still around him. "It is still perfectly legal to bring slaves onto the island of Zanzibar."

"But it is not legal to export them, sir," Ryan said. "And you will never be able to convince me that Zanzibar is consuming all of the twenty-thousand-and-more slaves a year that are brought to this island. Some are being smuggled off of the island somewhere. I only wish I knew where so I could stop it."

"We must all do what we can in our own way, Mr. Hunter," Livingstone said.

"Yes, you are right. When do you leave for the Continent, sir?" Ryan's question effectively ended the debate over the evils of slavery. Most of the other men turned to conversations of their own, but Trent held his position.

David Livingstone sounded weary when he replied, "I am hoping to leave by the nineteenth. I only stopped over here to collect some supplies for my trip inland."

"I am heading to the Interior myself. On the morrow, in fact. It has long been on my heart to take the gospel to the peoples of the Interior. I hope to be able to convince several of the warring chieftains to stop selling their captives into slavery."

"Indeed, that has been my goal for several years, sir," Livingstone said. "You will not find this an easy task. The natives don't view human worth in the same way we Europeans do. Once one has captured his enemy, he feels it is his right to do with that person anything he chooses. And the temptation of European trinkets is too much to withstand, it seems. This is why I have been trying to establish a trade route into the interior of the Continent for years. If the natives could get their hands on material, beads, and the other common trinkets in trade for legitimate items such as ivory or cotton, then the tendency to sell their fellow man would be much less enticing."

"What is this rumor I hear about the Royal Geographical Society asking you to locate the source of the Nile?"

Livingstone sighed. "It is true. Richard Burton returned to London proclaiming that he believed Lake Tanganyika to be the source. John Hanning Speke believes Lake Victoria, to the north, is the source. I have been sent with the disagreeable task of determining which of them, if either, is right. My heart is in establishing a trade route, but I have had a nasty time finding a passable route across the Continent, and so there is no brave soul who will fund another exploration."

Ryan gave a tired smile. "But if God is for us, who can be against us, yes?" Livingstone nodded with a smile of his own, and there was a slight pause before Ryan extended his hand to his fellow doctor. "May God bless your journey. I look forward to meeting you again someday."

"I will also look forward to that." The men shook hands.

Ryan glanced at his pocket watch. "Well, if you'll excuse me, gentlemen…" He gave a slight bow, a twinkle leaping into his gaze. "I had best go and dance at least once with my wife and daughters before the night is over."

Brayden led RyAnne to a golden brocade settee just inside the ballroom, and she sank onto it with a great deal of relief. Aching muscles released some of their tension, and a cool breeze from the French doors, which had now been propped open, wafted over her. Jasmine and Mother seated themselves in the two adjacent chairs.

"May I fetch you anything?" Brayden eased down by her side and bounced a glance between her, Mother, and Jasmine.

"Some punch would be lovely, dear. Thank you." RyAnne had no doubt Mother was just sending him off so she could reprimand her in relative privacy. But by the look on Mother's face, she was going to give her a good portion of her mind whether Brayden left or not.

So RyAnne offered Brayden a smile. "I'm actually rather parched and would love a cup of punch." It was true. Her mouth was quite dry. So she only allowed a tiny prick of guilt over the fact that she'd really sent him off to avoid the humiliation over whatever Mother was about to say and might have a moment to close her eyes. Which she did the second his back was turned.

"RyAnne Estelle Hunter, how could you bring so much embarrassment upon us…" Mother launched into her expected tirade, but RyAnne was adept at shutting her out and did so with ease.

Nonetheless, her head pounded. Oh to be abed with a cool cloth around her neck. *Please, Papa, hurry and come dance with me.* Her strength was fading even faster now that she'd allowed herself to sit, and she feared she might lack the strength to dance if he didn't arrive soon.

As if an angel had heard her thoughts as a prayer, at that very moment Papa's voice boomed out, "Well now, which of my ladies should I twirl about first?" As usual, Papa had already forgiven, if not forgotten, her social misstep.

A surge of thankfulness propelled RyAnne to her feet. Her chance had finally come. "Youngest first, I think, yes?" She offered him a bold wink she knew would sway him in her favor.

Papa glanced from her to Mother and Jasmine. Mother only huffed impatience, and Jasmine smiled her acquiescence. "Very well, you imp! Youngest first." Papa tweaked her nose before he swept her out onto the dance floor.

RyAnne knew she hadn't much time, so she pressed right into her request. "Papa, I've been searching for you all evening and wanting to speak to you."

A squint of exasperation was so fleeting she might have missed it if she hadn't been so attuned to his every expression.

She hadn't missed a chance all week to ask him to stay, but she hadn't yet revealed that she knew how sick he was. Still, she didn't want to start their conversation by annoying him. That wouldn't put him in an acquiescing mood.

But before she could even open her mouth to voice an apology, he was smiling down at her. "What have you been wanting to speak to me about, love?"

She ran her tongue over her lips and leveled her best pleading expression on him. "Papa, please. Don't go. I know you are not well."

His nostrils flared. "Not well? Whatever could you be speaking of?" But the evidence of the lie lay there on his face, plain for her to see.

She squeezed his shoulder. "I'm not a naïve child, Papa. I haven't served with you in the clinic on the plantation for all these years without learning a thing or two. And"—her voice hitched—"I need you, Papa. Please stay on Zanzibar?"

Papa's chin lifted slightly. His jaw hardened. And he blinked rapidly a few times. "I can't, child."

Despondency threatened to overwhelm her. But if he wouldn't stay for her, maybe he would stay for himself. "Papa, you are going to need me in the days to come. You are going to need medicines and care."

He looked down at her, and his features softened. "When did you grow into such a beautiful young woman?"

Good. Let him feel sentimental. Maybe that would sway him to her argument. "Papa, I'll take care of you. And Jasmine and

Rory, they deserve to have a good-bye." Her teeth clenched for a moment before she tacked on. "And Mother."

Papa's face became even more tender. "My sin has brought such a great deal of pain into your life, RyAnne. And for that my sorrow knows no boundaries."

RyAnne felt her eyes widen. The Hunter family secret was never spoken of openly where someone might overhear. She darted a glance around, but the music and rustle of skirts likely had prevented anyone nearby from taking heed of his words. She lowered her voice. "You've given me a good life, Papa, and I've nothing to regret." She swallowed. Except losing him too soon, and this was much too soon.

A sigh slipped from him. "I wish your mother could have learned to love you."

RyAnne pursed her lips. And only because she was trying her hardest to stay in his good graces, she offered, "She loves me in her own way, I suppose." Hopefully the Father above would look past the lie to see her heart was only in sparing Papa untold suffering at his end.

"Hmmm…perhaps, dear. Though she could better show it, methinks."

She seized on that opportunity. "She always treats me better when you are near. If you won't stay for yourself, mayhap you'll stay for my sake?"

Papa touched his cheek to hers, and she felt a shudder tremble through him. "There is none stronger than you, dear girl. Anne may not know it, but she needs you. And so when I go, I ask that you have patience with her." He must have felt her stiffen, because he hurried on. "You always do have patience with her, I know, but now, even more, you must bear with her impatience."

Discouragement was rapidly building a mound in her throat that threatened to block off her airway. She looked up at him again. "You must stay, Papa. There will be no help for you on the Continent."

Above her head, Papa looked over to where Mother and Jasmine still sat awaiting Papa's return. So many emotions passed across his face that RyAnne couldn't seem to pin any one of them down. Slowly, his features released their tension. His eyes were no longer so hard, his jaw not quite so set. And the longer he watched his family, the softer his countenance became. At long last his shoulders slumped in defeat, and he turned to study the ballroom floor.

Relief coursed through her. She had done it. Papa would stay. She dropped her forehead onto his shoulder and pressed her eyes closed hard to keep the tears of thankfulness locked away. Joy welled up inside her. She would have her papa for at least a few more months if he rested and convalesced well. Her happiness could no longer be contained. It bloomed into a huge grin that she turned upon him. "Thank you, Papa. You've no idea—"

"RyAnne, child. I cannot stay."

Like a wave had just crashed over her, all hope and joy disintegrated. Her feet stumbled to a stop, no matter that they were in the way of the other dancers. The song was coming to an end anyhow. "But I thought—"

"I'm sorry. There are many reasons you wouldn't understand. I simply must go." He started to lead her off the floor.

But she struck at his arm and dragged her feet. "And what about us!? Your family? You will just leave us and go off to the Continent to"—she checked the volume of her voice—"die alone?"

Papa took her elbow once more. Firmly this time. "Keep your voice down, child. My decision is made. Don't make this more difficult for me than it already is. Hush now. Jasmine approaches." Papa's face morphed into a beaming smile. He gave RyAnne a little nudge in the direction of her mother, and then Papa swept Jasmine into a waltz as the next song started up.

Effectively dismissed, RyAnne simply stood where she was. Her vision blurred against the large hand-painted vase that held a bouquet of island roses. She had failed. Now what was she to do?

"Oh, RyAnne, I do declare. You stand directly in the space where people need to walk as if you are the only person in this room." Mother snapped her fingers. "Do get over here and sit down, girl! You act as if you've never been taught manners a day in your life!"

RyAnne did move, but she knew from the chill spiraling through her that to sit would sap the last of her strength. She stood instead, behind Mother's chair, feeling as if the last pulse of life was draining from her.

Mother gestured to a cup on the side table. "Brayden asked that I give you his good-bye. He had an early appointment on the other side of the island at the plantation."

Thankful for something to do with her hands, RyAnne lifted the cup and drained the contents. Still, her tongue felt like a twig in her mouth. She must move or fall down, so she set to pacing. Surreptitiously, she used the sleeve of her gown to pat at the moisture dotting her forehead. Papa's refusal had drained her emotionally, which had apparently aggravated her symptoms.

She must stay strong. She must think. Consider what her next move must be. For no matter how much Papa seemed to wish it, she would not see him off to the Continent knowing it would be the last time they ever spoke.

Papa returned Jasmine to her seat and bowed before Mother. She rose regally and allowed him to lead her into the next dance.

RyAnne stood next to Jasmine, who was seated in one of the red velvet chairs. She trembled from the simple effort of remaining upright. But Papa always gave Mother one of the last dances of the evening. They should be heading home in just a few moments. Perhaps then, after some quinine and a short nap, she would be able to think what she must do.

At least her attempts to keep anyone from knowing she was sick seemed to be working.

Mother never paid attention to her. Papa normally would have noticed, but he was obviously preoccupied with the morrow's sailing. And Jasmine's mind was engaged with watching Captain Dawson's first mate, the tall, handsome Garrett Holloman, dance with Alicia Harcourt. His golden hair combined with deep-blue eyes and broad shoulders melded in a way that might make even the most reluctant of women swoon. Garrett said something, and Alicia stuttered a laugh accompanied by batted lashes. Jasmine turned her gaze to her lap, rubbing at an invisible wrinkle. But after only a moment her focus returned to the couple.

Garrett looked up suddenly from his partner and caught her eyes on him.

Jasmine darted her gaze on past him as though she'd merely been studying the room, but RyAnne didn't miss the dull flush that crept up her neck.

RyAnne tried to steady the fevered tremor in her voice as she said, "He really is very handsome, isn't he?"

"Who?" Jasmine asked innocently.

"Garrett Holloman, the man you haven't taken your eyes off all evening, who else? Rumor has it he's not only Captain Dawson's first mate but his cousin as well."

Jasmine groaned. "Is it that obvious? I had hoped I was doing an admirable job of hiding my feelings."

RyAnne smiled and couldn't resist teasing. "You probably shouldn't stare at him continually then."

Jasmine giggled, but then her face turned serious as she scanned the room. "Do you think anyone else has noticed?"

The dance ended, and Garrett left Alicia at the edge of the dance floor and strode their way. He met RyAnne's gaze and offered a bold wink, yet she knew without a doubt it was not her he was coming for. She pressed her lips together. So…rogue must run in the family.

"Maybe *he* has." RyAnne offered her sister the soft warning.

"Who—" Jasmine's question was cut short as her gaze landed on Garrett, who now stood before her.

"May I have the honor of this dance, Miss Hunter?"

Jasmine's mouth opened and shut like a sea turtle eating kelp.

Garrett only raised his eyebrows and clasped his hands behind his back, waiting silently for her to find her voice.

Finally Jasmine offered the man a wobbly smile and said, "It would not be proper, sir. I've danced with you once already this evening, and besides, I should not leave my sister standing here alone."

"Then allow me to keep her company."

RyAnne clenched her teeth as Captain Trent Dawson stopped beside her. Stodgy recriminations were the last things she wanted to deal with at the moment. Still, she wouldn't let that keep Jasmine from enjoying her evening. She nudged Jasmine in the back. "I'm sure Captain Dawson will be tolerably passable company, Jas. Please don't let me hold you back."

Garrett tipped a nod of thanks to his cousin, then held out a hand to Jasmine with a smile. His look said he would accept no more excuses. "Let's make tongues wag, shall we?"

Jasmine looked at RyAnne questioningly.

RyAnne nodded. "Go. I'll be fine."

Jasmine still looked uncertain when Garrett led her away. But RyAnne didn't have emotions to spare worrying about her. It was taking all her gumption to remain standing.

Captain Dawson took her elbow and directed her toward the settee. He seated her carefully at one corner and then sank onto a chair across from her, his quick scrutinizing glance taking in her trembling.

RyAnne expected him to launch into a lecture and was pleasantly surprised when he spoke in a compassionate voice. "May I get you something to drink?"

She passed her tongue over dry, fevered lips. The punch Brayden had left for her had only primed her thirst, it seemed. "That would be nice."

He was gone only momentarily and returned with a cup of hot spiced apricot juice. RyAnne wrapped her hands around the cup and could feel warmth begin to seep back into her body as she sipped the soothing drink. Who knew the man could be thoughtful?

He kept silent as she sipped carefully from her cup, but when she was done, he offered a faint smile and took the cup from her. "I think I shall rather miss your stubbornness when I set sail in the morning, Miss Hunter. Do try and take a care for yourself while I'm away, won't you?"

RyAnne sighed and started to tell him he needn't worry, but that's when the solution over what to do about Papa stopped her midword.

Captain Dawson set her cup on the table between them, a furrow creasing his brow. "Is something amiss?"

She brushed away his concern. "I'm fine, I assure you, Captain."

A moment of thought revealed the plan had some weaknesses, but this was the last remaining option she had now.

She angled the captain a glance. He seemed preoccupied with a stray thread on the arm of his chair.

Would sneaking aboard Captain Dawson's vessel even be possible? She bit her lip. All she would need to do would be to hide for a day or two. Then she'd let someone "discover" her, and Papa would be forced to bring her back home. It was an unstable plan because there were any number of things that might go wrong. She might be caught trying to leave the house. She might be caught sneaking aboard the ship. Papa might simply return her to port and then head straight back to the Continent without her. But Papa had left her no choices, and it was the only thing she could think to do. At the very least it would give her a few more days at sea to work her wiles on Papa—even if it meant facing the ire of the stuffy Captain Dawson when he'd be forced to turn his vessel around.

She studied him once more from the corner of her eye, and her chin lifted when she realized it wouldn't bother her to have a few extra days with him either.

The movement caused a wave of dizziness to wash through her.

Her fever was another thing that could go wrong…

She straightened her shoulders. She'd just have to stay strong long enough to make it onto the ship and keep hidden for a pair of the sun's rotations. After that, her fever would actually weigh in on her side. Papa was a doctor, and if anyone knew the toll a fever could take on a body, it was him. He'd want her back on the island, where he could offer her the best of medical care—just like *she* wanted *him* where she'd have access to his medical supplies.

Yes, she could make this work. She *had* to make this work.

Chapter 5
On the Wings of a Whisper

Trent clenched his teeth. Stubborn, contrary woman. She would exhaust herself into a serious illness if she kept up her belligerence.

"Listen." Trent cast a glance in the direction of her parents. "I know things with your mother could be better, but that's no reason for you to keep your sickness from her. Your father and I will be gone on the morrow, and I just want to make sure—"

"Captain." Exasperation touched her tone when she cut him off. "I already told you if I wasn't better by morning I would go see Dr. Kirk."

"What is the difference if your mother knows of your illness now or then?"

RyAnne sighed and tipped her head back. She stared at the ceiling for a long moment. "Things are…" She swirled her hand as though searching for the right word. "Complicated."

He suppressed a snort at her understatement and leaned toward her. "Yes, but—"

"Excuse me?" A young man wringing pale hands stood beside them. "May I have the honor of this dance, Miss Hunter?"

Dash it all! What was wrong with the lads in this port? It was obvious to anyone with eyes that the lady was unwell. Trent glowered at the boy, but his besotted gaze lay transfixed solely on RyAnne.

RyAnne stood to her feet with a smile for the idiotic intruder.

Trent lurched upright. "Miss Hunter, please." He kept his voice low so as not to draw attention.

But he didn't have time to say more. The smile left her face as though it had drained away with all her color. She swayed unsteadily and reached toward him as her eyes rolled back in her head and she began to topple. He caught her awkwardly in his arms and laid her gently on the floor.

"Get Dr. and Mrs. Hunter!" he snapped at the lad.

The young man only clutched the sides of his head and stared down at the lady's prostrate form. "D-did I say something wrong?"

Trent might have laughed outright under other circumstances. "No. Just get them!" Yanking off his coat, he placed it under RyAnne's head. He felt for a pulse on the soft hollow of her throat, and when the beat of her heart bumped sure and steady against his fingertips, relief washed over him.

Ryan and Anne pushed through the crowd that had gathered around Miss Hunter's still form. Rory and Jasmine hovered just behind them. Anne let out a gasp but made no move to help her daughter, and Ryan only looked at Trent and demanded, "What happened?"

Trent gave as brief an explanation as he could, not giving away the fact that she'd been sick since the ball began early in the evening, but only revealing she'd stood to accept a dance request and then fallen into a faint.

He glanced at the lad who had asked RyAnne to dance. He was wringing his hands and saying over and over again, "Oh dear. Dear me. What did I do?"

Ryan Hunter hunched forward in agitation as one of his coughing attacks took him. He groped for a handkerchief and covered his mouth. Then gesturing from Trent to RyAnne, he wheezed out between coughs, "Bring her. I'll fetch the carriages."

Trent placed one arm under RyAnne's neck and the other under her knees and lifted her to his chest. Jasmine gathered his coat, and he nodded his thanks, preceding her to the portico.

Rory assisted his mother into the first carriage, and Trent followed, angling RyAnne through the narrow entry. He started to lay her head in her mother's lap.

But Mrs. Hunter jolted back as though the girl might have a contagion. "Oh, no, Captain. Jasmine will sit here on this bench with me. You best keep RyAnne close to you in case the carriage slides on these dreadful roads."

Clenching his jaw, Trent laid her onto the opposite seat and then sat so RyAnne's head could rest against his leg. Jasmine draped his coat over RyAnne's thin shoulders and then tapped the carriage roof as she sank onto the bench beside her mother.

With a lurch they were in motion.

The ride to the Hunters' city home took twenty minutes, but RyAnne did not stir, and his anger at the mother studying the passing scenery and seeming so callous to the plight of her youngest child mounted with each passing minute.

When the carriage eased to a stop at the Hunters' front door and he stepped down with RyAnne, she moaned and rolled her head against his shoulder.

Relief washed through him. "There you are, Miss Hunter. I was beginning to think you may have gotten yourself into a bind I couldn't get you out of."

RyAnne frowned. Why did her head feel as though it must have been kicked by one of Rory's mules? Memory seeped in and she moaned. Mother and Papa surely knew now that she'd been taken with a fever again. Would Papa change his mind about sailing with the dawn now?

Another round of dizziness swept over her. And why was everything moving?

Opening her eyes, she looked up into Captain Dawson's face and frowned. It was most improper for the man to be carrying her around. It should be Papa, or at the very least Rory. She pushed at him and made an effort to get down, but she could not budge in the strength of his arms.

He was carrying her through the entryway at home.

"Put me down!" she demanded in a furious whisper.

The captain made no move to comply. He only looked into her face with the arch of one brow. "If I don't put you down, are you going to bite me?" The note of amusement in his voice reminded her of the incident in the bathhouse.

Not finding this situation at all funny, she glared up at him. "I will not bite you if you put me down this instant!"

"Is that a threat?" he asked with a grin, but in the span of a heartbeat all amusement left his face. He looked at her seriously. "I am sorry to disappoint. But right now I am under orders to carry you to your room, and that is what I intend to do. You need to rest."

Maybe he would know if anything had been said about delaying the trip. "Are you still sailing with the tide?"

He looked down, and if she didn't know the man better, she would have sworn there was a look of tenderness on his face. It must be the fever morphing her perception.

"As far as I know, the trip is to continue as planned. I do hope you'll have a care and take heed for your safety while I'm away?"

RyAnne couldn't help rolling her eyes. How many times had he expressed that same sentiment this evening? "You're quite used to having your way, aren't you, Captain Dawson?"

They had reached her room, and the captain entered, with Sarah bustling on his heels, and laid her on the bed. Mother stepped inside but remained by the door.

Bending over her for just a moment, he smiled, bringing a glint to his gray-green eyes. "I'm a captain. On my ship if someone does not obey my orders, I simply have him whipped."

With that he stood, lifted his jacket off her, slung it over one shoulder, nodded to her mother, and strode from the room. RyAnne sighed, closed her eyes, and ignored the feeling that the room had somehow grown colder with his departure. It was only because he'd robbed her of the warmth of his coat.

She gritted her teeth. For all he knew, he wouldn't see her again for months, and he hadn't even found it within himself to offer a farewell? She flipped over onto her side, ignoring Sarah's gentle ministrations with a damp cloth against her face and neck.

What did she care if he bid her farewell or not? The man had been nothing but a royal nuisance since he'd arrived in port two weeks ago. Besides, if she had her way, he would be confronting her with his imperial attitude once again only a few days hence.

But Sarah was going to be a problem now. Drat the troublesome timing of this bout with the fever. Sarah would be in and out of her room all night, fussing, and fluffing, and offering her water and cool cloths. Well, she would just have to think of a plan of escape. For no matter what, she must be on board *The Wasp* before it sailed at dawn.

At least she needn't worry about allowing herself to sleep a few hours. Sarah would wake her multiple times in the night to make her drink some of that vile quinine water Papa swore helped with the fevers.

She slept, woke, and drank the bitter tonic three times before she finally begged Sarah to give her some hours of uninterrupted slumber. "I'll drink the water every time I wake. My fever is much improved with the rest and your ministrations. Just leave me a bottle and the tin of quinine, but let me sleep."

Sarah grumbled and fluffed her pillow once more, but agreed, as RyAnne had hoped she would. She brushed aside her guilt at the deception. Not even Sarah would want Papa running off to the Continent to die all alone. And this was the only way to get Papa to see reason.

As soon as Sarah left the room, RyAnne rose, dressed in her practical green walking ensemble, and pulled her small satchel from the bureau. She couldn't take much with her, but she would need at least a few changes of clothes and a second pair of boots.

She studied her wardrobe. There was no sense in taking anything too fancy aboard ship. Pulling three walking skirts from the closet, she folded them and added the matching shirtwaists, petticoats, and underthings she would need. An extra pair of sturdy boots and a shift for sleeping in. To the top she added the tin of quinine, bottle of already-mixed tonic water, a packet of tooth powder, and a brush.

She studied the contents and ticked off the list on her fingers again, then gave a satisfied nod. That ought to do her for the week. She would have to wear at least one outfit more than once, but it couldn't be helped. She couldn't very well pack a full-size trunk aboard, and her little satchel was near to bursting as it was.

She penned a hasty note and propped it on the dressing table where she felt sure Sarah would see it come morning.

That done, she checked the time. Too soon to leave. The ship likely wouldn't even have the gangway down yet. She would just rest a bit longer. She sipped some bitter tonic and then sank down onto her bed. Intending only to close her eyes, she lay back against the pillows.

Seemingly only a minute later, she jolted awake. She rubbed her eyes and criticized herself for falling asleep at such a critical moment. If she overslept, she might miss the ship entirely.

That's when she noted the pale morning light seeping through her window!

No! She leapt to her feet. How could she have been so careless?! Had she missed her last opportunity?

Snatching up her satchel, she rushed to her door, but as she opened it and made for the stairs, she heard the sounds of the servants already stirring below! She would never escape unseen!

She hurried back into her room. What now?

Her heart thudded in her chest, and tears threatened to overflow. *Papa...*

Her gaze swept past her window. The trellis! She rushed across the room. Pushing open the window, she leaned out to double-check if all was clear. At least something was going her way, because no one lingered in the street below. She dropped her bag down. It landed with a *thud*, and she winced, sure a servant would come to investigate the noise. But after a moment when no one had emerged, she leaned past the sill, took hold of the trellis, and clambered out. A wave of dizziness crashed over her, and she gasped, clutching the trellis for dear life and pressing her forehead hard against one slat as she scrunched her eyes tight. After a moment, her equilibrium oriented itself, and she took a deep breath, forcing every muscle to relax. Trepidation trembling through her, she shut the window so a breeze wouldn't alert anyone too early to her absence, and then RyAnne scrambled down to her bag.

When she got to the docks, the smell almost overcame her. She literally wanted to gag from the stench but pressed the sleeve of her gown to her nose and forced herself to hurry on toward the slip where she knew *The Wasp* should be if she wasn't too late.

Please, God…

A larger ship currently blocked her view. She almost ran in her haste to get past it so she could see.

Rounding the end of the ship, she glanced across the harbor. She stumbled to a stop with a groan of defeat. For sailing out of the harbor at that very moment, its sails stark black against the golden dawn was—wait!

The captain's ship was a brig, not a dhow. Relief nearly took her to her knees. *The Wasp* still floated placidly at anchor just across the marina.

By the time she got to the pier next to the ship, the ammonia in the air stung her eyes to the point of tears. She eyed the ship. It was a sleek-looking vessel with two masts, sails furled, outlined against the ever-lightening sky.

She was so thankful to have arrived on time! She started to step from the shadows to hurry aboard, but just then noticed the sailor standing at the base of the gangplank checking the papers of anyone who attempted to board.

Her heart sank. To come so close only to be foiled by this! She narrowed her eyes. She gritted her teeth and calculated her options. She had not come this far to be turned away now. Her hastily hatched plan had involved stowing away, not purchasing passage—at least not until she revealed herself to Papa and the captain. She pulled back into the cloak of darkness.

Think!

She cast a glance about nervously. This wasn't the best part of town for a lone woman to linger. Thankfully the morning was still dark enough to offer some concealment in shadows.

Not too far away a young boy already offered his services to the stevedores for spare coins. One brushed him aside gruffly. "Outta my way, lad. I've no pieces small enough for the likes o' ye t' carry."

RyAnne stepped just far enough into the light to get the boy's attention when she snapped her fingers. "*Mtumishi! Kuja hapa!*" She called him toward her, then once more eased behind the barrel she was using for cover.

He scampered on willing feet, big dark eyes skimming her expectantly. But when he saw it was a woman who'd summoned him, disappointment drooped his features, and he skidded to a halt.

RyAnne held up a silver shilling. "So you've no desire to help a woman, have you?" she asked in his native Swahili.

At the sight of the coin, a huge white smile broke the dark plane of his face. He reached to snatch it, but RyAnne was quicker and lifted it out of his reach.

"First I need you to do something for me. Then you will come back and find this shilling sitting here atop this piling."

The lad twisted his lips up, as though determining whether his payment would indeed be there on his return.

"I will leave it. I promise you." She looked him right in the eye to ensure he'd understand she meant every word.

Finally he nodded. "What service may I offer the white lady today?"

RyAnne tilted her head in study of the sailor guarding the gangplank. "Well, lad," she murmured in English, "I know *what* I need you to do. I'm just not sure how to go about accomplishing it."

The boy cocked his head, obviously not understanding her words. But he followed her gaze and then gestured from her to the deck of the ship. "You need go? No ticket?"

She nodded. "*Ndiyo.*"

He chattered some words too quickly for her to grasp and ran off down the dock.

"No! Wait!" She stomped a foot. It looked like she was going to have to figure this out on her own. Maybe a fire in that canoe pushed toward *The Wasp* would buy her enough time to sneak aboard in the confusion? But she'd brought nothing to start a fire with. Perhaps she could pay two stevedores to start a fist fight? Yes, maybe—

Before she could even move a step in their direction, a little monkey scampered past her on the dock. He made a beeline for the sailor guarding the gangplank, jumped from the dock to his shoulder in one bound, snatched his hat from his head, and leapt away with a screech of triumph.

With a curse of surprise, the sailor was after him. "Come back here, ye little thief!"

RyAnne grinned. She set the shilling on the piling and scurried out of the shadows and up the gangplank.

But as she ascended the ramp, her smile quickly faded. She tried not to look at the foul, sewer-thickened water that lapped lazily against the hull, but her gaze was drawn to it like to a great disaster. She stifled a gasp as the unmistakable form of a bloated Negro corpse bobbed up not more than ten feet distant. Turning her eyes away in dismay, she forced herself to keep walking.

Yet, as though the horror cried out for her attention, her gaze returned to the desecrated waters. In all her wandering of the island, she'd never seen anything as appalling as this, not even in her ventures to the slave market. How could such an atrocity exist only minutes from their Stone Town residence, with her so naïvely unaware? Truth be told, the stench of the docks had kept her from venturing here before. And on any of their other trips to the mainland, her father had always insisted that RyAnne and Jasmine board the ship the night previous. He had not allowed them to come up on deck until they were three hours out to sea. She now thought she understood why. He had wanted to protect them from the awful scene that now stretched out before her.

As though in a trance, RyAnne moved to the stern of the ship, ascended to the quarter deck, and set her bag at her feet. She leaned her elbows on the taffrail. Her hand went to her mouth in silent horror as she eyed the dawn-washed harbor before her. Looking far out over the waves, she could see the frothy edge where the septic waste of the city ended and the murky waters of the Indian Ocean began. She had once heard Dr. Livingstone describe the stench of Zanzibar like a pie that could be sliced. Seeing these waters for the first time…it was no wonder.

And there amongst the filthy sewage of the city floated the remains of several bodies. When her eyes came to rest on the mangled body of a small child who could not have been more than six years old, tears came unbidden. "Oh, dear Jesus." The words slipped free on the wings of a whisper, the anguished cry of her soul.

She had heard that slavers dumped the bodies of sick slaves over the side of their ships just before port so they wouldn't have to pay duty for "goods" that would likely die. She'd heard. But she apparently hadn't believed.

Her eyes dropped closed. She suddenly did not want to be here. She was worried about her father, yes. But she wanted nothing more than to turn and run down the gangplank. Back to the isolated protection of her plantation home on the other side of the island. Her indigo-hued hills with their clean-smelling air. Her beautiful aquamarine ocean, white-sanded beaches, and sweet naïveté.

Papa had purchased many slaves to work on their indigo plantation. But he'd always treated them well. They had a roof over their heads, food, clothing, and a doctor when they were sick. Many of the young girls on the plantation she had viewed as friends.

But this… Her mind and body revolted at staying here amid the stench, with the horrid scene floating before her. She closed her eyes and leaned her forehead against her arms to quell the nausea pressing the back of her throat. How could Papa even own *one* slave when this was happening practically on their doorstep?

As though her earlier cry of anguish had flown to heaven and then back again, an otherworldly question resonated in her mind.

Whom shall I send, child?

From the main deck, she heard footsteps.

She jolted upright. She'd been so horrified by the sight of the bay, she'd forgotten to hide! The sun would peek over the horizon at any moment. She needed to get herself stowed away before then, but where?

Turning, she saw a tarpaulin-covered longboat strapped to the aft quarter of the deck. That would do! Hurrying to it, she lifted the canvas cover and pushed her bag inside the hull. Then with one last glance toward Zanzibar, she climbed in and pushed the tarpaulin closed behind her.

It was pitch black, but between two seats that stretched the entire width of the boat, she found a space large enough to curl up in. Resting her cheek against a mound of something she assumed to be netting, she closed her eyes. Her nose wrinkled at the distinct odor of fish mixed with the reek of the harbor.

Heaven's mercy, Papa had better be cooperative, seeing as how she was going to all this trouble for him. She felt a chill grip her and realized a fever was coming on again. She scrabbled her hand across the bottom of the boat until she contacted her bag. Withdrawing the bottle of quinine water, she drank as best she could, capped the bottle, and then laid back and closed her eyes.

The scene from the harbor would not leave her.

Again the question came to her. *Whom shall I send, child?*

She felt her brows pinch together. What could she do? She had no power or clout to stop slavery. She pondered the situation for several long minutes until she felt a lurch as the ship apparently left the dock. The rocking movement combined with her measly few hours of rest the night before lulled her to sleep.

She had no idea how long she'd slept, but when she woke, she was drenched in sweat and realized the sun must be baking down on her hiding place. The air was so thick she could barely draw breath. She must lift a corner of the tarp to allow a breath of fresh air in!

She listened carefully to hear if anyone might be near, but hearing nothing decided to chance the discovery—it was either that or die in here. And wouldn't that give Captain Dawson a start the next time he went to use his longboat? The thought brought an ironic smirk.

Tugging at the tarpaulin until it lifted enough to leave a three-inch gap where air could enter, she placed her mouth to the opening and sucked greedily at the fresh oxygen.

So thirsty! What she wouldn't give for a nice cool drink from the stream back home, but all she'd brought with her was the bottle of tonic water. It was warm, but she guzzled great gulps and was grateful for it. Despite the fresh air and water, weariness still weighed heavily on her. The fevers always sapped her strength with amazing totality.

She had the presence of mind to be thankful that something had finally gone her way. Surely Papa would listen to her now. He would see just how desperately she needed him and return with her to Zanzibar so she could care for him. She could hardly wait to reveal herself.

Lay Down Your Heart

Greater love has no one than this, than to lay down one's life for his friends.

John 15:13

Chapter 6

Lay Down Your Heart

Indian Ocean, off the Coast of Zanzibar
Midday
Early April 1866

ABOARD HIS SHIP *The Wasp*, Captain Trent Dawson leaned over a map in his cabin, studying the route Ryan Hunter had wanted to take to the Interior. Taking that route, they would have landed at Bagamoyo and traveled southwestward from there toward Lake Nyasa. It would have been a grueling trek—they would have had to make a hundred miles a week to reach the lake in five weeks' time.

The doctor was so sick that Trent tried to convince him to start his mission closer to the coast. He'd figured he could then continue his own operation to discover if Ali Khalifa, commodore of Harcourt Shipping, really was using his position to smuggle slaves. After he got the doctor settled, he'd planned to trek further inland to see what Khalifa was doing on the shores of the lake. But the doctor would have nothing to do with starting his mission closer to the coast. Trent had tried every means of persuasion at his disposal, but Hunter had been insistent.

"The good Lord has called me to the shores of that lake, Captain Dawson. And so to its shores I will make haste."

Trent rubbed the back of his neck and glanced out the porthole to the line of the horizon beyond. He didn't know whether to admire the man or curse him for a fool. Trekking so far into the interior of the Continent in his condition was naught but a death march.

One thing he did know...he wished they were traveling at any other time of year. It would be nearing the end of April by the time they arrived at the coast and made all their preparations for the inland trek, and the weather would likely be damp and sickly, although thankfully this week had been unseasonably warm and the winds were cooperating.

But the rains would come. And the rains caused more problems than just sickness. Rains always stirred up the rivers and made the crocs more dangerous due to hunger. Not to mention the sicknesses brought on by the combination of the damp, severe heat, and flash floods that contaminated drinking water.

He hoped the condenser he'd purchased on his last trip to England would hold up. He'd learned about the machine from Dr. Livingstone. The man had said during his last expedition, for over a month his crew had consumed only distilled water, and in that time not one day of sickness had plagued them.

Trent hoped distilled water would prevent Dr. Hunter from falling even more ill, and keep his crew healthy as well.

He ran his finger down the East African coast to Kilwa and then beyond to Cape Delgado. Thankfully, he'd been able to talk the doctor into taking that route. The Rovuma River wound west to its headwaters just east of Lake Nyasa. That would cut their overland route by hundreds of miles and shorten their trip by half, but it might also increase their run-ins with the dreaded crocodiles. Still, if they were careful, the river would be the faster and safer route to travel—especially for a man as sick as the doctor.

A movement at the door lifted his focus from the map.

John Knight, ship's bosun, stood at the door, his hat crumpled in his hand, looking most unsure of himself.

"What is it, John?"

"Well, Cap'n..." He gave the cap two twists. "It's really Garrett, sir...he's found...a stowaway."

Trent waved a hand of dismissal and turned his attention back to the map. "You know my rule when we find a stowaway and are less than a day's sail from a shore. Put him in a canoe with one canteen of water, an oar, and two rations of food."

"Aye, I told Garrett that. But he insists you'll want to see this one for yourself."

Trent sighed. Keeping order on his ship had often forced him to do things he hadn't enjoyed. Certainly it was harsh to turn a man loose on the sea with only one canteen and two rations, but he'd taken his life into his hands by sneaking aboard. Many a captain would make a stowaway walk the plank and give him nary another thought. "John, when was the last time you knew me to break one of my rules?"

John scratched his beard. "Never, Cap'n."

Trent gave a firm nod. "And I don't intend to start now."

John sighed.

Before he could turn away, Trent asked, "Oh, and who was on guard at the gangway this morning?"

John glanced down with a sheepish scuff of his boot against the deck. "That would'a been me, Cap'n."

Trent straightened and folded his arms. John had never been suspect of doing a half job before. "How do you suppose the reprobate got aboard?"

John couldn't seem to meet his gaze. "There was this monkey, you see, and 'fore I knew what it was about, it had snatched me cap and dashed off with it."

"A monkey?"

"Aye." John offered no more of an explanation than that.

"So while you were…retrieving your cap…you think this stowaway had time to come aboard?"

John's hat resembled a wrung-out rag. "Aye."

Trent suppressed the twitch that begged to lift the corner of his mouth. He'd have given every man aboard an extra week's pay just to see the well-padded bosun chasing that monkey. "Well, you've never been known to dally at your post, so I can believe nothing but that you were doing the best you could."

A sigh puffed out the man's cheeks. "Thank you, Cap'n."

"You may thank me, but the man who snuck aboard likely won't. Send him on his way. Dismissed." Trent resumed his study of the charts. It took him a moment to notice that John hadn't moved from his position at the cabin entry. He peered up at the man. "Is there something else?"

"Cap'n, beggin' your pardon, but First Mate Holloman told me not to return lest I brought you with me to administer the punishment yourself."

Trent's eyebrows went up at that. Garrett may be his cousin, but he was a first-rate second, and he'd never questioned Trent's orders before. Grabbing his hat, he thrust it on his head and gestured that John should lead the way.

Up on the quarterdeck, Garrett, hands clasped behind his back, paced before the longboat as though intent on producing a trench. Upon seeing their approach, he stilled and raised a hand to stop Trent before he could peer into the bottom of the longboat, where the man had obviously hidden himself.

Garret spoke, but in a voice so low, Trent could barely hear him above the wind. "Trent, I feel compelled to remind you of something Aunt Sally, God rest her soul, would say about now."

Trent cocked his head. It wasn't like Garret to break protocol by addressing him so personally while aboard ship. And his mother had passed from this plane when he and Garrett were ten and twelve, respectively. Not to mention, why was Garrett whispering? Had all of his crew gone mad?

Garrett cleared his throat and pressed on. "When we were lads, she used to tell us, 'There is no one in all the world so respected, admired, and revered as a gentleman.' Do you remember?"

Trent eyed him for a long moment before slowly saying, "Aye, I remember."

Garrett nodded and stepped out of his way. "Very well, then." He swept a hand toward the tarpaulin-covered longboat. "Please, take a look."

Trent jutted his jaw to one side, suddenly very leery of pulling back the canvas, for, heaven help him, he now had a very strong suspicion of who their stowaway might be, and if he was right, acting the gentleman was going to be the furthest thing from his mind.

In two swift strides he stood at the end of the boat, grabbed the tarpaulin, and heaved it back.

There curled among the nets on the bottom of the boat lay Miss RyAnne Hunter. Other than flinching at the first burst of light, she didn't even wake at the intrusion. Her long, dark curls had come loose of their pins and splayed in wild abandon around her head and across her shoulders. And an empty bottle that had been clutched in her hand rolled from her limp fingers.

He clenched his jaw and spun away to look out over the sea. *Of all the spoiled...* He didn't let himself finish the thought, but pivoted to look at her once more.

Her face was flushed, whether from heat or fever he did not know, but no moisture dotted her neck or brow. Her breaths were coming rapid and shallow.

Alarm shot through him, and he lunged forward to feel her pulse. Strong—but beating much too fast! He snapped his fingers at the young lad he'd taken on at the last minute this morning. "*Dabu, kuleta ndoo ya maji*! *Haraka*!"

The lad scampered off to fetch the bucket of water as Trent bent and unceremoniously lifted Miss Hunter into his arms. "Garrett, fetch Dr. Hunter. John, furl the sails, and make sure George is manning the helm, then bring her bag and get me some quinine and water from the condenser!"

Hurrying down the quarterdeck steps, he almost ran to the shade next to his cabin. Laying her out next to the wall, he scooped her mass of hair away from her face and neck, then rushed to remove her boots. They must cool her quickly!

"You've gone and done it now, Miss Hunter. I ought to keelhaul you. That would cool you down, and right quick." His head lifted, and he stilled. Of course! That would be better!

Dabu approached with the bucket, but Trent waved for him to put it down. "*Kamba*! *Kuleta kamba*!" Trent motioned toward the rope coiled near the mainmast.

Dabu ran to fetch it and returned just as Trent pulled off her second boot and John returned with a flask of drinking water.

They needed to cool her first! He motioned to the rope as he tugged off his own boots, hat, and jacket. "Tie me a stirrup, John."

"Sir!"

But Trent knew he needn't repeat his order, and John even fashioned a sling of sorts from a second short rope that would drape over Trent's shoulders and make it easier to hang on to her in the water. By the time he had stripped down to his breeches, his men had caught on to his plan and had everything at the ready.

John and Dabu helped lift her upright, and John slipped the sling under Miss Hunter's backside, and Trent draped the other end of the loop behind his neck and settled it along his shoulders. Then, his foot in the stirrup and clutching the rope with one hand and Miss Hunter with the other, his men hoisted him up and over the side of the ship and lowered them both into the bracing waters of the Indian Ocean as far as their shoulders.

"Come on, Miss Hunter. Put some of that stubbornness to good use and come back to us. Preferably before the sharks discover that we're here." He had no desire to risk an encounter with a shark in these waters. Many of them had developed a taste for human flesh because of the slave ships that tossed the sick and dying overboard between the mainland and Zanzibar.

He glanced around for any telltale fins and then dipped her back into the water until her head was submerged up to her ears. He shook her slightly. "Miss Hunter? Can you hear me?"

The first sensation RyAnne felt upon waking was the blessed coolness. The next was the realization that she was floating in water. With a gasp she jolted upright, only to encounter firm flesh and glinting gray-green eyes.

"Welcome back to the land of the living."

They were in the ocean! She was plastered against him and—Her gaze skimmed downward past where her hands rested on his bare shoulders, growing wider and wider as she encountered only flesh. "Captain Dawson!" She tried to push away, but she was tied to the man! "Sir! This is most inappropriate! Unhand me at once!"

"Aye. Most inappropriate. *You* should be back on the island, and *I* should be happily sailing toward the coast, where I will fill the hull of my ship with ivory that will make me a rich man. Instead here we are, saving your life."

"Saving…" If only she could remember what happened. The last thing she remembered was pulling back the tarpaulin slightly to get a breath of fresh air, and everything from that moment to this was a muddy mystery. She raised her chin. Then realizing how close that put her face to his, and the lift it gave to one corner of his mouth, she changed her tactic and looked at the side of the ship only a wave's crest away. "I can assure you, Captain, I feel most well. Why are we in the ocean tied together like a brace of fish bound for market?" She attempted to wet her lips, but her tongue couldn't seem to produce any moisture.

"Garrett, the fresh water!" The captain called toward the deck before looking at her and ordering, "Grab my neck."

Her hands already rested on his shoulders, and there was no way she was going to hold him any more tightly than she already was. "Captain, I'm already holding your neck."

"Have it your way." He let go of her with the one arm he'd had behind her and reached to grab a canteen snaking down from above.

As he did so, the rope holding her up in the water slipped off the back of his shoulders, and she plunged downward! With a squawk she lurched toward him, clambering and scrabbling until her arms were wrapped so tightly about his neck that they hung, pressed together, ear to ear.

He chuckled. "I thought you might come around to seeing it my way, Miss Hunter." He eased back and jiggled the canteen in the line of her vision. "Thirsty?"

Reluctantly, she had to concede that she was.

Something—could it be compassion?—glinted in his eyes. With his teeth he pulled the cork from the flask and then held it so she could grasp it with one hand.

She guzzled thirstily, taking such great gulps that some of the precious liquid spilled over to drizzle down her neck.

Thirst quenched, she ought to recork the canteen so they could return it aloft. However, the cork was still between the captain's teeth.

With her one arm clinging to the captain's neck and loathe to let go, despite the fact that he was now firmly holding her again, and her other hand holding the canteen, there was only one way— Her face blazed at the mere thought.

His lips took on a rakish tilt around the cork, and amusement furrowed up the skin at the corners of his eyes.

A passionate glare that ought to have put him in his place only raised a chuckle instead.

Well, she would rather face the sharks than give the captain the satisfaction of taking the cork from him with her teeth! Deliberately, she removed her arm from behind his neck.

He obliged the gesture by tightening his arm around her waist.

Careful to touch only the cork, she took it from his mouth and recapped the flagon.

He gave the rope tied about it a double tug, and someone from above pulled it upward out of her grasp.

For a long moment she stared at him, waiting for him to call that they too should be lifted, but he only stared back, a hint of ill humor tightening the skin around his mouth.

"Captain, *why* are we dangling in the ocean?"

He grinned, but somehow the light didn't quite reach his eyes. "That question brings up several very good questions of my own, Miss Hunter. The first being, what are *you* doing aboard *my* ship? And the second being, what under all of heaven made you think hiding under a tarpaulin in the blazing sun out in the middle of the Indian Ocean might be a good idea?! Especially when you're already sick with fever?"

Confound the tears that pressed at the backs of her eyes. She'd known he would be angry, but she hadn't counted on how much his anger would hurt. And if there was one thing she'd learned, it was that tears never solved anything. In fact, they generally made things worse for her. "I'm no thief, Captain. I brought money to pay for passage. I just knew you wouldn't let me aboard were I to try and buy a ticket in the usual manner."

"Well, you got one thing right, anyhow."

She blinked hard. But despite her effort to hold the moisture at bay, one tear spilled over.

A muscle ticked in his jaw. His throat worked, and his voice was low and raspy when he spoke. "I'm sorry, Miss Hunter. I shouldn't be so harsh. If I am angry, it only stems from a fear for your safety." His first knuckle brushed the tear from her cheek. "One day your rash decisions will lead you into a trouble from which I may not be able to save you."

His kindness heaped upon his anger only made more tears spill over. She gritted her teeth. He was going to think her nothing more than a weak-willed ninny.

"We are in the water because you had gotten overheated and I needed to cool you down quickly."

His finger skimmed the callus on her jaw where her violin had left its mark, and by all the water in the sea, every muscle in her body had surely just turned to jelly. And he'd thought she was overheated before!

"Captain—" Movement in the water beyond his shoulder drew her attention. A glistening black fin gliding leisurely toward them. Her eyes widened, and he was already turning to see what had caught her attention. "Captain, is that a—"

"Up!" he shouted. "Pull us up! Hang on!"

He clutched her tighter with his supporting arm, but she was taking no chances at slipping back into the water with a shark below! As the rope began a rapid ascent, she clamped both arms about his neck and her legs around his middle, squeezed her eyes shut, and hung on for dear life.

There was the feeling of racing air and then stillness, but she kept her face buried against his shoulder. After a moment, Captain Dawson reached up to loosen her arms. "You can let go now, Miss Hunter. We are safe on deck."

She pulled back slightly and looked down at him, but her arms seemed locked in place.

He swallowed visibly. "Miss Hunter?"

Her gaze roamed to the pleasant sight of firm lips surrounded by almost a day's worth of dark stubble, and she wetted her lips and reminded herself to breathe. "Yes?"

He cleared his throat. "I'd like to introduce you to my crew, if I may."

"Oh!" She scrambled down. But a wave of dizziness suddenly washed over her, and her legs tangled in her water-weighted skirts. She squawked and flapped her arms in a useless attempt to catch her balance.

Captain Dawson grasped her waist and held her steady. "Take a deep breath."

She suppressed a groan. This man would never see her as anything more than a flighty debutante. Still, she felt a great need for some air, so she followed his instructions.

"Good. One more."

Again, she obeyed.

Still supporting her with a hand at her waist, the captain turned her to face a group of motley men, all returning her look with varying degrees of incredulity. "Miss Hunter, I believe you know my cousin and first mate, Garrett Holloman?"

She nodded and curtsied, and that was when she noticed how her skirt was plastered against her. As subtly as she could, she pulled it away from her body. But a slurping noise accompanied each tug.

The captain didn't miss even a beat as he pulled his dry white shirt over his head. "And this is my bosun, John Knight."

The man who'd been guarding the gangplank that morning bowed to her as though they might be at royal court and she a countess.

Captain Dawson introduced her to the rest of the men, who stood stiff as statues in a perfectly straight line—all except the last. The last was a young boy with a nap of dark curls and skin so black his eyes shone. And he was fidgeting like a lad with a lizard in his trousers.

RyAnne's eyes grew wide as recognition dawned. "You!? Where's your monkey, then? Did you bring it aboard?"

Mr. Knight gasped and snatched his cap from his head. "That monkey! That was yours? Why, you imp! I ought to have you keelhauled!" He snatched the boy by the arm and propelled him a down the aft ladder, filling the lad's ear with recriminations.

RyAnne started after them. "Oh dear. I didn't mean to—"

The captain stopped her with a touch to her elbow. "Mr. Knight's bark is much worse than his bite, I can assure you. The lad will probably be eating spoonfuls of honey and drinking peppermint tea in Knight's cabin before the sun sinks below the horizon. For now, I believe your father waits for us in my cabin." He raised a brow at his cousin Garrett, who dipped his chin in acknowledgement.

Sickening realization washed over RyAnne. Why had Papa not met her on the deck? Dread gripped her. "Papa's well, isn't he?"

Captain Dawson looked grim. He started to say something but then snapped his mouth shut and simply held his hand toward the aft of the ship, indicating she should precede him.

Another thought penetrated. "Captain? How far out are we from Zanzibar?"

"Just over half a day's sailing."

Not nearly long enough!

Her plan to sneak aboard had been predicated upon the fact that she not be discovered too soon. She had wanted Papa to have a couple days to realize how much he missed them. How much he needed them, especially during these, his last days.

She sighed. Had she come this far only to have her plans foiled? Still…the closer they were to the island, the more likely he would be to turn back with her, so maybe all was not lost.

"Miss Hunter?"

RyAnne turned to see the captain's cousin holding out her valise.

He winked subtly. "I believe you might be needing this, miss."

"Thank you, Mr. Holloman. Indeed. And much sooner than I had anticipated." She lifted her heavy wet skirts in one hand and cast a disparaging look toward Captain Dawson as she reached for the bag.

"I'll carry that." The captain took the bag before she could.

As he said a few quiet words to Garret, she took a moment to study him. He looked quite different than he had the last time she'd seen him in his ballroom finery. Today he wore black breeches that ended just below his knees. His feet were bare, but he clutched a pair of boots in the hand unoccupied by her valise. His white linen shirt had grommets from collar to cuff and was laced with linen ribbing along the arms and at his throat. The wind plastered the loose material against well-defined muscles, and her face heated at the memory of the pleasant feel of his skin beneath her fingertips in the water below.

Before he could catch her looking, she focused her attention on the sea, an errant thought lifting one corner of her mouth. *It might not be such a hardship, were I to contrive heatstroke at some point in the future.* Pressing her lips together to stifle a giggle, she studied the decking at her feet and reminded herself what a drudgery life would be were she ever to be stuck with the man.

Yes indeed, Captain Dawson might cut a fine figure, but he was a bit stuffy and much too accustomed to having his way.

Trent paced the small area behind his desk, one hand cupping his chin, hardly able to believe what he was hearing.

"What do you mean you won't take me back?!" RyAnne gaped at her father, already lying near death's door on Trent's own bunk. "Papa! Look at you. You need to be home in bed, where you can rest and recuperate."

Trent planted his fists onto his desk. "She has a point, Hunter. And we certainly can't take her into the wilds of the Continent with us."

Ryan rasped for a breath. "You don't know my daughter, Captain Dawson. I didn't want my family to watch me die, but of all of them"—he fumbled for his daughter's hand—"RyAnne has the strength to face it. It is good that the Lord has sent her to me in my last days."

"Papa—" RyAnne's voice broke, and she spun away to stand near the porthole. She stared out at the ocean, but one hand plucked at her lower lip, and he could see moisture glistening in her eyes.

Trent thumped the desk and then turned his gaze toward the ceiling. How had he gotten himself into this predicament? While they'd been on the island, he hadn't known Ryan was so sick. But the man had come aboard and nearly collapsed straight away. He'd apparently been holding himself together for the sake of his family. Trent had tried to persuade the doctor to return home, but he'd insisted that he'd paid Trent to take him to the shores of Lake Nyasa, and he would have nothing for it but to go.

How could he deny a dying man's wish to die away from the grieving eyes of his family? He wanted them to remember him strong and steady, he'd said. Not wheezing and weak.

On top of that, this morning Trent had witnessed Khalifa's *Indigo Waves* pull from port just before he'd lifted anchor himself. If he turned back now, the man would have several days' jump on him, and he might lose the opportunity to discover what his business in the Interior really was.

And then weighting the other side of the scale, there was Miss Hunter.

He folded his arms over his chest and studied her in the light cast from the porthole.

She was still trying to keep her composure and doing a fair job of it. But he knew fatigue from the heat exhaustion would be hitting her soon, and one kind word or gesture was likely to put her over the edge. She needed to get out of her wet clothes, and he hadn't even one suitable place for a lady to dress on the entire brig.

That was only the immediate problem. He pinched the bridge of his nose. If he took her into the Interior, no doubt he would endlessly be chasing her down to rescue her from one dangerous situation or another. And there was the potential hazard to her health and even her life. Could he risk that, even in the face of all the other things weighing in favor of heading on to the Interior?

Ryan wheezed as though it might be his last breath ever, and RyAnne rushed to his side. Taking up a cloth, she soaked it with a bit of water and dabbed at her father's forehead.

Trent sighed. Maybe the man would die before they reached the coast and save him from having to make a decision.

He took in RyAnne's downcast expression and rubbed the back of his neck. *You're a callous lout.*

He remembered her mother's almost cruel treatment of her. It would be a burden most grievous for her to lose the only parent who seemed to care for her.

Miss Hunter's safety, balanced against knowing Ali's plans, would win out every time. But Dr. Hunter had been a good friend to him. And his dying wish that his daughter accompany them had to be given some weight. So for now they would press on as planned, whether he wanted to rush Miss Hunter back to the safety of the island or not.

Ryan's jaw slackened in sleep.

Trent took her elbow. She lifted eyes so full of grief he wanted to step back from the force of it. Instead he gently tugged her to her feet. "Let him rest. You need some yourself. You'll do him no good if you aren't well enough to care for him."

She sighed wearily. "Aye. I suppose you are right."

It was her compliance more than anything that sent a bolt of concern through him.

He strung a line from the hinge of the porthole to the handle of the bookcase behind his desk, cordoning off a triangular segment of the compartment. Flipping a blanket over it, he then tossed her bag behind the makeshift dressing room. With a nod to her, he stepped out into the passageway. "I'll fetch a hammock while you change."

When he returned several minutes later, knocked, and entered at her call, he was glad to see she had indeed changed and had even hung her wet things over the line to dry.

In his younger days, when *The Wasp* had been father's only ship, he had slept in here in a hammock and his father on the bed. The hooks for the hammock still remained in the beams, and it only took him a moment to hang it for her. Knight entered just behind him with a tray of broth, bread, and water.

Trent eyed the water glass. "Do you need more tonic?"

She shook her head. "I believe the fever has broken, but I find myself most exhausted."

Remembering her stubborn and insistent refusal to rest at the ball, he stepped forward and laid a hand on her forehead.

She stiffened. "Captain—"

Before she could say more, he cut her off. "Just seeing how candid you were being." At her outrage, he couldn't help a grin. "It appears that, at least this once, you have spoken truthfully." With a slight bow, he backed into the passageway and closed the door behind him.

Chapter 7
Lay Down Your Heart

Much to Trent's relief yet consternation, Dr. Hunter slowly regained his strength over the next three days' sailing, but he remained insistent they not turn back to return the stunned Miss Hunter to Zanzibar.

On this night, magnificent splashes of orange and turquoise colored the sky as he joined father and daughter in his cabin for the evening meal. From the moment he arrived, it was apparent that RyAnne was quite put out and that Dr. Hunter was having nothing to do with her persuasion. Yet if persistent didn't describe RyAnne, Trent didn't know what did.

"But, Papa, I don't have suitable clothing for a trek into the heart of the Continent."

Hunter met Trent's gaze across the table. "Oh, I'm sure Captain Dawson will happily assist with finding you a suitable wardrobe for the journey. I won't have you gallivanting around in skirts while we're traipsing through savage lands. For one, there are snakes, spiders, scorpions, and the like. For another"—the man leaned around the edge of the desk and peered at the girth of RyAnne's hooped hem—"those will be most unsuitable attire for traveling the narrow paths we will no doubt be faced with."

She gasped. "You can't be implying what I think you are implying!"

"I'm not implying anything, dear daughter. I'm stating it outright." Hunter calmly cut the fish on his plate. "'Tis breeches and sturdy boots you'll be wearing, or you won't be taking one step inland with us, young lady."

RyAnne's pretty little jaw dropped nearly to her chest. "Papa! This is most improper!"

Hunter pierced his daughter with a look. "So is stowing away on a ship, but that didn't seem to stop you."

RyAnne seemed unable to form a response other than to sputter incoherently, and Trent gulped from his glass to hide his amusement.

The doctor went on, undaunted. "Let us leave 'proper' to civilization and its courts, and think about *safety* and *practicality* while we are trekking the wilds of the Continent."

With a little huff, RyAnne tossed down her serviette and flounced from the room.

Trent shoveled in a mouthful of rice before his humor could be detected by his companion.

At least this was one battle he wouldn't have to wage with the little lioness himself, for he'd been thinking the same things. The savannah contained vast stretches of grass so thick and tall that two men marching side by side a foot apart might not know the other was there. And once they put his low-draft steamboat in the water to sail up the Rovuma, there would literally be no room to accommodate Miss Hunter's skirts.

Canvas pants tucked into thick sturdy boots had saved him more than once, and it would be nothing but foolish to head inland wearing the fripperies Miss Hunter considered her wardrobe. He was thankful her father at least had that much of a head on his shoulders, even if he did wish the man would order her back to Zanzibar.

Perhaps now would be a good time to broach that subject again. He cleared his throat. "Once we arrive at the coast, you and I could head inland and Holloman could take her back to the island."

The doctor sighed and wiped his mouth. For a long moment he stared at the darkening sky out the porthole. Then his words came slowly. "Rory will be out at the plantation working dawn to dusk. Anne insisted she and Jasmine would remain in town until I returned. So I left RyAnne home, because despite the way Anne treats her, perhaps because of it, she is the strong one who would have kept them all from falling apart when the word of my death arrived." He rubbed the back of his neck and hung his head. "It was my sin, Captain, which led Anne to detest the lass so much. I fear I brought a grievous curse on my family years ago, one that may never be broken. I've much to make up for."

Trent frowned at that revelation but held his tongue. The man's business was his own.

Hunter sighed. "Aye, I wanted her there, yet now that she is here…I fear my human frailty will not lend me the strength to part with her again." The man pinned him with a stare. "I fear I must ask a boon of you, my friend."

Trent straightened and set his fork down as sudden understanding shot through him. "I will watch over her and do my best to make sure she is returned safely home, if the time comes."

The doctor's face crumpled, and he lurched to his feet and faced the hull. After a moment, he rasped, "You lift a great weight from me, lad. I thank you."

Trent rubbed his palms together uncomfortably. "I will also ask Garrett to return to the island to watch over your wife and daughter."

Hunter dropped his head to study the floor at his feet. "Another weight lifted. You bless me in ways undeserved."

"It's only Christian duty, sir."

Ryan spun then to meet his gaze. "Is it?"

"I would do the same for anyone."

The doctor assessed him for a long moment. "Maybe. But she will make some man a fine wife one day."

Trent jumped up, his chair shooting out behind him as he held up his hands, palms out. "Christian duty, sir, that is all! Now if you'll excuse me, I need to relieve my helmsman."

Hunter placed his fingertips on Trent's chest before he could make his escape. "Promise me then that you'll do one more thing for me."

Leery foreboding seeped over him. He settled his hands on his hips. "If I can…"

"Promise me you'll not let Brayden Harcourt, or anyone of the like, marry her."

Trent couldn't stop the bark of laughter that escaped. "That may be like asking a mule to prevent rain from falling."

The corner of Ryan's mouth lifted. "Perhaps. But I've seen

you cross swords with RyAnne on more than one occasion, and generally you come out the winner. So I'm counting on you to give it your best shot."

Trent studied the decking at his feet. "*If* the time comes, and *if* you are not here to speak for yourself, I'll make your wishes known to her."

Ryan pulled his hand back and nodded. "That's all I can ask. And I appreciate it."

Trent made his escape before the man extracted any more intimate promises.

The lioness may be pretty and sleek, but he had no desire to spend the rest of his days fighting her sharp claws and biting wit.

RyAnne didn't do much except rouse to eat, and then sleep some more, for the next several days. Papa seemed to have turned a corner, resting most of the time himself, and her mind had been eased a small measure with regard to his condition.

But after several days of rest her strength had returned, and she feared she was beginning to come down with a case of "cabin fever," as Captain Dawson called it.

So she couldn't have been more relieved when the "land-ho" call had rung out over an hour ago, and Papa had gone topside to get the details. A little thrill rushed through her at the thought of getting to explore a new city.

RyAnne took advantage of Papa's absence to change into her only remaining clean dress, and now waited for him to fetch her once the ship had docked.

The port was called Bagamoyo. *Lay Down Your Heart.* Her brow furrowed as she primped her hair in the reflection of the tea tray. How odd that a town should be named such a thing. Whyever would they have wanted to call it that?

But—she set the tray down and smoothed her skirts—never mind the name. A town was a town. She was looking forward to doing a little shopping. Eating a fresh mango. And maybe even some roasted peanuts. She paced the confines of the captain's cabin, waiting for Papa to fetch her.

Memories of the Zanzibar harbor assailed, and her stomach turned a long, slow curl. Truth be told, if this harbor was going to be anything like that, she was happy to remain here belowdecks until she could escape the ship with as little exposure to the atrocities as possible. But she hadn't heard even one murmur about this harbor being similar to that on Zanzibar, so likely she needn't worry.

Finally she felt the bump of the ship against the dock. They had arrived! Soon her feet would be on blessed solid ground.

Slowly the minutes ticked by, but Papa did not come to get her. She peered out the porthole, but all she could see was the side of another ship in the next slip over. She poked her head out into the passageway. Empty and silent. Papa must have forgotten her. She would just go up and find him so they could go into town together.

Bosun Knight hurried toward her the minute she stepped into the thankfully pleasant-smelling air on the deck. "Miss Hunter. Your father asked that I instruct you to remain belowdecks until we can set sail once more this evening."

"Nonsense. Whatever for—"

An undulating screech sliced through the humid air. Much more than terror—so much more—reverberated in that short wail. It held a note of finality. A tenor of defeat. And the first was followed by a second and a third. The cries rose up together in chorus, and underlying them came deeper shouts, cold and uncaring, the crack of whip, and jangle of chain.

John Knight clutched at her sleeve. "Miss—"

She brushed past him, drawn to the starboard rail as if pulled by a lead rope. A dhow was tied up across from them in the slip that shared their dock.

On the shore, a line of poor woeful souls, shackled together, shuffled toward the gangplank of the dhow. None of them wore more than a breechcloth—man, woman, or child—all so thin that she could have counted their ribs. Two thickly muscled men strode along the dock, each holding a sharp prod in one hand and a whip in the other. These they liberally used on any of the pitiable, frail wretches they deemed too slow or uncooperative.

A whip descended across the shoulders of a hunched old man, leaving a crimson streak in its wake. RyAnne flinched and looked farther down the line.

A wide-eyed woman bent and frantically tried to disengage the shackle around her ankle. Bright-red blood and white bone stood in contrast to her dark skin. She'd obviously tried to remove the clasp before, to no avail. One of the slavers shouted at her, but when she was slow to rise, he jabbed her with the point of his goad. With a haggard cry the woman scrambled forward, and the slaver gave a satisfied nod.

RyAnne's hand rose to her mouth. She absentmindedly registered Mr. Knight by her side saying something. He took her arm, but she shook him off and gripped the rail.

At the top of the gangplank, two other slavers waited to receive the slaves being prodded their way. One held a key, and as each reached the deck, he bent and unlocked their shackles, then handed them off to another man. There were no slaves on the deck, so they were obviously being taken below. The dhow was small, smaller even than Captain Trent's brig, yet at least a hundred more slaves still waited to be taken aboard the vessel.

She'd heard of slave ships that gave only a meter of room between decks and packed the slaves in so tightly they lay shoulder to shoulder. But she was only now beginning to realize what a sheltered life Papa had ensured she had. Stories didn't compare to actually witnessing such atrocities.

How could people be so cruel to one another? She swallowed and absentmindedly rubbed her fingertips over her forearms. Had the woman who had birthed her faced something like this early in her life?

She remembered the question that had come to her as she had first registered the horrors at the Zanzibar harbor. *Whom shall I send, child?*

Something ought to be done! But what could she, a lone

woman, do about the injustice in the world? She couldn't take that whole ship's crew on by herself. And the law was not on her side—they were doing nothing illegal, provided they only shipped the slaves to Zanzibar.

She thought of Papa. First, she needed to return him to Zanzibar where he would have better medical treatment. She must convince him. But… She swallowed and scanned the dhow once more. What kind of person would she be to witness things like this and not at least try to do something?

She pressed the heels of her hands to her eyes as defeat washed over her. How had she lived in a land full of slavery all her life and never truly understood the dehumanizing origin of it? She'd even treated wounds at the slave market. However, nothing had struck her to the core like this sight.

The odds of actually making a difference seemed insurmountable.

Her desire to explore the town had vanished.

A pregnant woman in the line of slaves glanced back toward the shore and released a raspy keen that sent a chill down RyAnne's spine.

Lay Down Your Heart. The town's name made so much more sense now.

Exhaustion enveloped her like a heavy cloak. Listlessly she retreated belowdecks and crawled into her hammock.

Papa and Captain Dawson returned a few hours later, and they put out to sea without so much as a word. From the pinched looks they both wore, each was as happy to be away from that place as she was.

They sailed south along the coast, close enough in that the dark outline of the Continent remained a constant companion off to the starboard.

All RyAnne's energy had been sapped by the scene along the Bagamoyo dock. She spent several days pleading ill and sleeping most of the time. Which, if she were honest with herself, wasn't far from the truth. She was *heart*sick. She remembered nothing of her own mother, who had, in fact, died giving birth to her. But it chilled her to realize it could so easily have been her walking there in that chain gang of people. Once, when she slept, she dreamed a woman much like herself walked among the line of shackled humanity. She'd jerked awake with a start and lay in her hammock, heart pounding for a moment before reality settled into her mind.

Of course, the girl who'd birthed her would not have experienced such treatment. She had been the daughter of a Zanzibar clove plantation owner. Papa had purchased the girl directly from her father.

RyAnne rolled to her side and tucked her elbow under her head, staring at the hull.

That must have been painful enough for the girl—to have her own father sell her.

Papa had intended to use the girl as a house servant because of her beauty. But then he'd conceived in her a child, and the girl had died in childbirth. Papa could have taken RyAnne to the slave market. But instead, he'd insisted on raising her as his own. Her first soft mewl had driven a shaft of remorse straight through his heart, he'd told her years later. She was white enough to pass as his and Anne's own offspring. He'd even insisted Anne allow the use of her name to combine with his, as was common. And to save face in society, Mother had gone along with his plan. They'd promptly returned to England, and when family and friends expressed surprise over the new baby, Papa and Mother had claimed their letter about the impending arrival of a new little one must have gotten lost in transit. And by the time they returned to Zanzibar a few years later, the details of the timing of it all were a hazy blur in the distant past. Thus RyAnne's heritage had remained unquestioned.

RyAnne sighed.

It was no wonder Anne had spent the bulk of her life detesting her.

Finally sleep came that night, and when she woke, she set a resolve in her heart never to remain so naïve again. After she talked Papa into going home, she would find a way to make a difference. Even if she feared she could do naught.

She felt better after that, and when a few days later there came a knock on the captain's cabin door, she actually felt relief at the intrusion. "Who's there?" she called as Papa roused from a nap and rubbed his palms over his face.

"Begging your pardon, miss, but the captain has sent word. We'll dock at Cape Delgado by nightfall."

Finally, she would get to escape the wearisome rocking of this ship.

While at Bagamoyo, Trent had sent word to a friend at Cape Delgado that they would like a place to stay while they assembled the parts of the little steamship he and Papa had purchased for this trip. Tonight they were to stay in the home of his friend, a British commodore in charge of keeping the peace and battling slavery in the towns along the coast.

Surely there would be dancing and music, and maybe that would begin to erase the helpless feeling that had been hanging over her like a gray cloud for the past few days.

Music...

Her one regret was that she hadn't been able to bring her violin with her. She ran her thumb over the small calluses on her fingertips. Would they be gone before she had the chance to play again?

Papa excused himself so she could change her dress, and she'd just finished buttoning the shirtwaist of her yellow ensemble when a knock sounded once more. Papa must have returned to change into his evening coat. Her excitement had been building steadily since the announcement earlier.

Hurrying across the room, she flung the door open. "Oh, Papa, I'm so excited to hear music ag—"

Captain Dawson leaned in the companionway, one shoulder planted into the bulkhead, arms folded.

He'd been so busy for the past several days that she'd hardly seen him, much less spoken to him.

His eyes swept her, and a gleam leapt to life there.

She smoothed her hands over imaginary wrinkles. Why did she want his approval so much? "I'm sorry. I thought—"

Waving away her apology, he straightened. "I should have announced myself." He bowed over her hand, holding her gaze as he did so. "You look very…rested."

Rested?

She'd just spent over a quarter of an hour primping her hair and dressing, and the word that came to him was *rested*?

She pulled her hand free and forced a curtsy. "Thank you, Captain Dawson."

Dash it all. Why did she care a whit what this man thought of her?

"If you'll pardon me, I need access to my chest inside."

"Of course. I'll just go find Papa up on deck."

The next thirty minutes were occupied with the crew docking the ship along a rickety-looking wharf. A carriage had been sent down from the main estate, and a short ride later they arrived at a great house on a low bluff overlooking the ocean below.

Just a furlong or so away, small huts clustered near the Rovuma River, which flowed down the hill and dumped into the bay.

Trent introduced her and Papa to Commodore Llewellyn Cornwall, who seemed a pleasant enough fellow, if a bit drawn to his drink, and who in turn presented the dark-haired Arab already seated at his table.

RyAnne's stomach pitched.

"May I present Ali Khalifa? Here on behalf of Harcourt Shipping to…trade for supplies." The commodore and Captain Dawson exchanged glances full of some elusive meaning.

Ali Khalifa's eyebrows rose as RyAnne was introduced. He raked her with a look that sent a shiver of unease through her. He sucked at his front teeth, then picked at them with a dirty fingernail, glancing away and seeming to dismiss her from his mind.

Shaking out the serviette next to her plate, she tucked it into her lap. Khalifa here? What was the commodore of Harcourt

Shipping doing on an inland trading mission?

The whispered conversation she'd overheard in the Harcourts' garden the night of the ball came back to her with sudden clarity. She stiffened. Could Khalifa be one of the men she'd heard? She swallowed. If he was, then it was certain whatever plan they'd been discussing was ill gotten. Who had the second man in that conversation been?

After the long dinner trying to suppress her unease over Khalifa's presence, she could not even muster an ounce of disappointment that the meal was a short affair with no music and dancing afterward. In fact, RyAnne was to a great extent relieved when their host stood and indicated the meal was concluded, directing a servant to show them all to their quarters.

Trent stood along with her and Papa. He cast a cursory glance toward the repulsive trader before turning his attention back to their host. "Lew, I'll just escort Miss Hunter to her room, but then I'd like a word with you, if I could?"

"Certainly." Commodore Cornwall nodded.

Trent motioned for her to precede him out the door, and they followed the head house servant, who had been introduced as Kako, down a long outer veranda with guest rooms off to the left. Each room had a large window so guests could look over the terraced gardens to the beauty of the Indian Ocean beyond. As they walked, RyAnne admired the moonlight spilling like a milky gloss over the obsidian tabletop of the water. Far out in the bay, she could see the twinkling lights of a trawler, probably fishing. Cicadas had begun their evening serenade, accompanied by the chorus of rushing river water. And despite the fact that she'd done not much but rest for the past several days, weariness sapped her strength.

Trent paused just outside her room as Kako unlocked the door and handed her the key and then returned the way they had just come.

"Thank you, Captain. Good evening to you." She started into her room.

"Miss Hunter?"

Trent's words froze her on the threshold, and she turned to face him. "Yes, Captain?"

He rubbed the back of his neck, glancing down at the rattan mat under his feet before peering up at her. "Are you well?"

She lifted her chin and swallowed. "I will be fine, thank you."

"Yes..." He cleared his throat. "Let me remind you that over the next few days I'm going to be very busy putting our boat together and loading it with supplies. If you find yourself getting bored and have a yen to run off to a cockfight or a slave market, I hope you will take into consideration"—he glanced back toward the dining room where they'd just left Khalifa, and something dark rippled across his features—"that you are not in Zanzibar Town, where you have many friends, but are in a locale totally unknown to you and full of many dangers." He lowered his chin and gave her a pointed look.

Her jaw dropped. Did he think her so addlebrained? "Captain Dawson! I'm am not a child who needs to be mollycoddled and bossed about! I know how to take care of myself, and of course I would do no such thing!"

He clasped his hands behind him and headed back down the veranda toward the main house, then paused and glanced over his shoulder, his brows arched in apparent skepticism. "I, for one, hope you can prove those words to be true, Miss Hunter. Good evening." He offered a sketch of a bow.

She stomped into her room and slammed the door behind her. Of all the pompous boors in the universe, why did that one have to be so comely?

Kako directed Trent toward the parlor when he stepped back into the main wing of the house.

Lew sat on the settee nursing a finger of scotch. He indicated the decanter on the sideboard. "Help yourself."

Trent sat in one of the wingback chairs across from the commodore. "No thanks." He clasped his hands and leaned forward, resting his elbows on his knees as he studied his old friend. The many days of heavy drinking were wearing hard on the man. Veins etched trails across his bulbous nose, and wrinkles added years Trent knew were not there.

Lew turned the glass and assessed the amber liquid in the bottom. His lower lip protruded. "You are probably wise not to start, my friend. The old girl's not much of a companion." Despite his words, the man lifted the glass in a trembling hand and sipped unsteadily.

Trent studied the floor for a moment before looking up to meet Lew's gaze. "What news have you"—he turned to scan both entrances to the room and lowered his voice to ensure he wasn't overheard—"of Khalifa?"

Lew set his glass on the table by his side and rubbed a hand down his face. "He arrived day before yesterday. He and his crew have been loading casks of dried fish and tea onto his *Indigo Waves*." Lew pursed his lips. "Interesting thing is that Khalifa plans to take several of his crew inland on a 'trading mission' as soon as they finish loading the ship—probably in the next few days. His first mate is apparently going to sail the cargo to England."

Trent rubbed the back of his neck. "He'll have a good week's jump on me then. There's no way we can get *The Bee* assembled before then."

Lew nodded. "You'll have one thing on your side. He and his men are taking canoes. So perhaps your steamer will allow you to make up some time once you are underway."

"Canoes?" Trent cupped his chin and considered that. "That means he'll likely be taking any captives overland on the Trail of Chains to Bagamoyo, then. Using them to haul…ivory, maybe?"

Lew nodded. "Likely. I've seen at least two of his men with four bore rolling block rifles. And another three with the old sepoy Brown Bess."

Elephant guns. So Khalifa wasn't just here to take slaves but would likely use them to carry a haul of tusks to the coast also.

Trent gritted his teeth.

Despite the fact that he'd told Miss Hunter he was only here to score a ship's load of ivory himself, he had no stomach for destroying an animal for such a small portion of its parts. He'd seen more than his fair share of decimated herds cut down merely for their tusks.

But that wasn't the worst of it. Many times if women were captured with their children, they were forced to carry both ivory and babe. When they became too weak to carry both, the slavers often ended the life of the child, since they were of less immediate value than the ivory.

And he was supposed to follow Khalifa until he met up with the man he was working for? Trent's stomach pitched at the mere thought. He pierced Lew with a look. "I'll not stand by while innocents are killed just so you can discover who the head of this operation is."

Lew sighed. "Let us hope it won't come to that. If you can befriend him, perhaps you will gain his trust and can get the information we need before he can wreak too much havoc across the Continent. Just remember we don't get paid unless we put a stop to the whole ring."

Befriending such a man was the furthest thing from his mind. Trent stood. "No amount of money on earth is worth selling your soul." He started across the room.

"And yet—"

The tone of Lew's voice stopped him, and he turned back to look at the man.

Lew arched a brow. "I can't blame you for that sentiment. Do what you have to. However, how many more lives will be lost in the future if we don't find the ringleader and cut off the head of the snake?"

Trent clenched his jaw and headed for his room without replying. What had he gotten himself into?

For two days RyAnne kept to her room, only leaving for

meals and to check on Papa. She never lost an opportunity to cajole him to give up his mission. But no matter her pleas, he remained insistent that he would not return to Zanzibar.

Torrential rains had started late in the night of their first day on land and hadn't stopped. But it was more the fact that Khalifa was out there somewhere that kept her in her room.

By early afternoon of the third day, the sun finally emerged, and she paced her room like a caged animal. She must take a walk or go stark-raving mad. And she couldn't cower in her room forever.

She opened her door and leaned out to peer both ways down the veranda. No one was in sight.

Off to her left, far down at the mouth of the Rovuma where it dumped into the ocean, she could see the men had made good progress, for Captain Dawson's little steamship, *The Bee*, now floated, mostly assembled, on the waves next to *The Wasp*. And small ant-like crewmen carted crates and barrels across a gangway from the bigger ship to the littler one.

It looked like, unless she somehow miraculously changed Papa's mind, they would be on their way inland soon, and she hadn't even taken time to explore the beautiful grounds yet.

Kako stepped from the main wing of the house and set to sweeping the veranda with a thatch broom. If he was anything like Sarah, he would be able to tell her exactly where everyone staying at the house currently was.

"Good afternoon, Kako," she called.

He paused and bowed in her direction with a touch to his forehead.

"Where is everyone?"

Straightening, he glanced down toward *The Wasp*. Was that a hint of a smile he tucked away before glancing at the spot just in front of his feet? "Commodore Cornwall rests, madam. As does your father. Captain Dawson works with this crew to make small boat." He offered nothing more.

"And Commodore Khalifa?"

"He works at his ship, madam. Continuing to load supplies."

Relief edged out her concern. A little walk was all, and Captain Dawson would never be the wiser. Except, she hadn't brought a parasol with her, and if she got too much sun, the captain would certainly notice come dinner.

She remembered seeing a bumbershoot hanging on a hook in the entry. "Might I borrow the bumbershoot hanging by the front door, in case of more rain?"

Kako assured her it would be fine. She hurried to the entry, lifted it down, and headed outdoors. The metal handle and stout ribbing made the thing three times as heavy as her favorite parasol, but it would allow her to walk and still keep Captain Dawson happily ignorant.

She headed first to the garden, reveling in the beauty created by bird-of-paradise against a backdrop of palm bushes and acacia trees not quite in bloom. One stone pathway led around a circular bed full of red and pink roses in full glory. And another led past a trickling creek that spilled into a stone pond full of colorful blue and yellow fish that were flat and thin like little swimming saucers.

She bent to sniff the waxy white blossom on a gardenia bush, reveling in the warmth of the sun all around her.

Chapter 8

Lay Down Your Heart

Lugging a cask of flooring nails from the ship to the steamer, Trent glanced up toward the house. A glint of yellow movement in the garden snagged his attention. He stilled and looked closer. Something black hovered above the yellow. *Is that an umbrella?* He took in the cloudless blue sky, and then his eyes narrowed. Sure enough, only a moment later Miss Hunter stood to full height, she and her makeshift parasol clearly outlined against the white plaster of the house.

He sighed. Well, she'd made it a full two days. Much longer than he'd anticipated, probably thanks only to the constant downpour they'd been having.

He scanned the gardens around her. For the moment it looked like she was alone, but he hadn't liked the way Khalifa had stared at her during the evening meal the day before. The man had been kept busy loading his own ship, but he would likely be knocking off for the evening soon.

Trent carted the nails to where John Knight worked near the front of the steamer, and then used a rag to wipe the sweat from the back of his neck. Garrett trundled by, loaded down with a stack of decking boards, and Trent clapped him on the shoulder. "I'm going to head up to the house. I think we'll call it a night. Just set those up near the bow, and we'll get started on the deck tomorrow first thing."

Garrett offered a knowing grin with a tip of his chin toward the garden. "Go on then."

"I'm only doing my duty by the lass for the sake of her father, and I'll thank you to remember that."

"Mmmm… Would that every duty were as pleasant, aye?" He dropped the boards onto the small section of the deck they'd already assembled.

Trent glowered at him. "When I do take a wife, she will be complacent and domestic, not a prowling kitten always looking for mischief."

Garrett exchanged a glance with John Knight. "A woman such as that for the likes of you? You'd be bored and full of remorse after only a fortnight. Besides…marriage? Who said anything about marriage?"

Trent leveled him with a look that should have reminded him of his place, but his cousin and John only took great amusement from it.

Giving up, he leapt from the boat to the dock and trudged up the hill to see what Miss Hunter could be up to now.

The steady rush of the Rovuma grew louder the closer RyAnne got to the edge of the garden, and just ahead she could see the first of the huts that began the servants' quarters.

A breeze picked up, and RyAnne tilted her head back, enjoying the soft cooling caress. She hadn't realized how warm she'd become on her stroll.

Water would be just the thing. She pulled her handkerchief from her skirt pocket. She could wet it and cool her face and neck with it. She took two steps toward the river but then froze and glanced down the hill toward the bay. The crew still worked, passing back and forth from the larger ship to the smaller. And the river lay just ahead—only a few paces away.

She would just dampen her kerchief and then return to her room before dinner. Besides, she'd like to get a closer look at the river that would be home for the next several weeks.

She started forward but then noticed a young baby, not more than eighteen months, peering at her around one of the huts.

The combination of black hair twisted into tiny braids that poked from her head in all manner of directions, round pinchable cheeks, and sparkling eyes drew RyAnne a step nearer. Upon closer inspection, RyAnne tensed with a start. The child was totally and completely naked. But her skin was quite light despite her wooly woven hair. She was of mixed blood.

Just like me.

Her heart went out to the child, and she bent down. "Hello there!" She waggled her hand, offering a friendly smile.

With a giggle, the little face disappeared, only to reappear a moment later as though checking to see if RyAnne was still in the same place.

What a delightful child. She took another step, dipped her umbrella low enough to hide her face, and then quickly lifted it, making a silly cross-eyed grimace as she did so.

Gales of giggles erupted.

But an adult must have called, because the little one glanced over her shoulder, pulled back, and disappeared from sight.

A moment later, a woman balancing a pot atop her head stepped out from behind the other side of the hut and headed toward the river. One glimpse of her nearly naked body jolted RyAnne's gaze to the ground. Of course she had seen women naked before when she'd helped Papa doctor slaves at the market on the island, but it never ceased to give her a bit of a start. And the woman looked so much like the poor souls who'd been forced onto that ship the other day!

Other than a thin leather strap about her hips with two leather flaps, one hanging down in front and one in back, the only other clothing the woman wore was the strip of dirty cloth that held a baby to her back—the very child RyAnne had just been playing with.

RyAnne covered her mouth with one hand. If her own mother had not died giving birth to her, would Papa have left her with the woman? Her heart stuttered and then rushed as if to catch up. Would she have grown up the bastard daughter of a slave instead of the youngest child of a doctor who owned a successful indigo plantation?

The tot twisted around and grinned at her, then tucked her little face under the wrap of cloth, hiding in embarrassment.

RyAnne's heart squeezed. What would life be like for that girl growing up? Never fitting fully into one world or the other? Too white for the one and too black for the other.

The child peeked at her again, impish delight shimmering in her gorgeous eyes.

The helpless feeling that had consumed her as she watched the slaves being forced aboard that ship returned in full force. But this time things were different. Here were some people whose lives she could make a little bit better. It wouldn't be much, but she had to help her! At least offer the woman some cloth to make clothing for herself and the baby!

She followed down the dusty path toward the river. How would she even communicate with the woman? Would she speak the same Kiswahili spoken on Zanzibar?

The path descended down a gentle rocky slope toward a sandy stretch of beach along the river. The water looked muddy and fast, and she could tell it was higher than normal, because several plants clung precariously to their soil, and even as she watched, one broke away and washed downstream.

Stopping under a tree at the edge of the rushing brown river, the woman lifted the pot down from her head, adjusted the baby more securely on her back, and then stepped into the sandy slush at the edge of the muddy river to dip her bucket in the deeper water further out.

The water frothed. There was a flash of a leathery spiked tail and beady bulging eyes! And then the woman's feet jerked out from under her!

With an undulating wail that made every hair on RyAnne's neck stand at attention, the woman lurched for the tree trunk. The cloth broke loose, and the baby fell from her mother's back into the water at the edge of the raging river. With a shriek of shock, her little hands fisted and the toddler tried to stand, but the water sucked her feet out from under her.

The eddy was pulling the child deeper into the water! RyAnne rushed forward. And even as she ran, on the far embankment there was a splash, and she looked up just in time to see a spiky tail disappear into the mud-colored water. Dropping her umbrella, RyAnne plunged headlong into the river. Her fingers grazed the little one's leg, but before she could grasp her, she was out of reach. *Jesus!* RyAnne surged ahead, water blurring her vision. The girl had disappeared! RyAnne thrust her arms blindly through the brown water. And then—*blessed Savior!*—her hand wrapped around one little leg just before the child was swept out into the main current and lost forever.

Beside them the crocodile still had firm hold of the girl's mother. The woman thrashed and kicked, screeching at the top of her lungs and clinging to the mangrove tree for dear life! Red swirls mixed with the brown water where the crocodile's teeth remained clamped about her leg.

RyAnne swiped water from her face. There was no time!

Heartless as it was, RyAnne tossed the toddler toward the shore. She bounced on her backside, then tumbled over onto her belly, shrieking in terror.

"Run!" RyAnne screamed at her, even as she jerked her umbrella toward her. "*Kukimbia*! *Kukimbia*!"

That command seemed to penetrate, because the little child tucked her feet under herself and lurched farther up the embankment.

Wet skirts impeding every movement, RyAnne jerked the bumbershoot closed and gripped the top end like a club as she waded closer to the woman and the beast. Her heart clambered for release from her chest, and her mouth held no moisture. Surely at any minute her legs would give out from under her, but she couldn't leave the woman to such a fate without trying to help her!

Raising the umbrella high over her head, RyAnne brought the handle down on top of the beast's head. The creature didn't even budge. "Hold fast!" she yelled to the woman as she whacked the scaly thing again. And again. Still it did not release its grip but seemed to tug all the harder and loosed a low rumble from its throat.

Its eyes! She aimed her next swing at one of the bulging eyes, and with a hissing growl, the beast let go.

"Oh blessed Jesus!"

But with one rotation in the water, the creature righted itself and lurched right toward her! RyAnne scrambled backward, but not before the crocodile's teeth sank into the hem of her skirt! It gave a mighty tug, and her feet went out from under her!

"RyAnne!"

She'd never been more relieved to hear the captain's voice!

He tore into the water beside her with a feral yell. He aimed his pistol at the scaly head and fired.

The crocodile's eyes slipped shut, and its whole body went limp, but its teeth were still clamped around her skirt. And the rushing water pushing it was dragging her out into the current!

"Captain!" She clutched at him, and he grabbed her by her arm and pulled her back onto the beach. Snatching a knife from his sheath, he sank it into the material of her skirt and cut a quick *U* shape to release the croc's snout. Then planting his boot against it, he shoved it out into the raging water.

RyAnne scrambled toward the woman who had simply collapsed at the base of the mangrove. Her leg was still in the water and was bleeding profusely just below her knee. "Help me with her!" Then she remembered the second croc she'd seen slipping into the water. "There was a second one!" She pointed to the beach on the other side. "I saw it splash into the water from there."

But the captain wasn't even looking at her. He was facing the river, and his pistol was already held at arm's length. And something that could have passed, with a cursory glance, as a log slithered toward them through the water!

"I see it. Just get her up on the beach." He fired off two shots.

RyAnne unclasped the woman's fingers from around the trunk of the tree. Mercifully, it appeared she had passed out, whether from fear or blood loss, it didn't matter. They would be able to help her better while she was unconscious.

Up on the embankment, the little girl still wailed, although not as hard now. RyAnne glanced up. Several from the village had gathered along the embankment, no doubt drawn by the shrieking and commotion, and a black woman clothed like a maid was shushing and comforting the child.

RyAnne snapped her fingers at Kako, who stood among them. "Bring me a belt or rope or something. Quickly!"

Without waiting to see if he complied, she turned her attention back to the woman's leg. It was crushed severely below the knee. Splinters of bone protruded through several of the gashes of torn flesh. The foot canted off at an improbable angle. The leg would have to come off, but the knee looked normal, so they'd likely be able to save it, which was good. It increased her chances of survival. "I need that belt!" She glanced up, thankful to see the man standing beside her with a length of sash in his hands.

He handed it to her, but as she tied a tourniquet, using a small stout stick from the ground, he spoke. "She is gone, madam. You should let her travel to the other world in peace."

Happy to see the tourniquet seemed to be tight enough, she brushed Kako aside and tugged the woman further from the water. "She is not gone—she is only passed out. She will live, but I have to help her." Satisfied that she'd pulled the woman far enough from the river to prevent another unexpected attack, she knelt to examine the wound again. "Captain, I need water to make sure I've got the bleeding stopped! You," she snapped at the head servant again, "I'm going to need a table—preferably outdoors." She squinted at the rapidly descending sun. "But bring plenty of lanterns in case we'll need them. I'll need scissors, a basin of water, and a needle and thread—horsehair if you have it, but if not, the finer the thread is, the better." She glanced up at him. "Do you have all that?"

He nodded, but his lips were pressed together grimly.

She shooed him toward the house. "Quickly then, please. The captain and I will bring her momentarily." They would need a stretcher. She glanced around. The cloth the baby had been tied with floated in the brown river a few paces out, snagged on the branches of a bush.

Trent stooped by her side with the pot the injured woman had brought down to the river with her.

"Good, I need you to pour it slowly here at her knee." She

glanced up the embankment and pointed to two young men clad in nothing more than what the woman was wearing. "You two bring me the cloth there. We need to make a stretcher."

Both men folded their arms and shook their heads at her, neither moving from their spot.

"Oh, you are all a sorry lot!" She threw her hands in the air and dashed into the shoals to retrieve the cloth herself.

"RyAnne!" Trent barked. Two loud reverberations split the air as bullets slashed into the water to her right.

She jolted to a stop, cupping her ears in her hands.

"Get out of there! If the crocs don't kill you, I'll kill you myself!"

There was a splash of white water less than a cane's length away. *Heaven's mercy!* She snatched the cloth and leapt for the shore.

Trent fired again. But her feet were on solid ground now, and she tumbled to her knees next to the woman, panting more from the jolt of fear than from the short distance.

Trent had washed enough of the blood away for her to see that the tourniquet seemed to be doing its job. *Good.* "Captain, help me! We must get her to the house, and please make one of them go for Papa. I'm going to need his help. And he must bring his amputation kit."

Trent barked an order at a man on the embankment, even as he took one end of the cloth from her. He snapped something else at the two men she'd spoken to earlier. And they both came forward.

"I see they listen to you just fine," she groused.

Trent tossed aside a couple stones and spread his end of the cloth on the ground. "I'm not asking them to risk life and limb by wading into crocodile infested waters. And they"—he pinned her with a glare—"are not half-witted enough to do so."

RyAnne ignored his barbed tone as she gently slipped her hands under the injured leg. Trent took the good one, and each of the men took an arm, and they all lifted the woman over onto the makeshift stretcher.

RyAnne started to lift the material on her corner, but Trent brushed her aside. "I'll get this. You lead the way." Twisting the corners around his palms to form handholds, Trent spoke orders to the two men, who followed his lead and did the same.

RyAnne scrambled up the low little hill and rushed toward the house, hoping upon hope that Papa had received word and would be there to help her.

Papa stumbled from his room, clutching his doctor's bag and amputation kit in one hand but rubbing sleep from his eyes with the other. She barreled down the veranda toward him, Trent and the men following close behind.

"Papa, we need to do surgery, now! The leg has to come off, but I think the knee is salvageable."

Papa extended a trembling hand for her perusal. "I can't, RyAnne. My strength…it's not what it used to be."

She gripped his hand in both of hers. "Just come with me then. You can tell me what to do, and Captain Dawson will help us."

Papa cursorily assessed the woman, then nodded. "Fine. Yes. We must try."

Kako appeared and motioned them to a table set out on the grass just down the way.

RyAnne was relieved to find it clean and sturdy, and all the items she'd requested laid out on a tray beside it. "Bandages! I forgot I will need some strips of clean cloth. You've been most helpful, Kako. Thank you. But could you please get me cloth—preferably cotton or linen—and cut it into strips about three inches wide?"

The man nodded and rushed off as RyAnne directed the woman to be laid out on the table.

She glanced over at Trent and indicated the water. "Please, Captain, rinse as much of the blood from her leg as possible."

Trent held the chloroform-soaked cloth gently over the slave's face and watched RyAnne carefully examine her injured leg.

Had anyone offered him a wager, he'd have laid down money that the spoiled little heiress would faint dead away upon one glimpse of an injury such as this. But here she was about to perform surgery.

On top of that, she'd waded into a muddy river and fought off a croc to save the woman's life. And with only an umbrella!

When this was over, he was going to give her a solid piece of his mind about that. And maybe a gun and some shooting lessons—with her father's permission, of course.

Dr. Hunter drew an imaginary line on the injured leg just below the woman's knee with his finger. "Here, I think."

At that moment the woman stirred, crying out as though in pain.

RyAnne glanced over. "You can remove the cloth now, Captain. She's not awake. The excitement is an effect of the chloroform. She will be restless but will remember nothing when she wakes. You'll need to hold her still."

Trent set to rolling up his sleeves, ready to do as she asked.

RyAnne's hand trembled as she picked up the saw. She held it in a pleading gesture toward her father. "Papa, surely you can—"

A fit of coughing seized the man, and RyAnne's gaze flew to Trent's. He read increasing doubt there. *Father God, give her the strength to see this through. And please help us to save this woman lying here.* He glanced down at the blade quavering in RyAnne's hand.

He didn't know anything about amputations, but he did know that if she doubted herself, she might make a mistake. He offered a nod of encouragement. "Chin up, Miss Hunter. It was no mistake that the good Lord placed you where you were at just the right time. I've no doubt, with the help of God, you will bring her through this surgery to the other side."

"Truly?"

"Truly." Maybe distracting her would help. He glanced at the chloroform cloth. "Will I need to give her more of that?"

RyAnne brushed a lock of dark hair away from her face with a trembling hand. "No…not if I can quickly—" She swallowed visibly. "It's just…I've never done this part before. A surgeon's hands have to be strong and quick, to make the cut. And while I've helped with"—she swept a gesture toward the injured leg—"I've never before…" The blade in her hand lifted slightly. She pressed her lips together and took in the woman's still features. "It might already be too late for her."

Trent nodded. "But it might not." He pushed aside the fleeting thought of what the consequences might be if the woman didn't make it through the surgery. Her arm was banded with a bronze cuff. She was obviously someone's slave. Her owner would demand recompense, surely—and if she was the mother of the owner's child…

Hunter was still bent double, coughing.

RyAnne glanced from her father back to him, insecurity in her eyes. "Captain…"

He held up a hand and spoke softly, willing her to believe him. "We can do this. Together. You and I. But you must move quickly. We are losing light."

She still looked uncertain.

"If we don't try, will she even have a chance?"

The question was rhetorical. They both knew the answer, and he saw the moment she conquered her doubts. Determination tipped up her chin, and immediately she took control again.

"Papa, I need you to go rest. I can't worry about you while I'm trying to do this. Can you make it back to your room?"

The man wheezed an acknowledgement and tottered toward the veranda.

She set the saw within easy reach and lifted a thin, sharp blade in a steady hand. "Very well. Captain, say a prayer for me, if you would. I'd hate to have this woman's death on my conscience."

"Were it not for you, she wouldn't have even made it this far. And I've already said my prayers. Make the cut, Miss Hunter."

"Remember, keep her still as best you can."

He nodded and leaned over the woman, prepared.

Blessedly, although the woman cried out and thrashed a bit, once RyAnne started, she made quick work of it. She used a tool shaped like a hook from the doctor's kit, and the needle and thread to sew the vessels in the wound, checking carefully after snipping each thread to make sure she had stopped all bleeding. Lastly, she pulled a flap of skin over the whole stub and sewed it with fine stitches all the way around except for about half an inch, which she left free.

At his questioning look, she said, "For drainage."

Finally, she dropped the needle back onto the tray and set about rinsing her hands. She dried them swiftly and snatched up a roll of bandages, but then froze, biting her lower lip as she squeezed her eyes shut.

Trent watched her carefully, for her face had suddenly washed as white as the roll of cotton nestled in her palm.

Stepping around the table, he gently took the roll of cloth from her.

"If you will excuse me, Captain…I'll return momentarily." She spun, one hand going to her mouth as she rushed away.

He let her go, turning to wrap the stub of the leg with the bandage.

RyAnne Hunter was a barrelful of contradictions, and that was the truth of it.

Chapter 9

Lay Down Your Heart

RyAnne dashed toward her room, but the upheaval in her stomach made it clear she wasn't going to make it. She ran into the garden and leaned behind a leafy bush instead. When it was apparent she had nothing more to cast up, she wiped her mouth with a trembling hand and leaned her head back, pulling in a long full inhale.

Never again in her life did she want to be called upon to perform such a vile task. The horror of what had just happened refused to be held at the recesses of her mind any longer, and stepping back onto the path, she turned to look out toward the vast stretch of rippled water, now reflecting the last vestiges of evening light.

One moment the woman had been healthy and whole. The next moment, she and her child would have been gone if RyAnne hadn't happened to follow them. Taking the leg had been necessary. Yet, would the woman thank her for saving her life?

She brushed a trembling hand across her skirt and was surprised to note that it was already nearly dry and she felt no chill from the soft evening breeze, despite her little swim earlier. Her hands fluttered to her hair. It too was nearly dry, but likely her curls were quite the sight after taking a soaking and experiencing no brush. She shivered away the memory of the incident, wondering how the little girl was faring.

She straightened. Who was taking care of the child? She must check before dinner. But first she needed to bandage the leg. She glanced back the way she had come and pulled in a fortifying breath.

She hurriedly returned along the garden path. But when she arrived, it was to find that Captain Dawson had done a fine job on the wrap already. "Thank you, Captain. If you could see that she is settled in a room, I would like to go out and check on her child. I'm afraid in my desire to save her mother, I tossed her rather harshly toward the shore, and I'd like to make sure she is all right."

She lifted her skirts and started away, but he captured her arm, pulling her to a stop. His thumb stroked the hollow of her elbow, jolting her gaze to meet his.

He arched his brows. "If you are going anywhere, it will be with me and my pistol fast by your side. Wait here. I'll have Kako settle the woman into a room, but first he will have to secure permission from her owner."

"Secure permission? Whatever for? The woman needs rest and a comfortable bed."

A muscle pulsed in Trent's jaw. "You'll get no argument from me on that count, Miss Hunter. Wait here, please."

He was gone only momentarily and soon returned with Kako. "It seems Ali Khalifa owns her. He has not returned from his duties yet today."

Her eyes dropped closed. It figured that a man like that would be this poor woman's owner, and the child's eyes bore a striking resemblance to his, now that she thought about it.

Trent was still speaking. "Kako has a room where she can rest." He gestured for her to follow him, leaving Kako and two other house servants to move the woman.

Relieved that the woman would at least be well taken care of for the time being, RyAnne followed the captain.

As they walked the path toward the small village on the outskirts of Commodore Cornwall's estate, RyAnne kept her gaze glued to the ground. He must think her quite muddle headed—fixing the woman's leg and then rushing off the way she had. Perhaps she should try and explain…

"Trent—" *Trent?* She flinched. *Captain Dawson.* She must not think of him in such familiar terms.

He cleared his throat and ignored her slip as he plucked a blade of the hip-high grass growing beside the path and looked over at her. "I did not realize you knew aught of surgery?"

"Back home on the plantation, Papa often needed help with

surgeries or procedures of various kinds. Births. Accidents with hoes and the like." She swallowed. "But I'd never—" She blinked hard to keep tears at bay.

There she went again… Why was it she always seemed to be in some emotional state or another when the man was around?

He took her arm to guide her around a rock in the path. "This is a harsh country, Miss Hunter. It often requires brutal decisions and actions for the sake of survival. You did what the moment required for that woman."

"I cannot help but think she won't thank me for it."

He released her arm and tucked his hands behind his back. "Maybe not at first. But given time, we can pray she will come to see life can be joyous even without two legs."

"Joyous? Do you think a woman like her has had even a moment of joy in her entire life, Captain?"

They walked several steps before he responded. "We all have our trials to face in this life, Miss Hunter. Some more than others, to be sure. But I believe it a boon from the Creator that He offers the respite of joy to anyone who chooses to avail themselves of it. It is the *choosing* of it that comes so laboriously, at times."

RyAnne's gaze traveled involuntarily to meet his.

He looked back at her frankly.

She tucked her lower lip between her teeth. How could someone interested in nothing more than getting rich trading for ivory have such thought-provoking concepts bumbling about in his head? One of his brows winged its way upward. He was waiting for her to reply.

"That may be true, Captain, but I've no doubt it is much easier for people of our…*privilege* to realize it." She halted for a moment to study the golden sky along the horizon and only then realized how dark it had gotten. "Did you ever stop to wonder what your life might have been like if you were raised by a different family? How much of who we are is a result of those who surround us?" She looked toward the fires of the village just ahead. "I could so easily have—" She broke off, gritting her teeth lest she spill the whole dark truth.

He touched the small of her back, starting her down the path once more. Thankfully, whether he'd simply missed her near slip or whether he was being polite, he did not press for more details on what she'd almost said. "Admittedly, I have. But..." He smirked. "Sadly, I've not come up with a satisfactory answer other than we must put our faith in the fact that God loves us and placed us where He did, knowing what was best for us."

"What was *best*? How can a loving God be defended in the face of such misery as what I saw in the Zanzibar harbor just before the ship left port? Or after hearing the sound of broken hearts at the wharf in Bagamoyo? Why would a God who loves all equally place me in a home where I've been fed and cared for, but would allow another to be sold into slavery and then wouldn't step in to save that same poor sick soul from being tossed overboard like so much refuse? Is that what was *best*, Captain?"

He rubbed the back of his neck. "I fear your questions rise beyond the bounds of my meager theology, Miss Hunter. We tend to see any pain or misery as an evil, and thus it grinds against our concept of an all-loving God. But what if there are misfortunes that are mercies? Unless a seed becomes desiccated, for instance, it cannot be planted to produce new life."

RyAnne contemplated that as they walked the last few steps into the village. Was it God's mercy that her mother had died and thus she'd been raised by Papa and Anne? What good plan could God have had in that? And that poor woman lying back there, even now probably still unaware that she'd never again enjoy the simple pleasure of a walk such as this... What mercy was there in God allowing her to be used ill as a slave and then, on top of that, lose her leg?

She shook away her ponderings as they stepped past the first hut. She'd likely never get a satisfactory answer to the plaguing questions anyhow.

Several men squatted around a fire at the village's center, their feet planted flat on the ground and arms wrapped around their legs. Many times RyAnne had tried to imitate this position as a child, and she'd always ended up tumbling over in an unladylike sprawl. How they balanced in such a way was a mystery she'd never been able to ferret out.

Captain Dawson said a few words to them, and then one man rose and trotted across the way to a thatch-roofed hut. He stood outside the doorway and spoke to someone inside. After a moment, the wooden door opened, and the woman she'd seen holding the child after the attack at the river stepped out. She followed the man back to where they were standing, dipping her head and bending her knees in a show of respectful greeting.

The man sat back down at the fire without offering an introduction, and the woman only studied the ground near their feet, apparently waiting for whatever questions they might have.

"The child?" The captain spoke in Swahili. "The lady wanted to make sure she was not hurt at the river."

The woman clapped her palms together and dipped her knees again, still not meeting their gazes. "The child sleeps peacefully now. She suffered only some scrapes and fear."

RyAnne's heart twisted in pain. She met the captain's gaze. "I did not mean to frighten or hurt her."

He gave a quick nod of understanding, then spoke to the woman again. "The lady did not wish to hurt the child. She was trying to save her life."

The woman did look up then. She met both of their gazes with a wide one of her own. "Everyone knows what a brave thing the lady did for the child. It would have brought much distress on us all if Moyo had died." She jutted her chin toward RyAnne. "She is *mungu wa mamba* to be able to survive the attack of the beast without a scratch."

Amusement tugged at RyAnne's lips. She was no *god of the crocodile*! She opened her mouth to set the woman straight, but the captain took her elbow, squeezing firmly to silence her.

He spoke calmly to the woman but loud enough, RyAnne noted, for the men around the fire to hear. "The lady is not a god of the crocodile, but serves the One who is."

RyAnne gave a start at that. Did she? Serve God? She'd always seen herself as more of an addendum. Yes, she believed in God, but He didn't really need her help with anything, did He? He was God, after all. A God who had allowed Papa's sin against his slave to be conceived in the form of herself.

A whisper of memory prickled her skin. *Whom shall I send, child?* She wrapped her arms about herself and rubbed at the chill nipping her shoulders.

The native woman didn't look convinced by the captain's declaration, and a rumble of disagreement made the rounds of the men.

Captain Dawson stepped back. "We are happy to hear the child, Moyo, is well. We will let her sleep. In the morning the lady doctor would like to look at her scratches. Will you bring her down to the main house when she wakes, please?"

The woman dipped her head and knees in acknowledgement.

"Thank you." Trent touched RyAnne's shoulder, leading her away before she could form a coherent rebuttal to the woman's assessment of her.

They took the path back to the main house in silence. *God of the crocodile?* She grimaced. How did she get herself into these predicaments? If only Papa would agree to go back home. Within a fortnight she could be resting in her own bed, planning how she would sneak out to spend a little time with Valah and Halamme. She could forget her questions about God and whether He cared even a whit for anyone on this earth. She would talk to Papa again in the morning. Maybe now that he'd seen the toll travel was taking on him, he'd be more willing to return for rest.

When they reached the house, it was dinnertime, but RyAnne simply couldn't face sitting through a meal—especially not sitting across from Khalifa—after all she'd been through on this day. Exhaustion consumed her, leaching every ounce of her strength.

She paused on the veranda outside her door. "Captain, will you please offer my excuses at dinner? I'm afraid I simply must rest."

"I think that a good idea, Miss Hunter. I hope for us to be on our way inland tomorrow evening."

"Tomorrow!? That will be quite impossible, Captain. The slave woman is going to need more care than what I've given her."

He sighed and folded his arms. And after a long moment, he gave a curt nod. "The day after tomorrow then, but not a moment later. We need to be on our way, or we are going to be caught in the worst of the rainy season as we travel."

She gritted her teeth. The woman would need many more days of care than that, but for now, she would concede and take up the battle later. "Thank you, Captain."

His gaze skimmed her and lingered near her hem, and it was only as she glanced down to see what had caught his attention that she noted the large section missing from the front of her muddied skirt and remembered the crocodile tugging her feet out from under her.

A shudder coursed through her, and she wrapped her arms about herself. "You came at just the right moment today, Captain. If you hadn't…"

One corner of his mouth ticked up. "Saving you is beginning to be a full-time occupation."

Was that derision in his tone? She spun away lest he see the hurt his barbed wit had ignited. It was only due to the exhaustion, surely.

He caught her hand and gently tugged her back around to face him. A gleam of indiscernible emotion shimmered in his expression. His voice was low and gravelly when he spoke. "An occupation I find I am less and less loathe to perform." His thumb skimmed a warm trail across her wrist.

She held her breath and searched his face. Surely he didn't mean… She swallowed.

He took a step nearer and leaned toward her. He seemed ready to say something, but after only a moment, he dropped her hand and eased away, pressing his lips together and tucking his hands behind his back.

He looked down the length of the portico toward the main doors to the house. "I'll have Kako send someone with hot water for a bath and a tray of dinner, Miss Hunter."

She fumbled for the cool metal of her doorknob in the darkness behind her. "Thank you, Captain."

And with that she left the rogue standing alone on the veranda.

RyAnne woke early the next morning as the first rays of golden light brushed the ocean horizon. She dressed quickly and hurried down the veranda toward the little room where her patient rested.

She'd risen at midnight to check on her and had given her a clean gown, water, and some opium for pain, but now she worried that she should have checked on her another time between then and now. It had to be nearing the five o'clock hour! In her exhaustion she'd slept right through and had only awoken a moment ago.

She turned the knob and swept into the room. The woman was not there! She froze and searched the space. Everything was as she'd left it the night before…everything but the empty bed.

She lifted her skirts and stepped back out onto the veranda. Kako was just about to enter the doors to the main house. "Kako? Where is the patient?" She tipped her head to the open door behind her.

Kako pressed his lips together and looked everywhere but at her.

Dread tugged at her. "What happened?"

"Her owner has taken her. I told you it was pointless to try and save her." His Swahili was clipped with irritation.

"Taken her? She needs rest. Where has Khalifa taken her?"

His gaze skimmed toward the river, but he made no reply.

Her heart dropped, and horror washed over her. "He wouldn't!" She grabbed two handfuls of skirt and ran toward the Rovuma. "Get Captain Dawson and tell him to meet me at the river! Hurry!"

She leapt down the portico stairs and raced across the garden and up the path on the other side. By the time she reached the small strip of sand by the river, she was out of breath, but the sight that greeted her would have taken the strength from her legs even if she wasn't.

Pebbles bit into the thin flesh of her knees, but she barely noticed as she took in the horrific scene before her.

The slave woman had been stripped of the soft gown RyAnne had clothed her in the night before. The bandage around her leg had been removed, and she lay partially in the lapping water of the river's edge. She was crying, begging for her life and trying to scoot herself out of the water, but in her weakened condition her attempts were feeble.

And off to one side, offering no help whatsoever, Ali Khalifa sat on the low hill, chewing on a stem of grass and watching the sun glint off the rippling water.

RyAnne lurched to her feet and scrambled forward. "The crocodiles could return to finish her off at any moment. What are you thinking?"

Khalifa raked her with a derisive smirk. "She is no good to me without two working legs. You should have let her die."

A sick stillness came over her. "I should have let her—" Forget talking to the man. Had everyone on this godforsaken continent gone utterly and completely mad? She grabbed the woman's arms and tugged her back from the brown water.

She cried out in pain, but RyAnne dared not stop. They were too close to the muddy water that would conceal a croc until it was right on top of them. "I'm sorry. We need to get you away from the wat—"

"Hands off!" Khalifa leapt to his feet, jerked her grip loose from the woman's arms, and shoved her back, stepping between them. "She's my slave, and I will do with her what I want!"

The slave woman cried out and clawed her way a few inches further from the river's edge.

RyAnne gaped at him. "She is a human being. Not a *cow* to be sacrificed at your whim!"

Khalifa shook his head. "You are wrong, madam. She's black. The spawn of cursed Cain. No more human than a cow, nor is anyone with the vile blood of Cain running in their veins."

A chill raced down her spine. What would a man like this do if he discovered she herself was one of "Cain's spawn"? She took a breath and prayed her words would penetrate. "Only days ago at the Harcourt ball, you claimed we needed to rescue the natives from the dark influences of this continent. How are your actions those of the enlightened?"

"Ludlow held such a view. But if you think back, you'll recall it was never I who said such, Miss Hunter." His gaze slipped leisurely down the length of her, and a hint of lechery touched his expression.

Revulsion crawled over her, and she took a step back. Her mind scrabbled for something that might change his mind about the slave woman. "She is the mother of your child, is she not?"

Something seemed to still inside him. He swallowed and looked down, but then his chin lifted, and a glint of madness darkened his eyes. "Both are dead to me."

RyAnne's jaw dropped. Unable to comprehend a man so callous to human life, words failed her.

Trent sprinted toward the river, still strapping his pistol around his waist. Kako had been most unclear about what he would find—only that RyAnne needed his help.

Garrett panted, fast on his heels.

When he crested the little knoll, it only took him a moment to assess the situation.

Khalifa shoving RyAnne back, her chin tipping up like a lioness backed into a corner. The naked slave woman trying to pull herself farther from the water. Ali's hand sweeping toward the pistol tucked into the back of his pants.

There was only one way this ended without bloodshed. Only one language would reach a man like Ali Khalifa.

Trent motioned Garrett to stay hidden off to one side. He leapt from the little embankment and stepped between Khalifa and RyAnne, holding out his right hand to the surprised man even as he swept the exasperating Miss Hunter behind his back with his other arm.

Ali shook his hand out of reflex, and Trent hung on to it, pumping it like a madman, knowing if he let it go the man might reach for his gun again. "Khalifa! I'm so glad Miss Hunter found you."

Behind him he felt RyAnne lean her forehead into his back. And with his hand that still rested at the small of her back, he could feel she was trembling all over.

He gritted his teeth and forced himself to smile at the man he'd rather beat to a pulp.

Khalifa looked puzzled. "Yes?"

"Yes, you see, I'd like to buy this slave woman from you. Both she and her child, actually."

"What?" The man's face scrunched into a mask of incomprehension. He swept a gesture toward the woman sobbing at their feet. "A one-legged invalid?" His hand swept toward the village huts. "And a child too young to work? Why?"

Trent pushed out his bottom lip and gave a little shrug. "The galley on our ship will be small. She can do most of the cooking she will need to do from a chair, and in time she will learn to navigate with only one leg. Until then, the girl can do some fetching and running for her. And a female slave is always more content when her offspring are nearby. I think she will do nicely for what we need her for."

Khalifa scratched his chin. Then his lip jutted out, and he nodded. "It's partly your fault she still lives. So payment would be—how would you say?—just recompense."

Trent felt RyAnne stiffen and jolt upright. He tightened his grip on her, willing her to silence. His smile felt like it was carved in stone. If only there wasn't a woman present… He forced himself to speak in a calm tone. "I suppose you could look at it that way, yes. So what will you take for the pair?"

Khalifa named a sum twice and half again the going rate of a healthy woman in the Zanzibar slave market.

Trent gritted his teeth, knowing he didn't have any leverage when it came to bargaining. "A price I'm more than willing to pay. But if you'll forgive me, I left my room in quite a hurry, and my purse is still there. Come with me, and I'll pay you at once." Keeping the man's hand firmly within his own, he called over his shoulder, "Garrett, put down your gun and come help Miss Hunter carry my slave back to her room, would you?"

It gave him a measure of satisfaction to see Khalifa's face wash nearly as white as his kofia when Garrett stood from where he'd been crouching behind a rock, with his rifle in his hand.

Trent tugged the man forward. "Come, my friend. Your payment awaits."

Trent led the man to his room along the portico and retrieved his purse, and then followed him to his own room in the main part of the house, where they could sign the bill of sale.

Trent paid the man and sighed as he left the room with documents for one very expensive maimed slave and a child who would be nothing more than an extra mouth to feed. And all because of Miss RyAnne Hunter.

He stepped through the main hall to cut across toward his room, and paused at the sight of a violin case on a side table. He snapped the case open and took in the golden gleam of the instrument inside. The memory of the peacefulness that had settled over Miss Hunter's features as she'd been playing at the ball tipped up one corner of his mouth. He tapped the rolled-up papers against his chest as he studied the instrument. Perhaps he could talk her into playing it a little before they left? A derisive huff escaped, and he snapped the case closed.

He was going soft, for sure. Thankfully, he'd come to his senses last night before he'd said anything too revealing to her. The last thing he needed right now was the complication of a courtship. Especially not when they were headed inland, where he might very likely find himself in the role of her guardian.

Not to mention protector.

And if Khalifa and his slavers got wind he was tracking them, they'd hesitate at nothing to silence him, even going to the extent of threatening anyone they thought might mean something to him. Miss Hunter's stunt today could cost them later.

He'd have to be doubly careful with Khalifa. And yes, he'd best keep his distance from the lovely Miss Hunter. The problem was, she and her penchant for finding trouble at every cobble of the street were making that a nearly impossible feat.

But he'd promised to guide Dr. Hunter to his village, and nothing more. So once they arrived, he'd be free to explore the area and see if he could learn anything about the smugglers. And that would put him far from the woman, and any danger he might pose to her would be minimized.

He only prayed she'd be able to stay out of trouble long enough for him to track down the smugglers and get her back to Zanzibar safely.

RyAnne was resting in her room that afternoon, when a knock sounded at her door. She'd been sitting with her patient, who she'd learned was called Nyanja—lake, in the tongue of her people—all morning, and after her few hours of sleep the night before, exhaustion had caught up to her.

Rolling over, she ignored the intrusion, but when the knock came again, more insistently, she forced herself to rise.

Papa stood on the veranda with a grim-looking Captain Dawson behind him. And clutched in Papa's hands was a set of the loathsome clothing she'd hoped he'd forgotten about.

She pinched the bridge of her nose. "Papa. Let's just go back to Zanzibar. This whole thing is madness! You are so sick you can barely stand!"

Captain Dawson looked a little too hopeful as Papa brushed her out of the way and entered the room. He set the pile of clothes on the sturdy table by her bed. The captain only leaned a shoulder into the doorframe and crossed his legs, settling the toe of one boot on the floor.

When she looked back to Papa, he had sunk down onto the edge of her bed and supported himself against his knees. He hunched forward like a man well beyond his years. But when he spoke, his voice was strong. "There are regrets a man has in life, RyAnne. Regrets he'd like to make amends for before his departure from this plane. I've many a regret to amend. We will go on to the lake. And you will dress for safety and learn to shoot, or you will be escorted back to Zanzibar by Captain Dawson's first mate."

Escorted back to Zanzibar. Oh, wouldn't that be bliss. Yet her one desire beyond having Papa in a place where he could get adequate medical attention had always been that he not die alone. Tempting as it might be to give up her fight and flee back to the familiarity of home, she would never be able to bring herself to do so. Despair weighted her shoulders.

And then the other thing he'd said registered. "Learn to shoot!" Her shock spun her back to face the captain. Her eyes narrowed. "This was your doing, wasn't it?"

His gray-green gaze never wavered. "I suggested it, yes. But it is to your father's credit that he saw the wisdom in the suggestion. Being able to handle a weapon is a necessity where we are going."

She whirled back to Papa. "Papa, this is most—"

"Improper? Yes, I think we've discussed that already." He stood slowly to his feet and pointed at the pile of clothes and boots. "Get dressed and meet the captain at the end of the veranda in ten minutes. He's taking you out past the village, and both the clothing and the training are for your safety." He touched her cheek. "You are my everything. If I ask it, it is only because I love you so much, daughter."

RyAnne swallowed and tipped her head in a compliant nod, but when the men left the room, she ground her teeth and stomped one foot. Oh that she could pack her valise and hasten to *The Wasp* at once. But again, the thought of leaving Papa all alone stopped her. That and facing Mother's recriminations when she arrived back on the island.

Better face Mother's pet leopard than Mother herself. She snatched up the shirt on the top of the pile and held it to her bodice, smoothing it over herself in inspection.

She grimaced. If only Valah and Halamme could see her now!

Trent sat on the veranda stairs, one knee bent to prop up his arm. He chewed a stem of grass and studied the way the sunlight glinted off the expanse of the ocean. The way the clouds stacked up on the horizon like sheep at a feeding trough. The way *The Wasp* and *The Bee* bobbed on the rising tide down at the wharf. This was a good place Lew had chosen for his outpost.

Garrett would have *The Bee* ready to sail by tomorrow. But he'd seen Khalifa and his men set off up the river earlier. He sighed. The man would have at least a day's head start on him.

Behind him down the porch a door opened and closed, and soft footsteps headed his way.

He glanced at the shadow cast by the ebony tree to his left. It had been a bit more than ten minutes, but at least he hadn't had to go in after her. Tossing aside the blade, he stood and turned to face her.

The sight of her froze him in place, and he swallowed involuntarily.

She was much smaller than he'd realized. The shirt and pants belonged to the smallest man on his crew, but she'd had to turn back the cuffs of the sleeves and the hems several times, and the waist of the pants she'd cinched tight with a makeshift rope belt. The boots she held in one hand, and an apologetic look squinted one eye as she offered them toward him.

"I've tried, Captain. I really have, as you can see." She swept a hand down herself. "But I'd be much safer in my skirts than gallivanting in this getup." She flicked the rolled-back cuff at one wrist. "And these boots…I can't even cinch them tight enough to keep my feet from slipping around. I'll have blisters of a surety if I wear them. Will you please tell Papa that I tried, but it simply isn't going to work?"

Weariness weighed down her features.

His heart went out to her. She was trying. And in a tough

spot, to be sure, with her father dying and her disappointment at not being able to talk the man into going back home. Well he recounted the days before his own mother passed. He'd been much younger, but he remembered the uncertainty of what the future would hold, the dread of not having her there anymore, and the sorrow of looming loss.

And RyAnne carried the extra burden of the fact that her father seemed to be the only parent who cared for her. At least his own father had been loving, even though much of their time had been spent at sea.

Now as he assessed her once more, he realized he would need to fetch a set of Dabu's clothes, but even the lad's boots would be too big for the dainty feet visible beneath the turned-back cuffs of her breeches.

He took the pair of boots she'd held out. "You'll have to wear your own boots. For today those clothes will have to do, but I will bring something of a better fit tomorrow."

"I'm so touched by your generosity, Captain!" She laid a hand over her chest and batted her eyelashes at him.

He smirked at her dripping sarcasm. "The light is fading, Miss Hunter..."

She huffed and spun back toward her doorway. "Fetching my boots will only take me a moment."

When she returned, he was thankful to see that her boots at least rose to her ankles. They wouldn't be as safe as the calf-height boots he'd given her, but they would have to do until he could have another pair made for her.

Giving her a nod, he slung his Henry over his shoulder and then turned and led the way up the path through the village and to the other side.

Chapter 10
Lay Down Your Heart

RyAnne followed the captain, doing her best to push down her discomfort at appearing in public in men's attire. But the farther they went on the narrow path through tall grass that in most places soared above her head, the more she realized she would have constantly been fighting her hoops. And the thought of some creature crawling under her skirts sent a shiver through her that nearly jarred her teeth.

As they walked, the captain alternately talked and whacked vegetation with his machete. "When you are moving through grass like this, it is best to make as much noise as possible. Snakes will be afraid of the sound and move away from it."

Snakes? She shuddered and glanced down the path behind her, stepping so close behind the captain that she nearly tromped on his heels.

"If you come upon a lion, or cat of any sort, never turn your back on it. They are much less likely to attack if you are facing them. And once we are on our way, no straggling off away from the main group. Lions will stalk a herd for hours, waiting for one to wander off alone so they can pick it off."

She inched a little closer to him, tossing another check over her shoulder. Were the two of them a big enough "herd" to keep her from getting "picked off"?

With the machete, Trent whacked at a tangle of vines growing across the trail ahead of him. "The Cape buffalo, on the other hand, if you sense one getting agitated, don't look it in the face. They will take that as a challenge, and that is a fight you don't want to initiate!"

She frowned at his back. Weren't buffalo just large cows? How dangerous could one be?

He gave another forceful swing of the blade. "I've seen a man torn in two by the horns of a Cape."

Her eyes widened. *No challenging buffaloes, of a certainty.*

"Be careful of moving between taller bushes or trees without looking first. One bite from some of these spiders and there won't be anything anyone can do for you."

Ugh. Spiders were infinitely worse than snakes! She did tromp on his heel that time.

He stopped and faced her. "Miss Hunter. A little space, if you please."

She allowed her raised brows to reveal her irritation. "Captain, if you want *space*, you would do well to cease expounding on every dangerous creature that inhabits the Continent!"

Humor ticked up one corner of his mouth. "Well, if I succeed in ingraining some caution into that pr—" All amusement faded from his expression as quickly as it had arisen.

She rolled her lips in and pressed them together. What had he been about to say? Surely not…

He turned and resumed chopping his way through the vegetation. "I do not mean to make you fear, Miss Hunter. But a little caution goes a long ways toward safety. Something you showed a distinct lack of at the river the other day."

Her chin lifted. "Two lives were at stake!"

"There's where you are wrong. Three lives were at stake the minute you waded into that water."

"I couldn't just let them die!"

"I'm not saying you should have. I'm saying a gun and the knowledge of how to use it would have made a dangerous situation less hazardous. That's why we are here." He gestured ahead to a clearing under some flat-topped acacia trees. "And we've arrived." He stepped from the tall grass and sheathed his machete.

Dropping his pack to the ground and unslinging the rifle from across his shoulders, he thrust it toward her. "You familiarize yourself with the weapon while I get a target set up for you."

She started to turn the gun to examine it, but he grabbed the muzzle swinging his way and held it still. "Never aim your gun at something unless you intend to shoot it, Miss Hunter."

She quirked one eyebrow and swung the muzzle toward him once more, not all the way, but just enough to let him know what thought had occurred to her.

He grinned outright. "You shoot me out here, and my body may never be found, but then you'd have to find your way back to the estate through all those lion-, snake-, and spider-infested grasslands. And your body will likely never be found either."

She grinned and dropped the muzzle toward the ground. "Touché! But I would never shoot you, Captain."

He gave a mocking bow, touching his forehead in thanks.

"Then who would I call upon the next time I needed help?"

An ironic smile flattened his lips as he straightened. "Who indeed?"

For a long moment, he studied her with a warm gaze, his amusement slowly seeping from his features. His countenance softened, and he tucked one side of his lower lip between his teeth.

She held her breath, every muscle in her body tightening up as though ready to spring. Her mouth was suddenly as dry as Sahara sand, and she swallowed.

His gaze roamed to her upswept curls. He reached out to pluck something from her hair, stepping closer as he did so. He held up a bit of grass for her to see, twirling it in his fingers.

"Thank you, Captain."

"My pleasure, Miss Hunter." He flicked the grass aside and hooked his thumbs into the belt at his waist, but didn't step back. His searching gaze roamed over her face.

She could have counted every heartbeat loudly rapping in her ears, were they not skipping by so quickly.

His focus paused on her lips. "RyAnne…"

He said it so softly that she wouldn't have heard the word if all her attention hadn't been focused on him.

He lifted one hand to her cheek, but his fingers had barely made contact, when a muscle bunched in his jaw and he jerked back and spun away.

A strange disappointment drained her will to keep her eyes

open. She pulled in a long, slow breath and tipped her face to catch the bit of breeze coming from her left.

And she'd thought her mouth had been dry a moment ago!

What had just happened?

When she regained the will to open her eyes, the captain stood a few paces away, studying her as he rubbed the back of his neck. "I'm sorry." He lifted his hand in a helpless gesture. "There are reasons why it wouldn't be good to…" He turned his attention to the toe of his boot, methodically kicking at the dirt.

She wasn't sure how to respond. She'd been battling a rising estimation of the man for weeks now, but prior to that she'd always thought of him as a nosy big brother.

This was twice now he'd made advances, only to pull away at the last moment.

Then there was Brayden to consider… She dare not forget about Brayden. She'd promised him she'd consider his proposal seriously this time.

So, in truth, it was better this way.

And yet there was the disappointment and hurt still coursing through her. And the rapid pounding of her pulse still beating in her ears.

After all her years with Mother, she should be used to rejection by now. But try as she might with lifted chin and thrown back shoulders, she couldn't lessen the sting of it. "Can we just…" She raised the rifle and nodded toward the acacia trees behind him.

He cleared his throat, still studying her, but she refused to meet his perusal. Instead she turned all her attention to the gun in her hands, as though it were of utmost interest to her.

The stock was smooth, warm mahogany snugged tight between a brass magazine and a curved brass shoulder plate. She ran one finger over a dark indentation in the wood and rubbed her palm over the brass. If he and Papa wanted her to learn to shoot, she would show them she could do the job well.

When she looked back up, Trent— She gritted her teeth. *Captain Dawson!* Captain Dawson was digging through the pack he'd set down earlier.

He pulled out a canteen and offered it toward her. "Thirsty?"

She took it. "Thank you."

While she drank, he pulled out a large section of canvas and nailed it to one of the acacia trunks. Using a small chunk of red clay from the base of the towering anthill nearby, he drew a circle in the center of the material and filled it in with swift strokes. Then he paced off ten long strides and dug a line in the dirt with the heel of his boot. "We'll start right here."

Wiping her mouth with the back of one hand, she handed the canteen to him.

He took several long drinks and then set it down on a rock and met her gaze. He took the rifle from her but didn't step away. "RyAnne, I didn't mean to—"

"*Captain* Dawson, I am here to learn to shoot, and nothing more."

With a blink, he stepped back. "Yes. Good."

Pushing down the urge to apologize, she folded her arms and waited.

Telltale irritation bunched the muscles of his jaw, but he lifted the rifle. "This"—he tapped the back of the stock—"goes in tight against your shoulder." He illustrated. "Good and tight, because there will be recoil, and it will be painful if you hold it too loose." He lifted his right hand in the air. "Right hand goes to the trigger, like so. Left hand supports the rifle here under the brass. Don't hold the barrel, or you'll get burnt."

She sighed. So he was back to business. She smirked at her own wavering emotions. She'd just told him she was only here to learn to shoot, but she'd hoped he might have something more to say on the subject, she supposed.

He didn't miss a beat. "Your cheek goes here against the smooth part of the stock, and you sight down the barrel, lining up the two pins on your target. Jerking on the trigger pulls off your aim. Instead, take a deep breath. Let it out, and slowly squeeze the trigger."

He fired, and the sound was so loud she cringed, covering her ears. But a black dot now marred the center of the red clay circle he'd drawn earlier.

He looked over at her. "You'll get used to the sound. Here." Handing her the weapon, he motioned for her to step into his place.

And she was suddenly all thumbs. She gritted her teeth. She could do this. But the gun was much heavier than she'd anticipated, and the barrel wavered.

"Steady."

She adjusted her stance and put more effort into holding the barrel still. Biting her tongue between her teeth, she squinted along the sights, trying to form a line between them and her target. She held her breath, eased it out, and then put pressure on the trigger. The loud bang and the jolt to her shoulder happened almost simultaneously. She staggered back, rubbing at the pain but grinning from ear to ear because a second black hole now pierced the canvas. Not as close to center as his had been, but she'd managed to nick the red circle.

He nodded his approval but only said, "This time make sure the butt is tighter against your shoulder. Try again."

RyAnne changed back into her dress as soon as they returned, and had never been happier to put on a set of hoops in her entire life. Now she relished the feel of the material swishing about her legs as she hurried down the porch to check on Nyanja before dinner.

Both her arms ached terribly—the left from supporting the rifle and the right from taking the brunt of the recoil so often, but Captain Dawson hadn't let her quit until they'd shot all fifteen cartridges the rifle held, and his pistol several times after that.

A maid sat by Nyanja's bed when she quietly pushed the door open, and with a start RyAnne realized it was the same woman they'd spoken to in the village the other night.

She smiled at the maid and spoke in Kiswahili. "Hello again. What is your name?"

The woman stood and dipped her head deferentially. "Commodore Cornwall calls me June."

"June, I am RyAnne." She lifted the blankets to examine the stub of the leg. "How is she?"

"Her fever rises, madam."

"Yes. I expected that." RyAnne touched the patient's forehead. Warm, but not overly so.

The woman stirred and moaned in her sleep.

RyAnne looked at the maid. "I will mix her a tonic for the fever. Has she complained of pain? It has been a while since I gave her aught for it."

"Yes, madam."

"I will put some opiate in too, then. The bandage looks good. When did you last change it?"

"Only an hour ago."

"That's good. Thank you." RyAnne mixed the draught and then leaned over the patient, encouraging her to wake and drink.

Nyanja opened her eyes but rolled her head from side to side and moaned audibly.

"I'm sorry—I know you must be hurting. This will help with the pain and let you rest easier." She held the cup to the woman's lips.

The maid said something to Nyanja in a language RyAnne didn't recognize, but it seemed to penetrate the woman's fever-numbed senses, for she finally opened her mouth and drank the draught. RyAnne was just pulling away when the woman clutched at her arm.

"*Zikomo*." She whispered the word and then slumped back against the pillow, already sound asleep.

RyAnne lifted a questioning gaze to the maid.

"She says thank you, madam. I told her how you saved her from the crocodile and then purchased them from Khalifa this morning."

RyAnne smiled. "Captain Dawson did the buying, but when she wakes, you tell her she is most welcome. You speak her language, then?"

The maid nodded. "We are of the Chewa. Our tribe lives on the shores of the great Lake Nyasa."

RyAnne's smile widened. "More good news for her then. You can also tell her that we are just waiting for her to regain some of her strength, and then we are headed to that very lake. Captain Dawson has granted her freedom. She can go home."

The maid looked stricken. "You are going to Lake Nyasa? There is much turmoil and danger there. Many tribes quarreling and selling each other into slavery. Much death."

RyAnne's smile faded. "Yes. We've heard. But nevertheless, we go. Papa wants to start a mission there." She capped the powders and put them in a neat row on the table. "I will be back to check on her after dinner. You will stay with her until then?"

The maid dipped her knees. "Yes, madam."

RyAnne lifted her skirts and hastened to the dining room, fearing she was late. And when she arrived it was indeed to find all the men waiting for her arrival in the parlor. To a man, they rose when she entered.

"I'm terribly sorry. I needed to check on the patient before dinner and—"

Commodore Cornwall waved away her apology. "Think nothing of it, dear girl. You're here now, and all is well." He thrust out his arm, crooked at the elbow. "May I escort you to the dining room?"

She accepted his offer. "Thank you, Commodore."

As Commodore Cornwall pulled out her chair to seat her, he looked across the table to where Captain Dawson was taking his own seat. "Dawson, Kako tells me you took an interest in the violin in the hallway? It was my wife's. Do you play? Perhaps we could talk you into playing for us after dinner?"

Captain Dawson paused halfway into his seat, his gaze snapping to RyAnne's.

Her brows rose of their own volition. And a trill of anticipation washed through her. A violin? Here? Her hand tingled with an itch to hold a bow. She rubbed her thumb across her fisted fingers.

The captain's gaze flicked to where her hand rested on the table.

She tucked it quickly into her lap.

He sank the rest of the way into his seat and cleared his throat softly, glancing down the table to where Commodore Cornwall was just taking his own seat. "I did look at the violin, Lew. But I'm sorry to say, I don't play."

Beside the captain, Garrett Holloman grinned and fiddled with the fork by his plate.

RyAnne's eyes narrowed. What was that all about? She brushed the question aside, only thankful the captain hadn't volunteered her ability, like Mother would have.

Commodore Cornwall seemed oblivious to the undertones at his table. "Too bad. It's been quite some time since I heard real music."

Papa scooped a mound of potatoes onto his plate. "Oh, but RyAnne plays beautifully. I'm sure she'd be happy to entertain us after dinner."

The commodore gasped in delight. "Would you, Miss Hunter?"

RyAnne glanced at the faces around the table. The familiar quaver of fear gripped her stomach.

Captain Dawson shifted in his seat. "I'm not so sure the lady will be up to—"

"Of course RyAnne would love to play for us." Papa cut him off. "Splendid idea, Commodore! It's been far too long since I heard her beautiful playing."

Captain Dawson offered her the sympathetic quirk of one brow.

And a wave of warmth toward the man washed from the top of her head to the tips of her toes. She appreciated him wanting to prevent her discomfort, but the thought of having a violin in her hands after so many weeks eclipsed the trepidation. Dinner couldn't get over fast enough, and when finally Commodore Cornwall placed the beat-up case into her hands, a peace settled over her so profound it was as if the world had gone silent.

She opened the latch and traced her finger over the curve of one edge, surprised when emotion clogged her throat.

It took several minutes to tune the piece, but when she let the bow slide over the strings in one long sustained note, her eyes dropped closed. For one splendid moment, all was right with the world. The instrument's tone proved it had been crafted by someone with a great talent. Deep. Vibrant. Full.

Once again, she availed herself of the captain's advice and took herself elsewhere as she played, but this time it wasn't to a pleasant place.

A tune had been building inside her from the moment she'd taken the gangplank up to *The Wasp* and seen the carnage in the harbor. She closed her eyes and let it flow from her mind, down through her arm, and onto the strings. She played sadness for those who had been treated so ill as to be thrown overboard in their last hours—hours when they were in most need. She played anger for the wailing women who had been prodded up the gangplank of the ship at Bagamoyo. She played terror for Nyanja fighting for her life, first from a crocodile and then from a man so callous as to throw her back to the beasts a second time. Finally, she played sorrow for a world gone so terribly, terribly mad. And with a sigh of release, she let the last note linger long as she slowly pulled the bow along the final refrain.

And then she dropped the bow into her lap and eased out a long sigh. The song had been a prayer. A cry to the God of heaven to take notice. Did He even see this little piece of the world and know what was going on here? Did He know there was a town called Lay Down Your Heart on the coast not far from here? Did He care that all she wanted was to take her papa back home so he could spend his last days on this earth in relative peace?

After a long moment, she opened her eyes and realized that she'd closed them on the first note and hadn't opened them since.

The men remained silent. Papa was smiling with one hand over his chest. Commodore Cornwall's mouth was hanging open, and his gaze kept bouncing from her to the violin and back. Garrett was staring at a carved statue across the room without seeming to see it, a thoughtful furrow between both his brows.

And Captain Dawson was looking right at her. His eyes

shimmered, and he nodded approval. Had he heard the message of the song? Understood the cry of her heart?

It didn't matter, she supposed. There was only One who needed to hear her cry, and she was certain He had understood.

She glanced at the commodore and lifted the instrument. "It is wonderful. Thank you."

He smiled softly as he nodded. "It is *I* who should thank *you*, dear girl. The song was splendid. Simply splendid!"

RyAnne sighed in contentment as she tucked the instrument away in its case.

Trent watched her put the violin away, rubbing one finger over his jaw. He hated to break the tranquility of the moment, but Khalifa had a good day's start on him now, and they needed to head to the lake as soon as possible. Yet with the slave woman still recovering, he knew RyAnne wasn't going to like what he had to say one bit.

He sighed. There was nothing for it but to dive in and fight the battle head on. "*The Bee* is ready to sail. We'll start our inland trek at dawn tomorrow."

The only indication that RyAnne had heard him was the fact that she froze for a moment before she finished latching the case.

Trent pressed on as though he hadn't noticed. "Garrett, I've told the doctor that you wouldn't mind heading back to the island to watch over his family until we can all get back." He winced inwardly and glanced toward Dr. Hunter. The lie had slipped off his tongue so glibly. There would be no coming back for the good doctor. "I'll take John, but you'll have the rest of the crew with you. I've taken the liberty of hiring some of the men from the village to carry our supplies. And Lew has generously offered his man Kako, who knows the language of the area, so we'll have a good translator."

RyAnne clasped her hands in her lap. "Captain—"

He held up one finger to silence her. "Dr. Hunter, are you

certain, sir, that you want to press on with this mission?"

It would make his life so much easier if the doctor would agree to take Miss Hunter and go back to Zanzibar.

RyAnne seemed to hold her breath, hands clasped together in a hopeful pose.

But the doctor only nodded. "I've never been more certain of anything in my life, Captain. I would be a fool to turn back when the good Lord has made such a clear way before me. For I cannot find it a coincidence that the commodore has people in his employ from the very tribe I feel called to reach. Nor that he has agreed to let them accompany us as a means of introduction to our good intentions. Why, even the very woman RyAnne rescued hails from the lakeside Chewa."

Trent sighed even as RyAnne jolted to her feet and paced from her chair to the fireplace mantel and back. He couldn't blame her for her obvious distress over her father's refusal to return to the island. The man would be lucky to make it two days inland, much less the weeks it was bound to take them to get to the lake.

Still…he needed to catch up to Khalifa if he was going to accomplish what Lew wanted him to. He glanced at the man, only to find him glowering with an intensity that conveyed the urgency of his mission. He tipped the man a nod of acknowledgement. He hadn't forgotten what he'd been hired to do.

"Very well…then we leave at dawn." He gritted his teeth, waiting for the protest he presumed was coming.

She did not let him down. "Captain Dawson, I must object. The woman, Nyanja, is not strong enough to travel yet. And no provision has been made for someone to care for her child on the journey."

"Actually, I've spoken to Lew. It seems the woman we spoke to in the village the other day is from the same tribe as Nyanja. Lew has agreed to let her travel with us. Her name is…" The name escaped him, and he glanced to Lew for help.

"June."

"Yes. June. She can care for the child, since she is already familiar with her, and help you with the woman's care. And

Nyanja can rest just as well on the boat as she can here in the house."

RyAnne pinched the bridge of her nose and then spun toward the door to the veranda, blinking hard and obviously trying to hold her dismay at bay. "Very well, then. If we leave at dawn, I'd best see to packing the supplies we'll need for the patient."

Trent stood and reached past her to open the door. "Your father has already seen to that this afternoon. And Commodore Cornwall has a woman who will sit with Nyanja tonight. The trek inland will be grueling. Please get some rest while you can."

Cicadas and crickets serenaded the night as he followed her down to her room. He forced himself to keep his distance, even though he would have liked to offer her some consolation in the face of the emotions she was battling to keep bottled.

A thought occurred to him though. "Miss Hunter?"

She paused on the threshold of her room. "Yes, Captain?"

"Sick as he is, he's going to pass no matter what you try to do for him. Rest might prolong his days for a short time. But at least this way he gets the joy of following his last wish."

She pressed her lips together and nodded. "Yes. Thank you, Captain."

And with that, she eased the door shut, and he was left on the veranda with only the night sounds surrounding him.

RyAnne's feet dragged as she crossed the room. She flopped back onto her bed and stared at the ceiling, arms wide in defeat. Her last vestige of hope that Papa would return had just slipped from her grasp. She'd been so certain she could convince him to change his mind! She ought to have known his obstinate pride wouldn't budge. After all, she came by her own determined will quite honestly.

And yet…there seemed to be more to Papa's stubbornness this time than sheer determination. He'd mentioned several times that the Lord was calling him to go.

Father, do you see my papa? Do you see how weak he is? This trip will kill him even sooner.

Indeed, she feared he wouldn't make it a few days, much less the several weeks the grueling trek was likely to take. Would God really ask something so costly of a man?

Guilt immediately pricked her. Hadn't Jesus himself given everything, even his life, so that mankind might have a relationship with Him?

Greater love has no one than this: to lay down one's life for one's friends.

Papa had quoted that passage to her more than once when she was a child. He was but following in the steps of the One who'd set the example before him. And Papa seemed content enough in his decision.

She thought of Garrett Holloman returning to the island with tomorrow's tide. Papa wouldn't keep her from going with him. And yet…

Lay down your heart…

The words whispered through her, and she gripped a double handful of her hair, clenching her teeth tight.

She wouldn't be able to help Papa. He was dying, and she'd be forced to watch without recourse. There would be nothing she could do, just as there hadn't been anything she could do to save Nyanja's leg. And still might be nothing she could do to save the woman's life if infection set in.

Where was God's love in all of that?

The area they were headed to lay in the very heart of rampant slave-raid territory. Perhaps some of the people she'd seen being so mistreated on the docks at Bagamoyo had once lived carefree lives on the shores of the very lake Papa was so determined to reach.

Lay down your heart…

The natives at Bagamoyo were forced to lay down their hearts at the shoreline of their homeland due to the evil of people who were apathetic toward them. They had no choice.

But she could choose. It was either support a man she loved

with all her heart or walk away and never see him again. And in the end, that really wasn't much of a choice, was it?

Yet if she joined him on this journey, she must go with her heart in the right place. Could she truly leave behind her desires and go inland with Papa? Help him accomplish his last yearning on this earth? Could she serve him with genuine love? Forfeit her own wants selflessly?

And when Papa did pass on? Her heart broke at the certainty of it. Papa's time was not a matter of *if*, but of *how soon*. And it must be faced.

She would be alone in the heart of the Continent. Her thoughts flitted to Captain Dawson. Could she count on the man to help her get back home? Or would he be gallivanting about in search of more ivory to make himself rich?

Her stomach clenched so tight that she turned on her side and curled herself into a compact ball, wrapping her arms around her knees. *Please, God, don't ask this of me.* But she knew He already had—or at the very least, her own impulsive decision to stow away on the captain's ship had brought her to this point. Even in that, perhaps God had sent Dabu and his monkey to help her? She supposed it didn't matter exactly what had brought her to this place, only that now she had a decision to make and wanted to make the right one. Perhaps she hadn't made the wisest choices in the past. Perhaps she should have stayed on Zanzibar, as Papa had intended in the first place. But once Papa had seen her, he couldn't let her go again. He needed her.

Memories assailed her. The harbor at Zanzibar. The wails of the woman at Bagamoyo trying to free her bloody ankle from its chain. The blood swirling in the muddy river water as Nyanja clung to a tree for dear life. Papa, bent double and coughing up blood. Her whole body shuddered. If she went with Papa, she would be faced with worse. *I can't do it!* But in reality she knew she could.

Whom shall I send, child?

Someone else, Father.

But the plea lacked conviction. She already knew what her

decision would be. Tomorrow she would board *The Bee* with Papa, and she would do everything in her power to make sure he arrived at his destination with enough health to speak of the God he now loved. The God who had called him to the tribespeople. The God who had brought her to this place of choices.

Father, I lay down my heart…

Slowly her arms relaxed, and it didn't seem so hard to breathe anymore. Peace settled over her, and her eyes slipped shut.

Dear Reader,

Bagamoyo, the town called "Lay Down Your Heart," was the most important trading entrepôt on the east coast of Africa during the last half of the nineteenth century. While it is not exactly certain why the town came to be called "Lay Down Your Heart," it is speculated that one reason was due to the many slaves that passed through the town each year.

If you found it hard to believe that a slave owner would be angry that someone saved his slave's life when she was maimed, know that I did too. But Nyanja's story is only partially fictionalized. Dr. David Livingstone documented such a case in his book *Expedition to the Zambesi.* While I changed the details of exactly what happened to fit this story line and my heroine, a real slave woman was attacked by a crocodile, and some of Dr. Livingstone's fellow travelers rescued her. She lost her leg, however, and the next morning her owner had unbandaged her leg and left her to die. Livingstone wrote, "Her master was angry with us for saving her life, seeing as how she had lost her leg."

Still, in the midst of that dark time God was there, reaching *through* people *to* people, longing for relationship with them, just as He still does today.

I hope you'll persist in the journey with RyAnne as she continues to search for answers to her spiritual questions.

Thanks for reading!

Made Perfect in Weakness

And He said to me, "My grace is sufficient for you, for My strength is made perfect in weakness." Therefore most gladly I will rather boast in my infirmities, that the power of Christ may rest upon me.

2 Corinthians 12:9

Chapter 11
Made Perfect in Weakness

Rovuma River, aboard
***The Bee*, Headed Inland**
Dawn

RyAnne stood at the bow of *The Bee* and watched the dawn-gray water slip away beneath the hull of the steamer. She wrapped her arms about herself and added a long breath of her own to the breeze drifting past. All the effort she'd put into cajoling Papa to return home had been for naught. Now she must set her mind to a different course—that of helping Papa reach the village on the shores of Lake Nyasa, where he felt called to go. Last night she'd thought she'd come to peace with it. But this morning…

She sighed. *Papa ought not be so stubborn.*

RyAnne leaned over the side and glanced back the length of the boat to the disappearing ocean as the steamer and its passengers pressed forward into the mouth of the Rovuma. Zanzibar was getting farther away by the minute. As they chuffed forward into the covering canopy of trees, shadow seemed to wrap itself around them like the claws of a fish hawk. Now she couldn't see much more than a lighter shade of gray where the small steamship contrasted with the darker trees of the riverbanks streaming away behind them.

She rubbed her upper arms as she leaned against the rail and tipped her face into the cool breeze. The wind cut like a machete through the thin material of the breeches Papa and Captain Dawson had insisted she wear for the inland journey. For now, she was missing the warmth of the many layers of her skirts, but she knew that within an hour of the sunrise she would be thankful for the cooler clothing.

From somewhere along the southern bank she heard the distinct splash of a crocodile leaping into the river—probably startled by the steamer. The sound made her shiver. She'd never be able to see one of the creatures again without wanting to dispatch it forthwith. And her battle to save Nyanja's life was not at an end. The woman had been hot and delusional when they'd loaded her onto the boat this morning.

After a dose of opium, Nyanja was now resting on the bunk in the pilothouse, where June was also trying to get little Moyo, Nyanja's daughter, back to sleep. The only other warm space on the entire little boat was a common room just behind the steersman's cabin, where RyAnne presumed the rest of them would be sleeping on the floor come evening. Papa was already resting there on a pallet she'd made up for him. His breathing had been labored and thready this morning. Each inhalation rattling, each exhalation wheezing.

She shivered and turned back to face the ribbon of the Rovuma before her. How much longer did he have, her papa? And what was she going to do way out here on her own when he was gone? How would she get back home?

She'd written letters—one each to her siblings, Jasmine and Rory, and even one to Mother—telling them how Papa was faring, describing the journey thus far, and promising she'd be home just as soon as she could. Mr. Holloman, Captain Dawson's first mate and cousin, was returning to the island and would deliver the letters on his arrival.

A headache pinched at her forehead, and she rubbed circles at her temples, wondering if she shouldn't have been quite so forthright in her letters. But no. The family deserved to know that Papa probably wouldn't be returning to them. Then they'd at least have some time to prepare themselves for the impending news.

She forced herself to thrust the worries aside. She would deal with all of them when the time came.

The light of dawn had begun to invade the shadows. Along the banks of the river, large mangroves stood above the water like sentinels with long legs. The tall, arching roots tangled together to form misty hiding places for animals and birds of all kinds. A long-legged grey heron pulled his head out from under one wing to blink sleepily at them as they steamed by. And from the shadows of another root system, yellow eyes that belonged to an unseen cat of some sort reflected the light of the lantern hung on the long pole stretched out in front of the boat.

From the village on Commodore Cornwall's estate, firelight flickered orange and yellow against the backdrop of the new-gray sky. And somehow seeing the last of the estate solidified the immensity of what lay before her.

Ahead, a canoe paddled by four native men sluiced through the water before the steamer. A lantern on a pole rising from the center made them easy to spot as they led the way to the deepest sections of the river channel. The man at the rear of the canoe sang a long string of undulating notes, and then the other three responded with a singsong chant. The song was obviously a rowing song, because their paddles kept time to the beat, and when they needed to increase their speed, the rhythm of the song also increased.

The repetitive tune somehow soothed her. And, when all along the eastern horizon behind the boat a thin line of pink began to outline the land, she made her way past the pilothouse to the stern of the steamer to better see it. Soon shards of magenta, peach, saffron, and turquoise slashed across the canopy, creating one of the most fantastic sunrises RyAnne had ever seen. Were someone to put the colors into a painting, people would claim the artist much too fanciful. She smiled softly, letting the sheer beauty wash over her and remind her that God was still in heaven, still in control.

Movement beside her drew her attention to Captain Dawson settling his forearms against the rail next to her, his gaze fixed on God's magnificent painting. "Amazing, isn't it?"

She returned her own examination to the sky. "Breathtaking."

He hunched there for a long moment, his focus bouncing first from the array of colors in the sky to one embankment and then the other. He stood erect, folded his arms, and craned to see around the cabin to the path of the river meandering ahead of them, then returned his gaze to the sunrise as he leaned his hands against the rail. His thumbs tapped out a rhythm, and he seemed to be waging a battle within himself.

She put her back to the rising sun and tried to gauge what he'd been looking at. Ahead, the river narrowed and the embankments were dark and thick with foliage. "What is it, Captain?"

He sighed. "Unfortunately"—he swept a gesture at the magenta sky behind them—"it means we might be facing trouble downriver a bit. You'll need to keep out of sight in the common room for a couple days till we know if the trouble is past."

She frowned. "Whatever do you mean? How can such a striking sunrise possibly mean there is trouble ahead?"

"Smoke." He rubbed one hand across his cheek and down the back of his neck, giving her an apologetic look, as though he knew he was stripping her of a moment of peace. "Colors like that," he tipped his head toward the sky, "mean there is smoke in the air. And smoke likely means there's been a raid nearby. The river is narrow enough that anyone on the deck will not be safe from arrows should we come under attack."

Her jaw tensed, and she flicked one last glance at the sunrise. Not even this one glorious moment remained untouched by evil.

She clasped her hands and studied the toe of her boot, scuffing at a mark on the deck, as suddenly her emotions threatened to overwhelm her. She had been strong. Strong for Papa. Strong for her family because they would have wanted someone to care for Papa in his last days. Strong for Nyanja as she fought for her life, not once but twice. Strong when Papa demanded she wear these confounded men's clothes for her own protection. Strong before the captain because he expected nothing less. And now a simple little thing like the fact that the amazing sunrise was likely only the result of more death and destruction was nearly melting her into a puddle.

She blinked hard and tipped up her chin, forcing the tears to remain at bay as she said, "Alright, Captain. I will see to my father in the common room." But try as she might to prevent it, her voice broke on the last words, and as she spun away from him, he captured her elbow, stilling her.

"Miss Hunter." He gently tugged her around to face him. And the fingers of his hand skimmed a warm trail down her forearm.

Just when his touch whispered warm and soft against her palm and she thought he might entwine his fingers with her own, he yanked his hand away and propped it on his hip instead.

Her heart stuttered, but she forced herself to fold her hands serenely and meet his searching scrutiny.

His tongued darted out to moisten his lips. "I'm sorry. I did not want to steal this moment from you. But for your protection…"

If she allowed herself to start crying, she might just never stop. She snapped her teeth together. Tears solved nothing. If there were any truths she'd learned over the years, certainly that was among them, and yet here she stood, his form naught but a blur and every fountain deep inside her threatening to burst forth. She lifted her chin but couldn't quite bring herself to meet his gaze. "Confound you for being congenial just when I need you to be your normal condescending self, Captain."

He blinked, and if anything, his expression softened even more. He raised one hand to the back of his neck. "If ever I have condescended, it has not been to you. You are a woman of strength and virtue. If I am harsh, as I've said before, it is only for your protection."

A shiver of awareness prickled her skin even as her stomach tightened. Oh, the crazy extremes to which this man could send her reeling. Right at this moment she would like nothing more than to step forward and have him wrap her in a firm embrace. One that blocked out all the world and its deplorableness. Instead, she forced herself to step back. She needed to make an escape, and quickly. She started away, but once more he reached out to stop her. She jerked her elbow from his grasp. "Let me go, Captain, before I embarrass you with unnecessary tears."

"You could never embarrass me, and tears are not a weakness."

She sniffed. Mother would certainly contradict that statement. She folded her arms and refused to look at him. "Neither are they a strength."

"A heart that breaks when evil wraps its choking fist around the world certainly shows a strength of character, to my way of thinking."

She pressed her lips together, unsure how to respond to that. But after a moment, she conceded his point with a nod. "Thank you, Captain."

Dipping down to better see her face, he leaned closer. "I think, since we've known each other for quite some time, and since we are here in the wilds of the Continent far from society and all its mores, we could drop formality and simply call each other by our given names, don't you, RyAnne?"

The sound of her name spoken so quietly and tenderly from his lips jolted through her, and she pulled in a breath. Her eyes snapped to his. It would be so easy out here in the middle of nowhere, with no other confidant, to allow the man to woo her. She must stay strong and remember he did not know her true lineage and that if he did, it would likely change his feelings drastically. "Th-that would be most improper, Captain." She stepped away, once more aiming for escape.

"I see." He leaned into his heels, folding his arms over his chest. But his gaze never left hers, and a smirk ticked up one corner of his mouth. "I've never been much for propriety, so how about this…I will call you RyAnne, and you can stick to formality and call me Captain."

The connotation he gave the last word sent a spear of indignation straight to her marrow. "Why, of all the—" She reached to lift her skirts, only to be reminded she wore the blasted breeches. Giving a huff, she presented him with her back. But with her first step, the deck dipped out from under her foot, and she nearly sprawled flat. She caught herself on the gunwale just in time.

To the captain's credit, only the slightest hint of humor gleamed in his eyes when she glanced back at him.

Straightening her sleeves with a jerk, she made a retreat that would have had much more effect could she have accomplished it properly the first time.

Only once she reached the common room did she realize her pique with the man—and his dratted ship—had all but erased her near descent into tears.

In the makeshift cabin he'd set up under a tent on the bow of the deck, Trent sank into his chair. They'd sailed upriver for five days and now were anchored in a shallow inlet so that dinner could be cooked on a fire along the riverbank. None of the riverside villages they'd passed seemed to have experienced trouble. The scent and sight of smoke, however, had not dissipated all week, and now, while most of the inhabitants of *The Bee* were on land, he waited for the scout standing before him to give his report.

He pierced his scout with a look, and the man clapped his hands together in the custom of his culture, giving a little bow.

"It is as my white friend feared. Many villages ransacked and burnt."

Trent hunched over in his seat and scrubbed his hands down his face. He looked along the length of the Rovuma.

Could it be Khalifa? The man hadn't wasted any time, if so, and was being careful to keep his handiwork hidden from anyone sailing up the river behind him. Of course, Khalifa had known Trent and his party were coming along behind him.

Trent clenched his jaw. He needed more information. There was nothing for it but to leave the boat for a few days while he headed overland to see what he could find out. He had many suspicions and suppositions but not an ounce of proof.

Trent turned to John, the man who'd served as his bosun for the last several years. "Get our friend some food and his payment, would you?"

"Aye, Cap'n."

"And John?"

The man stilled. "Yes?"

"Prepare rations for three days for seven men, would you? And tell Kako I'd like for him to join me on the trip. I may need his knowledge of the tribal languages."

John looked resigned. "Aye, Cap'n."

"Sail during the day, and anchor well before dark. I will find you upriver once I know more."

John gave a tight nod.

Trent pressed his palms to his thighs and used the movement to help himself stand. Like an old man suddenly hit by weariness after only toddling in his garden, exhaustion took hold seemingly of his very marrow. This battle was not something he wanted to face, but since when had any man looked forward to taking up a war?

He needed to find RyAnne and her father and give them an excuse for his inland trip.

He found them on the riverbank, RyAnne squatting on the balls of her feet, with her father seated on a flat rock before her. She held a bowl of stew and was trying to coax the doctor to partake, but he kept waving the spoon away.

"It's really quite good, Papa," she urged, "and you need to keep your strength up." A touch of hopelessness etched her brow, but there was a cajoling tilt to her head.

Trent had to admire her attitude. She'd wanted nothing more than for her father to return to Zanzibar, where he could die in peace with his family nearby. But now that it was too late to change her father's mind, she seemed to have taken up a new cause—one of keeping him alive and well long enough for him to see his call fulfilled.

Trent's weary footsteps ground against the sand at the edge of the river, and she glanced up. Her cajoling expression turned stony the moment she laid eyes on him.

Perhaps he had twitted her one too many times about addressing him as "Captain" over the past few days. But the very thought roused the devil in him and touched the corner of his mouth with humor.

Apparently taking note of his mischief, she glowered at him. But it was fleeting. And that was when he noticed how pale and weary she appeared. She was working herself too hard trying to care for everyone. Nyanja's leg had grown infected and she'd been lying at the very gates of death since they had brought her on board. He knew RyAnne was spending many of the night hours caring for the woman and thus wasn't getting the sleep she needed.

He spun on his heel and went to the stew pot, filling two bowls and taking up two spoons. He was back by her side within moments, urging her to take one of the bowls. "Any chance I could trouble you to eat a bowl of soup yourself, Miss Hunter?"

A look of surprise on her face, she accepted the bowl he offered, her father's bowl still held in her other hand. He took it from her and pressed it into the doctor's hands, nudging the spoon closer to the man. "I'll sit here and eat with the good doctor so that you can partake of your own meal now as well."

He sat down on the stone next to the doctor and set to eating as though he hadn't a care in the world. And was quite pleased to see from the corner of his eye that the man lifted a spoonful of broth to his own lips, albeit with trembling hand.

Miss Hunter's jaw dropped slightly, and when she met his gaze, he offered her a wink.

She almost rolled her eyes.

He resisted an outright chuckle. No man, no matter how feeble, relished being coddled like a newborn babe. Her father would likely eat a sight more were she to leave the man to consume his victuals in peace.

And now it was time to get to the business at hand. "I've come to tell you both that I'll be…doing some scouting with a handful of our men over the next few days. I'll meet up with you all further up the Rovuma."

RyAnne sank down to sit in the sand and took up her spoon even as she leveled him with a scathing look. "Off to find your first herd of elephants, are you?"

"Something like that." He blew on a spoonful of the fish and rice.

She made a disgusted noise in the back of her throat.

"Before I leave, I have something I want to give you."

"Your last will and testament, perhaps?"

There was bite to her words, but he only chuckled.

She was curious—he could see that. But she managed to restrain any more of her questions and tucked into her meal.

They ate in silence, if an evening filled with the tympanic

rush of water over stones, lusty birdsong, and the chatter from a copse full of monkeys could be considered silence.

Trent emptied his bowl and noticed that Dr. Hunter's bowl was now half-empty as well. But the man didn't seem to be eating anymore, and exhaustion drooped his shoulders. Trent relieved him of his bowl and stacked the dishes together on a nearby rock. Then he took the man by the arm and helped him stand. "How about I help you to your pallet while Miss Hunter finishes her repast." He leveled a look on the younger of his charges. "If you'll wait here for me, Miss Hunter, I'll return shortly." Without giving her time to argue, he led her father back to the steamer.

Once he had the man comfortably situated on his bed, he made his way to his own pallet beneath the canvas at the front of the little ship. From the center of his bedroll, he withdrew the violin case and studied it for a moment.

Commodore Cornwall had given it to him to give to RyAnne just before they departed his estate last week. Trent had almost given it to her several times over the past few days, but the timing had never seemed right. Now that he was heading inland, however, he couldn't kid himself about the danger he might be walking into. And if he didn't return, he at least wanted her to have this one comfort to carry her through the difficult task of getting her father back home. Also, if he was honest, he wanted to hear her make it sing one last time. He really should have given it to her sooner. And now he regretted that. Each night he could have coaxed her for just one song—for her sake as much as for his own.

He tucked it beneath his arm and strode purposefully down the gangplank. Little Moyo was heading up as he was heading down. The child had been most reluctant—almost fearful—in his presence the first few days of the trip. But more recently she seemed to be tolerating him rather well. Something he wanted to foster. "Moyo." He called her to him. "Would you like to hear something beautiful?"

The little imp's eyes widened, and she nodded her head vigorously, even though he had strong doubts over how much of what he'd just said she truly understood. Her mother's dialect was quite different from the Kiswahili he spoke.

"Come on then." He motioned for her to follow him.

The bowls he'd stacked on the rock were missing, and Miss Hunter was not where he'd left her. Instead he found her farther down the river with June, washing up the dishes from the evening meal. They were standing within the temporary fence the men had erected to keep the crocs at bay. The site of RyAnne bending over one of the large cast-iron pots gave him pause, and he came to a stop. Had the doctor's daughter, who'd grown up with servants to do her every bidding, ever washed a dish one day in her life? He knew that each evening up to this one she'd gone straight back to the steamer to sit by Nyanja's side, while June had gone to do the washing up. But happily, Nyanja seemed to have turned a corner during the night and had rested fever-free all day today, so RyAnne probably felt like she could be put to better use helping June.

Moyo stopped by his side.

RyAnne watched June scrub one of the pots for a moment. Then her nose wrinkled, and she gave the pot sitting at her own feet a disgusted bump with the toe of her boot. It didn't budge. Casting one more glance at June, as if to verify she really was seeing what she thought she'd seen, Miss Hunter finally bent and scooped up a handful of the river sand, thrust her hand inside the pot, and set to scouring the iron with the handful of grit, just as June was doing. After a moment, still carefully mimicking June's every move, Miss Hunter made to lift the cast-iron pot and swirl some water into it. But the moment she tried to lift the cast iron, she let out a squeak and stumbled forward, losing her grip on the pot. It was obviously much heavier than she'd expected it to be.

Trent pressed his lips together to suppress a grin, but beside him Moyo held no such compunctions. She covered her mouth with both little hands, hunched her head into her shoulders, and giggled loudly.

The sound brought Miss Hunter's head around with a snap.

But as soon as she saw it was Moyo there laughing at her, her pique morphed into humor. She bent down and shook her finger at the little girl. "If you want to laugh, little Miss Moyo, I invite you to come and see if you can lift this pot!"

Moyo stretched her hands out wide and chattered something that neither one of them could understand.

Trent gestured to the pot with one hand while lifting the violin case with the other. "How about you trade me, Miss Hunter? I'll finish the pot, but as payment I expect you to play me a song."

As soon as her gaze lit upon the violin case, RyAnne's eyes widened. She quickly rinsed her hands in the river and then patted them dry on her breeches and hurried toward him. "How—" A sheen of appreciation glistened on her lower lids, and she couldn't seem to find any other words.

Something cinched up tighter than a bowline knot in his chest. He cleared his throat and laid the case into her outstretched palms. "It is from the commodore."

Softly, she swept one hand over the smooth surface of the case. "But it was his wife's!"

"He said she would have wanted it to go to someone well versed in the instrument and that he's heard none as well versed as you."

"Oh, Captain, this is…a most welcome blessing."

He took in the flush of excitement pinking her cheeks and the spark of anticipation in her emerald eyes. "Indeed." He stepped back and folded his arms.

Moyo chattered something again and stretched out her arms before her.

Miss Hunter laid the case into Moyo's outstretched arms and clicked open the latches. She folded back the instrument's covering of burgundy silk and cradled the violin to her chest like a mother welcoming a long-lost child.

Finally, just when he'd begun to think he might have to prod her to it, she reached for the bow and tuned the instrument briefly.

And then, standing on the shores of the Rovuma, with the

sounds of the camp and God's nature rising up around her, she closed her eyes and pulled the bow across the strings in one long and plaintive note that led to another and then another.

The melody flowed as though from her very heart, and he was so enraptured with watching her play that it was many moments before he remembered he ought to finish cleaning her pot. But when he turned to the task, it was to find that June had already completed it, and the pots were stacked neatly by her feet, waiting for someone to return them aboard ship.

Trent used that as an excuse to escape his building emotions. Lifting the pots, he strode up the gangplank and returned them to the corner of the deck where they were stored. Then he dropped onto his pallet, clasped his hands behind his head, and let Miss Hunter's songs serenade his soul.

She only played three, but even after she returned to the ship, all the camp lay in quiet, as though a holy hush had been brought on by her music.

Chapter 12
Made Perfect in Weakness

Trent and his scouts left camp just as periwinkle began to seep into the blackness of the night sky. Birds were already welcoming the dawn with hearty abandon, and the cicadas and crickets were singing their last duets before the heat of day drove them into silent hiding.

Trent paused at the top of the first hill and looked back toward the camp. He'd left a good contingent of men with the steamer, who should serve as more than adequate protection should the group come under any attack. But as adept as Miss Hunter was at finding trouble… With a grunt of disgust, he forced himself to walk away and not contemplate all the predicaments she could get herself into while he was gone.

The first village they came to remained intact, although at the outset, except for the hot coals still burning in several fire pits, they would have thought the village deserted, so hidden did the inhabitants make themselves at the sight of the strangers drawing nigh. Only when Trent and his men laid out trinkets for trade did one brave soul emerge from the brush behind a hut. After he successfully traded a small knife for a bag of sugarcane stalks, others slowly seeped from their hiding places, the last being the village headman, who invited them to stay for a feast that evening.

Word had traveled quickly from village to village of the men attacking settlements along the Rovuma, and the headman directed them toward the northwest—a track that would take them farther from the river. The next village they came to was not so lucky as the first.

Trent's stomach clenched when they crested the rise above the huts and saw the smoke wisping in misty tendrils from several piles of rubble that had once been homes. The mud walls of several huts still stood, but the thatch roofs had collapsed and smoldered within the circular walls. Next to the path that led into the village, an old woman lay sprawled, an arrow through her throat, eyes gaping in horror.

Just outside the door to a still-smoldering hut, a small child of just over two years lay dead. Too small to pack a load for the slavers, too big for his mother to carry both him and a tusk of ivory. A life cut down in the tight bud of innocence. Flies already covered the little body.

Defeat washed over Trent. He settled to his haunches next to the child and surveyed the carnage in the rest of the village. Gardens trampled. Goats, still penned, bleating in hunger. The old and young, dead where they fell. And everyone in between… *taken.*

His hand shook as he shooed away the flies and lifted the little body into his arms. "Release the goats so they can forage," he commanded. "And bring them." He nodded toward the other dead. "We will bury them and then move on."

For days they traveled, and for days they found no survivors. The path of butchery finally led back to the villages on the banks of the river. The man wasn't even bothering to disguise his actions now that he was farther inland—farther from any authority that might be sent for.

There was no proof. No one left alive to speak against the one who had committed the atrocious acts. But Trent knew. And what angered him most was the fact that the man's actions weren't even illegal. The only way to put him away was to either kill him—and if he was working for someone higher up, killing him would only result in a new "trader" being sent to replace him—or follow him to the coast and pray he made contact with his leader and that they tried to transport his slaves somewhere other than Zanzibar, which was illegal due to the Hamerton Treaty.

Late one night Trent lay in his bedroll, hands clasped behind his head, studying the myriad stars in the thick blackness overhead. The savannah grasses sang sibilantly, as if all was right with the world, and somewhere far off a lion roared, deep and low.

Llewellyn Cornwall, the British officer who had hired him for this mission, had warned him it would not be easy. He had cautioned Trent against moving too quickly lest the man at the top escape and hire new underlings to continue pillaging on his behalf.

Trent knew Lew was right. The only way to put a stop to this was to figure out who the lead man was. But God help him, he couldn't just stand by and let the carnage continue.

Khalifa had to have others working for him. With the number of villages he'd sacked, he couldn't be keeping all those people with him. He must be sending them off in groups to the coast, with men from his party or men he had bribed to help him along the way. Often natives could be bought off with as little as some bolts of cloth and the promise of their freedom. For such a small price they would turn on their fellow man and lead caravans of them to Bagamoyo, where they handed them off to someone appointed to close the deal.

His gut clenched as he considered the number of lives that could be affected if he didn't do something. "God, what am I to do?" he whispered into the expanse. Every instinct within him rang with urgency for action.

Yet, he had the doctor and his daughter to think about also. And he could only do one thing at a time.

He needed to get the Hunters to the lake and get them settled. Then he would worry about what to do with Khalifa. Already he and his scouting party were days late returning to *The Bee*. Tomorrow they would head back.

He closed his eyes and focused on the vision of RyAnne Hunter. A smile tugged at the corner of his mouth. After so many days of witnessing nothing but death and destruction, it would be good to see someone pure and lovely once more.

And that was when he knew.

His eyes flew open. He'd been fooling himself into thinking otherwise, but now it was quite clear.

The little lioness had firmly sunk her teeth into his heart.

Two weeks later RyAnne stepped off the boat and stretched the stiffness from her back. The days melded one into the next. It had been too long since the captain had taken leave of them with several men. Before he'd left that dawn, he'd said that they only needed to go inland for a few days to do some scouting and that she wasn't to leave the party near the river. The days since had stretched interminably.

Where was the captain? Had he been injured? Killed? The party of men who'd been left with the steamer were growing restless. She'd heard them grumbling to John Knight the evening before. She didn't know what the bosun had said to them, but whatever it was seemed to have appeased them for now. She only hoped they stayed so, at least until the captain returned.

She was thankful that, though he had to rest often during the day, Papa seemed to be holding his own.

The evening repast was generally cooked by one of the village men over an open fire along the bank, and either RyAnne or June would take a portion to Nyanja, who still recuperated in the captain's cabin.

The weather had remained mostly dry, but only two days after the captain's departure, a torrential rainstorm had come upon them late one night, and the stores of rice had been ruined. So for nine solid days they had eaten, unseasoned, either roasted hare or fish, accompanied by a tasteless thick porridge the consistency of day-old oatmeal. For each day's breaking of the fast, the porridge from the evening before was fried and eaten plain as they set sail for the day's journey. Sometimes there were crocodile eggs if one of the men had found a nest in the sandy banks of the river, but after her experience with the vile beasts, RyAnne wanted nothing to do with them, even if it meant eating their unhatched young. Besides, the eggs' taste—even though it was near-cousin to a regular chicken egg—contained a smack of something off that set her teeth on edge. At noon it was always so hot no one wanted much, save a few sips of cool water or a piece of fruit from one of the wild trees along the river.

Tonight they had anchored in a tranquil bend of the Rovuma, with a sandy shore. RyAnne's stomach grumbled even now. She hadn't eaten since the tasteless porridge slice that morning. But on this evening one of the native men had recognized a wild plant and dug up its roots, which turned out to be thick, potato-like tubers he had assured her were "most agreeable to stomachs."

Then she had come upon a small patch of wild vetches on the short walk she'd taken with June and Moyo, and they were picking what she hoped would be enough for a nice-size soup when combined with the tubers.

Moyo had grown accustomed to her now and chattered incessantly in her native tongue, skipping, and hopping, and spending more time at the wild honeysuckle vine next to the patch of vetches, sucking on blossoms, than picking the wild peas with them. But RyAnne couldn't find it in herself to scold the little one, and neither could June, it seemed—she was at this precise moment picking a honeysuckle bloom from the vine that Moyo couldn't quite reach.

RyAnne smiled and tossed another handful of vetches into her basket.

When they returned to the camp, the men were just setting about to roast several fish.

RyAnne spoke to the men using the few words she'd learned of their language and the few words they knew of Swahili, and managed to convey that she would like to do the cooking on this evening. The men quite gladly handed over the task once they understood her meaning. "June, fetch me the tubers and a bit of salt from the ship's stores, would you? And I believe I saw a braid of dried onions…bring one of those also."

The flour and cornmeal that was normally put to use for the porridge, she mixed with a bit of the salt, some oily drippings from the fish, and water. While the fish continued to roast over the fire, and the vetches, salt, tubers, and onions boiled in the pot, she formed the dough into flat rounds and set them on the hot rocks at the fire's edge, turning them every few minutes so they cooked evenly. When the fish were done, she flaked them into the stew.

It was neither the most satisfying nor the best-tasting food she had ever eaten, but it was a far cry above the fare they'd been consuming for the past few weeks. To a man, they thanked her, and Papa even went back for a second portion, which made it all worthwhile.

Hefting the now empty pot—she'd become quite used to the weight of it by this time—RyAnne rested it against her hip and started for the river. As they did each night, the men had built a fence, a makeshift safety zone of sharpened sticks pounded into the riverbed, forming an arc from one place on the sandy bank to another. It gave the camp a safe place to fetch water and wash clothes and dishes along the river without fear of another crocodile attack.

She set the blackened kettle in the sandy spot along the bank and caught sight of her arm as she took up a handful of sand and set to scrubbing. Her skin was becoming quite dark. She ought to be more careful. What would the captain say when he returned? Her face heated, and she shoved the thought aside. She had no business worrying about what the captain might think of her. Mother, however… Mother would have a conniption could she see how brown RyAnne had allowed herself to become. People would wonder, after all, how the daughter of a woman so blond and fair could darken so easily.

She finished scouring the pot at the river's edge and stood, pressing one hand into her aching back. Out here so far from everything, such worries seemed so paltry, yet she'd lived with such remonstrations her entire life.

Moyo ran, giggling, down the path and paused only long enough to throw her little arms around RyAnne's legs for a moment before dashing to the mango tree a few feet away and pointing chubby arms at a nearly ripe fruit hanging high overhead.

RyAnne glanced up at the fruit. "You want that, do you?" Her own mouth watered at the thought of the sweet, juicy pulp. She glanced back down the path. "Where's June?"

The child flapped her little hand downriver to where the steamer lay anchored, and chattered a few indecipherable words.

June must have taken Nyanja her evening meal. RyAnne glanced back at the little girl, whose large pleading gaze bounced from the fruit to her and back again.

With a capitulating laugh, RyAnne set down the pot. "Alright, let's see if we can't get ourselves a mango or two." She pointed to a rock. "You sit there. *Khalani*." She remembered the word for "sit" in the child's *Chewa* language.

The little one clambered up onto the large rock, plopped down, and rubbed her chubby hands together.

RyAnne chuckled and assessed the tree. Grabbing the lowest branch, she hoisted herself upward. The branches were close together, and it wasn't long before she found a fairly ripe fruit dangling just out of her reach. Wrapping one hand around a branch, she leaned far out and scrabbled at the fruit taunting the tips of her fingers. She huffed and stood on her tiptoes to lean a little further. "Moyo…if only my mother could see me now." The words were a grunt as she stretched full out.

"I'm sure she would be most impressed."

"Captain!" RyAnne sucked in a breath of surprise, but the fruit was firmly in her grasp now, and she plucked it, thankful his startling presence hadn't knocked her right out of the tree. Peering down through the leaves, she held it out for him to see before she dropped it into his waiting hands.

"'Impressed' is not the word Mother would use, Captain." She cleared her throat when the words emerged breathy and barely audible.

He winked up at her with a grin. "Likely not, I suppose."

She clenched one fist, willing down the racing of her heart. He was back! This time she was careful to keep any emotion from her tone. "I see you've returned no worse for the wear."

"And I see you managed not to get yourself killed while I was away…"

He squatted down by Moyo and handed her the fruit.

Jabbering something in her high-pitched voice, the child thrust it back at him. The captain used the knife on his belt to slice through the thick, tough skin and peel the fruit for her. Then rinsing his hands in the river and wiping them on his breeches, he glanced back up at RyAnne. "Since you are already up there, I'll take one too, if you please."

A green fruit lay ready to hand. She plucked it and tossed it down to him.

He eyed the hard, green oval and chuckled, tossing it aside.

Before she knew what was happening, he leapt up, caught a branch, and clambered toward her.

Her eyebrows lifted, and she clutched at the trunk behind her, sinking down to straddle the branch before she lost her balance altogether. The setting rays of the golden sun pierced her sanctuary, turning the leaves around her, which had only a moment ago been shades of green, to lemon and chartreuse.

The captain swung onto her branch and straddled it, facing her. Planting his palms into the section of branch between them, he leaned forward. Humor etching his expression, he scanned her face, his gaze lingering much longer than propriety allowed. Slowly his humor slipped away and something more intimate took its place in his expression.

Why was he looking at her in such a manner when only a few weeks ago he'd made it very clear there could be nothing between them? Yet, she couldn't deny the pleasure pulsing through her veins. She felt her cheeks heat.

He arched a brow, the glimmer in his gray-green eyes clearly revealing that her rising color hadn't escaped his notice.

Breathe. Just breathe.

After a long moment, he leaned toward her.

She ought to pull back and use the flat of her palm to remind him she was a lady, but with the trunk at her spine she had barely any quarter to give. And she wasn't sure she *wanted* to slap him. Her heart forgot to beat, and twisted into a knot of anticipation just below her ribs.

He was still leaning closer, his gaze holding hers captive.

Then at the last moment he turned his face aside and reached one hand past her shoulder. He was so close that she could feel the warmth radiating from his cheek against her own.

A small *snap* and he sat back and held up a red and yellow-green fruit for her inspection, one corner of his mouth pulled up in that maddening way of his. Yet somehow this time it wasn't so maddening as it was endearing.

Had he wanted to steal a kiss but changed his mind at the last moment and used the fruit as an excuse? Or had he been reaching for the fruit the whole time and only taunting her?

Pulling his knife from the sheath at his waist, he cut a thick slice of the fruit and held it against the blade with this thumb as he stretched it out to her.

She took the proffered fruit and hoped he hadn't noticed the trembling of her fingers. This was an entirely new sensation sweeping over her.

Frustration. Pique. Irritation. These were all emotions she expected to feel when the captain was present.

But this…she wasn't even sure what this new feeling was. Something akin to the time lightning had struck the tree across the indigo field when she'd been hurrying home through the rainstorm. The strike had knocked her from her feet and set every inch of her skin to tingling.

Yes. This sensation felt very similar.

She hadn't realized how much she'd missed him. He was much too easy on the eyes. She sighed and bit the inside of her cheek, the pain grounding her firmly to the branch lest she be tempted to float away on some airy, dangerous emotion. Someone needed to say something to break the spell that seemed to have fallen around them.

She scooped some of the tartly sweet pulp from the skin with her front teeth as she glanced down to make sure Moyo was still on her rock.

While the rays of the sun still reached them here in the treetop, shadows were beginning to cloak the ground. But she could still see Moyo where they'd left her. Good.

Keeping her gaze averted, she asked, "What can I do for you, Captain?" Her words were carefully controlled.

From her peripheral vision she saw him grin. He cut another thick strip of the fruit, and his voice was low when he spoke. "Oh, there are a great many things I can think of…RyAnne." He deliberately emphasized her name, causing her gaze to fly to his once more. Slowly he brought the fruit on his blade to his mouth, his twinkling eyes never leaving hers. He chewed leisurely, one eyebrow quirking up as if to challenge her to offer him anything he desired.

Involuntarily her focus dropped to where a bead of juice lingered on his lower lip.

Her mouth went dry, and she forced her attention to the slice of fruit in her own hands, then took another bite. But like a ship at the whim of the wind, her gaze returned to him of its own volition.

A breeze picked up and plastered his loose-fitting shirt back against the firm ridges of his torso.

The lightning-strike sensation returned in full force. She jerked her attention down to Moyo once more.

She must remember that there would be life after this brief jaunt into the heart of the Continent. Anything she revealed to the captain out here, no matter how tempting it may seem to do so, would soon find its way into the parlors of Zanzibar's upper crust. Mother would not take kindly to her revealing Papa's dark secret. And the captain deserved to know that much about her before…

She swallowed again. *Before what?*

A small thud in the brush below drew her attention. He'd tossed the mango down, and by the time she looked at him to see why, he already had his knife back in its sheath and had scooted so close to her that their knees were touching.

Heart thudding with a mix of both rapture and terror, she searched his face, breath abated. Golden light filtering through the leaves mottled half his face, leaving the other in deep shadow, which did much to hide his expression, but one emotion was clearly portrayed in his expression. Desire.

And good Lord have mercy, that same yearning thrummed in her own veins, and each moment she gazed into his eyes urged it to greater strength. Her mouth went dry at the realization. How was it she had fallen for this man who had tormented her in so many ways over the years?

Slowly, hesitantly, his hand lifted, and he skimmed his fingers across her cheek, tucking a stray curl back. "RyAnne…"

Was his hand trembling? Her heart beat as though seeking release from the bondage of her chest.

He settled his palm against her cheek. "I've seen so much death and destruction over the last few days… Seeing you again is like a breath of fresh air."

Barely able to see his expression in the deep shadows, she tilted her head for a better examination of his expression. "Captain—"

Tipping up her chin, he dropped a finger against her lips and then leaned closer and rested his forehead against hers. "Trent… say it…please?"

Her heart hammered. "T-Trent…"

Slowly, he eased back just enough to look her in the eye. "That wasn't so hard now, was it?" His words were barely audible above the rushing tumble of the river below them, and the warmth in his gray-green eyes as he studied her nearly snatched from her the balance needed to remain on the branch.

She swallowed and shook her head. Her gaze lowered to his lips, and she whispered his name again. "Trent."

"RyAnne…" His words were equally soft. He brushed the pad of his thumb across her lower lip. "Would that I could. But as I've already stated, I can't let this go further."

The words were firm. But there was a sadness, a regret that lingered in his eyes as he withdrew his hand from her.

She trembled, feeling that he wanted more than the brief contact they'd just shared.

Knowing that *she* did.

Yet, also at the back of her mind there lingered an agreement with his assessment, the reminder that she had so many secrets he deserved to be told before he committed himself to her more deeply. So much she wasn't free to tell him. She studied the branch between them, picking at the bark with the nail of one thumb. Took a breath to steady the crazy roil of emotions swirling through her.

The clang of something metallic suddenly drew his glance toward the encampment that was clearly visible through a gap in the branches. John Knight stood by the camp's fire, but he was looking in their direction. RyAnne doubted the bosun could actually see them from this distance, but it was as though a wall had suddenly appeared between her and the captain.

Trent sat back, tucking his fingers into his armpits and clamping them there with crossed arms. He looked down at the branch and clenched his jaw before looking back into her face. His throat worked, and he scooted several inches back before resuming his stoic arms-crossed position. He pressed his lips together and studied a leafy branch just to his right.

Confusion plucked at her brow as, once again, disappointment marched through her. Confound the man for… *For what?* She wasn't sure. *Well, just confound the man!*

Below them, Moyo finished her treat and stood to her pudgy little feet on the rock where she'd been sitting. RyAnne saw her means of escape. "Moyo, stay where you are, precious." She arched a brow at the captain. "If you'll excuse me, *Captain*?"

Slipping one leg over the branch so that both dangled from one side, she grasped another nearby branch and swung herself down to the ground below. There were at least some benefits to wearing men's attire.

She was helping Moyo down from her rock, when she felt the captain come to a stop beside her.

June stepped into sight up the path toward the encampment. The firelight from the campfire danced brightly behind her in the rapidly descending dusk. Moyo dashed toward June, chattering and gesturing back toward the mango tree.

RyAnne started after the child, but Trent called her name

softly. "RyAnne."

She frowned but couldn't suppress the double-time rhythm of her heart. Why did her name on his lips have to sound so appealing? "Captain—"

"I need to explain. Please stay but a moment?" He tipped his head, and she wished the rapidly falling shadows weren't so thoroughly concealing his features.

In exasperation, she tossed up her hands. A gesture that urged him to speak.

His feet shuffled as he took another couple steps away from her. He lifted one hand to grip the back of his neck, pegging her with a look. He kept his voice so low she could barely hear him above the rush of the Rovuma. "RyAnne, I have a confession. I'm not here on the Continent to seek my fortune in ivory."

Everything inside her tightened up like a drumskin. Whatever could he mean?

"There are other reasons, ones I'm not at liberty to reveal. Suffice it to say, were you and I to…" He broke off and cleared his throat. "The short of it is, I should refrain from…associating with you."

Those words shot as deep as a harpoon. She studied his expression.

Could he know Papa's secret? Maybe from Papa he'd found out who she *really* was. If Trent knew she was the product of infidelity, that the woman who had birthed her had been a quadroon slave, and that Papa and Mother had been lying to everyone about her for years, of course he probably wanted nothing to do with her.

No. That was not a possibility. Only the family knew. Papa had spent his life protecting her from that secret. And Mother's pride wouldn't give it up for torture. The only other person who had known was the woman who had died giving birth to her. So what could the captain's reasons for not associating with her be? Unless…

She frowned, and a sigh slipped from her. Both times that they'd spoken of this topic, he'd offered her the same excuse that there were reasons he was not at liberty to reveal. *I should refrain from associating with you…*

Did he have another woman waiting for him back in the Americas that she didn't know about? A shard of pain lashed at her heart, swift and sure as the strike of a mamba. That seemed a very logical conclusion, didn't it? And he'd been doing his level best to get her to use his given name!

Well!

Her chin lifted.

She had come to depend on him entirely too much.

She would *not* allow herself to be hurt by this man. "Tren—*Captain*… I must concur, because there is much you should know about me ere we ever…" Her face heated as she rolled her hand through the air. "Much *I* am not at liberty to reveal." Now why had she gone and made herself so vulnerable by disclosing all that to him? She ended with a quick, "Even if I were inclined to make it known to someone such as yourself."

She gritted her teeth and forced herself to stop talking, lest she turn into a blubbering ninny, or worse, a haranguing biddy.

He took another step back with a brief nod, jaw tight. "I see." Folding his arms, he turned to look out over the moonlight undulating on the passing water. "I understand."

She was quite certain he didn't see or understand any of it, but she let it rest.

Silence hung between them for a long time, and RyAnne tipped her head and just watched him, his silhouette stark black against the water.

His shoulders drooped, and he ran a hand over the back of his head. His words were ragged when he spoke. "I'm glad you didn't see any of the destruction, RyAnne. So much carnage and death. So much…*apathy* for the welfare of other human beings." He sighed audibly and continued to stare out over the rippling river as though he might still be processing all he'd taken in.

Finally, he gave himself a little shake and spoke, all business. "I wanted to ask about your father. And Nyanja? How are they? I want to press quickly for the lake over the next two weeks."

At the mention of her father she swallowed hard against the

desire to throw herself at the captain and beg for the comfort of his arms. Instead, she kept her hands tucked behind herself and her feet fast against the ground. "The long days with nothing to do but sleep have been good for Nyanja. She still has been fighting fevers, but the infection in her leg seems to be getting a little better each day. Every other day for the past week, we've been helping her off the boat, and yesterday she even made it a good distance with the crutches Mr. Knight made for her before June had to help her back to *The Bee*." She paused. "Papa…" She swallowed at the constriction suddenly gripping her throat. "Papa seems to be…about the same."

That was what she'd been telling herself, but the sharp look Trent turned on her with an upraised brow drew the full truth from her lips.

"He seems to be holding his own so long as he gets plenty of rest, but his cough may have worsened a little." Her eyes stung, and she kicked at an exposed stone beneath her feet.

"I'm sorry."

She nodded her thanks. The truth was, she knew she could lose Papa any day now. "All the more reason for us to press harder for the lake. I would hate for us to have come this far and for him to miss his dream."

"My men need rest tonight. We'll leave first thing in the morning."

Chapter 13
Made Perfect in Weakness

Trent was as good as his word. That evening he divided the men into two groups. One would navigate and sail by day and the other by night. Bosun John Knight was appointed captain of the day shift, and Trent would helm the ship by night.

Sitting around the campfire that night, the men, especially those who would have to navigate the river by canoe at night, grumbled and complained until Trent had to offer them an extra shilling a week to keep the peace. Then those who had been assigned to the day shift set to grumbling about the fact that they were getting paid less than the others. Finally, Trent brought all the men around and had them draw stones from inside a leather bag. A black stone meant they were on the night shift and got extra pay. A white stone meant they got the day shift. Each week they would repeat the process. This seemed to appease the men somewhat.

The next morning RyAnne rose early. She wanted one last moment ashore before she was consigned to the ship day and night over the next few weeks.

Slowly, she made her way through the thick grayness of dawn to the mango tree by the river. Leaning back against it, she watched the lightening horizon of the mountains ahead. One moment darkness covered the river valley, and in the next instant shards of light sprang over the mountaintops and cascaded into the valley below. The black water turned gray and then a dusky brown.

Something was different today. She frowned and tilted her head, trying to pinpoint what it was. Then her eyebrows rose, and she held her breath, listening. No birdsong accompanied the dawn.

The skin at the back of her neck tingled with tension. Something wasn't right.

And that was when a black mound floating in the river caught her eye. Squinting against the glare on the water, she leaned forward for a better view. The mass bobbed serenely, but there was something disquieting about it. Never taking her gaze off it, she turned and kept pace with it as it rode the current downriver. If it kept its course, it would float just past the far side of *The Bee*. She ran the last few yards, hurried up the gangway, and dashed across the deck, leaning far out to see if she could get a better glimpse.

There! It floated in a slash of glare but would soon be in the clear water next to the ship. She watched it come. This close, it only took her a moment to recognize the shape for what it was—a dead body.

She covered her mouth with one hand.

The broken shaft of a spear protruded at an upward angle from the right shoulder, and when a whim of current turned the corpse, she saw it was an old man, face wrinkled, hair downy and white.

Where had he come from? She glanced back up the river, and that was when she noticed the others drifting along. One was a small child of no more than three years. The others were all elderly.

"Dear Father." She closed her eyes and pressed a hand to her stomach, willing down the rush of nausea.

Someone stepped up beside her.

Trent grunted, obviously having just noticed the corpse. He took her elbow and pulled her from the rail. "I'm sorry you had to see that. Come away."

Before she could form a reply, John Knight jogged up to them, puffing from the exertion. "Cap'n, I reckon you ought to come see this."

Trent's hand rubbed a slow, comforting circle against her back, and she stepped away from it. The man was too much of a temptation for her in a moment like this.

Trent dropped his hands to his hips. "What is it, John?"

"It's the paddle, Cap'n. There's—" With a glance at RyAnne, he broke off and ended softly, "There's something stuck in it, sir."

RyAnne's horror grew. She pressed her lips together and

nodded to Trent that she would be fine and he should follow John, who was already heading back the way he had come.

RyAnne returned to her pallet next to June in the common room. She sank onto it, wrapping her arms about her knees and resting her forehead there. She rocked gently, willing the roiling in her stomach to settle, the pain in her heart to dissipate. But she was unsuccessful on both counts.

They set off as soon as they had cleared the paddle. For the next three days they had to pause repeatedly to remove bodies from the boat's wheel before they could resume their journey. It was midmorning of the fourth day when they came upon the burned-out village. John woke Trent, and he took a crew of men ashore to see if there were any who needed help. They came back, faces grim, shaking their heads. There were no survivors.

RyAnne stood, hands resting on the deck rail, and watched the remains of the village slip behind the thick vegetation along the banks of the river as the boat slowly lumbered away. Had anyone tried to fight for those people? Had anyone even spoken a word in their favor? The old man—the first corpse she had seen—had been killed from above. That was the only explanation for the angle of the spear. Had he been pleading for his life just before that fatal thrust? And what of those who'd been taken? Would they have been better off to have died? Who would help them now? Would anyone speak up for them along the way to Bagamoyo?

Exhaustion overtook her. She wandered to the stern of *The Bee* and settled into a cross-legged position on the deck, watching the Rovuma trail away behind them. Maybe if she studied only the water directly in their wake she wouldn't have to see any more bodies. Wouldn't have to contemplate any more painful questions that she didn't have the answers to. Wouldn't have to wallow in the helplessness consuming her. Surely someone needed to do something. But what could one person do?

Papa said he felt called of the Lord to help these people. But what could he in his weakened condition do about such atrocities?

She had no solutions. Such suffering! Such blatant disregard for humanity!

As the days passed, Trent's frustration increased.

The river grew narrower and narrower. Several times they came to impassable rocky shoals. The designs of *The Bee* had taken this into account, however, and all along the side of the ship there were slots into which short poles could be fitted. When they came to the shallows, everyone disembarked, and all the men stepped into the water, fitted the poles in, and lifted *The Bee* on their shoulders across the shallows until the river became deep enough to once again float the ship.

"On the count of three!" Trent counted off, and with a collective grunt the men hoisted *The Bee* and moved forward fifteen paces. A rest of ten seconds and the process repeated. "Again!"

At one place where the river climbed a series of falls, they had to transport the ship on dry ground up the hill until they could reconnect with the water.

Each new delay sent vexation coursing through Trent. With each destroyed village they passed, his resolve had grown. He needed to catch up to Khalifa and put a stop to his rampage.

And find out who he's working for.

And to do that he might have to pretend he liked the man for a while. The very thought set his teeth on edge.

Tonight he stood at the helm, keeping a keen eye on the lantern raised high from the canoe snaking through the river ahead of them. Well, keeping his eye on it most of the time…

RyAnne stood at the bow of the ship, moonlight gleaming off her dark curls as they billowed in the wind behind her. Beauty personified.

He gritted his teeth and jerked his gaze back to the lantern, adjusting the course of the little steamer. Why couldn't she just go to her cot and sleep like everyone else? He was doing the right thing keeping his distance from the lass. Khalifa's brutality had proven itself time and again over the past few weeks. And if the man ever had an inkling that RyAnne meant something to Trent, he wouldn't hesitate to use her for leverage.

If only Trent's heart would comprehend the message his head so clearly understood!

He swallowed. Distance was what he needed. A great deal of distance between the alluring Miss Hunter and himself.

But first he needed to get her and her father to their settlement, and this blasted river was not assisting him on that count.

So it was with great relief late one afternoon that they discovered they'd come to the mouth of the river and could take *The Bee* no further. Another fifty kilometers and they would arrive at the village where Dr. Hunter had arranged to start his mission.

Three more days.

"We'll have to walk from here." The captain's voice rang out loud and clear through the chilly morning mist.

RyAnne stood at the back of the group he had called together on the riverbank just after dawn.

"Everyone gather your packs and be ready to move out within the hour. Kako estimates it won't take more than three days for us to reach his village from here."

RyAnne swallowed and glanced at Nyanja leaning on her crutches. She had been doing very well for the past weeks, but her crutches would still slow her down. They'd need to make a rickshaw of sorts for her to be carried on. Though wheels probably wouldn't work on the terrain they'd likely be facing. A litter then.

RyAnne's gaze swept on to Papa seated on a stone, his hands propped against his knees as though he needed their assistance to keep himself upright. As much as it pained her to admit it, she didn't think he'd make it fifty steps even if he had nothing to carry.

Her jaw clenched. Two litters then. That was something she could orchestrate while the captain organized the rest of the party. She strode over to Kako. "I wonder if I might ask you to help me make two stretchers? One for Nyanja and one for my father?"

Kako bowed slightly and clapped his hands. "It has already been accomplished, Miss Hunter. Captain Dawson gave the word last evening, and they have been made." He gestured to two canvas litters lying on the ground a few paces to one side of the now dispersing group.

Touched by the captain's thoughtfulness, she swallowed. "Thank you, Kako." Now all that remained was for her to talk Papa into making use of the assistance.

She hurried to her father's side. "How are you, Papa? Can I fetch you anything?"

His eyes were rheumy when they met hers. "I've already had tea this morning, thank you. And if you've come to try and talk me into using one of those blasted contraptions the captain had made up last eve, then you can just take yourself right back to where you came from." Pique etched lines about his lips.

She squatted down and rested one hand on his knee. "Papa, you don't have the strength to walk for half an hour, much less all day." She was careful to keep her voice soft and undemanding.

He sniffed. "These legs have served me well for my entire life. I don't see the point in abandoning their use now. Besides, I daresay the fresh air and exercise will be a lot more healthy for me than the way you've kept me cooped up in that stuffy cabin all day long." He swept a disgruntled gesture to the little steamer that Trent's men were busily divesting of all conveyable items.

RyAnne dropped her gaze to the ground between her knees. His limitations were wearing on him. And how could they not? All his life he'd been healthy and independent. And now he was at the mercy of those around him for his care. Yet, despite his adamant wishes, she knew his strength would not sustain him for the arduous journey ahead. And she wanted nothing more than see him reach the village—especially now that they had come this far. So, how to convince him to make use of a litter?

The captain strode by. "Miss Hunter, a word, if I may?" He kept walking, not giving her opportunity to refuse.

RyAnne patted Papa's knee. "I'll be back in a minute. Just rest."

With that she rose and strode to where the captain waited for her, arms crossed over his chest.

"Yes, Captain?" Whatever could he want with her? He hadn't spoken more than a few words in a row to her since the night he'd first returned from his inland jaunt.

The captain held a pistol in a holster out toward her. "I would like for you to wear this in the event that you might have need of it."

Her eyes widened. It was one thing to go shooting with the captain. It was quite another to pack around one of his pistols on her hip. "You and Papa may have been able to force me into men's attire, Captain. But I assure you I have not lost all my womanly sensibilities and I'll not deign to carry a weapon like some"—she rolled her hand through the air, frustrated that no ready comparison came to mind—"trollop, that's the word! Trollop in a London alley!"

His gaze flickered over her, and for a brief moment there was a hint of something remarkably close to humor reflected there. But before she could lambaste him about it, he turned to scrutinize his hustling crew, indifference dropping over his features. "Very well." He draped the holster around his own hips and cinched it down. "As for your father, we'll take it very slow this morning under the guise of getting our traveling feet beneath us."

A frown tensed her brow. "I appreciate that, Captain. Thank you for letting me know." Though she had no idea why he was telling her nor why there was need for pretense.

The captain's gaze returned to hers, and then he practically rolled his eyes. "Every man deserves to keep as much of his pride as possible to the very end, Miss Hunter. Your father will be better served should he come to the conclusion on his own that traveling on one of the pallets will be best for all."

Anger shot through her, swift and sure. She was only trying to do what was best for Papa. "Oh, so you not only want me to abandon all the ways of civility, but you've been trained in medicine now as well, have you, Captain?"

He lifted his hands in a pose of surrender. "I can see that you strongly resist my assessment in these matters, so I shall leave you to do as you see fit, then." He strode toward the gangway, where two men were struggling to bring down a heavy trunk, throwing out as he departed, "You might at least pause to consider what I've said about your father before you barge ahead in your stubbornness, however."

RyAnne huffed and would have retorted, but he was already giving instructions to the men that the trunk was not coming with them and should be returned aboard ship.

She had every intention of ignoring the captain and badgering Papa to use one of the litters. However, as she marched back to Papa, it only took one glimpse of the dejected slump of his shoulders as he watched the frenzy all around him to realize that perhaps the captain was right.

What would it be like toward the end of life to lose all her freedoms and abilities? When someday her children were helping her old and feeble bones down a path somewhere? Would she want them making harsh demands? Or would she want them to give her a little space and as much dignity as her fragile state would in that moment allow her?

A weight settled over her, but she knew what she needed to do. It didn't mean she was going to like it, however.

Papa could walk for a little way and then he'd realize he wasn't strong enough, and likely he'd ask to be carried on one of the stretchers, and all would be solved without her having to force his hand.

Throwing her hands up in resignation, she turned toward the ship to gather her own meager accouterments, along with Papa's pack. The least she could do would be to carry that for him.

They departed within the hour just as the captain had stated, and the path at first was rather smooth and well worn. There must be villages nearby that used this trail to come to the headwaters of the Rovuma for water. However, nary a native came into sight as their caravan progressed westward.

RyAnne made sure to stick close to Papa. And despite the fact that she could tell Trent had instructed his men to go slow, Papa's tortoise-paced shuffle soon had them falling farther and farther behind the rest of the crew—even those men who were carrying Nyanja on one of the litters.

RyAnne resisted the pain and despair that threatened to drop her to her knees right in the middle of the path. She rubbed the back of her neck, commanded herself to take hold of her emotions, and minced her steps so as not to tread on Papa's heels. But the memories could not be vanquished.

When she was little and Papa had been gone to Stone Town for one of his fortnight trips, she used to stand at the edge of the yard and watch for the first sign of his carriage returning to the plantation. The moment she'd glimpse him coming down the road, she would run to meet him. He'd invariably leave the carriage and instruct it to go on without him. He'd put her on his strong, broad shoulders, and they would spend fifteen blissful minutes, just the two of them, traipsing across the indigo fields toward home. Papa would spin her around until he collapsed to the ground in dizziness, and they'd both laugh until their sides ached.

RyAnne's vision blurred. Oh, how she missed the hearty, vibrant version of her papa. The man who was full of laughter and tricks. The man who'd protected her and taken care of her and snuck her sweets long after bedtime.

Now he shuffled down the trail, his breaths so labored she could hear every inhale and exhale like the tempo of a sad song.

Surely at any moment now Papa would give in to reality and request to be carried. But his stubbornness held him fast to his course.

Every few paces Papa stopped to cough, and every third or fourth time, RyAnne took a moment to offer him water. And it was after one such halt midmorning that she glanced up while stoppering her canteen to realize she could no longer see even the last member of their caravan.

Gooseflesh prickled the back of her neck. She surveyed the vast prairie surrounding them. Shoulder-height brown grasses swayed everywhere, and while the foot-worn trail was still plainly visible for the moment, what if they came to a place where it wasn't so obvious which way to go? Somewhere far out on the prairie an animal barked a noise, half grunt, half growl, and the gooseflesh turned to a chill that slithered down her spine.

And once we are on our way, no straggling off away from the main group. Lions will stalk a herd for hours, waiting for one to wander off alone so they can pick it off.

The captain's words of warning came back to her as though he'd just spoken them to her this morning and not several weeks ago before they'd left the commodore's estate.

The grass here was so tall and thick. Would she even know if a lion was at this very moment creeping toward them? She took Papa's arm and tugged, urging him to his feet. "We'd best try and catch up to the others, Papa. They'll be stopping for the nooning soon."

Papa glanced around, seemingly for the first time realizing that the two of them were alone. His lips pursed out, and he ran a tired hand down his grizzled face. "I shouldn't have insisted on walking. I don't know what I was thinking."

"Nonsense." Now was not the time for recriminations, no matter how much she agreed with him. She nudged him forward, doing her best to keep her voice light. "We'll catch up, but I think we'd best try not to stop again for a time."

If only she hadn't listened to the captain's advice, Papa would be safely aboard a pallet at this very moment, and she would be surrounded by the comfort and safety of others.

She glanced over the vast expanse of empty savannah and blue sky once more. Oh, why hadn't she at least given in to safety over propriety and accepted the gun the captain offered her? Perhaps when they caught up with the others, she would be able to talk him into relinquishing it to her. Because indeed, if she lived through this, she was going to kill the captain, and maybe a bullet from his own gun would be just the ticket to get her point across.

Papa had only shuffled ten paces, and he was already huffing loudly.

RyAnne trod the path behind him, but a claw of apprehension kept reaching out to touch the base of her neck. Each time she cast a glance behind them, the path lay empty, but she couldn't shake the feeling that eyes were on them.

"Just a little farther, Papa."

Papa tried to hurry, she could tell. But his breaths wheezed like a punctured bellows, and his steps faltered. He staggered to one side before catching himself and coming to a complete stop.

"It's okay, Papa. Just be still and breathe for a moment." RyAnne's heart thudded in complete terror now. How long before the crew realized they were missing? Would the captain even send someone back for them? She was going to have to pack Papa on her back, or they were both going to die right here, probably eaten by some unsavory creature on the captain's list of animals to be most feared.

After five minutes when Papa's breaths had eased some, RyAnne slipped the pack off her back and stepped over beside him. "Okay, Papa, this is what we are going to do. You are going to hop on my back, and I'm going to carry you until we catch up with the others. It shouldn't be long before they stop to eat, and I think we'll catch up to them then."

"I'm sorry, daughter. I shouldn't have put us in this position in the first place. It's my stubborn pride that's put us here."

RyAnne wanted to assure him that this was all the captain's fault, but somehow she didn't think now was a good time to cast blame. "Let's just catch up to the others, and this afternoon you can ride on a litter and rest, okay, Papa?"

He sighed again and glanced at the flat emptiness around them. "Maybe you were right all along. Perhaps I should have stayed on the island and simply died in my bed. Now I've put you in danger."

It was the defeat in the words that terrified her the most. If he gave up now, he might never reach his destination. "Nonsense, Papa. If this is what you feel God called you to, then this is where you ought to be." She gritted her teeth, because what she *ought* to be doing was encouraging him to head back to Zanzibar with her this very minute. Yet, she'd given that battle to God. Or at least she'd tried to. And now she wanted to be a support to her father instead of a nag. So if he felt led to go to some village on the banks of a lake, who was she to stand in his way?

She put her back to him and leaned slightly forward, angling her arms backward, ready to take his weight. "One jump, and then I will carry you."

She braced herself to take the brunt of her father's weight, but before Papa even made a move, a whistle pierced the air. She glanced down the trail, hope burgeoning in her heart.

The captain strode toward them, followed by four of his crewmen, one of whom carried one of the empty pallets.

Relief nearly took all the strength from legs that had only a moment ago been prepared to go above and beyond their duty.

"Could use a lift, could you?" The captain's words were dry.

RyAnne was torn between giving him a dressing down and throwing herself into his arms with gratitude that he'd come back for them, and since she couldn't decide which to do, she merely clamped her jaw shut and held her silence.

The four natives helped Papa onto the stretcher and then hoisted him between them and started down the trail.

RyAnne was suddenly trembling all over, head to foot, and when the captain started down the trail after his men, she momentarily lacked the strength to put one foot in front of the other. Placing one quavering hand to her forehead, she turned her back on the men and studied the trail behind them.

She heard the captain's footsteps slow, and then still, and then return toward her. "Are you well?"

"Yes, fine. No thanks to you!"

He stepped around until he could see her face. Concern etched the firm, stubbled line of his jaw. "I'm sorry you fell so far behind. I should have noticed sooner."

Or not asked me to let him walk in the first place. But she didn't say the words. Somehow, though berating him had seemed something to look forward to when the terror had been pulsing through her, now that he was here, she couldn't muster the will or the words.

He unbuckled the holster with the pistol that he'd tried to give her that morning and held it out. "Will you at least take this now?"

Just as she took the holster from him, Kako stepped out onto the trail behind them. "Is it okay if I join the others now, *Mzee*?" he asked.

Trent stilled, and his jaw jutted to one side as he studied Kako for a moment as though he really wished the man hadn't appeared just then. Trent's head didn't move, but his gaze angled back toward her in a way that made every intuition inside her leap to life with awareness.

The eyes that she'd felt on them earlier…

She stepped close and used both hands to slam the holster into the captain's chest. "How could you!?"

Trent took a step back, and his hands came up on reflex to cup her elbows. His attention never left her as he calmly said, "Yes, thank you, Kako. You may rejoin the others now."

Kako skittered around them and trotted down the trail after his companions.

"You planned this!" RyAnne tried to step back, but Trent firmed his hands and held her close.

"Only for your own good, and that of your father."

She tried to muscle free again, but all with no fruition and hardly any effort on the captain's part. In frustration she smacked his chest with one balled-up fist. "He should have been on a pallet all morning instead of struggling along like he did."

"Indeed. But that was his choice to make. I simply orchestrated to make the decision easier for him from this point on."

"Manipulation and deceit!" She pummeled him with each word.

His lower lip pooched out slightly, and he gave a small nod. "I concede." His hands were still maddeningly gentle at her elbows.

She tempered her tone. "There would have been no need for manipulation if you had just left me to speak to him as we broke camp this morning."

He tilted his head. "Truly? You think you could have convinced your father—the same man who left behind his entire family to head to the Continent and die alone, and over much protestation from you, I might add—to lie placidly on a pallet and let others carry him? Without him having proven to himself that his strength simply doesn't suffice any longer?"

The probable accuracy of his argument drained the stiffness from her shoulders. "Maybe you are right. I don't know. I could have tried, but it doesn't matter now. What's done is done."

Slowly, he took the holster she still held pressed to his chest from her hands. He swung it around her and buckled it securely over her hips.

She gave him a withering glower. She really ought to stand by her refusal to wear it, simply because she knew her father wasn't the only one who'd been manipulated. The captain had purposely wanted her to wish she'd had the weapon!

But the man ignored her look and simply lifted her pack to his shoulder and swept a gesture down the trail. "Best we catch up to the others now, Miss Hunter."

She reached for the bag. "I can carry my pack."

But he angled it away from her. "I'll carry it for you until we rejoin the others."

RyAnne threw her hands up in concession and tromped down the path ahead of him. The man was the most stubborn creature she'd ever met!

Chapter 14
Made Perfect in Weakness

That evening they slept on the open savannah with the sound of a lion roaring in the distance and the sharp bark of zebras to wake them at dawn. The next day torrential rains set in, and they marched all day long, soaked to the skin. By the time a village came into view that evening, RyAnne had never been so relieved to see a grass-roofed hut in all her life.

And according to Trent, this was the last village they would need to stay in before they reached the one on the shore of the lake where Papa would build his mission. They only had half a day's journey on the morrow, and they would be "home."

They were exhausted. The whole band of them.

At the edge of the village, under the meager shelter of some palms, their group came to a halt.

With Kako by his side, Trent stalked through the downpour toward the center of the village, tossing over his shoulder, "Everyone wait here, and I'll see if I can find the headman. This will be a good place to make camp for the night."

He didn't even glance her way, and RyAnne pressed her lips together.

Dipping one shoulder toward the ground, she let her pack slide off onto the toe of one of her boots to keep it up out of the mud. She rubbed the sore muscles in her shoulders and rolled her head, feeling the release of tension all along her spine. She let out a sigh and glanced around the village.

They'd passed through several during their inland trek along the river, and this one seemed more rundown than the others, although thankfully she didn't see any signs of the brutality they had previously witnessed.

The huts here were unkempt, the thatching tattered, and the walls crumbling in places. The gardens they had come through along the perimeter of the village had been in sore need of weeding. And the paths were unswept and littered with detritus and debris. A couple pens for holding cattle appeared to be one bovine kick away from total collapse, and the cattle were so thin she could count the ribs of the poor beasts from here. None lowed. They simply stood, heads hanging. The only sign that they even lived was an occasional swish of a tail.

Trent returned a few moments later with a frustrated look gleaming in his eyes. "The headman says we can stay, but we'll have to feed ourselves, and there is only one hut at our disposal."

A grumble of surprise made the rounds of the soaking-wet natives. And Kako exclaimed something loudly to his companions in their native tongue.

Trent turned to the man. "What did you say?" he asked in Swahili.

Kako shuffled his feet and glanced toward the village, licking his lips, eyes wide. He laid a hand over his chest "I am the son of the great-chief of this area. The great-chief resides in the village of our destination along the banks of the great lake. This chief here"—he indicated the village before them—"is an under-headman. It is a great insult that he does not offer proper hospitality to the great-chief's son. But an even greater offense not to offer it to strangers." He jutted his chin forward, anger glimmering in his gaze. "My father will know of this before the sun is set tomorrow!"

They made out the best they could for dinner, and after they had eaten, Trent led the way to the little hut the headman had offered for their use. A fire burned in a pit in the middle of the floor, the smoke rising up to dissipate through a small hole at the peak of the conical roof.

RyAnne hovered over the flames for a moment as the captain helped Papa get settled on a cot. She was thankful that the room was at least warm and dry. Cold seemed to have seeped into her very bones, despite the fact that the rain had been rather warm throughout the day. She worried about Papa. He looked paler this evening. She crossed to him and settled one hand on his forehead. He was much too hot, and his breaths barely brushed the back of her hand when she held it before his mouth. She worried her teeth over her lower lip. Would he make it through the night? Should she try to remove his damp clothes? Or simply let him rest? In the end, she decided on the latter, for he already looked to be well on his way to sleep, and the warmth of the fire would soon have his damp clothing dry.

The captain said something quietly to June and RyAnne lifted her head. Nyanja's, Moyo's, and June's cots spanned the rest of the perimeter, and her own pallet took up the last remaining space by the door in the little room.

The door of the hut was nothing more than a rectangle cut into the wall. There was no actual door. The roof seemed to be holding most of the rain out, but was in disrepair just above the door outside, and the rain was slanting so that it would come right into the room. Bugs would also have free reign over them tonight if she didn't do something about that. From her pack she pulled a small roll of twine. She scanned the roof. Now if she could just reach the poles that held the thatching aloft, she could create a clothesline of sorts to hang a section of canvas from. That should keep at least some of the wet and bugs at bay.

Trent stepped to her side and took the ball of twine without so much as asking what she planned. He seemed to be able to read her thoughts. Standing on his toes, he tied one end of the twine to one of the poles and then stretched it tight over to another just on the other side of the doorway. Pulling a knife from his boot, he sliced off the twine and handed the ball back to her without a word. When he had finished tying off the string, she stepped forward with the length of canvas, and he helped her hang the cloth. It wouldn't be perfect, but it would be better than nothing. She felt pity for the captain and his men, who would be hard pressed to find any sleep in the conditions outside.

Trent stepped back and gestured to the canvas with a slight bow in her direction and a distinct glimmer in his gaze, as though he'd just built a bridge to help her cross a puddle.

She couldn't help but smile a little at his theatrics. "Thank you, Captain."

He tipped her a nod, and his gaze darted to Papa, his expression all seriousness now. "I'll be right outside. Call me if you need anything."

RyAnne followed his gaze, worry once again rising to the fore of her mind. Would Papa make it? He'd come so far, yet…

Realizing her attention had wandered from the captain, she turned to thank him again, but he was already out the flap of canvas and hidden by the darkness.

With a sigh, she collapsed onto her pallet. Slowly, she relaxed, and the exhaustion from the day's trek faded the world into the fuzzy haze of sleep.

She didn't know how long she'd been asleep when a sound outside her hut woke her with a jolt. She sat upright and looked around, blinking the fog from her thoughts. The rain had stopped, she realized, for all was silent.

June, whose pallet lay next to hers, was also sitting up, her eyes wide and white in the darkness.

And that's when RyAnne took note of the voices. Two men behind their hut, speaking in low tones. RyAnne could not understand the Chewa they spoke, but the gaps between the mud walls and the thatched roof left their words clearly audible.

RyAnne leaned toward June. "What are they saying?" she whispered softly.

June held up one hand and cocked her head to continue listening.

While June listened, RyAnne slipped quietly from her cot and crossed the room to check on Papa. Papa's skin was still much too warm, but at least his breaths were a little stronger this time, and his clothing seemed to have dried. There was not much more she could do for him but let him sleep.

After several moments of continued conversation, the men outside quieted and footsteps could be heard moving away from their hut.

June turned to her with wide eyes.

"What is it?"

"Kako…he has invited any who want to leave this village and

their lazy chief to come and take shelter in his father's village. He told them to be ready to leave with us at first light."

"That's good. These people need some help."

"Good, yes. But wars, they start over less, no? The chief, Wankulu, will not let his people go without a fight."

RyAnne swallowed and eased back onto her cot. Suddenly, she bolted upright. "We should tell the captain."

"I heard. Go back to sleep, Miss Hunter." His voice rose from just outside the canvas partition, so it was no wonder he'd overheard her conversation with June, close as they were to the door.

Miss Hunter… She suddenly realized he hadn't called her RyAnne once since that moment they'd shared at the mango tree, and on top of that realization came the recognition over how much she missed the sound of her name on his lips.

With a sigh, she lay back against her cot. She must think on something else or never sleep another wink this night. Her thoughts turned once more to Papa. If he didn't wake come morning what would she do? Would she travel ahead to the village Papa so longed to reach? Or would she turn back from here? She pressed finger and thumb to her eyes to stem the tears. This too was a subject she ought not think too long on if she wanted more sleep.

She punched her pack into a more comfortable pillow. Brayden. She would think on Brayden Harcourt and what answer she would give to his proposal the next time she saw him.

The trouble was, when she closed her eyes, it wasn't the vision of the man with blond hair and impish blue eyes that came to mind, but of the one with dark curls and green-gray eyes that held the power to stay her breath.

She gritted her teeth and flopped onto her side. It seemed her thoughts had come full circle.

Trent rose with the sun as it crested the horizon with prompt equatorial precision just after the five o'clock hour. Steam lifted in misty wisps off every rain-damp surface. The birds had been awake since the first hint of light had touched the sky, and the chorus they raised could almost be labeled a racket were it not so beautifully harmonic.

Trent gingerly gripped the rim of a scalding tin of the local tea. He would need the aid of the bitter black brew to power him through this day, since he doubted he'd slept more than two hours in snatches throughout the night. Sand seemed to line the backs of his eyelids this morning.

The villagers began to trickle into a small open area just outside the village proper with bundles and packs. One child carried a pot balanced on her head, and mothers had babies strapped to their backs, but none of them carried more than a handful of worldly possessions.

He gritted his teeth. The last thing he wanted to do was start a war with this chieftain, yet how could he deny these people a chance at a better life?

Of course they were going to accept the invitation of the great-chief's son to join his father's village, which according to all Trent had heard of the place, was thriving and well run.

Still, adding so many to their ranks was sure to affix time to their journey. He took in the number of women with small children strapped to their backs, and sighed. Likely they'd be pushing dusk, at this rate.

He'd wanted to arrive in plenty of time to get the Hunters settled in a good hut and ensure their safety so that he could take off promptly at dawn on the morrow to find Khalifa.

One more delay. He grimaced. Each delay could cost people their lives.

RyAnne emerged from the hut behind him, supporting her father, one of his arms draped over her shoulders. By the looks of her drooping eyes and the stretch of her yawn, it didn't appear she'd gotten much more sleep than he had.

Hurrying ahead of her, Trent readied her father's conveyance. He worked the inside of his lip as he watched RyAnne ease the old man down onto the sail-turned-stretcher. It was a miracle the doctor had made it this far.

As June assisted Nyanja onto the other pallet, Trent's gaze honed in on RyAnne where she leaned over her father fussing to settle a light blanket around his shoulders. At least the doctor had made it through the night. From what he'd seen of him the night before, he'd had his doubts. What was he going to do with RyAnne if the doctor passed away before he had all the information he needed about Khalifa? She wouldn't be safe all alone in the village.

Downing one last swallow, he tossed the grounds of his tea into the grass and forced himself to turn from her. He would deal with that when the time came.

Squatting down, he began thrusting everything into his pack, but his attention once again fixed on the villagers still trickling into the field.

One of the village women was very pregnant, and she had a tiny girl cinched to her back and a goat leashed with a rope trotting by her side. The goat bleated a protest when the woman pulled it away from a plant it wanted to nibble on.

RyAnne rushed to the woman's side and stretched her hands out, offering to carry the child for her. The villager seemed unsure whether to accept the white woman's help, but June stepped over and spoke a few words.

With a nod of understanding, the woman untied the cloth holding the baby to her and pulled the child around to her front, then held her out to RyAnne. The babe was totally naked.

RyAnne held the child at arm's length and glanced from it to the path they would need to travel today and back. The look on her face would have made a humorist good money at a circus sideshow.

Trent bit back a grin and quickly schooled his features as he strapped his hunting knife to his belt.

Hesitantly, RyAnne pulled the child closer, examining her from head to toe as though she might find some diaper cloth hidden somewhere on the little body. Trent could almost see the cogs turning in her head. She was obviously trying to decide how to avoid several good soakings during the day's trek.

The babe was still held a good ways from her body when she glanced over and caught him watching her. He raised one eyebrow and grinned at her.

This was one predicament she could get herself out of.

Lifting her chin, she wrapped the blanket carefully around the little one, pulled it close, and settled it on her hip. She quirked an eyebrow at him and then presented him with her back as she reached to sling her pack over one shoulder.

Trent laughed aloud. Her pride would receive its just reward many times over by the end of the day, he was sure.

A yell drew his attention and sent a bolt of unease down his spine that erased all traces of humor. A corpulent man rushed into the clearing from the direction of the village. Even at this distance, Trent recognized him as the headman he'd spoken to the day before. He jolted upright. This would not be good.

The man rushed straight for the pregnant woman standing next to RyAnne, yelling at the top of his lungs. He grabbed the woman by her upper arm and shook her like a dog might shake a snake.

She must be his wife. Trent shoved past a group of villagers just joining the crowd and jogged toward RyAnne through the milling throng of people. He leapt over a basket of maize and dodged the back end of a hump-shouldered cow a young boy prodded with a sharpened goad.

The chief leaned over the pregnant woman, yelling in her face and cowing her until she covered her head with both arms.

Trent pushed through a group of several women who had paused to watch the spectacle.

The chief suddenly noticed the babe in RyAnne's arms. He lunged for her, grabbed RyAnne by one arm, and jerked her closer, screaming so angrily that spittle exploded from his mouth with each word.

RyAnne's eyes were wide with a fear that shot Trent through with red-hot anger toward the man. Trent was too far away to protect her! Why had he let her wander so far from his side this morning?

RyAnne tried to jerk loose of the man, which jostled the baby, who burst into loud wails of terror. The pregnant woman hung on the headman's arm, crying and begging and, by her posture and gestures, promising to return to the village with him.

That was when Trent noticed the knife in the chief's hand—the knife arcing toward RyAnne's torso—and the gleam of hatred in the chief's eyes.

"RyAnne!" Trent hurdled a small hand-pushed cart and shucked his colt from its holster. The man was too close to RyAnne to chance the shot. Trent fired into the air as he leapt over a log lying in his path.

The sound of the shot had its intended effect. The chief froze for a moment, glancing around to see where the sound had come from.

The man's eyes widened as he focused on Trent barreling toward him, gun extended. He let go of RyAnne's arm and stepped back, dropping the knife on the ground by his feet and holding his hands wide, palms forward.

Trent stopped when he was only an arm's length from the man, stepping between the chief and RyAnne, who still clutched the screaming baby.

Trent pulled in a steadying breath, willing his heart rate to return to normal, never taking his eyes off the chief, who he suddenly realized was swaying unsteadily on his feet. "RyAnne, are you well?"

Behind him, she shushed and cooed to the baby. "Yes, I'm fine."

Trent met the man's gaze, jerked his chin back toward the village, and gestured with the point of the gun that the chief should return from whence he'd come.

The man's chin lifted, and his gaze grew more fierce. He slurred some words low and angry, and pointed to the general direction of the child in RyAnne's arms.

Trent swallowed. Like it or not, the woman and child were

obviously this man's family. "RyAnne, maybe you should give the baby back to its mother."

He heard her gasp. "But, Captain! That man is terrible! We can't make them go back to him."

The chief's wife still cowered with her head curled into her arms. Trent took in the scars all over her arms and shoulders. He gritted his teeth. RyAnne was right. And the woman was clearly terrified of her husband. Left to her own decisions, she would likely go back with the man. It had probably taken every ounce of courage she'd had to try and escape him this morning.

"June!" Trent called over his shoulder without taking his eyes or his aim off the man.

He heard her steps, but she stopped just behind him and only slightly off to one side.

"Tell this man that if he makes one move to follow us, I will shoot him. And tell the woman that she can come with us and we will protect her. She no longer needs to fear this man."

June swallowed audibly and then spoke a few tremulous words.

The chieftain growled and lurched toward Trent, but the menace was taken out of the action when he nearly lost his footing and had to flap his arms like a man on a floating log to regain his balance. He muttered an indecipherable protestation just before his knees buckled. His eyes rolled back in his head. And he slumped to the ground.

His wife studied him carefully for a long moment, and then she skittered around his prostrate form and hurried to gather her still-wailing girl from RyAnne's arms.

Trent squatted down and felt the man's pulse. Thready and erratic. Were he merely drunk, his pulse should be stronger. The woman had obviously drugged him with something this morning. He called over two of his guides and bade them haul the unconscious man back to his hut. The man might not live past whatever she'd poisoned him with, but at least he would die in his own bed.

When he stood, the woman was looking at him over the top

of the now silent baby's head. She said a few words, and Trent glanced at June for the interpretation.

"She says he will not die. Only sleep for a rotation of the sun."

He nodded his understanding and took RyAnne's elbow, leading her back toward her father. "What does a man have to do to keep you from finding trouble, Miss Hunter?"

Her only response was a huff of irritation as she jerked her elbow from his grasp.

He couldn't resist the smile that pulled at his mouth as he watched her fall in with the group that had begun to shuffle down the trail.

But his smile faded as he observed his men with the chief slung between them disappear into a hut. He had a feeling they'd not seen the last of the headman.

Jasmine Hunter sat on the piano bench in the parlor of the Stone Town residence. She closed her eyes and let her fingers drift over the notes on the keyboard. Drawing in a long, slow breath, she poured all the frustration she was feeling into the music.

With Rory off at the plantation house on the other side of the island, she and Mama were in danger of becoming two cats in a bag. She missed RyAnne. And despite Mama's constant complaints about how selfish she'd been to run off with Papa, she knew Mama missed her too.

And Papa… Tears pricked at the backs of Jasmine's eyes, and she let two mournful minor notes duel with each other.

Papa had claimed he would only be gone for six months. Yet RyAnne had left a note, found after she'd already stowed away and departed on Captain Dawson's boat, that claimed she thought Papa was more ill than he'd been letting on, and so she'd gone after him.

Was Papa really sick? And if so, why would he go into seclusion like that and keep them from being with him during his last days? Certainly it would be difficult to watch him dying, but wasn't that what family was for? To help each other through the hard times? Surely Papa would need them all?

She suppressed a sob and leaned over the keyboard, tilting her head to take in the plaintive high notes juxtaposed to the thunder of the low ones.

If only for the fact that Papa would have family with him during his last days, she was glad RyAnne had run off to be with him. And Captain Dawson would take care of her.

A hint of a smile tugged at the corner of her mouth as she remembered the way Captain Dawson had hovered outside RyAnne's room after the ball that night she'd collapsed. He'd nearly paced a trench until they were certain nothing too serious was wrong. Only once RyAnne had fallen into a restful sleep had he left his post outside her door. Yes, Captain Dawson was a good man who would take care of RyAnne and make sure she came home safely.

And then there was the captain's oaf of a first mate, Garrett Holloman. The man hadn't even bidden her farewell before heading off to the Continent to seek his fortune with his cousin. The last time she'd seen him had been during their second dance at the ball.

She banged out the notes a little more forcefully. So much for a second dance meaning anything anymore.

Behind her, the clock on the mantel chimed eight o'clock.

She was to meet Bishop Tozer at the mission in thirty minutes. Today would be her first day as teacher to the orphans in his care. Nervousness had prodded her wide awake just before the five o'clock hour. Many of her students had been rescued from the ocean after they'd grown sick and were dumped overboard by slavers. Several different tribes and languages would be represented. It was going to prove challenging, of a certainty, to teach the little mites. But she couldn't think of anything that had excited her this much since Papa had given her Mabel, her first pony, on her seventh birthday.

Movement between the music rack and the top-board of the grand piano caught her attention. Mama swept into the parlor, wringing her fingers, cheeks flushed, and a glimmer of indecipherable emotion in her eyes.

Jasmine's hands fell into her lap. "What is it?"

"Mrs. Corbel has just sent her servant over to let us know… *The Wasp* sailed into the harbor late last night."

A knock sounded at the front door even as Mama finished her sentence.

Excitement trilled through Jasmine. Papa and RyAnne had come home! Lifting her skirts, she hurried across the parlor toward the entry.

Jasmine heard Sarah unlock and open the heavy door just before she rushed from the parlor into the entryway. "Papa—" The words she'd intended died in her throat.

Garrett Holloman stood on the front steps, slouch hat in hand, a grim hardness clenching his jaw.

Her excitement guttered and died even as a rebellious thrill of another sort traipsed through her. His golden hair had grown since she'd seen him last—it curled just over his collar and ears. And he was dressed for calling. His bronze long-jacket cut away from the ruffle of his cravat and the trim fit of his slacks to reveal his knee-height black boots with brass buttons.

She swallowed. He looked as good as ever, but no one else accompanied him. *No one.* "Of-officer Holloman…" She licked her lips, studying him. Surely he was here to tell them Papa had passed on, but where was RyAnne?

He gave a slight bow, acknowledging her lame greeting. "Miss Hunter."

She peered behind him, but still no one else had emerged.

Sarah, still holding the door open, cleared her throat softly, and Garrett shuffled his feet, a hint of humor ticking up one corner of his mouth.

Realization jolted through Jasmine. She'd left him on the step for a dreadfully long time. "Oh, where are my manners? Do come in, please." She swept a hand toward the parlor. "Mama is waiting for you."

He strode through the portal but, instead of passing by and

on into the parlor, stopped directly in front of her. His warm blue gaze swept over her face, and a crinkle of pleasure edged one eye. "Your father was doing well when I left the party, Miss Hunter. Not improved, but still very much alive."

A breath of relief eased from her, and she nodded, pressing her lips together. "Thank you for telling me quickly."

His chin dipped in a very slight nod, but for the longest time he stood still, his gaze roaming her face.

She held her breath, unsure how to assess the emotions coursing through her.

Finally he glanced down, twisted his hat a couple times, and then stepped past her to lead the way into the parlor. Mama, seated on the settee in the sunlight streaking through the far window, rose when they entered. "Officer Holloman, what a pleasure to see you again." She pressed her palms together. "I fear the news you bring us won't bode well, however?"

Garrett bowed over Mama's hand. "Perhaps not as ill as you fear, madam, yet likely not as happy as you hope."

Mama gestured him toward the chair across from the settee as Jasmine took the space by Mama's side. "Do give us the good news first then, will you?"

Garrett eased into the proffered chair and hung his hat on one knee. "As I've just told Miss Hunter, your husband still lived when last I saw him. However…" He cleared his throat and fiddled with the leather thong tied around the base of his hat. "His health was not improved, either." He reached into an inside pocket of his coat. "I've brought letters to you from your daughter, and one from your husband also, conveying his wish that I stand in as your…protector here in Stone Town until such a time as"—he coughed uncomfortably—"I'm no longer needed."

Mama studied the letters Garrett held out to her. Her lips pinched together, and Jasmine could tell she was holding tears at bay.

Jasmine reached over and took the missives. "Thank you."

A muscle bunched in his jaw. But he made no reply, only nodded in acknowledgement.

The top letters were addressed to Mama—one in RyAnne's swirly script and the other in Papa's barely legible scrawl. There was a letter to Rory, and the last envelope was addressed to Jasmine. She set Rory's on the table and handed Mama hers before she broke the seal on her own letter and pulled the onionskin page from within.

Jazzy,

I hope you can forgive me for running off the way I did without letting you in on my plan. I know you'll understand that Papa needs me, is going to need me even more, in these his last days, and I couldn't risk Mother, or Papa for that matter, somehow finding out what I intended. I know you never would have told them, but the more who knew, the more likely they would have sensed something amiss.

I won't honey-coat the truth. Papa is not long for this world. His cough has grown worse, I fear, over the last few days. I've tried everything I can think of to get him to come home, all to no avail. We leave on the morrow for the lake Papa is so set on reaching before his death.

I will write in my journal every day so that when we find ourselves together again, you and Rory, maybe Mother too if she wants, will have the benefit of reading the firsthand account of Papa's last days.

I will send word with any news as soon as I can.

All my love always,

RyAnne

Jasmine blinked rapidly to hold her tears at bay as she folded the page and put it back in the envelope. So all was just as she'd suspected. She'd never see Papa again. A wave of despair threatened to overwhelm her. But one thing held her steady. Mama would need her to be strong. They would go on as though nothing were out of the ordinary until they heard otherwise. Then they would have decisions to make.

The clock chimed the quarter hour, and Jasmine realized how late the time had grown.

Mama, her letters still unopened and clutched in one fist, watched the bird-of-paradise swaying in the flowerbed outside the window.

Jasmine leaned over and kissed Mama on the cheek. "I need to hurry along." She stood, and ever the gentleman, Officer Holloman rose with her.

Mama acknowledged her words with a flutter of her fingers and an almost imperceptible nod of her head. Her gaze never left the yard.

Jasmine curtsied to the man across from her. "If you'll excuse me, sir. Thank you for the news and the letters. I'm sure I'll be seeing you around town, of a time."

Not giving him opportunity to respond, she started from the room, but she could hear him keeping pace behind her. Suppressing a huff of indignation, she gritted her teeth. She needed to be able to concentrate on her students' lessons, especially today of all days. She couldn't have him tagging along and distracting her. Irritation washed through her. She shouldn't even *be* distracted by the man, who obviously felt so little for her that he'd gone off to the Continent without so much as a fare-thee-well.

In the entry, she paused and faced him as she pulled on her day gloves. "Officer Holloman—"

"So it's back to officer, is it? I thought we were past that?"

She ignored the cajoling in his tone and jerked her gloves firmly into place. "*Officer* Holloman, I have classes to teach, and I don't want to be late. So if you'll excuse me…"

She reached for the door, but he leaned past her and beat her to it, his hand wrapping around the handle just before hers did. Instead of pulling it open, he stopped and looked down at her, waiting.

She cast him a glance of irritation.

Decided humor danced in his azure eyes—humor and curiosity.

Her chin lifted as her pique grew.

One of his eyebrows winged its way upward. "I can see that

I've somehow upset you."

She resisted a snort and studied a spot on the doorframe. The man didn't even realize his faux pas. "I'm going to be late." Lips pinched, she flicked him another glance.

A muscle at the corner of his eye ticked, but he pulled the door open and stepped back out of her way. "Good day then, Miss Hunter."

Thankfully, Azim had the carriage ready and waiting down on the drive. "And to you also, Officer Holloman." She swept past him, descended the stairs, and allowed Azim to assist her into the carriage. But as she settled her skirts, she couldn't resist one last glance back toward the house. Garrett stood on the top step, arms folded and leaning back into his heels, a frown of consternation on his brow.

She sat back with a huff. Let the man be confused. He deserved a little angst after leaving the way he had.

Chapter 15
Made Perfect in Weakness

Garrett watched the carriage disappear around the corner, puzzled by the lady's sudden lack of warmth toward him. He scratched the back of his head and ambled down the stairs to the drive, his gaze still on the spot where the carriage had disappeared.

What had changed between the last time he'd seen her and now? Had another suitor come along while he was away to the Continent? His teeth banged together. The least she could do was tell him straight out. But no, she had to go and be all coy and uppity.

He pushed out a breath of irritation. So much for the silver tea service he'd had that stevedore friend of Trent's deliver from the docks along with his parting letter the morning they'd set sail. He'd spent a good amount of coin on it. He laughed derisively at himself. He'd even paid extra to have that cluster of jasmine blooms engraved on it.

She'd probably enjoyed a good laugh at his sentimentality.

He kicked a pebble lying in his path and tromped back toward his quarters. It was going to be a long few weeks.

RyAnne heard the waters of the lake and smelled the sweet scent of it in the air before they crested the top of the last hill and saw the vast glistening expanse.

RyAnne closed her eyes and tipped her face directly into the refreshing breeze. They had made it. *Papa* had made it. Even now he stood, albeit shakily, beside her.

Thank you, Father. Tears of relief stung for just a moment.

Papa pulled in an unsteady breath and murmured, "Father in heaven above. You've preserved me and brought me here. May I serve these precious people whom You love with fervor and joy."

She opened her eyes and smiled at the joyous expression on

Papa's face, before she turned to study the village that would be home for the foreseeable future.

The lake had a surprisingly expansive beach with white sands that stretched as far as her gaze could travel in either direction. Along the horizon, a faint blue outline of the land across the water stamped a ragged line against the sky.

From their vantage point on the hill above, she could see that the village huts were set a smart distance from the waves licking the sandy beach. The sun hung low on the horizon, and early evening dusk smudged the valley. Smoke rose from chimneys, and from one of the dwellings the low rhythm of drums could be heard.

As villages went, this one was likely the most prosperous one she'd seen since leaving the coast.

The huts were arranged in large concentric half circles, with the flat diameter of the circle spread out along the beach. One hut at the center was twice and half again the size of the rest. It, and every hut both north and south of it along the beach, would have a wonderful view of the water from their doorways. Gardens stretched along the inland perimeter of the huts, green and vibrant. Coconut palms swayed in the breeze near the water, while other fruit trees grew in several locations throughout the village. A corral full of long-horned, hump-shouldered cattle stood to one side of the village, and smaller pens of goats and chickens lay scattered throughout behind various huts.

Trent stepped up beside them. "We need to go."

She gritted her teeth. The man was in such a hurry to get them settled and rush off. She wanted to lash out at him, but all she said was, "Come, Papa." She helped him back onto his pallet, thankful to feel that at least for the moment his fever seemed to be abated. She took up position at one of the corners herself, indicating to the man who had been at that post that he was free to go.

Trent motioned for the other three men to wait and stepped to her side. "I'll take it."

"I can do it. I'll be fine."

He brushed her back and shouldered his way in front of her and grabbed the pole. "You'll blister your hands, and I won't be around to doctor you."

She glanced down at her hands. She'd been helping to carry Papa off and on all day while Trent had been farther ahead in the entourage guiding their path. Blisters already covered the palm of her right hand. She held it up for him to see. "I've been helping to carry him all day."

A muscle bunched in his jaw, and he cast a scathing look at the three men at the other corners. "I told you lot not to let her help."

RyAnne lifted her chin. "Yes. So they said. I simply reminded them who has been cooking their meals each night."

Trent grimaced. "RyAnne, if one of those should burst and become infected…"

The worry in his tone sent a tremor through her, and she stepped back, acquiescing to his wishes. She swallowed. "I'll be fine, I'm sure. I've survived for many years without you to take care of me. So no need to worry."

Without another word, he picked up his corner of the pallet and started down the hill toward the village.

June and Kako had run ahead. And already the villagers were pouring from their huts and rushing to line the path into the village. The drummer was there, and a low song started at one end and grew as more and more villagers lined the way. They clapped and danced and sang in joyous abandon, obviously ecstatic to receive home some of their own and the visitors accompanying them.

Moyo ran to RyAnne's side, her eyes wide with wonder and a touch of fear at the loud song and undulating people. RyAnne lifted her and fell in behind the captain.

The smoky scent of cook fires filled the valley and added to the hazy pall of dusk.

Their entourage wound through the wriggling body-lined path to the center of the village and came to a stop in front of the largest hut, where a man with a thick iron bracelet, decorated with copper, sat on a carved ebony chair. His hair was braided into many plaits that hung down to his shoulders, and red clay had been used to mark a pattern on his right cheek and across one bare shoulder and part of his chest.

Trent lowered Papa to the ground and then dropped to one knee before the chief. "Keep your head lower than his," he said in a voice likely only she heard.

With a quick glance around, even as she curtsied to follow his orders, RyAnne realized that everyone in the vicinity kept their head lower than that of the chief seated on his black throne.

The chief welcomed them to his village and, at first, despite the fact that RyAnne knew Kako was his son, didn't seem any happier to see him than the rest of them.

However, later as they were all shown to various huts, she did notice that Kako's lay much closer to the center of the village, and thus the chief's own dwelling, than most of their group's, except for her and Papa's. The chief gave them the highest honor of the hut directly next door to his on the north side—after he displaced two of his wives to another a little further away.

Despite being evicted, the women looked none too upset as they exited with their meager belongings, even smiling at her as she waited to one side with Papa and Moyo.

The inside of the dwelling hung thick with smoke from the fire a few feet outside the door. With the wind blowing off the lake, the smoke wafted right through the doorway and filled the room in a nearly choking cloud. What had those women been thinking? No way could Papa sleep with all that in there. He was already bent double, coughing.

"Come, Papa," she took his arm. "Back outside for just a minute."

Outside, she eased Papa down with his back to the warm mud wall and his face to the lake and the setting sun. As soon as she felt sure he was as comfortable as she could make him for the moment, she sent Moyo to June, who was visible just down the beach, and then set about putting out the fire, which of course only created more smoke at first. But when she finally extinguished the last of each smoking ember, she returned to the inside of the hut and set about trying to remove the smoke from the interior.

There was a short grass broom leaning next to the door—a thick bunch of long blades folded in half and then bound tightly just below the fold to create a handle of sorts. She picked that up and set to shooing at the smoke, but only seemed able to swirl the roiling mass, not waft it out the door. Why didn't this hut have a hole at its peak like the one they'd stayed in last night?

After fifteen minutes, she was panting and sweating and, despite the fact that she'd now retrieved one of her petticoats from her bag to flap at the smoke, hadn't managed to clear the air even a tiny bit.

With a growl of frustration, she chucked the broom into one corner and her petticoat atop her valise, then propped her hands on her hips and glowered at the hazy cone-shaped ceiling.

Behind her, Trent chuckled.

She spun around, wide eyed. How long had he been watching her?

He stood in the doorway, arms folded, trim hips and broad shoulders clearly outlined against the crimson-and-gold sunset splashing across the sky and lake behind him. His face was in shadow, so she couldn't read his expression, but a glint of humor twinkled in his eyes. A gentle breeze ruffled his shirt and hair.

She swallowed and returned her attention to the ceiling.

So he'd come to say good-bye, like she'd known he would. She pushed away the worry fisting her stomach at the thought, and couldn't even muster up any anger to throw his way for sneaking up on her. She hadn't seen which hut he'd been given by the chief, but knew that regardless which it was, he wouldn't be needing it for long. "So you've come to say your farewells."

His feet scraped against the ground, but when she looked at him, he still stood in the doorway. "That and to tend your hands. Come outside. Give the breeze fifteen minutes to do its work, and the hut will be as smoke free as you'll ever get it with all that commotion and bluster of yours."

She glowered at him and waved a hand toward the hazy interior. "Papa can't sleep in these conditions."

He nodded. "Fifteen minutes. The breeze picks up in the evenings off the lake. But later when it dies down, the mosquitoes come out in droves. They"—he tipped his head in the general direction of the village—"prefer the smoke to the bugs."

Understanding dawned. So the fire had been strategically placed to fill the hut with smoke and ward off the mosquitoes...

She brushed past him, pulling in a full breath of the fresh, sweet air coming off the lake. "My hands are fine. I need to find Papa something to eat."

Trent captured her hand, stilling her, and nodded toward her father. June already squatted before him, a bowl of broth in one hand and a spoon in the other. Papa held a corn cake in one trembling hand and slowly took bites between spoonfuls of broth. June glanced up, and RyAnne nodded her thanks. One corner of June's mouth lifted as she returned the gesture.

Trent still held her hand in his, and now his thumb stroked a warm trail that swept a tingle of awareness across her skin. Her eyes flew to his. There was an ember of heat gleaming in his gaze that fanned her awareness into blatant desire, and she snatched her hand back to her side lest she throw herself into his arms and beg him not to leave.

He settled into a relaxed stance, thumbs hooked into his belt, and his gaze kept hers captive. "I'll only be gone a few days. Two weeks at the most."

She clenched her jaw, crossed her arms, and forced herself to study the sunset across the way. "I'm not your keeper. Take all the time you want."

A small puff of impatience escaped his lips, and he reached out and unfolded her arms, tugging her blistered palm into the space between them. He studied the angry red sores. But the light was fading quickly, and it only took a second for him to release her hand and stride back toward the village, tossing over his shoulder, "Wait here."

He was back in a moment with Kako and a lantern. Arching

his brows, he held one hand out palm up and waited this time for her to place her hand in his.

With a sigh of reluctance, she complied. She might as well appease him, for in his stubbornness he would just hound her until she conceded. But she wasn't looking forward to the harangue she was about to receive. One of the blisters had broken open only a few minutes ago when she was trying to clear the smoke with the broom.

She was right that it only took him a moment to notice the split skin, but the chastisement she'd feared did not materialize. Trent glanced at Kako. "Can you fetch the doctor's bag from inside the hut, please?"

"Yes, *Mzee*."

RyAnne held her breath, still expecting a lecture. But to her consternation, the man simply retrieved a pot that sat next to the door and strode down to the lakeshore to fetch some water.

The village here had employed the same type of fencing Trent's men had used while traveling along the river to gate off a segment of the lake for safety, she noted.

June had finished with Papa now, and RyAnne noticed her helping Nyanja get some exercise with her crutches. Little Moyo trotted along behind them, clapping chubby hands and chattering a mile a minute. RyAnne smiled softly, love for the sweet girl swelling her chest. And then there was June. Such a genteel woman. Always going out of her way to help and do for others. She had to be near exhaustion. RyAnne made a note to try and take on more duties so June would be freed up a little more.

Papa seemed perfectly content, his face tipped into the last golden rays of the sun. So she let him sit quietly for the moment.

Kako returned with Papa's medical bag.

"Thank you, Kako. I'm sure you are tired. You may go if you like, but leave the lantern please. Captain Dawson will need it again."

"Aye, madam." He gave a little bow of deference and set the lantern on the ground near her feet.

June and Nyanja had stopped after only a few paces and turned back. Nyanja was probably too tired tonight after the day's long trek. RyAnne eyed the stump of Nyanja's still-bandaged leg as the women headed toward the hut they would be sharing down to the south a ways. RyAnne would need to check that before she slept tonight.

The golden orb of the sun hung low in the sky, the bottom lip of its circumference just kissing the surface of the water along the horizon. Out over the water a large fish eagle, only a charcoal silhouette against bright light, dove feet first into the water and emerged with an unlucky fish dangling from its claws. Near her, the leaves of several tall palms rattled together in the gentle breeze coming off the lake.

Trent trudged her way, the pot filled with water now. Her gaze wandered past him to the fence in the lake.

As Trent stopped at her side, she asked him, "Why didn't the village near Commodore Cornwall's place have a fence like that in place, do you think?"

"There probably was one normally. But it had rained straight through for a couple days before, if you'll recall. The fence likely washed away, or the river rose so high the crocs just swam over it."

RyAnne sighed. "I wish I could have done more for her."

He gestured for her to sit on a large rock to the side of the fire pit and, when she complied, held out the pot of water, motioning for her to wash. She lowered her blistered hand into the coolness. Pain zinged through her palm when the water seeped into the open blister, and she bit back a wince. But after only a moment, the sharpness of the pain eased, and the refreshing water actually felt good.

While she soaked her hand, Trent dug through the medical bag. "You did a sight more for that woman than anyone has ever done for her before, I daresay."

She pressed her lips together and glanced over to where the women were just disappearing into their hut. Guilt niggled at her. "I didn't want to come. From the moment I climbed the gangway to *The Wasp* and saw the horrors of the harbor, I wanted to run back home to the plantation house. I only came because I knew Papa would need me. Yet, if I hadn't…" She couldn't voice the fact that if she hadn't come, Nyanja and Moyo both would be dead now. "But still, I often feel like I didn't do enough. Perhaps I should have tried to save her leg."

Trent squatted before her with a roll of clean white bandages in his hand. For a long moment he didn't reply, only stared at a spot a long way down the beach.

Finally he spoke quietly. "I daresay, Miss Hunter, that feelings like those are what keep people from doing good for others more often. We feel we can't do enough, or be enough, or give enough, so we don't even take the first step. When in reality, offering the best we can is better than offering nothing at all." He tipped her a look. "You gave her the best you could, and don't be forgetting it. Had you tried to save her leg, she wouldn't have survived. You made the only decision you could."

RyAnne eased out a breath and had to concede with a nod.

Trent dipped his chin in affirmation and peered at her firmly. "Don't let what you could not do make you feel that what you could do was tainted by lack." He took the pot from her lap. "Now then, let's see that hand."

His fingers were warm and gentle as he carefully wrapped a length of the bandage around her palm and then cut it and tied it off. Still squatting before her, he folded her fingers down over the bandage and covered her hand with his own. "Take care of yourself while I'm away, will you?" His gaze captured hers and held steady.

Her chest refused to expand for any incoming breaths. She tore her gaze from his and looked down to where his hand remained wrapped around hers.

The expanse over his knuckles was broad and brown and sturdy. A seam-work of veins drew her free hand before she thought better of it. But as soon as the warmth of his skin grazed her fingertips and penetrated her consciousness, she clenched both fists and withdrew from his touch.

She ought to offer a witty comeback about how she could survive just fine without his help. But she couldn't seem to get the words to form on her lips and had to settle for a simple nod instead.

"Well then…" He stood and held Papa's bag out to her. "I'll return within a fortnight."

She rose, accepted the bag, and cleared her throat, unable to meet his scrutiny. She missed him already and didn't dare say more than, "Good traveling, Captain."

He turned as though to leave but then spun back around to face her. "I've asked Kako to remain with you. If any need should arise, just send him to fetch me. He knows the route we plan to take."

RyAnne's gaze skittered to Papa before returning to his. "Thank you, Captain."

He bowed slightly. "Very well. We are on our way at first light, and I'll see you in a few days when I return." He stopped and squatted by Papa's side. He gently touched Papa's shoulder and, when he roused, said a few low words to him.

The *shush* of the waves on the shore prevented her from hearing their exchange. Unfortunately, it didn't prevent emotion from clogging her airway.

She looked toward the horizon.

After a few moments, she heard the captain rise. He took two steps across the sand and then stilled.

She spun to face him.

He stood quietly, hands clasped behind his back, studying the ground. He pushed at a rock with the toe of his boot, and then his gaze lifted to hers, sending a jolt of awareness through her. For a long moment he studied her, his focus roaming across her features as though he was set on memorizing each contour and shadow.

Her heart thudded against her rib cage. Perhaps she should tell him how she truly felt? She swallowed away the dryness parching her tongue. No. She must be considerate of the man's reputation. He at least deserved to make a well-informed choice in the matter.

Besides, before any words would have had time to form, he tipped his head, gave her a bold wink, and without another look in her direction, strode off into the village.

RyAnne eased a breath through her lips. She allowed her gaze to linger until he disappeared into the cloak of dusk, and then she cleared her throat and forced herself to resume business as normal.

As she returned to the hut, prepared Papa's pallet, and then helped him to it, all she could think about was how likely it was the captain would never lay eyes on her dear Papa again. How frail this man, who'd always been so strong for her, had become. His skin, translucent as parchment, revealed every vein. His coughs had grown more thin and reedy over the past few days. Even as she eased him to his pallet and placed one of her rolled-up petticoats beneath his head, her heart lay heavy within her. Would this be the last time she helped him to bed? The last time she ran her fingers over thinning hair and smiled tremulously into his blue-gray eyes? The last time she would get to speak with him?

She smoothed the covers over his chest. "I love you, Papa."

He lifted a trembling hand to her cheek. "You look so much like her. Your mother. Her name was Arabella."

RyAnne held her breath. He'd never spoken of her mother this way before.

Too weak to keep his hand aloft, he dropped it back to the coverlet. "What I did to her was wrong in so many aspects. Wrong against Anne. Wrong against her. Wrong against you." He sighed.

RyAnne smoothed his hair. "Don't fret yourself, Papa."

He shook his head. "No. You must listen." He wetted his lips. "It was wrong. And I've asked the good Lord to forgive me a thousand times or more."

"He does, Papa. He does."

"Yes, child. But will you?"

RyAnne blinked. She hadn't expected that. "Whatever do you mean, Papa?"

"Your life hasn't been easy, child. And though God brought good from my sin by opening my eyes to my need of Him, the consequences of my actions have still run me through with grief many a day." He shuffled his hand across the blanket until it could clasp hers. "Don't hold Anne's anger against her, child. She will need you in the days to come. The anger she directs toward you is really with me."

Tears stung RyAnne's eyes. No words would form, but she managed a nod.

"So you see…much of the difficulty in your life stems from my sin. So I must seek your forgiveness."

The tears spilled over and trickled down her cheeks. "Of course, Papa. I forgive you."

He sighed and seemed to relax. "Waves of mercy." The words were barely audible as he patted the back of her hand and gave a little nod. "Indeed, the Father above keeps sending them my way." And then his eyes dropped closed. It was only a moment before his breaths deepened, though the rattle of the consumption gargled in his throat.

RyAnne dashed at the moisture on her face. *Father in heaven, I know I don't perhaps approach You as often as I should. But please, for Papa's sake… All he's wanted for years was to serve You by starting a mission here. Give him time? Time to see that dream fulfilled?*

She paced the room until she was sure Papa indeed slept, then grabbed up the medical bag and hurried down to check on Nyanja.

RyAnne was pleased to find that Nyanja's leg appeared to be well on its way to healing, and rewrapped a clean bandage around it. "Only a few more days and then you won't need the bandages anymore." She offered the woman a smile.

And when June translated the words to her, Nyanja gave a slight stretch of her lips in return. Though her lips barely formed the smile, her eyes showed her pleasure with a quiet certainty that warmed RyAnne's heart.

"Well, I'll just be on my way."

Nyanja stretched out a hand and spoke softly.

RyAnne looked to June for the translation.

"She asks if you have a moment, Miss Hunter."

RyAnne nodded and returned her focus to Nyanja.

With June translating, the woman spoke, never taking her eyes off RyAnne's face. "I owe you much thanks."

RyAnne blinked. She had often wondered what the woman felt, especially since RyAnne hadn't been able to save her leg. Words failed her, so she simply nodded.

Nyanja picked at a loose piece of bamboo on the woven mat she would sleep on tonight. "My people have a saying, 'No matter how long the night, dawn always comes.'" Her gaze lifted to RyAnne's as June translated, then she continued, "Before you came to Commodore Cornwall's, I had nearly given up on seeing the dawn… Khalifa, he is a hard master. A man who cannot be pleased, no matter how one tries, not even by his own daughter." Sorrow tugged at the corners of Nyanja's eyes as she cast a glance to where Moyo already slept on a pallet across the way.

RyAnne felt her own emotions threatening to flood her eyes.

Nyanja pressed her lips together and seemed to gather herself for a moment before going on. "I lost my leg, but I gained my freedom. And Moyo gained hers also. This is a gift for which I can never repay you."

"Oh, Nyanja." RyAnne squeezed the woman's hand. "I would never expect repayment from you. I only wish I could have saved your leg. I'll always regret that."

Nyanja leaned forward, her eyes intense. "Nothing behind us can be changed. It is better to walk forward than to curse the road. This I have chosen. It was what you chose the day you took my leg and saved my life. Because you walked the road put before you, I was taken off a wearisome rutted path and placed on a new smoother one. Now, you must choose again."

RyAnne sighed and nodded. There was much wisdom in her words. She would not have chosen this road. But it seemed the good Lord had chosen it for her. So now she had another choice. Either walk or curse.

"Thank you, Nyanja. You have done my heart good with your words tonight."

The woman nodded, and RyAnne rose to take her leave.

After a quick peek at Moyo and a squeeze to June's shoulder, she returned up the beach on weary legs and fell onto her own bed.

She'd thought her weariness would drag her to the depths of sleep swiftly tonight, but her mind didn't seem to be as exhausted as her body.

She prayed again for Papa. And then added a prayer for Mother, Jasmine, and Rory. Soon she would have to send them disturbing news. But she prayed it would be a few weeks rather than the days she feared it would be. *Please, God.*

She pondered the captain's words from earlier and realized they were quite true. She considered Papa. Certainly he was here because he hadn't wanted his family to watch him die, but he was also here because he felt the need to help these people despite his obvious limitations.

Had she ever truly wanted to help someone out of a pure motive? She'd helped Papa doctor people back on the island, but mostly because it allowed her to spend time with him and gave them a common bond. And she'd come after Papa on this trip. But truth be told, she'd only come after him because she'd wanted to convince him to return home with her. Because she needed him in her life. Needed his love so badly.

She pondered… Helping Nyanja might be the first truly selfless thing she'd done in her whole life. And yet, what she'd been able to do seemed to have fallen so short. And yet Nyanja had been content, even pleased, it seemed, with the outcome.

Across the room, Papa's breaths rattled in his throat.

Her own throat clogged with terror and sorrow. When his time came, she knew she wouldn't have enough to offer him. There would be no tonic she could give. No healing she could supply. Consumption took whom it would with nary a request for permission.

Father in heaven, You ask too much. I know I must be strong.

But I feel so alone. So helplessly inadequate.

Bishop Tozer often said that if you waited silently and listened carefully, the Almighty would sometimes speak to you. But even though RyAnne lay awake long into the darkness, she heard no heavenly response to all the prayers she'd directed God's way that evening. And yet, a verse she had memorized in one of Bishop Tozer's Sunday classes came to her mind as clearly as though she were reading it on the page. *And he said unto me, "My grace is sufficient for you for my strength is made perfect in weakness." Therefore most gladly I will rather boast in my infirmities, that the power of Christ may rest upon me.*

And with that reminder came a wave of peace. She could worry about her lack of ability to make Papa better, and fret over what she'd do once he passed, until she was naught but a tight ball of twine. Yet none of it would do her a whit of good. For perhaps it was only once she totally gave up reliance on her own strength that the Lord could best use her.

Father, forgive me. Perhaps it is I who asks too much. I am weak. Weak in knowledge. Weak in fear of the unknown. Please make Your strength perfect in me. I don't know how to glory in my infirmities. I think that's something You'll have to grow in me over time, but I will try not to fret so much.

As she continued to pour out her heart, her eyes grew heavy and her consciousness gave way to rest.

A Walk Through the Waters

When you pass through the waters, I will be with you; And through the rivers, they shall not overflow you. When you walk through the fire, you shall not be burned, Nor shall the flame scorch you.

Isaiah 43:2

Chapter 16
A Walk through the Waters

Lake Nyasa
At the Dawning of a New Day

The sun was just cresting above the horizon when RyAnne woke and stepped onto the sand outside her and Papa's hut. The breeze off the lake cut through her blouse and breeches in a way that reminded her she could probably resume wearing proper women's attire now that they'd arrived at the village. And yet, after wearing the men's clothing for the past several weeks, she'd found them to be quite freeing—certainly much less restrictive. Perhaps she would grant herself a few more days' reprieve from corsets and hoops.

She folded her arms against the chill and enjoyed the orange and pink hues of dawn spreading across the dome of the sky.

Trent and his men were already gone. Even though she'd known they would be, she felt as though another weight had just dropped onto her shoulders.

It was nonsense for her to miss him. The man had made it perfectly clear on numerous occasions that nothing could grow between them. And if she wanted to be fair to him, and she did, she wouldn't pursue a relationship with him. For to do so would require her to be honest with him about her heritage. And if word ever got out about her ancestry, it would be the death knell to Mother's social standing and to the captain's business workings on Zanzibar. Not that she feared the captain would say anything to anyone, but still… Right at this moment there were exactly four other people in the world who knew that Anne Hunter was not RyAnne's real mother, and those were the immediate members of her family. The more people who knew, the more likely the news would somehow leak to the public. She had to be mindful of that and consider carefully before she said anything to the captain.

She wrinkled her nose. She simply wouldn't think of him. Instead, she wrapped her arms about herself and forced her concentration to the clean scent of the morning breeze wafting off the lake. The birds had already been warbling for the past half hour, and it appeared, by the bustle of activity she could observe from all the huts around theirs, that the villagers were not far behind.

Papa's breaths had rattled in his throat the whole night long, but he seemed alert and excited when she went back in to check on him.

"Would you like some porridge, Papa?" She offered him a hand and lifted him into a sitting position.

"I think tea will suffice this morning. Thank you, daughter."

She didn't like to see him skipping a meal, but had learned over the past few weeks that if she left him to his own choices, he would eat eventually. She placed his Bible next to him on the cot and set about to quietly prepare his tea.

When she brought it to him, he said, "See if you can't find Kako, would you, dear? I want him to arrange a meeting with the chief for me. I'd like to put up a shelter of sorts for chapel services. Part of it can be used as a clinic also."

"Shouldn't a clinic and a church be separate?" She helped him draw on a clean shirt and handed him his boots.

He smiled. "I think the good Lord will forgive us for being frugal with our construction, for the time being."

That was probably true enough.

After breakfast, she left Papa seated on a rock near the fire pit outside their door, and made her way through the chatter of a village just coming to life to see if she could find Kako.

Two women, walking toward the lake with clay pots, giggled with each other and altered their course when they took note of her. Both women stepped right into her personal space, and one was even bold enough to reach out and finger the linen of her shirt. The other—apparently emboldened when RyAnne, in her shock, could come up with no appropriate negative response to the first—reached out to touch RyAnne's hair. She gave a vocalization of awe that drew her companion's hands to RyAnne's hair also.

RyAnne grimaced but bore the relatively intimate inspection with as much grace as she could muster. She felt rather like a baby baboon being groomed by a troop of boisterous mother baboons. But she realized that their behavior was born of simple curiosity, and let them finger a curl for a moment longer before offering them each a smile and taking a purposeful step back. One woman seemed reluctant to release RyAnne's hair, and RyAnne had to somewhat forcefully extract the curl from between the woman's fingers. Next time, she made note, she would pin her hair all the way up.

But this time she pasted on a smile. "My name is RyAnne." She laid a hand on her chest. "And you are?" She waited, bouncing a glance between the two women.

But they only looked blankly at each other and then back to her. They apparently did not understand the Kiswahili that she spoke fluently.

And RyAnne felt her hopes deflate a little more. It was one more weight that pressed on her. If Papa passed away, she didn't even know enough of the language to communicate, much less get herself back to the coast. Oh why had the captain had to rush off the *moment* they'd arrived?

She bade the women farewell and found Kako down near the shore and led him back to Papa.

Papa explained what he wanted and was quite pleased when Kako assured him there was no need to talk to the chief, for the man had already indicated Kako should give them every possible concession. Papa was even further pleased when Kako had a crew of the village's men working to erect a small shelter near the beach by that very afternoon.

The walls were naught more than strips of bamboo split the long way and then woven together to form a matting of sorts, but the roof was thickly thatched and sturdy, and the bamboo weave would allow a breeze to flow through to cool the building's occupants. Even before the last wall had been tied into place, Papa insisted on being helped into the building. There were tears shimmering in his eyes when he stood at the front and turned to face the room.

RyAnne swallowed, once again thankful that she'd given her all to help her father fulfill his calling. She was blessed to have a man such as this one for her papa.

The next day and for a week afterward, Papa's energy seemed to be in peak form. Each day a couple hours before noon, he would ring a gong he'd fashioned from an old piece of iron tied to a string outside the shelter, and as many as were free and wanted to come hear him speak made their way to the chapel-clinic near the beach. After Papa read from the Bible, he would, with Kako translating, answer any questions the people had, and then he and RyAnne would doctor any wounded who would accept their help.

Mostly, they only bandaged small cuts and abrasions, for any serious illness was considered too important for the white *azungu* to handle. For those sicknesses the people went to the village doctor, who was more likely to cast a spell over them than heal them. The man, with his large ivory nose ring and body piercings shot through with porcupine quills, made a chill run down RyAnne's spine each time she saw him.

Each day fewer and fewer villagers came to hear Papa speak, and finally Kako informed Papa that the village doctor had made it clear it would displease him greatly if the people continued to listen to the white man's lies about a nonexistent god.

But, though RyAnne was tempted to despair, Papa refused to give up hope. He reminded her to put her trust in the God who had brought them here.

And then one day just when Papa was saying the closing prayer over the chapel hour—two men had been brave enough to ignore the medicine man's instructions—there arose a great commotion outside.

"Miss RyAnne! Miss RyAnne!" That was June's voice rising above all the hubbub.

RyAnne rushed out to see whatever the matter could be.

June motioned madly for her to come. "It is the wife of Chief Wankulu. The babe faces the wrong way. And the village doctor says to leave her alone and that they will both die!"

RyAnne's eyes widened.

On their trip here, they had taken rest in a village just a day's journey back along the trail. The chief of that village had misused his people terribly, including his wife. And when their party had left his village the next morning to continue on their way here, many of the people of that village had accompanied them, including the man's wife, who had been full with child.

RyAnne rushed back into the chapel. "Papa, we are needed right now." She snatched up his doctor bag and reached for his arm to help him rise. But he was so slow to gain his feet, she changed her mind about her approach. "Kako, you bring him down, would you? I'm running ahead to see what I can find out."

As she rushed out the door, one thought pounded over and over. If that baby died in this village, not only would the people's belief in their sham of a doctor be shored up, but a war would begin, of a certainty.

Wankulu would not let an offense like that stand. Especially not after the way Trent had allowed the man's abused wife to accompany them to this village. Wankulu had already been livid over that.

The woman's hut was far back in the concentric circles of the village. Outside it, a crowd of women already keened the way they might over a corpse. RyAnne pushed through them and into an interior so dark and smoky that her lantern did little except to illuminate wafts of churning gray clouds. Finally she was able to locate the moaning woman, who squatted against the wall near the door. She met June's wide, terrified gaze.

"Remind me of her name?"

"Yani."

"Okay. We're going to need to be able to see. We need to move her outside. Lay a blanket in the shade of the banana tree, and we'll move her there. And"—she motioned through the door toward the crowd of wailing women—"that keening must stop! She's not dead!"

While June made those preparations and remonstrated the

crowd to silence, RyAnne laid a hand to Yani's forehead. She was warm, but not overly so. Probably only from her exertion. A contraction must have gripped the woman, for she suddenly gave out a gritty moan and clutched at her womb in anguish.

"There now, Yani," RyAnne soothed, rubbing the woman's shoulder. "My father is a doctor." Likely Yani couldn't understand her any better than the two women along the path the other day, but RyAnne hoped her tone at least conveyed a reassuring message. "All will be well. We are going to help you."

Or at least give it their best attempt. She set to rolling up her sleeves while she waited for the preparations outside to be completed.

June returned and indicated that the blanket was ready, and they helped the agonized woman out to it, but Yani refused to lie down and instead squatted in the middle of the blanket. RyAnne was thankful to see that at least the woman's waters had not broken open yet. Now that she could see better how to help, RyAnne realized she was trembling all over. If Papa couldn't save this baby…and maybe its mother… She swallowed and pushed the thought aside for the moment.

Just then Papa shuffled up holding on to Kako's arm. RyAnne blew out a breath of relief. If anyone could make this better, Papa could. But instead of pitching in to help her, he motioned to a log-round by a nearby fire pit, and Kako fetched it for him. Papa sank onto it, panting.

Movement just behind Papa drew RyAnne's attention. The village doctor, his face smeared white with a mixture of ash, glowered so angrily RyAnne felt the look like she would have felt the thrust of the long feather-decorated spear he held in one hand.

"Papa?" RyAnne's tremors had ratcheted up to full force.

"Calm yourself, RyAnne. You must trust in the Lord and pray for His protection. There is great power in the name of Jesus against a spirit such as that." Papa spoke some words low to Kako, who in turn strode across to say a few words to the medicine man.

Though Papa bowed his head and RyAnne could hear his low supplications, she couldn't seem to take her eyes off the confrontation taking place, nor lift up any other prayer except *Jesus*... The village doctor started toward her and Papa. Kako stepped into his path and placed one hand to the man's chest. There was a fierceness in Kako's stance that RyAnne didn't remember seeing before.

Behind her, Yani moaned loudly. June cooed a few soothing words and fussed over her, but the woman did indeed sound like she might be dying.

RyAnne's fingernails bit into her palms.

At the sound of Yani's great distress, the medicine man threw up one hand and said a few angry words, but Kako stood his ground, and after a moment the man turned and stormed away.

Despite the fact that June had managed to shush their keening, the whole village, it seemed, still stood gathered about the hut and had just witnessed the medicine man stomp off in a fit of rage.

Papa lifted his focus from his prayers and returned his attention to RyAnne. He continued as though nothing out of the ordinary had just happened. "'Tis just a birthing. Now you must get her to lie down."

June passed the instructions to Yani, who reluctantly collapsed onto the blanket as requested.

Papa nodded. "Now palpate her stomach and tell me what you feel. Remember? We've done this before, you and I. The head will be firm, hard, and round. Feel for it." Papa placed a hanky over his mouth and coughed into it a couple times.

Helplessly, RyAnne looked down at the woman, who writhed and whimpered and rubbed her belly. Her faith was so lacking, yet it seemed that once again God was asking her to simply offer what she had. Limited though it might be. Heaving in a fortifying breath, RyAnne complied with Papa's order.

"The head is high, Papa, just under her ribs. The babe does indeed face the wrong direction." The feel of that little head so high up sent a wave of certain fear shooting through RyAnne.

The medicine man might be right, in the end. But the first rule of medicine Papa had taught her was to never let your patient see your fear. No matter how strong it might be.

"Is there room to turn the child? Or is it already too far down?"

RyAnne assessed the situation, and as another contraction bore down on the woman, she realized with dread the babe was too far into the canal to turn. She shook her head at Papa, doing her best to keep her breaths from banging against her teeth.

But Papa remained as calm as the placid lake. "Fine, then we'll have to carefully watch that the cord doesn't get clamped off at the last, but 'tis not impossible to deliver." Papa smiled. "You yourself came into the world in this manner. You always have been determined to do things your own way."

That bit of information did not help calm her tremors, since her mother had died in childbirth.

Papa seemed to be able to read her thoughts. "Not all endings are the same, child. Now"—he motioned her back to the task at hand—"get her on her hands and knees."

As soon as that task was accomplished, the woman's waters broke.

"Good!" Papa's voice soothed over RyAnne. "Now then, reach in and grasp the feet gently. Think of your work as more that of a guide. You are not to pull, at least not yet."

RyAnne followed his instructions and felt the soft smoothness of the baby's feet beneath her fingers. She offered a tremulous smile to June. "You can tell her to push now."

June spoke quietly to the woman, and with the next contraction, Yani's face stretched into a grimace as every muscle in her body tensed. She pushed with all her might.

Jesus, you know my limitations and lack of faith, and yet I do believe that you can work wonders when you choose to step in. Please, let this be one of those times. So many lives are at stake if I fail here.

Two little feet emerged into the daylight, but RyAnne's heart nearly stilled in her chest. "Papa, the cord."

Papa dabbed at some moisture on his upper lip with the back of one hand. "All you can do is get the babe out as quickly as you can, child."

RyAnne's breaths came short and fast. *Jesus, please...*

When you walk through the water, I will be there.

The words were so clear it was as though someone near had spoken them aloud, yet RyAnne knew no one nearby had said the words. *Jesus...* A quaver coursed through her, and with it a need to hurry the birthing along as quickly as she could.

"June, tell her she must push with all her might!"

June bent over Yani and whispered into her ear, speaking low but urgently.

And with the next contraction, RyAnne was satisfied to feel the babe emerge a few more inches. She tugged gently to hasten the process as best she could. Still, she feared for the child. Was the cord pinched? Was it getting the life-sustaining support it needed during this critical time?

"Again," she urged the woman as she saw the next contraction tightening the woman's abdomen. "Push!"

After three more contractions, the baby boy's head and shoulders were all that was left to birth. She gently hooked two fingers around the umbilical cord. The part she could feel felt cold. Lifeless. The babe's wrinkly body was limp and cool. Despair threatened to overwhelm her. *Jesus, please...* It was the only prayer she could seem to formulate. With the next contractions, RyAnne gently eased out first one shoulder and then the other, and with one more contraction and a bit of help on her part, the baby slid into her hands.

The tiny boy lay in her hands, without response. His little mouth hung open, but he made no move to try and breathe.

A ripple of sound filtered through the gathered crowd. And despite the fact that she couldn't understand any of the words, the tone was one of acceptance of death.

"Turn the child upside down, RyAnne. Rub his back firmly. Now!" Papa hadn't sounded so forceful in a long time.

Hands shaking, RyAnne turned the boy. She hooked two

fingers on either side of his neck and curled them over his shoulders to hold on to him, and she rubbed his little back hard. "Come on, little one. Father in heaven, life, please, for this child." She rubbed him again and gently whacked his back with the heel of her hand.

The baby flinched and gave a tiny bleat of protest.

From the crowd, a sound of awe lifted.

The awe was echoed in RyAnne's own spirit. "Oh, thank you, Jesus!" She turned the baby over.

At the bright light in his face, the infant balled up his fists and screamed in earnest.

RyAnne couldn't withhold a soft chuckle. "That's right, little one. That's right. Just breathe." Joy pulsed through her.

A baby boy. Whole and beautiful in every way. A grin stretched RyAnne's face from ear to ear as she tied off and cut the cord and laid the baby against his mother's chest. "You have a fine, strong son." The woman seemed content despite the communication barrier, and she clutched at one of RyAnne's hands in thanks.

Yani then turned to face her son. She murmured and cooed to the baby, and such a swell of happiness rose up in RyAnne she had to step away from the intimate scene.

Papa looked all done in.

"Kako, if you wouldn't mind, could you please see Papa back to our hut while I wash up?"

The man nodded, and RyAnne was so thankful for his help.

Down at the lake, she sluiced water and soap over her hands and arms. Her sloppy grin didn't seem to have anywhere else to be. *Thank You, Jesus! We did it. Together. Thank You…* She had just saved a life. Maybe two. And maybe had prevented a war!

Certainly sometimes God seemed shockingly silent in the face of appalling evil. But today she had felt Him almost nearer than Papa had been.

And certainly sometimes her gift would not be enough. But sometimes it was enough. Today, combined with a bit of prayer, and God's help, it had been enough.

Trent swung the machete with vigor as he and his men blazed through a large marsh full of tall grasses. Pillars of smoke had appeared on the horizon, and the local guide had insisted the fastest way to get there was across this marshy bog instead of cutting all the way around the large hill that stood between them and their destination at one end of the marshland. But he was beginning to think the man might have led them astray. His feet had been wet since midmorning, and twice they'd had to fight off a crocodile—thankfully, small ones. He was more concerned for the condition of his men's feet than his own. He was in the best getup for traipsing through land like this of all his men, none of whom had any shoes on.

He was just about ready to call a halt and question the man further about this shortcut, when ahead their guide gave a triumphant shout. "*Ti na fika*!"

Trent hoped that meant they had arrived, and wished for the umpteenth time that day that Kako could have accompanied him. He certainly could have used the man's translation skills, but had felt it more important to leave Miss Hunter under the guard of a man he trusted. He did have one man with him who spoke rudimentary Swahili, so he was able to communicate with his men.

They climbed out of the bog, and he gave the men thirty minutes to rest and dry their feet before they would be required to traipse across the rocky terrain. The smoke was dissipating now, so likely they would be too late to be of help, but maybe someone would be there who could give them some more information about who was attacking the villages and where they were taking the people.

If he could just catch up to the man so he could verify if it was indeed Khalifa or not, that would give him a better idea of how to proceed. It was not unheard of for tribal chieftains to go to war with one another and sell the captives to traders passing through. Perhaps Khalifa wasn't the instigator but merely the beneficiary of all these uprisings. Yet, somehow, Trent doubted the man had nothing to do with the terror that had been ripping a path across the Continent. And the most infuriating part? Even if he had instigated every attack, Khalifa was doing nothing illegal, yet.

Which in itself was a slap in the face of God. Abetting the trade in human flesh was the fact that the Anglo raiders had dehumanized the natives in the eyes of much of the world. Trent had never understood how someone could think so low of another human being.

The stockings he'd laid out on a rock had dried quickly in the heat of the sun. As had his breeches. His boots were still damp, but they'd have to do. They needed to get moving.

He gave a call, and the men roused from their rest and were ready to march before he had tied the last lace on his boots.

When they arrived at the village, it was to find it had been decimated. Kraals kicked in, nearly every hut set afire, many people slain where they'd fallen as they ran to escape.

Trent's heart sank, and his teeth clenched in anger at the destruction and horror all around him.

All the deceased were either old or young, just like at every village they had passed for the previous several weeks.

Trent squatted next to a small girl who had fallen backward with a spear in her chest—just before she would have reached the cover of tall grass at the edge of the village. She couldn't be more than five. She apparently had turned to face her attacker at the last moment. Her eyes were wide and terrified.

He fisted a hand and placed it over his mouth as he gently closed her staring eyes. A knot of anger formed in his stomach. What he wouldn't give to be able to get his hands on the men who had done this right about now.

He thought back to RyAnne's questions. How could God allow such evil to go on unchecked and not step in? Where was the good in something like this? He sighed. *Father, forgive me, but when I see pillage like this, I have to question why You allow it. What did this child do to deserve a death like this?*

The heavens rang with silence.

Next to him the grass rustled. He leapt back and drew his machete in one hand and pistol in the other, ready to defend himself in case an animal emboldened by the scent of death was set for an attack.

A soft gasp and another rustle of grass was all he encountered, however.

There was a survivor! "You." He sheathed his machete and snapped his fingers at his translator. "I have a survivor here. Tell them it is okay to come out, that we won't hurt them."

The man approached and squatted down. He murmured some quiet words toward the stand of thick brown grass, and after a moment there was another rustle and the blades parted to reveal a small tear-stained face.

The girl was young and terrified. She didn't move fully into the open but examined Trent carefully from head to toe and then asked the man squatting next to him a question. She was obviously nervous that he might be another slave trader come to finish what the previous raiders had left undone.

Trent unslung his canteen and held it out to her with a little shake and a gentle smile. This child could be the break they'd been hoping for. Could she have seen anything? Surely she had?

The girl took a hesitant step away from the relative safety of the concealing grass. She eyed the canteen with a frown, obviously unsure what it was.

Removing the cork, Trent tilted back his head and poured a splash of water into his mouth in demonstration, then held it back toward her. She had to be thirsty. It was straight up noon, and she'd probably been hiding for hours.

Eyes widening as she realized what he was offering her, she clutched at the canteen greedily and tipped it back, taking long, desperate draughts of the revitalizing liquid. After a moment she wiped at her mouth with one tiny palm and handed the canteen back to him with a slight bend of her knees in thanks. The girl couldn't be more than seven or eight.

Trent reached into his rucksack and pulled out a mango he'd plucked along the path early that morning. He squatted down and held the fruit out to her.

The girl didn't hesitate this time but took the fruit and bit through the skin without ceremony. She used her teeth to quickly pull back the thick skin in a half circle around the mango and then ate the pulp with gusto before moving on to the other half. Once again, when she had finished and tossed the seed and skin away into the thick brush, she dipped her knees and pressed her palms together in the tribal way of saying thank you.

Trent tipped her a nod, then looked at his guide, who had sat quietly by, waiting for the girl to finish. "Ask her if she saw the men who raided her village."

The man spoke low to the girl.

Her eyes widened, and she chattered a few phrases with a trembling voice.

Trent waited patiently for the guide to translate for him.

"She say, the raid came just as the sky's day lamp lifted above the horizon. Many men attacked from all sides. She and her sister"—he pointed subtly to the dead child— "ran."

"Did she see the leaders?"

The translator murmured to her again.

Tiny hands gesturing, she responded.

The translator turned a surprised look on Trent. "After the chaos at the first of the attack, the raiders made all the villagers gather in the *bwalo*. She says there were two men. Two leaders."

Trent leaned forward. "Can she describe them?"

The translator spoke to the girl again.

She responded with a bit of a warble in her soft voice.

The man looked to Trent. "She says one man is very tall with very dark skin and a white patch in his hair. The other is an Arab wearing a gray kofia."

Trent's stomach clenched. Khalifa wore a gray kofia. And he recognized the description of the other man as one of the Zanzibaris who had been with Khalifa at Commodore Cornwall's estate.

"The Arab is in charge of a caravan of women only. The other was taking anyone, man or woman strong enough to work, that the Arab passed over. The first man only took those women who were fat."

Trent frowned. "Fat?"

The translator scratched his head as though unsure of the correct Swahili word to use. "It is the village way to say…how you say…good teeth, good skin, young, no babies yet."

"Beautiful virgins?"

The translator snapped his fingers in recognition. "This is the word. Harem women."

Harem women. Trent stood slowly and let his focus blur into the horizon. The sultan got his concubines from Oman. Any women from here wouldn't be destined for the palace on Zanzibar. Which meant…whoever Khalifa was working for really was involved in an illegal smuggling of slaves. Because current laws only allowed for the transport of slaves to Zanzibar and no farther. Lew was right. They needed to figure out if Khalifa was using Harcourt ships to smuggle with their full knowledge or if he was working for someone else right under Harcourt noses.

In the meantime, it had been over two weeks since he left RyAnne and her father, and his men were too few to confront Khalifa anyhow. The best he could do was send runners ahead. Something he should have thought of earlier.

He glanced at his translator. "Send men ahead. They must hurry and get ahead of the slave caravan and its raiders. Go to every village in their path and warn them they are coming."

The man looked skeptical. "This is the way of things here, *mzee*. The word has already spread. The villages will already know of the raiders."

Trent scrubbed at the back of his neck. "I know. But it is our human duty to try to warn them further. Send the runners. And send some men to hunt. We should eat meat tonight."

"Yes, *mzee*."

The men were dispatched with haste, and Trent felt only a fraction more relieved. He wouldn't rest easy until he had the cowards bound hand and foot and headed for Her Majesty's courts. Would that all slavery could be made illegal. He glanced around the village once more. He wasn't naïve enough to think a law would stop all of this, but it might put a stop to such open desecration and destruction and save the lives of many.

It took them the rest of the day to bury the dead. After the last corpse had been laid to rest, the men gathered around the small cook fire to eat the *nsima* and meat from the gazelle the hunting team had returned with earlier.

Trent made sure the young girl, who told them her name was Nyimbo—song—received the first plate. Her eyes looked weary beyond their years, and he knew grief must be tearing her up inside. He gently laid a hand on her head and then squeezed her shoulder. It appeared Miss Hunter would have another charge once they returned to the village.

He left the girl to her food and took a portion of his own. "We return to the lake at first light," Trent informed his men. "For now, we will rest." This village, pillaged though it was, would be as good a place to do so as any. The raiders wouldn't be returning here, at least not so soon, and there were at least a couple roofs still standing that would serve well as shelter for the night.

Chapter 17

A Walk through the Waters

One evening, just as the sun was dipping below the surface of the lake for its nightly swim, RyAnne found Papa sitting on the beach, taking in the golden glory gilding the surface of the water. RyAnne sank down next to him and handed him the bowl of *nsima ndi ndiwo* June had prepared for them. Tonight's corn-flour patty was accompanied by stewed game and tomatoes.

Glancing into his bowl, Papa asked, "What manner of animal is this?"

RyAnne crinkled her nose. "I was afraid to ask."

His warm chuckle drifted across the dusk. "Probably better that way. Say the blessing, would you, child?"

RyAnne thanked God for the benefit of hot food to eat, even if it was of unknown origin, and this brought another chuckle from Papa, which warmed her heart. It had been too long since he'd laughed so freely.

A soft sigh slipped from her father's lips as they set to eating in cicada-serenaded silence. After a moment he gestured to the sunset. "Beautiful, isn't it?"

The champagne light had puddled into distinct swatches of guava and mango now, and with the palm tree just to their right silhouetted against the sky, it had been some time since RyAnne had seen anything so beautiful. "Stunning," she agreed.

Papa dipped another morsel of the corn patty into the stew. "Your mother loved sunsets."

RyAnne stilled, knowing instantly that he was speaking of the woman who had given her birth, not the woman she had called "Mother" all her life.

Setting his half-finished bowl aside, Papa licked his thumb and offered, "Did I ever tell you that her mother came from this tribe? This very village, in fact?"

RyAnne's brows lifted. "My mother's mother?"

Papa nodded. "Aye. She was captured from here back in the

early twenties. Silas Coventry bought her from the Zanzibar slave market. Silas was your mother's father. He sold Arabella to me in 1845."

The bottom seemed to drop from her stomach. She'd only ever known that her birth mother's father had been a plantation owner, but never his identity. "Silas Coventry is my grandfather?"

Papa nodded.

RyAnne set her own bowl aside, not sure she could stomach any more food on top of the bitter taste currently in her mouth. Silas Coventry was one of the cruelest men on the whole island of Zanzibar. His plantation thrived on the backs of slaves who were often abused to the point of death. "Is my grandmother still alive?"

Papa shook his head. "I'm afraid not. It was her death that caused your mother to rebel to the point that he sold her to me to be shut of the trouble of her."

RyAnne felt a little sick to her stomach. "Did Silas kill her, do you think? My grandmother?"

Uncertainty hissed from between his teeth as Papa rubbed the back of his neck. "I'm not sure. Arabella never wanted to talk about it."

RyAnne glanced around the village. "So partly the reason you are here is out of guilt?"

"Nay, child. I came to terms with my guilt many years ago and am ever so grateful that all my past sin is covered under the blood of the Savior. We can't escape the consequences of our sin, but we can be free of the guilt with the help of the Lord." He rested his forearms against his knees and continued, "Nay, I'm here because I felt a distinct call of the Lord to come preach to these people. One day while in prayer, I clearly saw this lake." He swept a gesture to the orange waters before them. "And along the shore of this lake I clearly saw this village. It was like a map had been sketched for me. And a voice said to me, 'Matthew 28:19.'"

"What does that verse say, Papa?"

"'*Go therefore and make disciples of all nations, baptizing them in the name of the Father and of the Son and of the Holy Spirit.*'"

Papa sighed and took up a twig from the sand beside him. He set to breaking it into small bits. "That was many years ago, child. I tried to talk Anne into coming with me, bringing the family. But she would have nothing to do with coming here to live in the wilds—especially not to reach the village of the woman who was your mother." Tossing down what was left of the twig, Papa spread his hands. "So when I knew I was dying, I thought what better way to solve two problems at once? I could fulfill what I'd felt the Lord calling me to these many years, and I could free my family from having to watch me slowly die."

RyAnne squeezed her father's hand. "I'm sorry she wouldn't come with you, Papa."

The silence lingered for a moment before Papa said, "I hurt her, most severely, child. I broke our vows and misused her trust. Not much can amend for that, no matter that I've attempted to apologize in innumerable ways and tried to prove myself worthy of her trust once more. Now in these my last days, I can only pray that she will be able to let go of her bitterness ere she passes on into eternity. It grieves me that my sin might be the cause of her separation from God for all of eternity, for she's never been able to forgive me for what I did."

A frown furrowed her brow. "Whatever do you mean by that? Surely you can't mean—"

"Just as I say, child." Age-spotted hands scrubbed over his wrinkled face, and then he draped his arms wearily over his knees. "It's part of the Lord's Prayer. 'And forgive us our debts, as we forgive our debtors.' Then Jesus also said in the verses following, 'For if you forgive men their trespasses, your heavenly Father will also forgive you. But if you do not forgive men their trespasses, neither will your Father forgive your trespasses.'"

Puzzlement tugged at RyAnne's brow. "Yet aren't we saved by grace alone?"

Papa nodded. "And yet, if we can't bring ourselves to respond in obedience to commands so clearly laid out in God's Word for us, can we honestly claim that we've fully placed our faith in God?"

RyAnne thought of Khalifa, who had first attacked her in the Harcourts' garden and then so abusively maltreated Nyanja after she lost her leg to the crocodile. Could she ever bring herself to forgive a man like that? And what about a man like Chief Wankulu? Did a man who would whip and browbeat a woman deserve forgiveness?

The next thought stilled the breath in her lungs.

And her mother? The woman who had constantly belittled her and made her aware of how inadequately she measured up. Could she bring herself to forgive her?

Apparently seeing the quandary expressed in her features, Papa rested one hand at the back of her neck. "Do you remember the parable of the unforgiving servant, RyAnne? He owed the king of his country a great debt, but when he begged for forgiveness, the king granted it to him. Then the servant promptly went out and beat a man who owed him only a few cents. Word got back to the king, and the man was brought back before him, declared wicked, and delivered to the torturers. The lesson that parable points out is that we who have been forgiven so much in the face of God's perfection ought to realize how little harm has actually been done to us by people who misuse us. When God has forgiven us for so much, and in fact made us perfect in his sight only by our belief in him, how can we in turn refuse to offer that same forgiveness to others? It is out of a grateful heart for what our Savior has done for us that we pass on that forgiveness. And if we can't find it in ourselves to offer forgiveness, then it is questionable whether we've actually understood the magnitude of what Christ did for us on the cross."

Realization of how far she had to go to become more Christlike washed through RyAnne.

Papa sighed. "I don't say all that to make it seem like what I did to Anne was negligible. I understand it was a horrendous thing I did. And yet, her burden now rests in finding the strength to step out into forgiveness. This is my prayer for her."

RyAnne's tears transformed the scene before her into an orange blur. All these years she had resented the way Mother treated her. Always angry about little things. Always keeping RyAnne at arm's length. Never satisfied with anything RyAnne had tried to do to impress her. And now, suddenly, even though RyAnne had known in the back of her mind all these years where the bitterness must stem from, it became clear *why*. She put herself in her mother's place, having to raise the child brought forth from an adulterous affair perpetrated by her husband. And she suddenly had a magnitude of sympathy for the woman. What pain Mother must feel each time she looked at the child that resulted from that affair. What bitterness. And yet, if she could have brought herself to forgive Papa, what a better relationship they could have had with each other. And if *she* could bring herself to forgive *Mother*? They too would have a better relationship. The kind RyAnne had longed for all her years, growing up.

Maybe it wasn't too late.

RyAnne dashed at the tears coursing down her cheeks. After a long moment, she whispered. "I will join you in praying for her soul, Papa." *And for my own.*

Somewhere in the brush behind them, an owl hooted, and the guttural cry of a startled bush baby grated across the night. Waves caressed the shore, and a breeze rustled through the leaves of the palm trees. And for the first time in months, RyAnne felt content.

It had been two weeks and a half since Trent and his men had left the village. Dusky pink tendrils of the sunrise still wisped across the dome of the sky, even though the sun floated well above the horizon now. RyAnne stood at the edge of the lake and let the coolness of the morning water lap over her feet.

Several times over the past few days, she had looked in on Yani and the new babe, and the boy seemed to be thriving well. After the safe birth of Yani's baby, Kako's father, Chief Banda, had sent a runner to tell Wankulu about the birth of his son. The messenger had returned with Wankulu, and he'd been given a special dispensation from Chief Banda to enter the village, despite much grumbling from those of his tribe who'd traveled here to escape the man's poor management of his own chieftainship.

Also since the safe birth of the baby boy, more of the villagers had been emboldened to attend Papa's services. Not as many as Papa would have liked, but more than had been coming previously.

And yet, despite that seemingly good news, RyAnne's heart was heavy today.

This morning she had awoken in the wee hours before any of the birds had even decided to greet the new day. At first she hadn't been able to place the reason she'd woken so suddenly. She'd lain in the darkness, listening, but her straining ears could pick out no sounds.

And that was when it hit her! She lurched out of bed. "Papa!" She dashed across the room. The breaths that had rattled in his throat every night for the past few weeks were still and silent.

Terror clawed at her. Not yet! She wasn't ready to lose him yet!

"Papa." The word was barely audible as she crept closer. She was almost afraid to touch him, could barely make out his shadowed form in the dim glow of moonlight filtering under the door.

She held her breath. Forced herself to reach out.

Papa jolted at her touch, flipped over, and grabbed her arm.

She gasped, half in relief, half startled at his quick movements. "It's me, Papa. Just me. You were breathing so quietly, I came to check and make sure you were all right."

"I'm fine, daughter." Papa squinted at the amount of light coming under the door. "Try to sleep some more. It won't be morning for another few hours yet."

"Yes, Papa."

But despite her attempts to do just that, sleep had evaded her for the rest of the night, and the certainty of her impending loss had grown heavier with each passing hour. One time she was going to check on him, and he would not be fine—he would be gone.

On top of that realization was the weight of what had happened when she'd gone to check on Yani and the babe this morning.

Eyes gritty from her lack of sleep, RyAnne had set out at first light with a small basket of things she had made for the baby. A soft blanket she had cut down from one of Papa's old shirts, a pair of booties she had crocheted with her last length of yarn, and a small and very deficient doll for the baby's older sister, which she'd made with the scraps left over after making the blanket.

Despite her scare over Papa, her heart had felt fairly light this morning. And she'd been at the edge of the clearing before Yani's hut, with the basket on her arm, when she'd heard the screeching and the tiny wail of the newborn baby.

Without thinking, she burst into the hut, certain something was very wrong. It took but a moment for her eyes to adjust to the dim interior after the weak dawn light outside. And when they did, it was to find Yani cowed against one wall with Wankulu leaning over her, grinding out a stream of words RyAnne was, for the first time, glad she could not understand. The babe lay on the mat across the room, with his big sister—not quite yet two—doing her best to shush and comfort his crying. RyAnne's eyes adjusted a little more, and that was when she noticed Yani had fresh blood marring the arms she'd curled over her head and Wankulu had a whip in his hands.

RyAnne's anger bubbled up and boiled over the top so quickly, she hardly knew what she was doing. One moment she was standing in the doorway with a basket of gifts over her arm, and the next moment she was by Wankulu's side with the captain's pistol pressed to the man's temple. "Drop that whip this instant, you miserable cur!"

The man's eyes widened slightly, though whether it was because no woman had ever dared to speak to him thus or due to the volume of her order, RyAnne wasn't sure.

The man's hand twitched, and the flails of the whip lurched her way.

But RyAnne thumped the point of the pistol into the man's

head with a good deal of force. "Don't make me!" She prayed he could not detect her trembling in the dark of the room.

Slowly his fingers relaxed from around the handle, and the whip fell to the ground near Yani's feet.

"Now, out!" RyAnne tipped her head toward the door. "And you had better believe that Chief Banda will hear about this the moment I have the opportunity to tell him!" She didn't care if the man couldn't understand a word she said. She felt certain her tone conveyed her massive displeasure.

With a grunt, he exited the hut.

And while Yani scrambled across the room and gathered the wailing baby into her arms, RyAnne eased out a tremulous lungful of air and kept her gun trained on the doorway, lest he should change his mind and come back. Yani crooned softly to the little one, and after only a moment, his wails turned to soft snuffles.

After calming the babe, Yani managed to convey that Wankulu was trying to force her to return to his village with him and she had told him she didn't want to go.

RyAnne went straight to the chief's hut after leaving Yani's, and the man was livid when Kako translated her story of what had just happened.

Kako had assured RyAnne that Wankulu would be escorted from the village the moment he was found and that he would not be allowed to return.

Now, the waves grew a little stronger and tugged at the tops of her ankles. She lifted her skirts—she'd gone back to wearing skirts almost two weeks past—and tipped her face to catch a bit more of the breeze.

And it struck her—Wankulu was doing to his wife what RyAnne had wanted God to do to some people. Wankulu had been trying to force his wife to return to his village with him, just as RyAnne had wanted God to forcefully intervene in some of the atrocities she'd witnessed recently. Yet force was no proper way to show love. The ultimate sacrifice of true love was giving people free will. Free will meant that sometimes one man's choices would bring hurt upon someone else.

She considered the questions she had lifted to Captain Dawson just after the attack on Nyanja that had left her a cripple with only one leg. Some bad things that happened were not a result of man's choice to harm another. Some, it seemed, should be easily preventable by a loving God.

How could a good God let such things happen? Nyanja losing her leg, for instance, yet Nyanja had told her not long ago about how grateful she was to be free of Khalifa's abusive ownership. She would not have gained her freedom had she not lost her leg. So it could be said that God had used the bad to bring about a greater good for Nyanja and Moyo.

But then there was Papa. Certainly he'd made his share of mistakes. One of them had resulted in her birth. But from those mistakes he'd realized the error of his ways and had given his life over to God. He'd dedicated his life from that time to this, to serving others. But God had allowed him to be struck down by a disease that was slowly eating away at him day by day.

She recalled the verse that had come to her as though spoken from the very mouth of God as she'd been delivering Yani's baby boy.

When you walk through the waters, I will be there.

God promised to be there, to be a comforter, to be present in the hard times. And she believed it. Another verse spoke about God working all things for the good of those who were called by His name. And she believed that too. The struggle was in seeing *how* God was doing that. Perhaps if Papa had never grown sick, he never would have worked up his courage to come to this village where he so strongly believed God had called him? It was quite possible, but for the moment, RyAnne gave up on the answers.

"Father, I don't suppose I have to know all the reasons why. Just help me to keep my trust in You. To know that You will never leave me nor forsake me, no matter what You ask me to go through."

Slowly, as she prayed, her heavy heart began to ease, and finally she felt ready to face her day, though she knew by the end of it she would be feeling her short night and stressful morning to their fullest.

She retrieved her shoes and headed toward the hut to awaken Papa. They needed to get on with their day.

It was midafternoon, just after she and Papa had shut down the clinic for the day, when a commotion rose from the outskirts of the village. RyAnne's heart lurched with hope. Was the captain returned? She rushed from the clinic, drying her hands on a scrap of toweling. And there he was, striding into the village at the head of his men, his gaze drilling into hers.

As though he were a compass needle and she were north, he strode straight to her. He searched her over from the top of her head to the swaying hem of her skirt. "Miss Hunter." He touched his forehead and offered the sketch of a bow.

Her hands trembled with the desire to pull him into a welcoming embrace, so she thrust them behind her back before she could do something inappropriate. "Captain."

Commotion swelled around them as villagers poured into the clearing from every direction, but for RyAnne it was almost as though a curtain of privacy had been dropped around just the two of them.

The captain leaned closer, a devilish grin tipping up his lips. "No matter how I try to prepare myself to be stoic at the sight of you, your beauty always takes my breath away. It mocks me and makes me realize what a weak-willed man I am."

RyAnne's mouth went dry at the blatant compliments that were so unlike him. She clenched her hands even more tightly around the towel behind her back, feeling the warmth of pleasure that brushed her cheeks. And yet, she knew without a doubt that were she to reciprocate his attentions, he would backpedal faster than if she were a swaying cobra.

"Let's not forget about your woman in the Americas, Captain."

The captain startled. "My what?!"

She let her upraised brow reveal her pique. Could he really be trying to deny it? After he'd just made it clear to her a few weeks past that he had reasons why naught could grow between them? What other reason could there be?

His scrutiny remained steady, but she had no desire to meet him in a challenge at the moment.

Her gaze dropped, and that was when she noticed the wide-eyed child practically clinging to the captain's side. "Who's this?" She softened her tone.

The captain rested a hand on the girl's head. "This is Nyimbo." He cleared his throat. "She lost her family. So I brought her home with us. But let us not get off the subject. I don't know what you think, but—"

RyAnne ignored the man and squatted down to put herself more on the girl's level. She extended one hand. "*Moni*," she greeted.

The child bent her knees as she took the proffered hand. "*Moni-thu*," she responded.

RyAnne stood and spoke to the captain, even while extending one hand to the girl. "She looks hungry. And could certainly use a bath. I'll take care of her. Good afternoon to you, Captain."

The little girl followed her lead without hesitation, and RyAnne led her across the sand toward the hut she and Papa shared.

"Miss Hunter?"

The captain was only trying to waylay her escape. She kept walking, pretending she hadn't heard him.

"RyAnne!" A touch of irritation burnt the edges of the word even though it was accompanied by a chuckle.

She almost halted, but then clenched her jaw and forced herself to keep walking. She refused to allow the man to toy with her emotions!

Chapter 18

A Walk through the Waters

The next day, just after chapel, only two patients waited to be treated. Both injuries were minor, and she had them cleaned and bandaged within a few minutes. Papa declared he was heading back to the hut to lie down for a bit, and since that was not unusual, RyAnne let him go without worry.

She stepped out into the zephyr that kissed the shore, and shaded her eyes from the bright sunlight. Just down the beach, Nyanja practiced on the crutches she'd become quite adept at using, June by her side. RyAnne hadn't spoken with either woman for several days, even though they almost always attended Papa's chapel services, for generally she and Papa went straight to working the clinic after chapel.

And now she suddenly realized how much she was missing female company. Oh what she wouldn't give to be able to walk into the Stone Town house right this moment and share a silly conversation with Jasmine, or even a stolid one with Mother.

With a huff that reminded her to return to reality, RyAnne called out to the women and hurried after them, intent on asking after Moyo and seeing how Nyanja was tolerating pain now that she'd quit taking the opiates.

The women waited for her, and when asked, Nyanja assured her that she was well and Moyo was thriving here in the village. She and Nyimbo were currently playing together at the water's edge down the beach. RyAnne was glad to see her new young charge at least out of the hut. She'd hardly cajoled two words out of the girl yesterday. Likely not surprising, considering what she'd been through so recently.

June and Nyanja leaned close to one another and resumed their conversation in low tones.

Disappointed that the interaction had been so short and that she seemed to be intruding on their conversation, RyAnne folded her arms against the breeze that had picked up quite briskly off the lake. "Okay, well, please let me know if you need anything." She offered a parting smile that she hoped didn't look too self-pitying and then turned to go.

Behind her, June said something, and Nyanja replied.

"Miss Hunter?" June called her to a stop.

Hopes soaring, RyAnne turned. "Yes?"

"Perhaps you could answer a question for us?"

An uneasy feeling lodged in RyAnne's chest. She brushed a strand of hair from her face. "I can try…"

June motioned for her to join them as they walked. "Nyanja and I have been talking about your father's words from the chapel."

RyAnne's heart rate picked up. They wanted to know about spiritual truths? Oh, she certainly wasn't the best one to help them with that! Yet something kept her walking with them. "Yes?"

"Yesterday your father spoke about Jesus loving the world so much that He died on a cross for us."

RyAnne nodded. Papa had drawn a cross in the dirt floor of the chapel to show the villagers what one looked like, and then he had explained, using his medical knowledge, the horrifyingly slow death that took place on a cross, and he'd ended with the challenge for the people to take up their own crosses and follow Jesus, along with an explanation of what that meant.

June pressed on. "I used to attend the chapel on Commodore Cornwall's estate, so I have heard this story before. But Nyanja says maybe this God is only for the *azungu* and not for the Chewa, or any other black tribe. Is this so?"

"No!" RyAnne suddenly longed more than anything for them to believe her next words. "Jesus died for everyone!"

The two women looked at her skeptically. "Then why don't we know any of our people who are serving this God?"

RyAnne swallowed. "You do." The words were out before she could think better of them.

"We do?"

RyAnne nodded. Her heart was beating from the region of her throat now. If she continued with her explanation and told them of her heritage, there would be no going back. Word would spread. Captain Dawson would learn of it, and that might be the final brick in the wall of rationales that seemed intent on keeping them apart. And yet…perhaps this was the very reason the Lord had directed her path to this village? This was something she could offer that not even Papa could.

She swallowed. Took a breath. "Did you know that my mother's mother was from your tribe? She lived in this very village, on this very lake." She swept a gesture to the water.

Both June and Nyanja came to a stop. June's voice was incredulous when she asked, "You carry the blood of the Chewa in your veins?"

RyAnne smiled. Nodded. "My grandmother was taken as a slave from these waters. And my mother was my father's slave before he gave up his own ways and started living for the God he now tells you about. I can assure you that Jesus loves all people, no matter the color of their skin or the blood that flows in their veins."

June and Nyanja laughed incredulously and chattered a few phrases to each other.

"This news makes us very happy," June said.

RyAnne smiled. "Yes, it is good—"

"RyAnne!" From down the beach, the captain dashed toward her.

RyAnne's heart plummeted in her chest. She turned to face him, but resisted voicing all the fears pounding through her.

Trent came to a stop before her and pulled in a breath. "It's your father. You need to come now."

Without a word, she lifted her skirts and took off at a run toward the village. "Where? Our hut?"

"Yes." Trent jogged at her heels.

She was too afraid to ask any more questions, and when a moment later she burst through the door and found Papa lying on his bed, looking pale, but alive and breathing, her strength left her. She collapsed on her knees by his bed. "Papa. What is it?"

His hand trembled as it fumbled across the coverlet to find hers. "It's time, dear girl. I can feel it." The words were barely a wheeze across his lips.

It couldn't be! He'd stood at the front of the chapel and preached a sermon only a bit ago!

RyAnne wanted to protest. She wanted to urge him to fight. But nothing she thought to say seemed right in that moment. She clamped her teeth against the wail that wanted to escape her. "I'm here, Papa. I'm right here."

His fingers tightened around hers. "God gave me…more time… than I expected." He struggled for the breath to say the words.

"Shhh, Papa. Don't speak. Just rest."

"Yes… rest." His eyes drifted closed.

And this time RyAnne couldn't suppress a sob. She knelt by him until her knees were almost too cramped to move, and then she worked her way to her feet and paced the confines of the room.

Captain Dawson sat on a stool across the room, elbows on his knees as he whittled a small stick with his pocketknife, his face grim.

Papa's breaths rattled, but at least they remained mostly steady. Every once in a while the wheezing would stop and RyAnne would freeze, certain this was the end, but then Papa would start breathing again, and her relief would set her to pacing anew.

After several hours, the captain strode from the room and returned a few minutes later with a bowl of broth and a corn cake. He took her arm and led her to her cot, urging her to sit as he held the bowl out to her. "You are going to need your strength."

She tried to push the food away. "I can't."

"Yes. You can." His words left no room for compromise. He took the bowl she handed back to him, and he squatted before her. Lifting a spoon of broth, he gave her a pleading look.

"Captain, please…"

He used her speech as an opportunity to slip the spoon between her lips, and she gave up. It would take less strength to comply—and would certainly be less messy—and she was too weary to fight him on this. She swiped at the broth on her chin and took the bowl from him, broke the corn patty into the broth, and set to eating, giving him one last glower for good measure.

With a satisfied nod, he left her to it and stepped over by her father's side.

They passed the night hours together. Fitfully dozing, pacing, pausing when Papa's breathing stopped, and starting up again only when he resumed. The rattle of death's looming victory gargled at the back of Papa's throat, and RyAnne wanted to put her hands over her ears, or maybe run from the room, more than once that night.

Then just as dawn was breathing light against the horizon, RyAnne lay down next to Papa's pallet and rested her head on the side of his blanket. Papa's hand fumbled across the coverlet and found her, patting gently.

Hope burgeoning, she rose up and took his hand. "Good morning, Papa."

"RyAnne." His voice was dry and scratchy, and she scrambled to fetch him a drink of water, holding the cup carefully to his lips as the captain lifted him slightly and held his head steady. But after only two swallows, he waved a hand weakly to indicate he'd had enough. The captain settled him back against the pallet. Papa's gaze found hers.

"Would you read to me?"

"Of course, Papa."

He eased out a rattling breath. "Psalm ten."

RyAnne started to rise to fetch the Bible, but Trent was already by her side, handing her the book. She accepted it from him. "Thank you."

The captain squeezed her shoulder gently in a gesture of support, and she flipped through the pages until she found the psalm. Then in as steady a voice as she could muster, she began reading.

> "Psalm 10:
> 'Why do You stand afar off, O Lord?
> Why do You hide in times of trouble?'"

A sob gathered at the back of her throat and threatened to

prevent her from finishing the Psalm, but the captain's steady hand on her shoulder gave her the strength she needed to go on.

"'The wicked in his pride persecutes the poor;
Let them be caught in the plots which they have devised.
For the wicked boasts of his heart's desire;
He blesses the greedy and renounces the Lord.
The wicked in his proud countenance does not seek God;
God is in none of his thoughts.
His ways are always prospering;
Your judgments are far above, out of his sight;
As for all his enemies, he sneers at them.
He has said in his heart, "I shall not be moved;
I shall never be in adversity."
His mouth is full of cursing and deceit and oppression;
Under his tongue is trouble and iniquity.
He sits in the lurking places of the villages;
In the secret places he murders the innocent;
His eyes are secretly fixed on the helpless.
He lies in wait secretly, as a lion in his den;
He lies in wait to catch the poor;
He catches the poor when he draws him into his net.
So he crouches, he lies low,
That the helpless may fall by his strength.
He has said in his heart,
"God has forgotten;
He hides His face;
He will never see."
Arise, O Lord!
O God, lift up Your hand!
Do not forget the humble.
Why do the wicked renounce God?
He has said in his heart,
"You will not require an account."
But You have seen, for You observe trouble and grief,
To repay it by Your hand.

The helpless commits himself to You;
You are the helper of the fatherless.
Break the arm of the wicked and the evil man;
Seek out his wickedness until You find none.
  The Lord is King forever and ever;
The nations have perished out of His land.
Lord, You have heard the desire of the humble;
You will prepare their heart;
You will cause Your ear to hear,
To do justice to the fatherless and the oppressed,
That the man of the earth may oppress no more.'"

By the end, RyAnne's voice was so choked that she could barely speak the words.

Papa's hand found hers and squeezed gently. "God…will…do justice to you…child. Do not…be…afraid."

Tears streamed down RyAnne's cheeks, and she set the Bible aside, lest she soak the pages with her grief. She leaned over Papa. "I'm going to be just fine, Papa. You go." She held her breath against the cry of protest and the compulsion to beg him to fight for life.

"Captain?" Papa raised one hand feebly.

Trent stepped around RyAnne and took his hand. "I'm here."

"Remember…your…promises."

Trent wrapped both his hands around Papa's. "I won't forget."

"Letters…" Papa stretched a weak finger in the direction of his trunk. Foam flecked his lips now.

"Yes, Papa. I will find them."

He seemed to relax then. His eyes dropped closed, and his hand went limp in the captain's grip. Carefully the captain laid it down.

Papa roused. "My Bible." He flexed his fingers.

RyAnne retrieved it and handed it to him, and with his last remaining strength, he pulled the book onto his chest and hugged it to himself. Then his eyes closed, and sleep once more claimed him.

Time passed, one agonizingly slow second after another. RyAnne stayed by Papa's side, wiping from his lips the death foam that indicated he was slowly drowning, and trying to keep him as comfortable as possible. The captain tried to get her to leave the hut for a few minutes at noon to eat, but she adamantly refused him, and he gave up without too much protest—but only when she took a few bites of the roast venison he'd brought to her. She felt numb, and barely tasted the food.

And then late in the afternoon, Papa finally drew his last breath, and the hut rang with silence. Kneeling by his pallet, RyAnne waited, half hoping he would rally and half praying that his battle on this plane was completed.

After a few minutes she wearily reached out to feel for a pulse, and found none. She dropped her head onto her arms, too overwhelmed to even cry just yet.

The captain placed a hand gently on her head and then stepped outside, presumably to let those gathered know that Papa had passed.

After a few long minutes, RyAnne rose from her knees and looked down at the only man who'd ever known everything about her and still loved her. Taking up the towel, she wiped the foam from his lips one last time. She'd never felt such despair and desolation before. They draped her like a clinging fog—inescapable and heavy. How was she going to go on without him?

Carefully, she brushed Papa's hair back from his face and straightened the collar of his shirt. She pried the Bible from beneath his limp fingers and laid his hands one atop the other.

Her fingers rubbed at the smooth sheen his daily use had given to the leather of the book. Only this morning… Her fist curled around the spine of the Bible until it shook.

Outside, the piercing keening she ought to have expected started up. First one lonely high-pitched voice, and then as others joined in, a chorus of them. All screeching shrilly at the top of their lungs. The sound of the village women mourning grated on RyAnne's nerves and made her want to rage at the world.

Before she realized her own intent, she hurled the Bible

across the hut with a guttural cry.

Splayed pages splatted against the mud wall and then fell to her bed.

She stared at the ruffled mess, feeling immense guilt for having treated something so precious in such a manner, and then the first sob heaved up from inside her, followed by a second and a third.

Her knees started to give, but then Trent was there, wrapping her in a firm embrace and pressing her head to his chest. She hadn't even known he'd returned. "I'm here, RyAnne. I'm sorry. I'm so sorry."

She clung to him like he was life itself, gripping handfuls of his shirt and crying so hard no sound escaped except when she heaved for breath. How long they stood that way, she had no idea. But Trent stayed with her, murmuring soft words of comfort against her hair. Time seemed eternal yet dead all in the same moment. Finally she stood quiet, her cheek resting against the beat of Trent's heart, his shirt still fisted in one hand, but more loosely now.

He smoothed her hair from her forehead and damp face, then dropped his cheek against the top of her head and simply held her, rocking gently.

Through the open door of the hut, she could see Nyanja balancing carefully on her one leg as she stood respectfully in the crowd of wailing women. Moyo and Nyimbo sat, with forlorn expressions, in the dust at Nyanja's feet.

RyAnne stirred and swiped at the moisture on her face, but she couldn't pull herself away from the comfort of his embrace just yet. "Did you hear the verses I read to Papa this morning?"

Trent stroked her hair again, burying his fingers in the curls at the back of her head. "Yes. I heard."

She rested one palm against her cheek. "My faith is weak, Captain. I haven't had a chance to tell you about Chief Wankulu. He came while you were away, and I caught him beating Yani, his wife. He wanted her to return to his village with him, but she didn't want to go. And I realized that was how I had been wanting

God to deal with the slavers. To force them to his bidding. But in that flash of a moment when I saw Wankulu leaning over Yani with that whip in his hand, I knew true love would never force someone to do something." She paused, thankful to hear that the keening outside seemed to be coming to a stop. How did she assemble all her jumbled thoughts together to make sense of them? Finally she continued, "I know that Nyanja is likely better off now that she is free of Khalifa, and perhaps that wouldn't have come about if she hadn't lost her leg. And I know that Papa is in a much better place now, with no pain or suffering. And as stated, I know that true love never would use force. Yet still my heart wants to demand why God doesn't do more?!" She gestured to the two little girls still visible out the door. "Nyimbo, for instance. Why did she have to lose her entire family? Couldn't God have sent someone to help them in time?"

Trent eased back and crooked one finger under her chin, lifting her face to meet his gaze. "I think you've just hit on the key. What if someone was supposed to step in and help? Yet, in the freedom of choice God's love demands, they chose not to act?"

RyAnne's eyes widened a little at that. Would all her resentment and frustration toward God for failing to step in, better be directed at people who had failed to fulfill their calling?

Trent's gaze bore steadily into her own. "I confess I've had the same questions. When I see the destruction slavery brings, I fear my doubts arise. And yet, God chooses to use people, RyAnne." He tipped his head toward the village outside. "He sent them you. He sent them you, and me, and your father." He followed that with a gesture toward Papa lying so still on his pallet. "And he sent him *you*, to be an encouragement and support in his last days."

She blinked. And her thoughts returned to the conversation she'd been in the middle of with June and Nyanja when the captain had fetched her to Papa's side. Perhaps God had used her concern over Papa's health to bring her along not only to take care of Papa, but to take Papa's place once he was gone?

Trent caressed the line of her jaw, but his gaze wandered to the scene beyond the doorway. "You and I, RyAnne, we came kicking and screaming. But your father, he came with a willing heart, and look how much good he did in the short time he was here. There's already a chapel and a clinic of sorts. What does the last part of the Psalm say? Do you remember?"

She pulled in a shuddering breath. "'To do justice to the fatherless and the oppressed, that the man of the earth may oppress no more.'"

He murmured his agreement. "I think the time when earthly mortals will oppress no more is yet to come, but in the meantime, we are here. And God wants to use us. We must take up our crosses—give our fleshly desires over to God so He can show us what He wants of us, just like He did for your father. Let us defend the fatherless and work for the oppressed, as willing tools in His arsenal."

RyAnne nodded. "As said, my faith is weak. Yet who else but God holds the words of life? I don't see how we can do anything else." She glanced at Papa, and another wave of tears coursed over her. "On the other hand, I don't know if I have the strength to aid anyone."

Trent lifted her face once more, brushing her tears away with his thumbs as he cupped her cheeks in his hands. "I'm here. I'm not going anywhere. Lean on me, but mostly lean on the Lord. He will be your strength. The One who carries you through the trials of this life to the end of your days."

She nodded. "Yes." A wave of weariness, so strong that it nearly took the strength from her knees, tugged for her attention. She rubbed her eyes and willed herself to think.

But Trent took her arm and directed her over to her bed across the room. "Rest, RyAnne. I will take care of preparing him. I promise to wake you in a few hours."

She gave in to him, too weary to fight.

RyAnne was asleep almost before she could swing her legs up onto her pallet. Trent brushed her hair back from her face and felt the heaviness of the burden he now bore for her safety. Only a bit ago when he'd stepped out to let the village know of the doctor's passing, Kako had confided to Trent that RyAnne had told June and Nyanja that she carried native blood. The news should have surprised him, but it hadn't, because suddenly so many things about the Hunter family had clicked into place—RyAnne's dark looks compared to her siblings, Anne's constant aversion to and abrasive behavior toward RyAnne, and Ryan Hunter's bent toward giving RyAnne anything she cajoled him for.

No, the news hadn't shocked him. What it had done was send a wave of terror through him, because now, with Ryan Hunter passed on, it would be legal in every way for anyone to capture RyAnne and sell her, providing they did so only on the island of Zanzibar. Or, once they returned to the island, for Anne Hunter to put RyAnne on the auction block. Would the woman do something like that? He scrubbed one hand down his face, then shook his head. No. Anne Hunter was much too concerned with her own reputation to sully it with such actions.

But any of the natives… Trent clenched his teeth. A woman as beautiful as RyAnne would fetch an exceptional sum that might be enough to entice even the most upright of souls into betrayal.

RyAnne stirred restlessly, and he laid a hand against her head. "Shhh, RyAnne. I'm here. Just rest." His touch seemed to calm her, and she settled into sleep once more.

Trent wrapped one of her curls around his finger and stroked it with his thumb. Four months ago he would have scoffed at anyone who told him he would come to care for the girl, and now all he could think about was that he must do everything in his power to protect her. He would get her back to Stone Town as soon as possible.

But for now, he needed to get her father's body ready for burial. He rose quietly so as not to disturb her.

Wankulu had been escorted from the village, at the point of several spears, and sent along his way with a firm invective never to return. Now he stood by the side of the path, hands clasped behind his head, and watched the path that had remained empty since the headmen had returned to the village. He pivoted and scanned the path in the direction of what had once been his own prosperous village—before the *azungu* had come along and encouraged the rebellion of all his subjects, including his wife!

Bah! He needed to think.

A large baobab grew to the side of the path, casting a long patch of shade, and he strode to it and squatted to his haunches to think. He was still sitting thus when two men on their way out for a hunt stopped by to give him the news. The *azungu* doctor was dead. And it had come to be known that the *azungu* woman carried some blood of The People in her veins. Because of this, her father was being given the highest honor of burial in the graveyard of the chiefs.

Wankulu grunted his acknowledgement of the news, but as the two men walked away, he plucked a blade of grass and tucked it between his teeth, a gleam of satisfaction in his eyes.

So…the *azungu* woman who had run him out of his hut at the point of her gun wasn't so *azungu* after all? And it was obvious this woman was of great interest to the *azungu* captain, who had encouraged both Wankulu's wife and his people to abandon him. He was also friends with Kako, son of the great-chief, and the one who had planted the seeds of the rebellion in the hearts of Wankulu's people. And what hurt the *azungu* captain was sure to hurt Kako.

Thus the answer to Wankulu's problems had been handed to him as though already dangling from the end of a spear. Now he knew exactly how to repay them, and he wouldn't even be required to expend himself to do it.

Rising, he strode from the shade and started out at a trot on a path leading toward the place where the sun lifted into the sky each morning.

Chapter 19
A Walk through the Waters

RyAnne clutched her violin case to herself and watched numbly as the four men lifted the stretcher that carried Papa's enshrouded body.

Trent stepped up to her side. Concern etched his features. "Ready?"

She nodded, but the truth was she would never be ready for this moment.

Trent motioned the men to proceed.

They made their way through the village, and from every direction people stepped out to join the procession. A woman about halfway back down the line once more broke into a loud *lulu*ing yowl that sent a jolt through RyAnne at the first piercing cry. Soon women all along the procession picked up the wail. Even though the loud sound of their traditional keening was a sign of respect for Papa, it was almost more than RyAnne's nerves could take.

Only the captain's steady hand at her back kept her from screaming for them all to be silent. Her feet felt made of lead, and her heart also, as they strode past the last huts at the edge of the village and headed down the path to the thorn-bush-fenced graveyard of the chiefs. To prevent animals from sneaking in later and disturbing the graves, the gate in the thorny wall was opened, and then closed as soon as the procession had passed through.

When they arrived at the grave site, RyAnne once again nearly came to her undoing as she stared at the hole in the ground. All around her, everything seemed blurry—the keening, the colors, the people—everything but the hole dug into the sandy taupe earth. The hole that was so deep, only shadow delineated the bottom. The hole that would soon hold the body of her dear, dear Papa.

The wind picked up and whipped a strand of hair across her face, and with relief she closed her eyes.

The captain had volunteered to say a few words, and she was

ever so grateful because she didn't think she could have found her voice were the task left up to her.

Holding Papa's Bible, the captain stepped to the front, and slowly the wailing died off as the people prepared to listen.

As the silence descended, RyAnne felt the release of some of her tension. She pulled in a calming breath, brushed her hair from her face, and turned her gaze to the swaying fronds of the palm tree overhead. She didn't want her last glimpse of Papa to be one of him being lowered into the ground. But she couldn't block out the sounds of scuffing and the swish and soft thud as Papa's body slid from the stretcher into his grave. She blinked hard to hold the tears at bay, knowing that if she let them start, she would have a hard time putting a stop to them again. Finally the four bearers stepped back, and RyAnne allowed her focus to descend from the treetops.

With Kako by his side as translator, the captain spoke. "For the past weeks the doctor has talked to you in his chapel of a God who wants only the best for you." He paused, waiting for Kako to translate. "That same God has a place of peace for us to go when we die. The good doctor is there even now, because the Bible, God's Word, assures us that to be absent from the body is to be present with our Lord. The doctor feels no more pain. Will never again experience sickness or death or tears."

A murmur traversed the villagers at this apparently odd teaching, but the captain didn't seem fazed. He opened Papa's Bible, and as he began to read, RyAnne recognized the passage from the twenty-first chapter of Revelation, describing heaven. And with each new verse about the lack of pain and sorrow, the peace, and the beauty of the place, RyAnne found herself imagining Papa there even now, perhaps receiving the grand tour from Jesus himself. And as much as she was going to miss him, she couldn't begrudge him the joy he must be feeling.

The captain concluded his short talk and nodded to her. She had requested to play her violin for her papa one last time, but now as her fingers trembled against the latches of the case, she wondered if she would even be able to draw out the first note.

Her gaze skittered to the hole and then to the captain.

There was a world of understanding in his eyes. He tilted his head as though asking if she wanted him to continue without her song.

No. She would do this for Papa.

With firm resolve, she snapped open the latches and smoothed back the velvet cover. The wood was like hardened silk beneath her fingers as she lifted the instrument out. She tightened the bow and tucked the chin rest close, shutting her eyes at the familiar feel of it. A sob was almost her undoing, but she clamped it off, sniffed, and pulled in a fortifying breath. For Papa. One last time.

She played his favorite hymn, "When I Survey the Wondrous Cross." She repeated the tune four times and sang each verse silently in her mind.

When I survey the wondrous cross
On which the Prince of glory died,
My richest gain I count but loss,
And pour contempt on all my pride.

Forbid it, Lord, that I should boast,
Save in the death of Christ my God!
All the vain things that charm me most,
I sacrifice them to His blood.

See from His head, His hands, His feet,
Sorrow and love flow mingled down!
Did e'er such love and sorrow meet,
Or thorns compose so rich a crown?

Were the whole realm of nature mine,
That were a present far too small;
Love so amazing, so divine,
Demands my soul, my life, my all.

And Papa had given his all.

She pulled in a breath, and this time she played straight from her heart. Releasing the cry of anguish that had been building slowly there since she'd first figured out that Papa would not be recovering from what they'd thought a chill. She let all her sorrow whisper through her bow, and then she let it speak, and then she let it shout, building to a crescendo that had her closing her eyes. *Do you hear me, Lord? What now?* Softly, once again she played her prayer.

And this time she wanted to look at the people her papa had given everything for.

She turned her body slightly so she could study the villagers as they listened. These were her people. Was she related to any of them? After Papa had told her about her grandmother being from this village, she hadn't even thought beyond that. But now…

The notes from her violin lifted on the breeze and melded with the soft song of the palm branches.

All along this journey she had thought that the moment Papa passed, she would head back home to Zanzibar. But…perhaps God had prepared the way for her to come here for just this moment—to continue Papa's ministry after he was gone. The gentle wind kissed her face, bringing with it the sweet scent of the waters of the lake. She closed her eyes once more, but this time… This time the notes of the song transformed from minor to major as a little of her despair lifted. A brighter tune flowed as a fraction of her sorrow drifted away.

Mother and Jasmine didn't need her. Rory certainly didn't need her. But these people. Yes. These people needed her. This was her call. Here God could use her, and hopefully, as she stepped in to fill the need, her response, her *choice*, would bring blessing and prevent some measure of evil from befalling these people. *Use me, Father, as You wish, to lessen the pain in this sin-sick world. And help me to hear Your directing voice.*

With a sigh she drew out the final note long and slow and then dropped the violin to her side.

A murmur of appreciative awe swept over those gathered. This was the first time any of them had heard her play. And RyAnne determined it would not be the last.

Hadn't the captain said as much just the other day? *We must take up our crosses—give our fleshly desires over to God so He can show us what He wants of us, just like He did for your father. Let us defend the fatherless and work for the oppressed, as willing tools in His arsenal.*

RyAnne nodded to the captain that she was done as she tucked the violin back into its case.

Captain Dawson closed Papa's Bible and lifted it in one hand for the people to see. "The same God who gives us these promises can be spoken to just as you and I speak with each other on a daily basis." Kako repeated the words to the people, and then the captain continued. "Let us speak to Him now." Captain Dawson bowed his head and committed Papa's spirit into the Lord's hands. Afterward, he stepped over to her side.

RyAnne reached out and squeezed his arm, offering a weary smile. "Thank you, Captain. Your reminder about heaven was a great comfort to me." Behind them, two men set to filling the grave, and each thud of dirt felt like the impact of a fist against RyAnne's chest. She closed her eyes, once more willing herself to keep a rein on her emotions.

The captain pressed his hand against her back. "I'm sorry. Let us return to the village."

She nodded and stepped out ahead of him.

The captain tucked his hands behind himself as he strolled beside her. "The second song you played. It was beautiful, but I didn't recognize it. What was it?"

RyAnne brushed a lock of hair from her eyes. "It was mine."

The captain looked over at her. "Truly?"

She nodded. "Sometimes a tune has just been building inside me, and I have to let it out."

"Do you ever mark them down?"

RyAnne shrugged. "I'm no composer, Captain."

They had arrived at her hut, and they paused outside the door. "The song you just played belies your words. You have a wonderful talent, as I've told you in the past. You should mark the songs down."

RyAnne had no rejoinder for that, so she merely looked down at her clasped hands.

The captain's feet shuffled. "We've plans to discuss, but I can see you are weary. Rest for a while, and I'll return this evening?"

RyAnne was weary. But there was no need for the captain to make any plans. She set her violin case inside the door, and spoke to him over her shoulder. "I've decided to stay."

He actually jolted, then folded his arms over his chest, his white shirt billowing in the breeze. "You've what?" Challenge radiated from his every pore.

"You said it yourself. We must take up our crosses and serve as the Lord asks us to."

"Yes, I said it. But…things have changed." He kicked at a stone, then looked out toward the waves cresting onto the shore.

RyAnne felt something go still inside her. "What has changed?"

The captain's jaw bunched. "You were only here for your father, not for the Lord. Don't mistake duty for calling."

RyAnne tilted her head and studied the village huts she could see spread along the perimeter of the lake. "Perhaps." She waved a hand. "I've no will to argue at the moment. Can we talk about this another time?"

His lips thinned. "Rest for now, but yes. We will speak of this again."

She ought to tell him her decision was made and there would be no profit for him in further discussion, but her capacity for keeping her composure was just about expired. She needed some privacy. She retreated into her hut. "Thank you, Captain."

And with that she closed the door, strode across the room, and collapsed onto her cot. She gave in to the wave of grief pulsing over her, and great sobs shook her.

Wankulu found the men he'd been searching for, just as the sun rose above the mountains to the east. He had run from one village to the next all day and all night, but now he would tell his tale, and then he would sleep most peacefully knowing his enemies would be repaid for their wrongs against him.

The slavers were just rising, and the Arab squatted near the fire, holding his hands to the flames as a pot steamed in the fire's center.

Wankulu approached the edge of the light, dropped to one knee, bowed his head, and clapped his hands. The deference grated, but it would hopefully gain him favor.

To his right he could hear the clang of metallic links *tink*ing together. The sound sent a jolt of trepidation through him. Perhaps this hadn't been the wisest move on his part. It was rather like marching up to the outskirts of a pride of lions and then announcing himself. Perhaps he should retreat and rethink his intended revenge?

But before he had time to move, the call for him to enter the circle of light rang out. "*Lowani*."

To retreat now that he had been acknowledged would have the lions chasing him down, so pressing down his panic, he stood, scooted forward a few steps, and then lowered himself to one knee again.

If he played this right, perhaps the spirits would ensure that he didn't end up chained to the line of slaves.

"Speak," one of the traders prodded. "What is your purpose?"

Wankulu kept his face turned toward the ground. "It is my understanding that you are not only searching for strong healthy slaves but for beautiful women also?"

A quick glance showed the Arab appeared more interested in picking at his teeth with a stem of grass than in Wankulu's news.

He felt a bead of sweat slip between his shoulder blades.

Finally the trader responded. "What of it?"

"I know of a village that is very prosperous. Their chief works his people hard, so their gardens grow lush, and they are a vigorous and strong people."

"There are many such villages all along the way." The disinterest in the man's tone was leaning toward irritation now.

Wankulu willed away his trembling. “Yes. This is true. But in this village there is a woman of great beauty. One who would fetch three, maybe four times the amount that any of those might fetch you.” He tipped a nod toward the sound of the chains.

The Arab lowered the grass stem and tilted his head. “Tell me more.”

Wankulu licked his lips and pressed down his excitement. “First, let us speak of my price…”

Far to the north, a coastal town, along the Gulf of Aden, lay baking in the sun. A ship flying the flag of England, but most freshly from trading their goods in Oman, pulled into the harbor, but no stevedores strode out to meet her. The captain docked the ship, and for a long moment he and his crew stood in the breeze on the deck, staring at the seemingly abandoned docks.

A gull whined far above them, answered by another. Waves sloshed against the underside of the dock in a constant rhythm. And off to the right a mongrel sat on its haunches, eyeing them. But not a soul stirred.

The captain tested the scent of the wind. Fetid fish. Briny water. Moss. Mold. Dust. All scents common to a wharf. But missing were the scents of alehouse meals and woodsmoke.

After a moment, one sailor covered himself with the sign of the cross. “’Tis an omen, Cap. Ought to be movin’ onta th’ nex’ town, we should.”

The captain was never one to go in for superstition, however, and he brushed away his crewman’s concerns. “We’ve need o’ water, Jonesy.” He snapped his fingers at his first mate. “Send a crew ashore to see what’s about. Look sharp.”

The market square, which should have been filled with the bustle of activity, lay silent as a grave. Only the scuttle of a leaf scooting along the cobbles created any sound.

One of the sailors bumped into the first mate from behind. “Gives me an eerie feelin’, this does, sir. Let us water up, and right fast, so's to be on our way."

"I concur." The first mate shuddered and motioned back toward the ship. "Bring the buckets."

The city well lay in the market square close to the harbor side. And while several men dashed back to the ship to fetch buckets, two others set to drawing up the first fresh water from the depths. Never had the brigade worked so quickly, or so smoothly, with each other. To a man they were all eager to be shut of the place. Above them a buzzard loosed a loud cry that set several of the men to crossing themselves, and the buckets moved down the line even faster after that.

By the time they left the town, still not a soul had come into sight, but the wind was strong and filled their sails like the overfull cheeks of a hungry babe. They sailed for fifteen minutes in utter silence, and then Charles Cottrell, the newest member of the crew, socked the man next to him in the arm. The two men looked at one another and burst out laughing as relief at being away from the place set in. Soon the men all along the deck were laughing and joking and jabbing one another.

Comfortable and relieved now that they were away from the place and back in the familiar vastness of the sea with nothing having gone wrong, they settled into their routines.

Charles Cottrell died two days later.

Jasmine Hunter was still laughing at the antics of one of her students as she pulled on her gloves and stepped from the small cottage they were using for a schoolhouse.

Garrett Holloman, dressed in tight black breeches and a free-flowing white shirt, was leaning, arms folded, against the nutmeg tree at the edge of the school yard.

Jasmine halted, gave her gloves an irritated tug, and then strode toward him. "I told you I didn't need you to walk me home."

He straightened languidly and leaned into his heels. "And I

told you I would be here. You may walk several paces ahead of me if you don't like the idea of being seen with me."

She sniffed. "It has nothing to do with not wanting to be seen with you." She spun and started down the road at a fast clip. Maybe he would get the message and leave her be, for her heart was certainly taking a beating each time he came around, and she didn't know if it would last the month if he insisted on showing up every day to walk her home from classes.

"Doesn't it?" His brows lifted, and he fell into step beside her. "Well, hope lifts all ships."

Jasmine spun toward him. "What does that mean?"

Garrett batted away her question and then lifted his hand to work the muscles in his neck. "Nothing. Forget I said anything."

"You may be a man who can easily forget things that are said, but I assure you I am not of that ilk!" Jasmine took a calming breath, her cheeks heating over the fury coating the words she'd just flung at him. And before he could take note of it, she spun away and resumed her smart march toward town.

He wasn't far behind. "And now it is my turn to ask what you mean, Miss Hunter."

"Nothing. Forget I said anything." She tossed his own words back in his face, aggravated that he seemed to be casually strolling and yet still kept pace with her.

"So! It appears we are at yet another impasse. Shocking, I must say." The sarcasm dripping from his words could have drowned an army.

She spun toward him and stopped, no matter that they were right in the middle of the road. "We would never have needed to be at *any* impasse if your word meant something to you!" She would not cry! She wouldn't! She started to spin away from him again, but this time his hand shot out and gripped her arm.

He stepped closer and leaned in. "My word means everything to me, Miss Hunter. And if you are suggesting I lied to you about something, I certainly would like to know to what you are referring!" Anger glinted in the depths of his blue eyes.

Jasmine sniffed and lifted her chin, blinking hard but

refusing to look away. The problem was…she couldn't very well say anything without revealing too much of her heart. And she would rather die than let this pompous, arrogant knave know he had hurt her. "It was nothing."

His hand tightened on her arm, and he tilted her a look. "Jas."

"Don't call me that! You have no right!"

"Don't I?" He stepped closer, his countenance softening. "I thought the time we spent together meant as much to you as it did to me."

"And then you left without so much as a fare-thee-well!" The words were out before she could rethink them. It was his confounded eyes! She couldn't look into that velvety blue without falling headlong into honesty.

"Without so much as a fare—" He stepped back and lowered his chin, folding his arms. "So the silver tea service I sent over—the one that I paid a good bit of coin to have your name and a cluster of Jasmine flowers engraved on—that counted for nothing? And the letter that accompanied it, asking you to wait—oh, dash it." He swiped a hand through the air as though wishing he could erase this entire conversation, and started off toward town. "Never mind."

But Jasmine wasn't going to let him off so easy. Whatever was he talking about? "I have no idea what you mean, but I can assure you that I never received such a gift from you. Nor a letter!"

He paused and spun toward her. "Come again?"

Jasmine felt the hard and stony places inside her turn soft like Mama's sponge cake sopped in strawberry juice. Could the man really have sent such a gift to her? And what had he said in the letter? Asked her to wait…wait for what? Her heart rate picked up at just the thought of the answer. It could have changed everything she'd been feeling for the past months if it was true. Could change everything now. Her mouth went dry. She lifted her skirts and stepped past him.

"I think this conversation has run its course, Mr. Holloman. Let's just head into town, if you please."

The irritating man muttered something as he strode out after her. She couldn't quite make it out, but it sounded like he said, "Oh, I'll head into town, and that's for certain."

Chapter 20

A Walk through the Waters

Two weeks later Trent intercepted June as she was bringing some dinner to RyAnne at her hut. On every occasion that he'd set himself to the task of convincing RyAnne it was time to return home, his conscience had pricked him to give her a few more days to grieve. But now the task could be delayed no longer.

Reports of unrest in the surrounding villages were growing. Runners came daily to report another village had been sacked. Either a new slave trader was making his way through the area, or Khalifa had reversed his course and was backtracking.

And no matter which it was, it didn't bode well for RyAnne.

So despite her protests, for the past two weeks Trent had bedded down outside her hut, and he'd gotten little sleep. He'd seen too many greedy looks cast upon RyAnne to let his guard down. It would take only a moment of inattention on his part and RyAnne could fall to the mercy of some villager bent on profit alone. She was far too trusting of everyone, just as she had been back home on the island. Despite her grieving, she'd continued to open the clinic each morning and had run the services at the chapel each afternoon. And yesterday he'd nearly been in a panic when he'd stepped away from the clinic for two minutes and returned to find her gone. His relief when he'd found her tending to the newest village baby had nearly taken the strength from his knees.

And then last night, as he'd lain with his hands clasped behind his head studying the stars above, it had hit him… During their long months of travel, he had been careful to keep his growing estimation of RyAnne hidden for her protection. But now, since she'd made the news of her heritage known, his publicly staked claim on her might be the only protection she would have.

Holding the bowl of vittles in one hand and the cup of tea in the other, he studied the door of her hut with some trepidation.

Why did he have a feeling she wasn't going to take the news at all well? Swallowing away his concern, he knocked on the flimsy wood door with the toe of one boot.

"Come," she called.

He entered and then froze. She obviously hadn't been expecting him. Though she was fully clothed, she sat cross-legged on her mat, with her hair tumbled about her and a hair brush in one hand.

"Captain!" She scrambled to her feet, rapidly gathering her mass of ebony curls at the back of her neck. "I thought you would be June."

Trent swallowed and strode purposefully to the small table on the other side of the room. He hadn't been in here since her father's passing. He'd expected that she would have rolled up her father's mat and gathered his things into his trunk, but every item lay almost exactly as it had the last time he'd been in here. Trent rested his fingers against the table and kept his back to her, giving her time to put herself together. The vision of her hair cascading all about her slender shoulders returned to him, and he closed his eyes against it.

After a moment she spoke. "What can I do for you, Captain?"

Taking that as permission, he turned to face her. She stood quietly, hands folded before her. No fancy silks or lace, and with nothing but a mud wall behind her, and she was still the most beautiful woman he'd ever seen.

His first instinct was to blurt out that she should marry him, but that wouldn't do at all. He bit one side of his lip. Blast this infernal wasteland with no priest or pastor for hundreds of miles. He must think his next words through carefully, or she would laugh him right out the door, and rightly so.

He folded his arms. Perhaps he could quietly stake his claim on her among the villagers without even having to bring her in on the plan? Yes. That might keep her safe in the short term. But his main goal needed to be in talking her back to Zanzibar. "Before your father passed, he asked that I do all in my power to protect you after he was gone."

At the mention of her father, she blinked several times and smoothed her hands over her skirts. "Yes. I know that. And I thank you."

"Since your father seemed to trust me, I would ask that you also trust my judgment and heed my council."

She tilted him a look, one eyebrow cocked and her lips twisted in a way that made it plain she was admonishing him to return to reality.

But he wouldn't be dissuaded. "RyAnne, you must go back to Zanzibar."

She stiffened and lifted her chin stubbornly.

He reassessed. The words had come out more forcefully than he intended. To soften their impact he added, "Your family will be worried about you once they hear of your father's passing."

She brushed the thought away with the swipe of one hand. "I will write to them so they know of my well-being. My place is here, Captain. If you yourself want to return to the island, I release you from any perceived commitment to my safety, and I thank you for your concern."

"Perceived commit—" Trent snapped his teeth together before his surge of frustration got the better of him. "You've no need to thank me."

"Nevertheless, I do, Captain. And I've quite made up my mind so…" She let the rest of the thought trail away as though the matter was settled.

Perhaps a reminder of what she'd so stubbornly wanted only weeks ago was in order. "Think back to the time we spent on Commodore Llewellyn's estate. You would have done just about anything to return to Zanzibar then."

She sighed and pressed her palms together. "Yes, but that was before"—a sweep of her hand encompassed the village—"I met these people. Before I knew they were *my* people, and recognized how much I could do to help them. You yourself said just the other day that perhaps much of the evil in the world happens because people don't heed God's call to step in. My family will be fine without me, Captain, but here they need me."

"You are the most stubborn woman on the face of the earth!" The words burst forth before he could lay hold of them.

Her gaze flew to his, her mouth falling open slightly.

He scraped one hand through his hair and gripped the back of his neck. "I'm sorry. I shouldn't have spoken so harshly. I just feel the burden for your safety quite heavily." He worked his teeth over his lip. Perhaps the best thing was to tell her his feelings outright. He softened his tone. "My commitment is not out of duty to your father's request. Even had he asked me to leave you to your own devices after his passing, yet I would be here still." He held her focus steadily, willing her to see the true meaning of the words shining in his eyes.

She licked her lips. "Captain, perhaps you have not heard. I've wanted to tell you many times but couldn't quite decide how to approach the subject…"

When her voice trailed away, he decided to make it easy on her. "Kako has informed me that your birth mother was a slave."

She squinted at him, as though trying to assess how he felt about the information. "You know? And still you are here?"

He frowned. "Why would I not be here?"

"It's just that most men would have—" She pivoted partially away from him, rolled her lips in, and pressed them together, then paced to the door he'd left open upon his entry, and stared out toward the lake. "Only a couple months past, you informed me naught could grow between us, Captain." There was a beat, and then she continued, "I've resigned myself to this reality."

The words were like a spear-thrust to his heart, yet the hand she laid against the doorpost at her shoulder trembled, and that gave him hope. "All that has changed now. Where once my veneration of you might have brought you danger, now that you have made your heritage known, a relationship with me might be your only safety."

Her hand on the doorpost clenched into a fist. "I see. So 'tis only for my safety that you…" She tossed him a glance, then folded her arms. "I knew full well the danger I might be placing myself in when I disclosed my secret, Captain. And I'll not have you sacrifice all you hold dear simply because you are concerned for my well-being."

Whatever was she talking about? A few swift strides placed him at her side, where he took her hand and turned her to face him. "Apparently I have not made it clear enough that all I hold most dear in the world stands directly before me." He raised one hand to touch her chin and heard her take in a small breath.

"Trent, please don't toy with me."

He felt one side of his mouth lift on the tug of a smile, for she'd said his name on her own without him having to beg her for it. Her chin was soft under the caress of his knuckle. "Always I have endeavored to honesty, yet now you would accuse me of toying, little lioness?"

"Back along the trail I got the impression you were courting a woman… in the Americas perhaps? What about her?"

Trent didn't even try to prevent the bark of laughter that burst forth. "Courting a woman in the Americas? Whatever gave you such an idea?"

Her lips turned petulant. "When you said you couldn't see me, I presumed there was another."

He drew her hand against his chest. "My reasons for not seeing you were to keep you far from danger, as stated. But trust me when I say that on many an occasion my heart has protested the requirement for distance I laid upon myself."

She still didn't look convinced.

"There is not, nor has there ever been, another woman in my life, save my mother, God rest her." He tucked a wayward strand of her hair back into place.

RyAnne tilted her head. "Do you only woo me in an attempt to gain my capitulation to return to Zanzibar?"

He shook his head. "Never."

Her lips quirked. The first inclination that he might have been ensnared in a trap zipped through him.

"Good then, for I am quite determined to stay."

As she giggled, he growled. "If that pleading look you are casting my way elicited in your father anywhere near the same desire to satisfy you as it does in me, it is no wonder the man constantly let you have your way."

A gentle blush touched her cheeks, and she fanned herself with one hand. "Will you walk with me along the shore? I've a sudden desire for some fresh air."

Trent's sudden desire had more to do with bumping the door closed and kissing her until they were both out of breath, but for now he contented himself with tucking her hand against his arm and leading her out into the evening breeze.

From a fishing canoe out upon the lake, Khalifa peered through his field glasses toward the hut at one end of the village where Wankulu had assured him this "woman of most unusual beauty" lived.

Beside him, Wankulu prodded for the hundredth time. "Can you see her yet?"

Khalifa lowered the glasses to glower at the man. "Stop pestering. I will let you know if I see anything." Before resuming his scrutiny, he rolled his neck first to one side and then to the other. This wait with the heat of the sun beating down on him and the sweat dripping out from beneath his kofia was beginning to wear on him.

Wankulu couldn't be setting him up in some way with false information, could he? It was not the first time he'd had the thought, and for that reason he'd brought an extra guard with him in the canoe. But he suddenly realized that Wankulu could have bribed the man, for which native ever had been faithful and trustworthy? He eyed his guard carefully. The man sat, arms folded and stoic, at the back of the canoe.

Deciding he was being paranoid, Khalifa lifted the glasses back to his eyes just in time to see a flash of motion near the door of the hut. Someone had entered the abode, and he'd missed seeing who it was! The door was left open now, but the interior was too dark for him to make anything out.

With frustration, he lowered the glasses again and swiped at a trickle of sweat slipping down the back of his neck. Wankulu had been able to tell him very little about the woman other than that she was fair skinned and had recently arrived at the village. But he'd been most adamant that she would fetch a soaring price on an auction block. Perhaps the woman was descended from one of the tribes far to the north. Many of them were quite light skinned.

He caught a flicker of movement and lifted the glasses. Someone was in the doorway but standing just far enough back to remain mostly hidden in shadow. Blast this heat! He scooped his kofia into the lake and dumped a measure of the cool water over his head, shaking away the drippings from his eyes. He would be dry within moments, and likely be hot again, but for now the coolness brought great relief.

Wankulu finally settled into silence, and for several moments the only sounds were the cries of the fish eagles diving for their dinners, the occasional splash from a blue trout leaping at some unlucky bug, and the chattering from the troop of monkeys in the palm trees along the shore. On the beach to the north, a hippo and her calf emerged from the lake to snort through the long grasses at the back of the sand.

And then more movement caught Khalifa's eye. He swung the glasses back to focus on the hut. His eyes widened, and he cursed all the crazy gods who had made him believe Wankulu's foolish story.

In an instant he'd dropped the binoculars into his bag on the bottom of the canoe and leaped over to take Wankulu by the throat.

The man's eyes bulged as he clutched at Khalifa's wrist and tried vainly to take in air. Khalifa glanced over at his guard. The man must be faithful after all, for he remained in his stoic pose, simply watching the two of them. Khalifa returned his focus to Wankulu. "You fool! That woman is whiter than your teeth! Her father is a doctor and indigo plantation owner on the island of Zanzibar, and her mother is as blond as a Dane!"

Wankulu shook his head pitifully and tried to speak. But Khalifa was having none of it. He had sat baking in the sun for the entire afternoon! And he'd returned miles along the trail! He could have been days farther along the way toward the coast and a comfortable bed, but instead he'd agreed to check out the rumor, only to find this!

RyAnne Hunter, a black woman! The man was mad. And that had been Dawson at her side. Khalifa had no desire to go up against one such as that.

Wankulu's feet scrabbled feebly across the bottom of the canoe now, but Khalifa squeezed all the harder. The man had drawn his last breath on this side of the abyss. It was only a moment more before the man's body went limp, and Khalifa motioned for the guard to help him. Together they heaved the man over the side of the canoe. He would be crocodile fodder inside of ten minutes.

Khalifa adjusted his kanzu and sank back onto his seat. Thankfully, Wankulu had not soiled it. "Return us to the shore," he ordered.

Without a word the guard set the oar into the water and started them forward, but after several strokes, he lifted his gaze to Khalifa and jutted his chin toward the village. "This woman's father died not long ago. There is a rumor among The People that her mother was a slave descended from this region."

Khalifa blinked. He turned his gaze first toward the shore where he'd last seen the tiny dots of Miss Hunter and Captain Dawson walking along the beach, then back to the place where Wankulu's body had disappeared below the blue waters of the lake.

Perhaps the poor fool had been right after all. At least it appeared the story ought to be checked out. For if it were true, Miss Hunter would indeed fetch an astonishing price on the Chinese market. And wouldn't that be sweet revenge for the way she's spurned him all those months ago in the Harcourts' garden!

Khalifa scooped another capful of water over his head. A smile split his face. The good doctor might not have been so good after all, ay?

RyAnne could hardly believe the giddy emotions swirling through her. With her hand tucked into the crook of Trent's arm, she tilted her face to catch a bit more of the breeze off the lake. He had no other woman in the Americas! His actions had been for her benefit all along. And now, just when she'd resigned herself to losing him forever, he'd made it clear his interest in her went far beyond simply keeping her safe and returning her to Zanzibar.

How far did his intentions go, however? For unlike Brayden, who had asked her to marry him at every opportunity since they were children, the captain had made no such request or even a close proclamation.

She angled her gaze toward the man. Today he seemed more relaxed than he had been in the past several weeks. The breeze caught at his hair as he looked over the cerulean waters. She followed his gaze. Far out on the lake a canoe of fishermen sketched an almost imperceptible outline against the horizon. Her gaze returned to the captain's face. Did he have marriage in mind?

Her face heated at the mere thought.

He glanced at her. "You are getting overheated in this sun. We should return you to your hut."

When he tried to turn them back, she tightened her grip on his arm. "No. I'm fine. Really. Let's keep walking a little farther." Maybe she could tease a few more of his intentions from him while they walked. "I know you want me to return to Zanzibar. However, I can't help but honestly feel that this is the place where I can offer the most help, at the moment. Perhaps it was the Lord who orchestrated to bring us both here?"

He inhaled slowly, then pulled her to a stop and turned her to look at him. "There's no easy way to say this. So I'm just going to come out with it. You do realize that since it is now known your mother was a slave and you carry native blood, any one of these people might betray you and you could be taken captive?" His throat worked, and concern etched his features. "One drop. That's all it takes. One drop of native blood and you are considered free game on the markets. 'Tis madness, I know, but I fear for you nonetheless."

Yes, she did know that. Had considered it more than once since she'd told June and Nyanja the truth. Had even worried over it a time or two. But she'd always felt it was such a remote possibility.

She squeezed Trent's arm and started them walking again. "I admit that I've considered that danger. But I don't think any of them would do that. I'm here to help them!" She tilted him a look. "Besides that, even were I to return to Zanzibar, what would stop someone there from doing the same?"

"Your parents were wise to keep your lineage a secret, if only for your safety. But there are other ways to ensure your safety."

RyAnne clenched her teeth. Still the man didn't outright mention marriage.

Trent seemed to misjudge the reason for her agitation. He covered her hand where it rested against his arm. "I know it shouldn't have to be that way. In a perfect world it wouldn't be that way. But since we don't live in a perfect world, it was best."

She sighed. "Perhaps."

"You've taught June so much. She's helped you constantly in the clinic. We can leave her your father's medicines and know that the people here are in good hands."

RyAnne stopped beneath a palm tree and lifted her face to study the branches. "How does one determine the will of the Lord for their life, do you think?"

Trent rubbed the back of his neck with one hand. "I suppose there's no pat answer. God probably speaks to each person with as much individuality as He used in creating them."

"So then… How am I to know what is from the Lord? What if He used Papa's sickness, and my concern for him, to bring me here to help these people? To witness to them in a way that no one else likely can?" She turned to survey the village, which now lay far behind them on the beach. "But then…" She waved a hand. These questions were so complicated she wasn't even sure how to voice them.

Trent stepped in front of her and cupped her cheek. "But then what if He is speaking through my urgings for you to return to Zanzibar, is that it?"

"Yes. Exactly." When he said it like that, it made the quandary seem rather simple.

His lips curled up at the corners. "I can tell you which one I think is right."

She couldn't help but smile in return, though she dipped her chin and gave him a *be serious* look.

Expression turning somber, he stepped closer to her. His gaze roamed leisurely over her face, from her hairline to her lips, where it paused. He swallowed and inched nearer. "Often you ask me questions that test the bounds of my theology, RyAnne. I know not the answers… I believe God can speak audibly. I believe He can speak through dreams. I believe He can speak to us in many ways. And I think that as long as we are looking to Him with hearts that long to do His will, we need not fear whether we are doing it or not. Perhaps God leads us by our desires in some cases. First by your desire that your father not be alone at his passing. And now by your desire to help these people who are connected to you in ways you never knew before. So…" He slipped one hand behind her back and tugged her toward him until they stood pressed together. "If this is where you feel the Lord is calling you, I will endeavor to trust the Lord in that and will labor here by your side. Only first return to Zanzibar with me so we can be married?"

Sardonic humor twisted her lips. "Was that a proposal, Captain?"

His grin bloomed full. "It was rather a bad one, wasn't it?"

She lifted an eyebrow and touched his chin with one finger. "I've had better."

"From that whelp of a pup, Harcourt, no doubt," he growled.

She tipped her head back on a giggle, but when she returned her face to the fore, Trent had brought his so near, she stopped short.

"Perhaps a proper proposal should begin with a kiss? What say you, RyAnne?"

She angled her head, pretending deep thought, but her heart was racing so that she felt sure he could hear it. "I believe you may be right, Captain Dawson."

He leaned forward until his lips hovered just above hers, grousing quietly, "What happened to Trent?"

She capitulated without protest, suddenly wanting more than anything for him to cease delaying. "I believe you may be right, *Trent*."

His mouth tilted into a satisfied smile, and then he kissed her, and she feared she may have moaned softly at the bliss of it. His kiss was gentle and sure. Smooth and commanding. Full of ardor and yet full of restraint. His hand at her waist, he tugged her closer, and footsteps crunched across the sand behind him.

Footsteps? She jolted back to peer behind Trent.

Trent must have heard the telltale sound too, for he spun around, clutching her to his back in a protective gesture.

Over Trent's shoulder she saw a native man with a knife in one hand nearly upon them!

"Trent!"

Trent swiped the man's arm to one side and threw his knee into the man's groin. The native doubled over with a cry.

"RyAnne, run! Back to the village." Trent never took his eyes off their attacker, who was slowly getting to his feet.

RyAnne's boots felt mortared into the sand.

The native lunged at Trent again. And again Trent slapped his arm to one side. This time Trent slammed the man's wrist down against his knee, and the knife flew off into the long swaying grasses growing close by. Trent swung hard, and his fist connected with the man's jaw. Spittle caught the last rays of the sun as it flew in an arc from the man's mouth. Their attacker fell to the sand, and Trent was instantly upon him, his knee pressed firmly against the man's chest. Trent's shoulders moved rapidly as he fought for breath.

Seeing that Trent had the upper hand with the man loosed RyAnne's feet from their roots. She turned to flee toward the village and ran straight into a solid wall of flesh.

Khalifa wrapped bony hands firmly about her arms.

"You!" RyAnne tried to jerk away.

But Khalifa was strong and able to hold her without struggle. "Oh yes, it's me." The man grinned, his too-long teeth yellow beneath the hooked beak of his nose.

"Let her go!" She heard Trent scrambling across the sand behind her.

Khalifa's expression hardened, and he spun her around to wrap one arm across her neck. Something clicked next to her head, and she felt the cold press of steel against her temple. "Not another step, Dawson!"

Trent skidded to a halt without even arguing. He lifted his hands, palms out, and all the starch seemed to slip out of him.

Seeing that Trent was under control, the native scrambled across the sand and scrabbled through the tall grass where his knife had disappeared.

"I hear you have been keeping secrets, Miss Hunter." Khalifa ground the pistol a little harder against her temple but said the words as if they might be having tea in a Stone Town parlor.

Trent's shoulders slumped even farther at those words, but his eyes never left Khalifa.

With a grunt of triumph, the native man held his recovered knife above his head. In a flash, he was back before Trent, a gleam of hatred in his eyes as he laid the tip of the blade against Trent's belly.

Panic gave RyAnne voice. "No! Please, Khalifa! Tell him not to hurt the captain! I'll come with you." She couldn't disguise the pleading in her tone.

She met Trent's gaze, feeling all the despair in the world drop onto her shoulders.

When you walk through the waters, I will be there. And through the flames.

God's Word said it, but how deep did the waters have to get before He showed up? For the first few weeks after Papa's passing she had felt like she might just shrivel up and die herself, but now… Facing the death of the man she loved raised pain from places in her heart she'd never felt before.

"Please, Khalifa," she pleaded.

Khalifa said a few short words to the native. And the man reluctantly stepped back, but not before he let his blade cut a slow, deliberate slice across Trent's stomach.

Trent hissed but held his ground. A deep-red ooze seeped into his shirt from the cut, but Trent kept his hands raised.

With a taunting smirk, the native melted into the tall grass at the back of the beach, and Khalifa started to pull RyAnne in that direction also. Relief that they were going to let Trent live was all she could focus on at the moment. She willed him to see her love in her eyes.

He tipped her a reassuring nod, as if to tell her to hang on, he would come for her.

And then Khalifa stretched out his arm and shot Trent.

Trent took a step back and glanced down at himself. Blood blossomed with a gush this time, and Trent clutched at the wound with both hands.

For one suspended moment RyAnne felt frozen, and then she was screaming. "No!" RyAnne threw an elbow into Khalifa's ribs, satisfied to hear his grunt of pain. "No!" She must reach Trent! She scratched and clawed and kicked, determined to escape and go help him.

But Khalifa's arm could not be budged. He dragged her backward despite her best efforts.

Trent's knees collapsed, and he glanced down at his chest as he dropped to the sand.

And then the grasses sprang back into place and blocked her view of him.

RyAnne's heart despaired, and she gave up the futile fight.

So all her questions about God's will had come down to this. She was to forever be lonely, wretched, and heartbroken. And she would be sold as a slave to the highest-bidding lecher willing to put down money for her.

Were some waters too deep for even God to penetrate?

The Trail of Chains

He brought them out of darkness, the utter darkness,
and broke away their chains.

Psalm 107:14

Chapter 21
The Trail of Chains

RyAnne pressed her face into her hands but didn't bother wiping the tears that tracked down her cheeks. The manacles around her wrists and ankles were padded on the inside with leather, presumably to keep her skin from scarring. RyAnne had hoped the padding would give some leeway that might allow her to pull herself free, but all her efforts had been fruitless—the blood seeping along one of her wrists was proof of that—and the other end of the chain had been locked to the sturdy, thick trunk of an acacia tree.

Khalifa had chained her a ways back from the village, with a spear-carrying native standing guard. But even though she was in a sheltered thicket of acacia with an occasional baobab, she was close enough to smell, and even see, the thick black smoke lifting from the roofs of the village huts and to hear the cries of the people she had come to think of as *her people*, as they attempted to escape capture. For Khalifa hadn't contented himself with merely capturing her. Moments ago he'd sent his men in to ransack the village with instructions to "capture only the healthiest and strongest."

Though her tears cascaded, a numbness had started in RyAnne's chest the moment she'd seen Trent fall, and had steadily been spreading through her in a chilling wave ever since. She should be worried about Nyimbo, Moyo, Nyanja, June, Kako, and the other villagers, like Yani and her newborn baby and young daughter, yet all she could think about was Trent, who at this very moment lay dead or dying, while she remained impotently powerless to help him.

As she vainly tried to free her wrists once more, a cry of sheer frustration rose from inside her.

The guard's expression remained impassive.

Another roil of belching black smoke billowed into the sky. RyAnne shuttered her gaze, feeling the bite of the manacles against her wrists as she clutched handfuls of her hair in both fists.

Thank God Papa had passed on before Khalifa's attack!

It seemed forever, and yet it seemed as though hardly any time at all had passed, when Khalifa reappeared. The violin that Commodore Llewellyn Cornwall had gifted to her through the captain landed with a thud at her feet.

"It is done. Stop blubbering. You will carry this on our journey to the coast. Once the bidders hear your talent on the instrument, the price we'll get for you could double."

RyAnne glowered at him. She would sooner hurl the instrument into one of the fires raging behind the man than play it and give him even a shilling more of profit.

Khalifa sank to his haunches before her. He jabbed a thumb in the direction of the sacked village. "You do realize the fault for all this is yours, Miss Hunter?" He said the words with a touch of disparaging joviality, as though it pleased him greatly to deem her at fault.

Indignation lifted her chin. "I sit here in chains at your hand, yet you attempt to blame me? I had absolutely nothing to do with it, and well you know it!"

"Oh, but I beg to differ, Miss Hunter." He folded his hands and tapped his first two fingers against his lips, studying her with that stomach-sickening humor in his eyes. "Not long ago, did you not confess to some of the village females that your grandmother hailed from this tribe?" He tilted a nod to the burning village.

RyAnne's stomach pitched.

But Khalifa didn't give her time to sort through the muddle of emotions swirling through her and to come up with a reply.

He nodded. "Oh yes. I can see the truth dawning in your horrified eyes, Miss Hunter." He leaned closer, as though about to impart the most important of secrets. "You see…a man named Wankulu came to me. Apparently you did something to get him banned from the village, hmmm? But"—he waved a hand through the air—"that is not important. What is important is that he somehow became privy to your secret, Miss Hunter. And he came to me with it. And of course, knowing the kind of price I would get for a woman of your beauty, I had to come see for myself. So you see…the fault is undeniably yours, Miss Hunter. If your blood wasn't so tainted…if you weren't so beautiful…" He gave a little shrug, and his gaze slipped over her form.

Revulsion riled in the pit of her stomach and whispered a chill along the back of her neck.

A lecherous smirk twisted his lips. He reached out and fingered one of her curls.

RyAnne jerked back and slapped his hand away, her chains clanking loudly with the motion. "Don't touch me! This is no more my fault than was the broken flowerpot I smashed over your head back in the Harcourts' garden!"

Before she could blink, she was knocked to her back with his hand wrapped around her throat. He squeezed hard enough to cut off her air.

RyAnne clutched at his hand. Tried to kick at him with her feet. But her chains hampered her effectiveness. And his brute strength prevailed. The edges of her vision blurred, and everything inside her ached for just one sweet breath of oxygen.

This was it then? Perhaps she would be reunited with Trent sooner than she'd realized.

And then just as suddenly as he'd attacked her, he released her.

RyAnne's body convulsed, and she gasped for air.

Khalifa straightened his sleeves as he stood to his feet.

She turned on her side, feeling like she might retch, but all she could do was cough and wheeze. Pain seared through her. Weakness tremored in every muscle of her body. For a long moment she lay there, her cheek pressed against her bound hands, then slowly she climbed to her feet, dusted off her skirts, tugged broken bits of grass and twigs from her hair, and lifted a scowl to Khalifa. He might have control of her body. But he would never be able to take her mind from her.

Khalifa took in her defiance with another smirk. He lifted one hand and snapped his fingers. "Asha, come." Khalifa pierced RyAnne with a look and tipped his head to where a man stepped out from behind a baobab with Moyo, wide-eyed and tearful at his side.

"Moyo!" RyAnne stretched out her hands to the child, who barreled toward her and buried her face against RyAnne's stomach.

Khalifa's eyes narrowed. "The girl will also travel with you. And if I have any trouble from you, *she* will be the one to suffer for it, do you understand?"

Moyo sobbed, her face pressed into the material of RyAnne's skirt.

RyAnne's chains clanked garishly as she attempted to wrap her arms around the little one. Her gaze drilled into the man as she rasped, "She's your own daughter!"

Khalifa's gaze flickered to the girl, and for just the fraction of a moment RyAnne thought she saw something human reflected there.

But then he threw back his shoulders and lifted his chin. "And with her light-colored skin and those tawny eyes, she ought to fetch me a good price at the market now that she's older!"

"You are a snake of the lowest form!" The words were not harsh enough to convey the depth of her feelings about the man. The child was barely four if she was a day! RyAnne tightened her arms about the little one as best she could.

Khalifa's expression mocked her. "You wound me most grievously, Miss Hunter!" With a guffaw of laughter, he turned his back on her. "Be ready to travel in five minutes." He snapped his fingers at the guard he had called Asha, and the man stepped forward and clapped two tiny manacles to Moyo's wrists, unlocked RyAnne's leg chains from the acacia, and then nudged them both to start walking.

RyAnne took Moyo's hand in her own. And tempted as she was to hurl the violin toward the flames that now engulfed the brush behind the last row of huts, something made her wrap her palm around the case's handle and hang on tight instead.

A loud outcry suddenly arose from Khalifa's men. "*Moto*!" someone yelled. And RyAnne realized the breeze off the lake was pushing the flames. The fire was hungrily racing through the brush and devouring everything in its path.

The guard behind RyAnne and Moyo jabbed RyAnne with the blunt end of his spear. "*Kimbia*!"

RyAnne recognized the Swahili command to run and knew that Moyo wouldn't stand a chance at outracing a fire. She squatted down and instructed the child to quickly climb onto her back. Moyo complied, clinging to her for dear life. Her chains gouged into RyAnne's spine. Tiny manacles grated against shoulder blades, iron conquering bone. Despite the pain, RyAnne shuffled forward, clutching her violin to her chest as she followed the guard before her. The chains around her ankles made anything more than a cantering gait impossible.

Ahead she could hear cries of terror and clanking of chains. The other prisoners Khalifa had taken from the village were obviously terrified of the fires also. And RyAnne knew the wind off the lake would only pick up faster over the next hour. They could all be overtaken and burned alive!

Her legs ached, yet she ran on. Time and again her one-handed grip on Moyo's legs slipped as her loping run yanked her chains one way or another. But a wall of flames fed by the long savannah grasses rose like a hungry orange dragon behind them. She must not stop!

The brief thought that in this chaos she might chance upon the perfect opportunity for Moyo and her to escape flitted through her mind. And then the guard ahead of them disappeared into an enveloping cloud of smoke.

Trent came to with a moan. His eyes flew open. "RyAnne!" He lurched upward but didn't quite make it to a sitting position before his body rebelled. He gasped at the shock of the pain.

Someone pressed a hand to his chest and kept him from trying to rise once more. "Be still, *mzee*. Much hurt has come upon you."

Kako. Relief eased a breath through Trent's lips. Maybe the situation was not as bad as he feared. He cracked open one eye and peered into Kako's concerned face, leaning over him. Water droplets glistened in the man's hair and cascaded in rivulets down his bare chest. Beside him, June was equally wet, but her horror-filled gaze was fixed on something in the distance.

Trent lifted one hand to the persistent pain pulsing beneath his skull. But as he did so, shards of shattered bone ground against each other in his shoulder. A loud moan escaped him, and with a wince he gingerly lowered his arm to the ground.

Kako snapped a few words at June in the Chewa Trent was yet endeavoring to learn, and she seemed to give herself a shake as she turned her focus from whatever horror lay in the distance to examining his wounds. And horror it must be, for there existed no other word to describe the expression on her face.

Trent's brow furrowed. "What happened?" His every thought felt muddied. But at the back of his mind lingered a strong concern for RyAnne.

Kako shook his head as though still processing the events himself. He responded in the Swahili Trent spoke fluently. "The village was raided. June and I were both down by the shore. We hid in the lake. But the rest…" He let the words trail away.

June flicked a glance of sheer anger Kako's way. "You should have let me go to them!"

Kako made a sound of disgust. "You would have been captured!"

"Go to who?" Trent inserted.

June returned to examining the wound in his shoulder, but tears now tracked down her dark cheeks. "The young ones Moyo and Nyimbo were both taken."

There was another flicker of pain in her gaze that indicated something deeper still. Trent's gut rolled. "And Nyanja?"

June blinked hard a few times, pressed her lips into a tight purse, and wrinkled her nose. The pain in the expression was unmistakable. She shook her head. "*Anafa*."

Trent's eyes fell closed. Though it was Chewa, that was a word he knew. Nyanja had been killed. RyAnne would be so devastated.

He couldn't believe how quickly things had changed. One moment life had been full of hope and joy as he'd walked with the woman he loved along the beach. And now… His one hope fell to the fact that Khalifa would treat her somewhat carefully because she would be worth so much.

"I couldn't save her." He rolled slightly to one side to remove the painful bulge of his pistol from his lower back. "I didn't even have time to draw my gun."

Kako obliged him by tugging the weapon free and laying it on the ground next to him.

Trent nodded his thanks. "How long have I been out?"

June still studied and prodded his shoulder gently. "We just came upon you. But the raiders have been gone for at least an hour now. Be still a few moments more so I can clean and bandage your wounds."

Trent clenched his teeth and gave in to her ministrations only because at his current levels of pain, he would be no good to RyAnne, or anyone else for that matter. Every breath sent waves of fire through his chest. Every movement produced the same affect in his abdomen and shoulder.

June spoke a few words to Kako, and he helped lift Trent partially so she could see the back of his shoulder.

Pain swept through Trent, causing waves of dizziness and nausea, but he gritted his teeth and bore the anguish, willing his stomach to cease its churning.

She said a few more words.

Kako eased Trent back to the sand, then touched his good shoulder gently. "You have broken ribs and a broken bone at the back of your shoulder. The spirit you speak to must have been watching out for you. June says we must cut out the bullet, but with a sling you should recover fully in time. The slice across your abdomen is deep, but Dr. Hunter showed her how to sew such a wound closed. You will live, mzee. Courage."

With that, Kako slipped quietly away.

June offered a sympathetic look. "He goes to see if he can find a knife or any of Dr. Hunter's supplies. I fear to make you better, I must first hurt you worse, mzee."

Trent nodded. "Yes. I understand."

He would take any level of pain if it meant he would sooner be able to head out to rescue RyAnne.

Chapter 22
The Trail of Chains

Just as RyAnne's hopes soared that she might indeed be able to make an escape with Moyo—and she'd turned to flee in another direction—a hand wrapped firmly around her upper arm and yanked her forward. "No one escapes Asha."

The guard had doubled back for them.

Despair threatening to overwhelm her, she stumbled to keep up with the man.

Relentlessly, Asha prodded her onward, and yet the flames never seemed more than half a furlong behind them. Hampered as she was by the heavy manacles, it seemed they could not put enough distance between themselves and the encroaching crackle of the devouring blaze.

Earlier her fears had revolved around her capture and wondering if Trent had suffered much before he died. She had beaten back the hopeful question over whether he was really dead. For of course he was. There had been so much blood! And she had never been one to linger in a fantasy of hope. But now her fears turned to keeping herself from getting burned to death. And worry for Moyo.

Her legs begged for rest, but still she pressed onward. The chains felt heavier with each step. Moyo also. RyAnne demanded just one more step from her muscles. And then another. She ran until her legs gave out from under her and she crashed to the ground. Moyo's face smacked into her shoulder, and RyAnne heard her whimper. The fire wheezed a scorching belch against the skin of her legs exposed by her fall. Terror zipped through her.

"Moyo, we have to run!"

The child was yanked from her back, and RyAnne started to protest the separation until she realized Asha had swung the little girl onto his own back. He bent and used a key to unclasp her manacles. Yanking them off, he thrust them into a leather bag angled across his chest. And then he prodded RyAnne to rise and run. RyAnne managed to get her legs beneath her and stumble forward, but every breath pulled in only a lungful of smoke. She coughed. Her eyes watered, and she squinted to see where to place her next step.

All thoughts of escape momentarily left her. Her only thought was of survival, and there was only one direction to move at this point. The conflagration marched surely and steadily behind them.

The ground beneath her feet began to quake, and off in the distance she heard the dull roar of something like thunder.

The guard cursed angrily and yanked RyAnne's arm to angle her movement in a line tangential to their current direction.

The roar grew louder, and suddenly they were running in the midst of a herd of wildebeests, gazelles, zebras, and ostriches. Every creature on the plains seemed to have congregated together in an attempt to outrace their looming deaths. And yet they were running in a line almost parallel with the flames. If they kept going this direction, the fire would catch up to them of a certainty! And yet there was no way to dodge through the herd and keep going away from the fire without getting knocked to the ground. So she raced along with the herds, like all the other people around her.

Do not fall. Do not fall. Do not fall. RyAnne chanted the words with each step. For a fall now would mean being trampled to death by the terrified animals careening along behind her. RyAnne tried to think what the captain might have told her to do in a situation like this. But in all his lectures on safety, he'd never once covered how to respond if she was running in the middle of a stampeding herd of wild animals with a grass fire chasing hot on her heels.

Tears stung her eyes. What she wouldn't give to hear him barking orders at her in that moment!

Just ahead of her she heard the guard, Asha, give an exultant shout. And then she heard the distinct splashes of the animals leaping into water! A gust of wind momentarily cleared the smoke from the plain. And blessed sight! A river, wide and placid, stretched before them. The animals had instinctively known where to head!

Asha hoisted Moyo to his shoulders and leapt down into the riverbed, turning to raise his hands to help RyAnne down after him. Grateful for his help, RyAnne leaned forward and took his hands, then jumped down into the water.

Asha gave her a nod, turned, and waded out into the river, grasping onto the neck of a wildebeest as he kicked out into the main flow of the water.

RyAnne followed suit without a second thought. It was only after she was in the middle of the current, clinging to the mane of a wild-eyed zebra, with the danger of the fire behind her, that her thoughts turned to what creatures might be lurking beneath the surface of the water and ready to take advantage of all the meals swimming above them. She had but a fleeting moment to fear however, for just then her feet hit ground, and she released the zebra and slogged toward the shore.

As soon as she was free of the water, she fell to her knees and crawled toward Moyo, whom the guard had left seated on a rock. RyAnne gathered the sobbing child into her arms and tucked her head beneath her chin. She glanced around. Where had the guard gone? Maybe this was their chance to escape?

Her gaze skimmed the chaos in the river, and for the first time she saw the other slaves from the caravan were also struggling to cross the deep watercourse. But the heavy chains that bound many of them not only hand and foot, but from one to another, were making it difficult for many to swim. It was a miracle so many had even made it this far, bound as they were.

She spotted Asha then. Swimming in the center of the pandemonium, helping people across.

RyAnne's hopes of escape soared, but then a woman cried out, and her head disappeared beneath the muddy surface of the water. Only a second later she bobbed up again, but from her flailing arms RyAnne could see she was struggling to remain afloat. She couldn't just run off while other people drowned. She had to help!

RyAnne kissed Moyo's head and took her face in her hands. "*Khalani pompo*!" She dipped her chin to make sure her order not to move registered with the little one.

Moyo nodded, her wide, tear-filled eyes flitting from one struggling swimmer to the next.

As RyAnne dashed back into the waters, she wondered how much the child had seen today. The way she had searched the faces of those who scrabbled their way onto the bank gave RyAnne the distinct impression that she was searching for her mother.

What had happened to Nyanja? RyAnne remembered Khalifa's instructions to capture only the healthiest of the villagers. So what had happened to those deemed unfit? A shudder coursed through her. Well she knew Khalifa's practice was to leave no survivors. Hopelessness threatened to bring her to collapse right there in the water. Had Moyo witnessed the death of her mother this morning?

RyAnne took the arm of the woman struggling to find her footing and tugged her to shallower water. Offering what few words of encouragement she knew in the tribal language, she tugged on the chain to pull the next woman forward as well. She didn't know how long she stood in the shoals helping people from the muddy water, but when there was finally no one left to assist, she lifted her gaze to the far side of the river to see that night was almost upon them, aided by the clouds of smoke still rising from the dying embers. All along the far embankment, small fires continued to blaze here and there, but even they would soon be out of fuel.

She slogged her way back to Moyo and took the little girl's hand to lead her farther from the river.

The feel of Moyo's delicate fingers clasped in hers returned her thoughts to Nyanja. The resurgence of her anger filled RyAnne with the hope that perhaps Khalifa had been killed in today's mêlée. And then she immediately felt guilty for wishing the death of anyone, even if it was Khalifa. Even so… She glanced around. She hadn't seen him since they had started running from the fire.

Moyo was shivering, and RyAnne realized that a damp chill had sunk into the very core of her own bones as well. Her wet dress was sucking the warmth right out of her.

Asha stopped before her and clapped the leg irons around her once more. So much for a chance at escape. With a sigh, RyAnne held out her wrists, but the man stepped back, deliberately stuffed the wrist cuffs back into his bag, and then resumed his stoic stance nearby.

RyAnne thanked God as she sank down and pulled Moyo onto her lap. Having her hands free would be so helpful in caring for Moyo. She glanced around. She scooted over to put her back to a tree so she could hold Moyo more comfortably. Her leg irons rattled at the movement. Moyo recoiled at the sound. Already the child had come to realize what that clanking represented.

Loss of freedom.

Loss of personhood.

Loss of hope.

All around them other guards prodded the surviving slaves together and ordered them to sit. And all around them chains rattled as the newly captured slaves complied.

Moyo squirmed with each jangle and clank.

"Shhhh." RyAnne soothed a hand over the child's back and wrapped her arms tighter, trying to offer as much warmth as she could.

A couple of the guards set about making some fires, and RyAnne was thankful for the relief of the warmth.

A loud curse rang out, and Khalifa stormed into the center of the circle. "How many did we lose?"

So much for her hopes that he might no longer walk among the living.

None of the guards replied, and none of them looked at him.

"How many?!" Spittle flying, he fisted Asha's tunic into his hand and yanked the man forward.

Moyo whimpered, and RyAnne tightened her embrace.

Asha mumbled a few words that RyAnne couldn't make out.

But Khalifa was apparently very unhappy at the report. He went still.

RyAnne felt a prickle along the back of her neck, for it wasn't a calm stillness. It was a stillness fraught with tension. A tension that might explode at any moment.

The guard also seemed to hold his breath.

And then with a feral yell, Khalifa slugged the man's face.

RyAnne flinched at the brutality of it.

Asha stumbled back a step and fell to the ground.

Khalifa leapt forward and kicked him. Fists clenched, tendons in his neck stretched taut, kofia askew, Khalifa bent over the man, screaming and bellowing in a language RyAnne did not know. His face turned red. His eyes bulged.

The guard curled his arms over his head and tightened into a ball to protect himself.

Temper unabated, Khalifa kicked Asha again. He spat on him, still cursing and screeching. And then he raised one boot and stomped fiercely on the guard's head.

RyAnne thrust Moyo to one side and scrambled forward. "Stop!"

She tried to insert herself between Khalifa and the prone man, but Khalifa backhanded her out of the way.

Her cry of surprise and pain must have somehow penetrated the fog of his rage, because he froze and turned to look at her, a dazed confusion slacking his jaw.

The left side of RyAnne's face pulsed with pain, and she gingerly felt of her cheek. Her fingers came away bloody.

Khalifa blinked. "What have you done?!" He was upon her in an instant, taking her face in his hands to angle it toward the firelight and examine her wound. "Stupid woman! This might leave a scar!"

"Good! Let it scar! Let it disfigure me till no one wants to offer you even a penny for me!" She batted his hands away, but he slapped her with an open palm. Her head jolted back, and before she could even gather her wits to continue her fight, he once more took her face firmly in his hands. She met Khalifa's gaze steadily, without flinching, as he prodded and wiped at the wound.

"Jabir! I require you! Now!"

Footsteps scrambled toward them from the other side of the fire, and then a turbaned man with thick, bushy brows and a pointed chin stepped into sight.

Khalifa thrust her toward the man none too gently. "This one is going to need stitches. Make them small and perfect, for after the auction, if I feel I've lost any money on her due to a scar, I'm going to take every penny out of your hide!"

The man called Jabir bowed but didn't speak a word.

Khalifa stomped off then, and there was suddenly the soft rattle of chains and the release of breaths as everyone around seemed to relax at his departure.

Jabir stepped toward her, but RyAnne turned her face away. She pointed to Asha, who remained prostrate, unconscious on the ground. "You don't get to touch me until you have helped that man." Despite the fact that the guard worked for Khalifa, the man had likely saved both her and Moyo's lives today. She wouldn't just stand by and let him die.

Jabir glanced at the guard but then stepped toward her again. He stretched out his hands in a placating way, indicating she should let him treat her first.

Why did the man not speak?

RyAnne scooted back from him, lifting her chin. "The guard first!"

Jabir merely sighed and turned a look on two other guards who stood nearby. Both men stepped over, and each took one of her arms and dragged her over to sit on the rock. One grabbed a handful of her hair and jerked her head back, angling the cut on her face so that Jabir could see it. The other held up a lantern.

Calmly, Jabir set to cleaning and examining her wound. Beside them the unconscious guard moaned.

"Well, at least he's alive." RyAnne glowered at the doctor. How could he leave a man so injured to treat a little cut?

Asha rolled over to his back with a groan, and RyAnne caught a glimpse of a large gash across his forehead.

"He needs help."

Still Jabir spoke not a word. With careful precision, he stitched the short cut on her cheek. His needle was so sharp and thin that RyAnne barely felt the prick each time. After he had finished and given a satisfied nod, he motioned to the two guards who had been holding her to bring Asha and seat him on the rock.

RyAnne rose and turned to watch.

With each movement he was forced to make, Asha moaned quietly as though intent on keeping Khalifa from knowing how much pain he had inflicted.

Even with one of her eyes swelling shut, RyAnne could see that the man's left arm was broken. White bone protruded through ebony skin. She winced. That would make it all the harder to prevent infection.

RyAnne had expected the guards to seat the man on the rock, but instead one knocked him to his knees before it, while the other strode to one of the fires and thrust the flat metal point of his spear into the flames.

RyAnne frowned, trying to guess why the healer might require a hot spear for setting an arm.

Jabir quickly wrapped the strap of a leather whip around Asha's wrist and stretched his broken arm out over the rock, passing the handle of the quirt to one of the guards.

Asha screamed in pain, no longer able to tamp down the expression of his discomfort.

One of the guards pulled the arm taut while the other guard placed his foot just above the elbow.

Asha cried out again, but through gritted teeth this time—the sound a reluctant acceptance of what they were about to do.

RyAnne felt pity for the man and couldn't help but admire his acquiescence. It was good. Setting his arm would go easier if he tried to relax as they did it.

Jabir tied a tourniquet above the guard's elbow.

She frowned. What sort of medicine had this man studied? They didn't need a tourniquet for setting an arm.

The healer took a step back and then withdrew a large machete from his belt. This he also thrust into the fire, its light reflecting on the grim set of his pointed features.

Horror swept through RyAnne. They weren't preparing to set his forearm! They were going to cleave it off and cauterize the stub!

Jabir stepped toward Asha.

"No!" She threw herself between Jabir and his patient. "It is only broken. It does not need to be amputated!"

Jabir glowered at her and motioned for her to get out of his way.

"Give me a week!" RyAnne spread her hands and prayed there was a scrap of decency inside the healer someplace. "Let me treat him. If he's not well on his way to mending within the week, then you can take the arm. Please just let me try. He saved my life today."

Jabir raised the machete a little higher and leaned toward her menacingly.

RyAnne swallowed down the tremor of fear that threatened to steal the strength from her knees, and lifted her chin. "To get to him you are going to have to go through me. And what will Khalifa have to say about such further injury to his property?"

Jabir grunted, thrust his machete back into its sheath, threw his hands into the air, and stalked away.

One of the other two guards cast her a perturbed look, as if she might have just robbed him of his evening's entertainment. He unwrapped the quirt from around Asha's wrist and followed in Jabir's footsteps.

The other guard stepped back and folded his arms across his chest, waiting as though he thought she might need his help.

A fact for which she was thankful, since she would indeed need him to help her set the bone back into place.

"Thank you." She unwrapped the tourniquet and motioned for the guard to hold the lantern so she could see. Though the bone had broken through the skin, it did not appear to be shattered and was not as bad as she'd first feared.

She pointed the guard to Asha's arm just above his elbow. "I need you to hold it tightly there. See this lump? That is where the bone has separated. We must pull until the bones fit back together." She cast the man a questioning look, and he nodded that he understood. RyAnne squatted down and met Asha's gaze. "This is going to be painful, but if we can do it right, it will save your arm. Bear with me for just a few minutes, yes?"

Asha pushed a breath out between pursed lips and nodded.

"Very good. Let us begin." RyAnne took hold of the man's wrist while the first guard took hold where she had showed him just above the elbow, and she pulled with all her might. Her manacles clanked and rattled, and Asha gritted a moan through his teeth, but he did not fight them, and it was only a moment before she felt the bone snap satisfyingly back into place. Panting for breath, RyAnne sank to her knees. She looked at the guard who had helped her. "Thank you. I will need four straight sticks the length of his forearm." She indicated the length with her hands held about a foot apart. "Can you get them for me? And some leather lacing?"

With a nod, the guard headed off.

The guard who had earlier stalked off with Jabir returned just then and thrust a small roll of bandages and a pot of hot water into her hands. "From Jabir," he said and then walked away.

Thankful for at least that small blessing, RyAnne set to cleaning the broken skin and then wrapped the arm with the bandages and tied it off. That at least would keep it somewhat clean.

RyAnne then turned to the problem of the large gash where Khalifa's boot had split Asha's forehead. Her dress was still wet, and she had no other material, so she used part of her skirt to wipe away some of the blood. She winced. The man needed stitches.

When the guard returned with the four sticks she'd requested and some leather thongs, she took them up and set to placing them around Asha's arm. She asked the question on her mind. "He needs stitches. Will Jabir stitch him as he stitched me?"

The guard shook his head.

As she'd feared. RyAnne tried a different tack. "I want to thank you for your help. What is your name?"

The guard folded his arms and swept her with a suspicious look. But after a moment he offered, "Jelani."

RyAnne tipped him a nod as though they might be meeting in any number of normal social settings. "And I don't suppose, Jelani, that there's a way for you to fetch me some thread and a needle?"

Again, the man shook his head. Then he strode away as though his job here were done.

RyAnne grimaced. How was she to help Asha without proper medical supplies? She cinched the last of the leather thongs into place around the splints, pleased to at least have that much done. She had just decided that a compress was going to be the best she could offer, and had assisted Asha to a seat with his back to the rock, when Jelani returned. He stretched something out to her, lifting the lantern so she could get a good look at what he held pinched carefully between his fingers.

RyAnne's eyes widened.

The man held the body of one of the large black pinching ants of the region.

RyAnne quaked at the memory of the time she'd stepped into the path of an army of them and gotten a few under her petticoats. The creatures were the length of half her little finger and just as thick of body. And their pinchers were strong enough to draw blood when they snapped together.

Now the guard thrust the lamp into her hands and instructed her to hold it so he could see the cut on Asha's head. He pinched the skin on Asha's forehead together and thrust the head of the ant at the cut.

RyAnne winced when the creature clamped its pinchers shut on either side of the wound.

With a quick twist, Jelani severed the head of the ant from its body, leaving the head with clamped pinchers closing the wound.

He spread his hands as if he'd single handedly solved every

last one of her problems. He raised his brows, as if asking if she wanted him to find more ants.

Despite the churning in her belly at the method of treatment, she had to admit it solved her problem of trying to keep Asha from bleeding throughout the night.

Reluctantly, she nodded. “We’ll need at least five more ants, maybe six.”

The guard grinned and headed off to fetch them.

RyAnne shuddered.

Weak light prodded at Trent’s eyelids the next morning. With a grunt of pain, he squinted open one eye. The seep of dawn filtered through the branches of the acacia tree they had taken shelter under the evening before, after June had prodded the mangled bullet from his shoulder. Normally he would roll over and go back to sleep at least until the sun crested the horizon, but today the searing torture pulsing through seemingly every muscle in his body would not release him back to the gentle oblivion of sleep.

He sat up slowly, doing his best to withhold the strangulated groan the pain lured from his throat, and failing rather miserably. June was by his side in an instant, urging him to lie back down, but he brushed her aside and propped himself gingerly against the tree trunk. Perhaps he would just sit here for a moment. He didn’t think he would make it more than a few steps without some help.

Near the fire, Kako stirred the coals and offered him a grim look of sympathy.

Trent ground his teeth. The last thing he wanted was sympathy. Blast his frail flesh for failing him at a time when he needed it to be stalwart and indefatigable. Each moment he sat here like an invalid, RyAnne grew farther and farther away.

Why had he not pulled his pistol and used it to defend her? Because there hadn’t been time. First the native had been on him before he knew it, and then Khalifa had held the gun to RyAnne's head. These things he knew, but now he wondered if he couldn't have done more.

June pressed a cup of hot tea into his hands. Much of the food stores in the village had been destroyed, but Kako had managed to find a few items that had escaped the worst of the flames, the tea tin among them. And Trent could honestly say that he had never been more happy to see a cup of tea in his entire life.

Accepting the cup, he tottered the few steps to the log Kako had dragged near their fire the night before, barricading a hiss of agony behind his teeth. He huddled into his coat, realizing as the warmth of the fire met his skin that a chill was trembling through him.

June gave him a glare and motioned he should return to his pallet.

When the cup cradled in his hands blurred around the edges, he assessed that she might be right, but he couldn't just sleep the days away with RyAnne being carted off to who knows where. He had to go after her!

He took a sip of the tea, savoring the warmth of it slipping down his throat. "Kako, I need you to fashion a cart. I have to go after Miss Hunter. But I won't have the strength to travel on my own power for a few days."

June snorted and gave him a look that made it clear he would be indisposed for more than a few days.

Kako only nodded blandly. "I will set about to make this cart. But for a few days you must rest, mzee. Even a cart will be too much for you right now."

Trent sipped more of the tea and pinched his brow. Mzee… Wise one. Somehow he didn't feel very wise today. How had he let Khalifa get the drop on him? He'd known from the moment RyAnne admitted her heritage to the villagers that she'd put herself in grave danger. Yet he'd foolishly let his vigilance go lax, and it might have cost RyAnne everything. Had almost cost *him* everything.

Now he needed to assess his strength. For to come upon

Khalifa before he was able to mount a rescue could result in the man gaining the upper hand yet again. Much as he hated to admit it, he did need to rest, at least for today.

He offered Kako a nod of agreement and drained the last of the tea. When he stood, a wave of dizziness washed through him, and he stumbled a sideways step. Kako leapt to his side and took hold of his arm, guiding him back to his pallet.

Okay. Maybe he would need more than one day's rest before attempting a rescue.

The roaring of a lion woke RyAnne the next morning at dawn. The throbbing in her cheek made her gasp when she sat up.

Asha, who was already squatting near a crackling fire just a few paces away, cast her a sympathetic look, obviously in a great deal of discomfort himself. His splinted arm cradled carefully against his chest, he used the long stick in his other hand to prod some of the glowing coals beneath a pot perched on three rocks.

Moyo lay curled on her side next to RyAnne, her tiny hands tucked beneath her cheek, her soft breaths sonorously sibilant against the backdrop of birdsong and wind-stirred savannah grasses. At the moment the child looked so peaceful, and yet RyAnne could plainly see the dried salty tracks her tears had left in the smudges of smoke that coated her chubby cheeks. Long into the night RyAnne had comforted and shushed the mourning child until she had finally drifted off, aided by a quiet sonata from RyAnne's violin. If for that reason only, RyAnne was glad she had not chucked the instrument into the fires when she'd been tempted to the day before.

The roar of the lion came again, louder. This time it was accompanied by screams, the loud clanking of chains, and the guttural shout of one of the guards. A moment later the *boom* of a gun cracked through the dawn prelude.

Moyo jolted awake, and RyAnne gathered her into her arms.

There came a beat of silence, and then several shrill shrieks pierced the air. Asha leapt to his feet and trotted off, presumably to see what the commotion was about.

Moyo buried her face against RyAnne's chest, and a shudder coursed through Moyo's little body. RyAnne's heart plummeted. All of the evening before she had longed to ask the child what she had seen in the village, but she hadn't been able to bring herself to make the child face the terror yet again. But she and Moyo had been kept separate from the rest of the villagers captured. And it was almost more than RyAnne could bear not knowing who had been taken…and who had not.

Nyanja was ever the one heavy on her heart. Had she been captured? Or would Khalifa have determined her too much of a bother and health risk since she only had one leg? Considering that he'd tried to murder her immediately after the loss of her leg, RyAnne feared she knew the answer. Feared she understood what kept the normally chatty child in her arms so quiet and taciturn.

What of June though? And Kako? Yani and her two small children?

With each name and face that flitted through her mind, RyAnne's spirit grew heavier and her heart more despondent.

Her eyes fell closed. How were they to bear this load? *Jesus?*

Whom shall I send, child?

I came! I was reluctant at first. But then I was ready to stay and try to make a difference! Look where that got me? She actually lifted one manacled foot to draw heaven's attention to her chains, as though God didn't already know of her plight.

She remembered the apostle Paul's words in his letter to the Corinthians about how the Lord had denied his request and told him His grace was sufficient for him.

RyAnne gritted her teeth. She didn't want *sufficient*. She wanted rescue! She wanted justice. She wanted retribution. She wanted to turn back the hands of time and walk with Trent along the shores of Lake Nyasa just once more. Instead, doing what she had thought God wanted her to do had brought her here. She had always presumed that if she did what God wanted, it would bring blessing into her life. Peace. Comfort. Joy unspeakable. None of those things were hers. More like sorrow, discomfort, and heartache unimaginable. And yet…perhaps this was exactly where God wanted her to be?

She opened her eyes. Looked around at the trampled grass beneath flat-topped acacia trees.

Even though she and Moyo had been kept separate, she knew the many others who had been captured were close by. Was it to them the Lord was asking her to go?

The smell of burning porridge wafted to her, and she looked up to see a tendril of black smoke lifting from the pot that Asha had abandoned on the fire. Giving Moyo a quick kiss, RyAnne set her aside and stepped over to the fire, the chains binding one ankle to the other making even that short distance a mincingly difficult task.

The porridge was too thick and charred, but she spooned some out for Moyo nonetheless. Mindlessly, the child scooped the thick mash into her mouth, her eyes glassy and vacant.

Asha had only been gone for a few minutes when a loud outcry arose from just beyond a knoll. "*Tieni! Tieni!*" *Let's go! Let's go!* The shout carried a hint of panic as it was repeated over and over by several who RyAnne presumed were guards.

RyAnne studied the area to one side of the knoll, and soon a line of slave women shuffled into view. Along either side of the line, several guards swung their arms to crack short whips as they hurried the women along. After the line of women came a line of young girls and then another of young boys. Each was marched into the center of the encampment.

Asha reappeared at her side and thrust her toward Moyo. "Bring the child quickly."

RyAnne lurched over and urged Moyo to her feet. "What is happening?"

"There has been a lion attack. One of the slaves has been killed."

RyAnne barely had time to grab her violin before he shoved them toward the cluster of people. "Everyone together. The lion will not attack again soon, but there is more safety when all are in one place."

RyAnne craned her neck to get a better look at the line of women. She recognized two of Chief Banda's wives—women who had given up their hut in order that she and Papa might have a place to stay when they'd first arrived at the village. And then her gaze found Yani. Quickly she skimmed the rest of the line, but didn't recognize most of them, other than cursorily. She focused on Yani once more. Yani returned her look, but there didn't seem to be any life in her eyes. Her newborn was strapped to her back, but another search of the rest of the lines did not reveal the woman's other child, a little girl who had been only a couple years old. Her gaze returned to Yani's, and the woman gave a slight shake of her head.

RyAnne's feet stumbled to a halt as she pressed one hand to her throat and blinked back tears.

Asha prodded her from behind. "Keep moving."

RyAnne didn't want to look around after that. She pointed her face toward the ground and kept Moyo tucked close by her side. In her chest, her heart pumped death. *Gone-gone. Gone-gone. Gone-gone.* Everyone gone. She hadn't seen Nyanja. She hadn't seen June. Nor Kako, or any other man, for that matter. Where had all the men gone?

She heard a distant clanking of chains then, and only a moment later the chain gang of men shuffled into the clearing. One man, the last of the line, was barely able to keep to his feet as he stumbled along. And behind him, a pair of empty but bloodied manacles dragged along the ground.

Khalifa stormed into the clearing and scanned each group of slaves in a quick assessment before grabbing the nearest guard by one arm—Jelani, who had helped her treat Asha the evening before.

"How many did it get?" Khalifa gave the guard a shake.

Jelani swallowed. "Just the one. And"—he motioned to the slave at the end of the line of men—"left another quite injured."

RyAnne looked to that man again. At that moment he turned

to show Khalifa his injuries. Deep, bloody claw marks angled from the man's shoulder almost all the way to his waist.

Khalifa cursed the lion and spun away. "Now that it has had a taste of flesh, it will likely stalk us for miles. We must be extra vigilant not to lose any more bucks or does. I won't have a blasted lion eating my profits!"

RyAnne blinked. For a moment she'd thought he'd been speaking of the lion attacking antelope. That he was referring to those he had captured like they were nothing better than animals sent a sick churning through her middle. The man cared nothing about the fact that a *person* had been killed by the rogue lion, only about the fact that he had lost money because of it!

RyAnne lifted her chin and stepped forward. "The man will need tending. I can see to his wounds."

Khalifa shook his head. "No. Even should he recover, he will be too much of a speed liability over the next few days." He snapped his fingers at a guard near the line of men. "Dispatch him, and let's be on our way."

"No!" RyAnne gasped even as the guard lifted his gun and shot the injured man in the head. "Oh!" She spun away, clasping Moyo to her. Moyo shuddered and pressed her face into RyAnne's skirts.

From the line of women a high-pitched wail of total despair pierced the morning. RyAnne too well understood the timbre of the cry. It was as though the woman's soul had burst through a seam in her throat and followed her loved one into the next life. It was the same cry that had been beating for release from her own chest since the moment Trent had fallen to the sand.

Had that truly only been yesterday?

Chapter 23
The Trail of Chains

A GREAT THIRST woke Trent that evening. Either that or the sound of crying.

Crying?

He rolled slowly into a sitting position and gingerly swept one hand down his face to clear the clutter of disjointed dreams from his mind. He scrunched his eyes tight and then stretched them wide open, willing them to grow accustomed to the evening light. And then he held his breath and listened.

Yes. Crying.

Neither Kako nor June were in sight. But the crying was too delicate to be either of them. It was coming from a child. Gritting his teeth in preparation for the shards of pain, Trent slowly tottered to his feet. He supposed it fell to him to find the child and see if he could help. But just as he started to shuffle a few steps toward the sound, Kako emerged into the clearing by the fire with a little girl in his arms.

Relief swept over Trent. "Nyimbo."

Her snuffling increased anew as she lurched from Kako's arms and launched herself against Trent's legs to wrap frail arms about him.

"Whoa there." Trent flapped his arms.

Kako shot out one of his hands and captured a handful of Trent's shirtfront. Trent would have gone over backward if not for Kako's lightning-fast reflexes.

Kako grinned at him as he pried the child's arms from around Trent's legs and then squatted in front of her. He spoke in the girl's Chewa language. "We must be careful with mzee. He has been injured and requires time to heal."

Nyimbo bounced Trent a terrified look.

Kako ruffed a hand over the nap of her hair. "Don't worry. He's much too stubborn to let a mere bullet bring about his end."

A tearful smile of relief peeked through.

Trent nodded reassurance at the girl and then asked Kako,

"Where did you find her?"

Kako handed the girl a guava from the small basket of food near the fire. He stood, folding his arms, looking more weary and worn down than he ever had since Trent had known him.

"I've been..." His jaw bunched, and he bent and plucked a blade of grass. "All day I have been digging graves and burying my father's people." He swallowed visibly. "And my father."

Trent reached out one hand and clapped the man on his shoulder. "I'm sorry." Chief Banda had likely been killed so that he couldn't urge his people to rebellion on the long journey to the coastal city where the slaves would be auctioned off. From this region, that was likely Bagamoyo.

Kako remained dry eyed and brushed the sympathy away, as was the custom of the men of his tribe. No more would be said of his father until he was ready.

"The child was captured along with Moyo. But she says the Arab in charge took only Moyo, and as he left, commanded his guard to kill Nyimbo. The guard shot into the ground and then instructed her to run and hide. She did and remained there quietly until fear and hunger overwhelmed her. I found her only a few minutes ago."

Trent gritted his teeth. He turned to study the child who had gobbled down the guava and now lay curled atop his bedding, with her hands tucked beneath her cheek. She was already sound asleep. "The man is a devil."

Kako nodded his head. "*Inde.*" The simple agreement carried with it a world of grief and despondency.

June returned from foraging through the remains of the village and nearby gardens for what food and supplies she could find.

Kako was not in sight, but the captain was on his feet near the fire, and the sight filled her with relief. This was good. She nodded her head in satisfaction. The captain would go after Miss

RyAnne and rescue her from the terrible slavers.

June's search for food had turned up only a few potatoes, one corn stalk with two small ears of corn, and a clay pot that had somehow been spared destruction during the sacking of the village. Today she had managed to net one decent-sized fish. But if they moved away from the lake, what would they do for food on the morrow? She sighed. Bad news they had plenty of. So she would try to be thankful to see the captain on his feet and for the fact that many fruits were in season this month.

Giving the captain a nod of greeting, she bent down on her knees near the fire pit and leaned close to the coals to blow on them. They would need the fire built up to cook the few bits of food she'd found today. She fed in a few twigs from the pile nearby and was glad when they easily caught flame. She added a few stouter sticks and then sat back on her ankles.

That was when she noticed the child lying on the captain's blanket. She gasped, and a thrill of happiness coursed through her, but her relief sapped all her strength. She remained where she was. Besides, exuberance would do no one any good. She darted the captain a questioning look.

He swayed slightly on his feet. "Kako found her and brought her in a few minutes ago."

Nyimbo was sleeping soundly on the only bedding they had. And the captain looked about done in. He needed to lie back down.

She gestured to the child. "I will move her." She started to rise.

But the captain swiped away the suggestion with one hand. "No. She needs the rest more than I do."

June doubted the truth of that. The man's color was not much better than that of his tattered shirt.

"At least sit, mzee."

He complied, sinking rather clumsily onto the log Kako had dragged near the fire.

Half keeping an eye on him and half watching the sleeping child, June worked at creating a fish stew with the potatoes and corn and fish.

The water hadn't even started to boil yet when the captain slumped forward.

"Mzee!" She lurched toward him and grabbed his shoulder just before he slumped all the way forward and fell into the fire. She pulled him backward off the log, away from the flames.

The man trembled all over. He should not have left his bed! She needed to move the girl and get him back onto his blanket. That would at least keep most of the dirt out of his wounds. Dr. Hunter had told her that dirt in wounds was a bad thing.

The captain's trembling ceased, and his body went completely limp and still.

Let it not be! She placed her hand under his nose to see if he was breathing. At first she felt nothing. Her pulse pounded harder. She tilted her head, kept her hand there, and willed the man to breathe! Finally she felt the faintest puff of air against her hand.

Kako stepped back into the clearing just then.

June scrambled to her feet and kept her eyes trained near Kako's feet, as was respectful of the man who was their tribe's new chief. "The captain has collapsed. I think it is best if we move the child and return him to the blanket."

Kako hoisted a singed piece of canvas into her line of sight. "I found this today. The child can sleep on this. Lay it out, and I will fetch her."

June dipped her knees and clapped her hands in acknowledgement of his suggestion. Then she took the canvas from him and settled it over the pile of dried bamboo leaves she had slept on the night before.

It was only a moment before Kako brought the child over and laid her down. And then together they worked to lift the captain and half drag, half carry him to his pallet.

Bright new blood seeped into the shoulder of his shirt. And when June lifted the bandage to see if there was something she might do, the stench of infection greeted her. She clucked and fussed over the wound, trying to clean it as Dr. Hunter had shown her a few times in his clinic.

But she knew it was pointless. Never had she seen someone

with a wound this infected recover.

Kako waited quietly nearby.

She knew he was waiting to hear her assessment. Her gaze flicked up to his for just a moment before she remembered he was now the chief, and she pulled it into proper obedient subservience. "I fear the captain will not be long with us."

Kako turned from her, propped his hands on his hips, and tipped his face to the sky. But after only a moment he spun back to face her. "Wake the child. We must pray to the great spirit of the English. He's the only one who can save him now."

June bent her knees and clapped her hands. She woke Nyimbo. And the three of them knelt beside the captain, as they'd often seen Dr. Hunter do when he beseeched his god. They folded their hands and bowed their heads. June stared down at the place where a breeze ruffled the captain's shirt and waited for Kako to begin to speak. Kako shuffled back and forth on his knees for a moment, then cleared his throat.

"June, say the prayer."

June felt her eyes widen. What if she said the words wrong? She thought back. Had there been any special way Dr. Hunter prayed each time? She didn't think so. She remembered the talk she and Miss RyAnne had shared on the beach when Miss RyAnne had told her that the English god could be her god too. Miss RyAnne had not said they needed to do anything special. Just believe as the doctor had spoken of in his message.

She cleared her throat. "Great spirit of the English. We know we are not English. But today we are not here for ourselves. We are here for this man who is yours already."

Kako nudged her.

June debated between offending the spirit she was talking to or offending her chief.

Kako nudged her again.

June decided that offending the chief kneeling by her side was probably more dangerous than offending the spirit she could not see. She glanced over at Kako.

His expression held apology. "Perhaps, like a chief, this spirit will not hear the case of anyone who is not his?"

June shrugged. "How should I know?"

Nyimbo yawned sleepily.

Kako rubbed both hands down his face and then back over his hair to clasp them behind his neck. He glanced down at the captain, whose chest was barely rising and falling. "Great chiefs like to receive great gifts. I think to be safe, we need a gift to offer this spirit."

June pondered that. "Just before Dr. Hunter died, Miss Hunter did tell me that this god could be ours too. Nyanja seemed to believe it. I was not so sure. But you might be right."

"So how do we ensure this spirit will listen to us? Chiefs will only hear the cases of people from their own villages. And they expect large bounty before they grant new people admittance into their villages."

June thought back. "The doctor said in his chapel that last morning that the son of this spirit came down to earth and died—"

Kako made a noise of disgust and started to climb to his feet. "How can a god who let his son die be of any help to us then?"

June captured his arm before he could tromp away. "But then the son came back to life again! And that makes him very powerful, yes?"

Kako sank back to his knees between her and Nyimbo. "If it is true, I suppose it does. So what gift do we offer?"

Nyimbo tugged on Kako's arm. "A servant is a big gift," she said. "You can tell this spirit that I will be his servant if he will heal my friend."

June nodded. "We should all say that. Flattery might help also. So we should tell him that we've heard of his great power and that we all want to be his servants."

"Yes." Kako nudged her, and a gleam of triumph spread across his face. "And if he wants us to be his servants, he needs to use some of his power to heal our friend."

June folded her hands again, as she'd seen the doctor do. "Fine. But if you want to barter with him, then you need to pray to him yourself. Bartering with a spirit does not seem so wise."

"All great chiefs love a good barter."

June only offered a skeptical look as response.

Kako threw up his hands. "Fine. Pray to him your way then. But don't blame me if the captain dies."

Satisfied, June tried her prayer again. "Great spirit of the English, it has been told to me that you would be our spirit too if we choose you. We have heard of your great power, and we have agreed that we will all be your servants. And Kako wants me to say that if you accept our offer of service, you will please use some of your power to heal our friend, the captain." She paused. There was some way the doctor had always ended his prayers, but she could not remember the words. So she finished with. "That is all. Thank you."

They all stood, and Nyimbo rubbed her eyes sleepily. "How does one go about being a servant to a spirit?"

June looked to Kako.

He shrugged.

June nudged Nyimbo into a seat on the log near the fire. "Perhaps the captain can tell us that if he gets better."

Nyimbo looked sadly toward the captain. "Do you think this spirit knows we are serious? I want the captain to get better."

June touched the child's head and then set the fish stew away from the fire. It would need to cool for some time before they could eat it with their fingers. "Spirits know much more than we, Nyimbo. I'm sure this spirit does also."

For days they marched.

Two weeks ago, after the caravan stopped one evening, Jabir had come by and removed her stitches. He'd studied the cut on her face and then grunted in satisfaction and stalked away. He hadn't bothered even once to examine Asha, but thankfully the man seemed to be well on his way to recovery.

Today, the sun beat down with such merciless heat that

RyAnne could see the shimmer of its fervor cavorting on the horizon, as if to taunt her. Sweat poured from her until everything from her hair to the hem of her skirts felt limp with the dampness of it, and still the march continued.

The manacles around her ankles chaffed persistently, and today a large blister had burst open.

After so many days of walking, she had assumed her body would eventually grow used to the strenuous task required of it. But today when the call had gone out for the evening's rest, she'd never felt more relieved to be able to collapse to the ground. Moyo did the same and promptly fell asleep.

RyAnne took off her boot and examined the large, oozing blister. Infection would set in if she didn't care for it. But she knew that asking for medical supplies would only be greeted with a grunt of cynical laughter.

With a sigh, she tore off part of her petticoat, soaked it with a bit of the water from the creek they had settled near tonight, and wrapped it around the wound. Hopefully that would keep it clean and keep her from getting an infection. It felt a little better after the initial sting of the cool water. Even so, she dreaded tomorrow's long day of walking. It would be compounded by Moyo's weight because her little legs simply couldn't keep up with the grueling pace Khalifa had set for them. RyAnne knew she would be carrying the child for much of the trek to the coast.

Asha stepped into the light of the fire he'd made for her and Moyo earlier. It had become quite clear that Khalifa had assigned Asha to keep her and Moyo separate from the other slaves. They were treated with more care than the others—fed more and given bedding to separate them from the cold ground each night. Asha had even packed Moyo on his back for several hours today, but only after RyAnne had fallen when her foot slipped into a rut on the trail.

Each evening when RyAnne curled into her blankets, she heard the rattle of chains as the rest of the captured settled onto the cold ground, and guilt pricked at her. But for Moyo's sake, she was thankful for the small luxuries they were given. For despite the heat of the days, the nights were quite cool. Cool enough that she often woke with cramped muscles that had tightened against the invasion of the chill. Moyo had taken to curling up against her for the past several nights. That had helped Moyo, at least, to sleep a little better.

For RyAnne's part, she hadn't slept well for weeks now, for every time she closed her eyes she saw the face of the captain. She saw the quirk of his brow or pulse of his jaw when he'd been frustrated with her. She saw the exasperated expression of the valiant hero who had come to her rescue more times than she could count. She saw the soft eyes of the man who had consoled and comforted her after Papa's passing. She saw the gentle crooked smile that had touched his lips just before he kissed her that last day. And always…always…the last thing she saw was the blood blooming on the front of his shirt after Khalifa shot him.

Now, Asha held out two bowls to her and indicated Moyo with a dip of his head. "Wake her. She must eat."

RyAnne accepted the food and set it on a rock next to her. "I will. If you want, I can look at the cut on your head."

He brushed her concern aside. "It heals well."

"And your arm?" She was thankful to see the man still wore the splints as she'd requested.

He lifted it. "The pain is much less now." His gaze darted across the encampment to where she could see Jabir smoothing a salve on the whip lashings of one of the other slaves. Jabir's act almost looked compassionate if she hadn't known it for what it was—simply keeping Khalifa's "investment" healthy.

She returned her attention to Asha. "Why does the healer never speak?"

Asha gave her a sharp look and then transferred his attention back to the healer. For a long moment he didn't answer. Then finally he said, "Two years past, Jabir voiced disagreement with Khalifa over the way he was treating the slaves. Khalifa cut out his tongue."

With a gasp, RyAnne raised one hand to her mouth. She swallowed down the bile at the back of her throat. "Why would he still work for a man who did something like that to him?"

Asha blinked. "You do not know? He is Khalifa's slave. As am I. We do the bidding of our master."

RyAnne's gaze returned to Jabir, but this time she saw the man in a new light. "I'm sorry. I did not know."

Asha made no response other than to pluck a round blade of grass and roll it between his lips.

RyAnne moved the conversation back to a safer topic with a gesture to Asha's splinted arm. "I'm glad the pain is less."

Asha only grunted with a nod of thanks.

Willing away the depressing thoughts about just how deep the scars of slavery ran through the world, she scooted over next to Moyo. She touched the girl's shoulder. "Moyo, I have food."

While Moyo ate, RyAnne prepared her pallet, and Moyo had just settled back to sleep when in the far distance a lion roared.

Asha's brow puckered, and he tilted his head to listen to the sounds more carefully for a moment. With a flick of his tongue, he tucked the stem of grass into the corner of his lips. "It stalks us."

RyAnne nodded, a tingle of horror creeping across her scalp.

For the past several nights they'd heard the creature. Each night it seemed to grow closer. Bolder.

She didn't want to dwell on it. "How long until we meet up with the next caravan?"

Asha shrugged as he settled down against the base of the acacia tree, tipped his head against it, and shut his eyes. "Soon."

RyAnne would have liked to have drifted off to sleep right away. But her mind wouldn't let go of the thoughts tumbling about. Asha and Jabir, slaves themselves… Surely they understood better than most the horrors of what they were inflicting? And yet they were forced to help their master make slaves of others. Khalifa was a terrible man, yes. But she had no doubt that he was just a garden-variety slave runner. All up and down the eastern coast of Africa, men just like him plundered and spoiled and pillaged.

Tears slipped from the outer corners of her eyes and ran back into her hair.

Back at the village, she'd had the lofty thought that staying there and helping the villagers might make some sort of impact on slavery. She'd even told June and Nyanja that her grandmother had been a woman from their tribe, thinking to help them see that the color of their skin did not have to hold them back from anything—not a relationship with God, not education, not happiness. What a fool she'd been to think that she could make a difference. In fact, if Khalifa could be trusted, that very admittance was what had caused the village to be plundered in the first place. Her attempts to help had only made things worse.

If she had just stayed out of it…gone back to Zanzibar with the captain when he'd asked her to, none of this would have happened. Trent would still be alive. The village would still be intact. She wouldn't be bound in chains and headed for an uncertain future.

And yet…hadn't the upper echelons of society's propensity to "stay out of it" been the very foundation stone upon which today's rampant slavery had been built?

She thought again of the question that kept rising from the moment she'd walked the gangway up to *The Wasp*. And remembered her earlier thought that perhaps this was exactly where God wanted her to be. Yet what could she do here that might make a difference for poor people like those lying in chains all around her?

So many questions. Questions she had no answers for.

She pinched the bridge of her nose and closed her eyes, willing the tears to remain at bay. *Father, I don't understand. Please make it clear to me what you are asking of me. I'm tired, so tired, of fighting for my own way.*

A thought jolted through her. What was she thinking? She had lost all freedom to make her own decisions. And if she was tired of fighting for her own way, she was certainly in the right place, because nothing was going her way. That would be even more compounded once she was sold as a slave. So who was she to think that God wanted anything from her at all? Perhaps she'd only been fooling herself into thinking He had plans for her.

She scrunched her eyes shut. *No!* She wouldn't let this trial steal her faith. Hadn't Christ Himself faced the trial of the cross? She opened her eyes and studied the stars above. Yes. God had a plan for her. And apparently this journey was a part of it. So for now, she would just have to keep on trusting and trying to help those around her as best she could.

Her thoughts turned to Mother. Papa had asked her to forgive Mother. To try to understand what had driven her spitefulness over all these years. And now she might never see her again.

Father, help her to know that I forgive her.

The tears did come then, slipping back into the hair at her temples as she studied the moisture-distorted stars spangled across the velvety blackness of the heavens. If she could just see Mother one last time, she would tell her how utterly sorry she was for the pain her presence had brought each time Mother looked at her.

Asha's "soon" turned out to be five days. They came upon the larger caravan midafternoon on a sticky humid day that had kept RyAnne busy swiping at her brow to keep the sting of sweat from trickling into her eyes. Exhaustion clung like a heavy burden. This was multiplied as they crested the top of a hill and caught sight of the vast stretch of valley teeming with long lines of people chained together, most of them packing a tuck of ivory on their heads. The adults she had expected, but it was the vast amount of children that stole her ability to put one foot in front of the other.

Asha prodded her from behind. "No resting yet. We must reach the valley." He tossed a glance behind them, and RyAnne recognized his concern over the rogue lion.

As they descended the trail into the valley, RyAnne couldn't help but voice her shock. "So many children, Asha. So many boys."

He turned his gaze to the valley, let it linger, his lips pressed together grimly. "They will be made into eunuchs. Sent to the palaces of the East."

"But that's illegal!"

He gave her a look, eyes narrowed to point out her naiveté.

RyAnne swallowed and returned her focus to the valley. This was what Trent had been searching for—evidence that Khalifa was involved in illegal activity, and if so, whom he worked for. She clenched her teeth. Trent was no longer able to carry out that mission. But maybe she could find out more and somehow get a message to Commodore Cornwall.

"Asha, you must let me sleep near the children tonight. Some of them may need medical care."

He nudged her forward. "I must do nothing. And you should not get close to the children. Nine out of every ten of those boys will die from the castration."

RyAnne gasped. Surely he exaggerated? "How did you come to be the slave of such a man, Asha?"

He swept a hand down his face, and a look filled with so much emotion crossed his expression that she felt the impact of it.

"I was one of the boys who lived."

The port of Mombasa bustled with activity as stevedores unloaded a fleet of ships recently in from India.

The scents of curry and sandalwood mingled with other not-so-pleasant odors common to any port city—sewage, bilge water, and decaying wharfs. Along the beach, a string of camels being loaded with supplies bellowed and grunted their displeasure, while men alternately yelled and prodded or cajoled the beasts to cooperate.

In the dark hull of one of the ships, Hakim Chadha hefted another crate of spices and thanked the gods he'd been assigned this task instead of the one of sluicing down the last slave ship that had docked.

He emerged on the deck and made his way toward the gangway, but Anju, the stevedore ahead of him, had stopped and was staring out to sea. Hakim adjusted his hold on his crate and looked to see what had caught Anju's attention.

A galleon flying a British flag tacked toward the wharf—a sight not strange in and of itself. It was the speed at which it approached that was strange!

Anju glanced over. "It comes with too much speed, yes?"

Hakim swallowed as he nodded. He assessed their position in relation to where the ship was going to crash. "Clear the docks!" he yelled to those below. Boatmen, porters, and hawkers carried on about their business. Hakim dropped his crate and ran to the ship's rail. "Clear the docks! You there! Move!" The turbaned sailor glanced up. His eyes grew round as he screeched warnings to those nearby and scrambled to escape the quickly looming disaster.

The ship plowed into the docks, sending wood, crates, and men flying in all directions. The ship Hakim and Anju stood on shook violently and heaved on the waves, but thankfully the ties stuck fast.

The British galleon now had a gaping hole in its hull and was rapidly taking on water.

Simultaneously, Hakim and Anju rushed toward the injured ship. They were halfway down the gangplank of their own ship when, from the pilot house of the other, a man stumbled to the rail. Even from this distance Hakim could see that his face was gray and pasty with sweat. The man leaned on the rail for a moment, and then he collapsed, slipping out of sight behind the gunwale.

He was dead by the time Hakim and Anju reached the deck.

Had the choice been left to Hakim, he would have tugged the galleon out into the water and set the ship afire. But the choice was not his. Seeing as how there wasn't a living soul left aboard the ship, the port master claimed the contents of its hold as recompense for damages to his wharf. He set several men to unloading the galleon, while others were immediately dispatched to fetch new lumber for the repairs that would be needed.

Hakim once again thanked the gods that he'd drawn

lumber duty. He didn't get paid enough to have to deal with dead bodies—especially ones that stank as badly as a few of the corpses aboard the galleon. The last man alive had obviously been weakened enough by the sickness that he couldn't hoist the corpses overboard.

Hakim was even more thankful that he'd been sent off on lumber duty when, three days after the unloading of the galleon, the first of the dockworkers assigned to that task fell ill. When the man died two days after that, Hakim packed up his rucksack and hired aboard the first ship that would take him.

It was headed to Zanzibar with the morning's tide.

Good enough.

Life was too short for him to stick around this cursed port.

He would have one last drink with his comrades, and then he would move on to bigger and better things. Hakim found them at their regular alehouse and sank down at the table with them, ordering a draft.

Little did he know that the keg he was served from had only last week arrived in port aboard the British galleon.

Chapter 24
The Trail of Chains

Trent awoke with a groan. So much pain. He didn't dare open his eyes yet. First he must assess. Remember. Where was he? What had happened? Everything seemed to be moving, and he just wanted it to be still. To let him rest. There was a repetitive squeak, squeak, squeak and…heat. So much heat. His head lolled first to one side, then to the other, and a jostle of whatever bed he was lying on zinged pain through his shoulder and forced a gasp from his lips.

The jostling stopped. And suddenly blaring sunlight hit his face.

Even though his eyes were still closed, the light made him scrunch them tighter and lift a hand as a shield.

A moment later a deeper shadow settled above him.

Slowly Trent squinted open one eye. A worried face hovered above his own. Trent tried to say "Kako? Is that you?" but he feared it came out more like a garbled moan.

"The god you serve has saved you then?" Kako poked him in the chest, a quick jab almost as though he half expected Trent to be a spirit being.

"Ow!"

With a gasp, Kako leapt back.

The sun slammed into Trent's eyes once more.

"Ah!" Trent winced and covered his face with both hands. This lying on his back with the sun blazing directly above him was no good. He'd be blind as well as half dead if he didn't find the strength to sit up soon. Whyever was Kako acting so strangely? Trent stretched out one hand. "Kako, help me sit up, please?"

"He *has* saved you!" Kako took his hand and gently pulled him into a sitting position.

Trent didn't have the gumption to try and decipher Kako's strange behavior. His tongue felt like a stick in his mouth. "Water. Please." He pried his eyes barely open, wanting to give himself time to adjust to the bright sunlight.

He wasn't sure why the light would be so bright. The last thing he remembered… What *was* the last thing he remembered? Nyimbo had been on his bedroll. He'd been sitting by the fire.

Kako pressed an open canteen into Trent's hands. "We have been traveling for days, mzee. We thought we had lost you."

Trent pondered on that while he lifted the canteen to his lips. His hand trembled. Since when had a canteen grown so heavy?

His eyes were more accustomed to the light now, and he glanced around them. They were not in their encampment back under the trees by the village. He took another swallow from the canteen, savoring the liquid as it spread over his tongue despite the warmness of it. After a moment he pegged Kako with a look and realized that June and Nyimbo were standing on either side of him. All three of them had eyes nearly as wide as the mouth of the canteen in his hands.

"We are not at our camp." He frowned. It wasn't like him to so blatantly state the obvious. He tried again. "Where are we?"

June clapped both hands to her mouth, and a look of glee filled her eyes. "He lives!" she exclaimed.

Trent actually tossed a glance over his shoulder to see if she might be talking about someone else, but no. It was apparent her comments were made with regard to him.

"What happened?"

Nyimbo threw both her small hands into the air and danced a little jig as she spun in a circle. "He lives! He lives! He lives!" she shouted, hips swaying and knees protruding at odd angles.

With a degree of frustration, Trent tamped home the cork of the canteen. "Yes. I live. Now if one of you could be so kind as to fill me in on where we are and why you are so happy to see me alive, I would greatly appreciate it."

Silence and wide eyes were all the answer he received.

Realizing his strength was fading quickly, he gave up and plunked the canteen down on the wooden board that had apparently been his bed for the past few days. He eased back onto his elbows and studied the contraption he was lying on. It was a rickshaw of sorts with a tented frame above it. Tied over the frame was a somewhat burnt-about-the-edges piece of canvas. It had several charred holes in it but had apparently been his shelter from the sun as they'd been traveling.

He gave his head a little shake, trying to dislodge any memories of the past few days from the depths of his mind. But all he could conjure was blankness. "So weak." He let himself collapse all the way back to a prone position, no longer even caring about the sun in his face.

He heard some bustling about and then blessed shade covered him. But June crawled up onto the plank beside him. She jostled his shoulder. "Before you sleep, mzee, you must eat a little. For days you've had nothing but a little broth dribbled between your lips."

"Too tired, June." He tried to brush her away.

"Only a few bites. Then I will leave you to sleep again." She nudged his lips with a wooden spoon, and he tasted the bland cornmeal mush that was a breakfast staple in these parts.

If only to get her to leave him alone, he took the first mouthful. But then it was as if his body realized its need for sustenance, for he greedily slurped the next spoonfuls that she offered him.

"Not too much. Here, have more water." June held the canteen for him this time, and he drank several more swallows.

She said something else to him, but the black tug of sleep had already too far encroached for him to make sense of her words.

The next time Trent awoke, he was cognizant of only one thing: he couldn't fellowship with his own odor for even one more minute. He needed a bath, and he needed it now. The cart wasn't moving, and the air felt comparatively cool, though he could see it was still light outside the charred canvas covering. "Kako?"

The flap of canvas flipped back, but it was Nyimbo's face that peered in at him.

"Kako." He gestured for the child to go get him.

She only shook her head.

"June then?"

Nyimbo shook her head again.

Trent frowned and struggled to sit up. The effort took all of his strength, and he was puffing for air by the time he got his spine straight.

The cart was parked beneath a lone acacia tree in the middle of a vast plain of brown savannah. Whatever direction he looked—north, south, east, or west—there lay nothing but sepia swaying grasses. But there to the south he could see a dip in the grassland, and now that he could see it, he also heard the dulcet trickle of water.

Blessed water! Perhaps God yet remained on His throne. The irreverent thought brought an immediate prick of conscience. He angled a glance toward the heavens. *Forgive me, Father. But I think even You would admit that my circumstances of late haven't offered the best proof that You watch over the righteous and promise to bring about the destruction of the wicked, aye?*

He judged the distance between himself and the stream. Considered how much strength it had taken for him just to sit up, and realized the water was too far for him to make it there and back again.

Nyimbo stirred something over a small fire not too far distant.

"Where are they?" he called to her.

She looked up, shrugged, then chattered something in her native Chewa, spoken too quickly for him to grasp. He caught "Kako" and "June" but couldn't decipher anything until she said, "Miss Hunter."

A sheer jolt of energy infused him. Had they caught up to the slave caravan? How many days had he been slipping in and out of consciousness while they traveled? He glanced around again as he tested his ability to move his injured shoulder. There was still pain when he moved the limb, but nothing like it had been at first. With time and continued limbering by movement, the shoulder would be next to new again.

Movement caught his eye. Several miles to the north he

could see two people picking their way through the grass. June and Kako were returning. So whatever news the child had just been chattering, he would soon have it from Kako himself.

Nyimbo brought him a bowl of thin stew. There wasn't much in it but broth, but he used his own hand, shaky though it was, to spoon the sustenance into his mouth and was thankful for the bolstering of it. He had just finished when Kako and June stopped next to the cart.

June's smile stretched like a white moon across her face. "You have come back to us from the very teeth of death."

Trent returned her smile and tried not to feel too keenly the pain pulsing through his newly worked shoulder. "That feels about right." He handed his empty bowl and the wooden spoon to Nyimbo with a nod of thanks, then took in Kako's grim expression. "What do you find?" He pointed with his chin in the direction they had just been.

Kako and June exchanged a glance.

Kako's words were measured when he said, "Less than half a day's journey to the north and east we have come across a wide trampled path made by many people."

That had to be the slave caravan. But Trent's strength was nowhere close to what it needed to be to win out in a confrontation with Khalifa. "How far behind them are we?"

Kako shrugged. "Perhaps eight suns? But they seem to be moving fast. So…it may be a few more."

Eight days. Much too long. And yet, when he assessed his injuries, not nearly long enough. And then there was the other looming dilemma they were up against. "How many days until they reach Bagamoyo?"

Kako looked grim. "I spoke to a man once who told me of this trail to Bagamoyo. He described that mountain there, the one with the smoke coming out of the top."

Trent glanced over at the small volcanic mound wisping steam into the sky. "Yes. And?"

"He told me that from here it was less than ten moons to Bagamoyo."

Terror clambered through Trent's chest. They must mount their rescue before the caravan reached the town, for there would be too many in Bagamoyo who would side with the slavers, no matter that RyAnne was more white than black, or that most of the other slaves had neither been at war nor part of a raiding party when captured.

Trent's heart thudded in his chest. Less than a week and he might be able to pull RyAnne into his arms once more, or he would lose her forever! "We must reach them before they get to Bagamoyo. We must travel a little further than normal each day. And I must exercise and begin to get my strength back. We can also travel for a portion of the cooler nights."

Kako shook his head. "That would be most unwise, mzee. I found the carcass of one who had been attacked by a lion, and our party is small."

Trent swallowed. A rogue lion would definitely be a reason to stay in camp close to a blazing fire each night. He slammed his palm against the wood of the rickshaw. Could nothing go his way lately? He sighed. There was naught for it but to press on and pray he wasn't too late to save her.

He nodded at Kako. "Fine. Right. We should not travel at night in that case. But let's try to make the best time we can during the days. For now, help me." He motioned to the streambed. "I intend to rid myself of this deathbed stench."

Kako, June, and Nyimbo were all staring at Trent when he awoke the next morning. He blinked sleepily and scrubbed one hand over his face, hating the itch of the several-weeks-old beard.

He sat up, finding that after having eaten the nourishing stew the evening before, he was much better able to handle that task this morning.

Still the three of them stared at him.

Trent lifted a hand of question. "What can I do for you?"

Three pairs of feet shuffled, and June and Nyimbo turned

their focus onto Kako.

Kako cleared his throat. “You must tell us what we have to do as servants of your great spirit.”

Trent’s brows lifted. “Truly?” Wouldn’t Dr. Hunter be overjoyed if he could hear this conversation? How many times had they sat about the fire on their way inland to Kako’s village with Dr. Hunter expounding on the truths of the Scriptures to the men traveling with them, yet none of them had ever shown the slightest inclination of turning from their traditions. Yet now this…

Kako rubbed the back of his neck, seemingly a bit uncomfortable with the subject. “When you lay dying, we promised your great spirit that we would become his servants if he would use his powers to save you. As you can see”—Kako swept a gesture the length of Trent’s body—“you appear to have been saved. Thus, we too must hold up our end of the bargain.”

Trent grinned. “I see. Well, I can tell you that it gives me a great thrill to hear you say it. But if we are going to engage in such a theological discussion, first I’m going to need a cup of tea, aye?”

Nyimbo scrambled to fetch the gourd they’d been using to drink from. She dipped it into the steaming pot over the fire and hurried to his side with the drink.

Trent sipped, relishing the feel of the hot liquid sliding down his throat. “Very good. Thank you. All right… How about we get on our way, and I will tell you of my God as we travel?” And perhaps that would keep him from worrying so much about whether he was going to arrive in time to save RyAnne from being sold and shipped off.

It was agreed upon, and it only took them a moment to gather their meager supplies and head down the trail.

From his position sitting on the board of the rickshaw, Trent said, “Let’s begin at the beginning.”

All that day, as they followed the wide trampled swath of grassland leading toward the coast, he told them of creation. Of Adam and Eve—that God created them because He wanted to have fellowship with mankind. Of how the devil deceived them, and how they sinned and were removed from paradise, and their relationship with God was broken. He told them of Cain killing his brother Abel. Of Noah and the flood.

Kako voiced the opinion that perhaps there should be another flood to wipe the evil slavers off the face of the earth.

So Trent explained that the rainbows that could be seen in the sky of a time were a symbol of God's promise that He would never again flood the earth.

They stopped for a short time at noon to eat and refill their canteens from a small stream. While they ate, Trent told of Abraham and Sarah and of the promised child, Isaac, whose name meant laughter and who would be the seed from which a whole nation would spring.

When they started on their way again, he walked for a bit. This time he told them of Joseph and his brothers. Of Moses and how his people were enslaved in Egypt by Pharaoh.

Partway through that story, June tsked in disgust that this new spirit they were planning to serve had let his people become enslaved. But when Trent got to the part about the plagues and Pharaoh's army drowning in the Red Sea, she lost her recalcitrance and opined that perhaps this spirit would be worth serving after all.

By the time he'd made it to David's fight with the giant Goliath, his voice was giving out, and it was time to make camp for the night. "I will tell you more of my God and his people tomorrow," he said.

And he did. All that week as they traveled, he walked them through the Scriptures. Through Jesus's death on the cross and subsequent resurrection, and on into the book of Revelation, which promised all mankind would one day stand before God—some to live in heaven and some to face eternal damnation.

All three listened intently. Nyimbo seemed ready to believe anything he said—a fact that made Trent all the more careful with his word choices. But the stubborn logic he kept bumping up against from Kako and June was the fact that there were many spirits in many places, all of which men had to be mindful to please, and it was a "weary lot indeed for people to try and keep all the spirits appeased."

Finally in frustration at the fire one night, Trent threw up his hands. "Look at me. I am well and whole. I even walked for several hours today. Have any of the spirits you have known before this one done such a thing for you as to bring a man back from the very brink of death?"

June pierced Kako with a look. "Never have I seen a man as sick as he was live to tell about it."

Kako begrudgingly agreed.

At last perhaps they were getting somewhere. Trent lowered his hands with a breath of relief. "That's because there is only one God. He is above all other spirits, of which there are many, to be sure. But we do not have to fear them, since we serve the One who rules them all. The One, in fact, who created them all."

This logic seemed to satisfy, and they were less resistant to the truths of the Scriptures after that.

RyAnne woke while it was still dark, and lay in the night silence, listening to Moyo's soft breaths on the thin blanket beside her.

The day they had crested the hill and seen the large caravan stretched out in the valley below them seemed so long ago now. For many days already they had been traveling with the much larger caravan. RyAnne and Moyo had been segregated from the main group once again, but this time there were other women with them. Each of these women had some special feature that made her physically attractive and thus worth more on the market. Some were of mixed blood like RyAnne and Moyo. Others simply had striking features that set them apart from the rest. But all of them would likely be sold as concubines to the palaces of the East, RyAnne had learned.

Fear quaking through her, RyAnne settled one hand over Moyo's little head. What did the future hold for this little one whose father was so calloused as to sell her? She trembled, as she did every time she thought about the future.

Just as before, they continued to receive special treatment—they were fed twice a day instead of only once, and their guards stopped to water them every two hours, where the others only got water three times a day despite the merciless heat of an uncaring sun that scorched them from the moment of its rising till going down again.

The children of the main group had long-since ceased to even have the strength to cry, and RyAnne's heart broke each time she glimpsed the empty vacant stares as they marched forward, simply putting one foot before the other. She had tried several times to sneak over and offer some of the children a bit of the extra fruit she took from the relative bounty she and the other segregated women were given, but twice she had been caught and dragged back, and the one time she had succeeded, she'd only had three tangerines to share. She'd run out of segments within moments, and the pitiful looks she'd received from the children who were unlucky enough not to get a section of the fruit had literally taken her to her knees in tears. Asha had found her there sobbing into her palms, and dragged her back to the segregated women, and this time he'd chained her ankles to those of two other women, one on each side of her.

"I told you nothing good could come from you letting yourself care about them," he growled.

At least Moyo was still free to come and go, so each night the child continued to snuggle next to RyAnne and curl into her side for warmth. And no doubt for comfort also. RyAnne could still hardly coax more than two words at a time from the girl.

With a sigh, she turned on her side to relieve one ankle from the painful press of the manacles.

The first rays of gold-kissed coral light seeped along the edge of the eastern horizon, and RyAnne had just loosed a prayer of thanks for the privilege of seeing such beauty even in the midst of her circumstances, when the lion's roar split the damp dawn air.

RyAnne jolted upright, prickles of terror tingling across the back of her neck, for the creature was very close this time.

She darted her gaze around, trying to pin down exactly which direction the horrifying roar had originated from. Not across the encampment. Not behind the hill.

Next to her one of the women mewled loudly.

The terrified sound sent RyAnne's heart into her throat.

What was that there?!

She saw the flicker of movement—more that of darker shadow shifting within a lighter one—and then, when the beast lifted his head and she could see the outline of his mane against the coal-blue dawn sky, she realized that the mound of blackness she'd first thought a knoll was actually the lion.

The creature was stretched out on its belly in the grass not more than a stone's throw away!

Moyo whimpered by her side, and RyAnne urged her to her feet and pushed her behind the line of women who were all now clambering to their knees. "Stay behind us!"

Languidly, the lion turned its gaze upon her. Tongue lolling, it panted as though it might be a family dog sprawled out on the back porch.

Down the line, others also located the lion and noticed how close it was. Another woman screeched, and then another.

Asha and the other guard were there now, bellowing at them to get on their feet. The second guard hurled his spear at the lion, but in his haste he missed the mark, and the spear went wide. RyAnne waited for Asha to throw his, but he did not. He stood his ground just behind the line of women, watching carefully to see what the lion's next move would be. Why would he not throw it? With no guns provided to them, there wasn't much more help he could offer than that.

More terrified yelps emanated from the women down the line.

RyAnne scrambled to her feet only to be immediately yanked off of them when the woman next to her panicked and tried to run. The chains clanked garishly and pressed painfully into her shins as she righted herself, never taking her eyes off the creature.

Agitated by all the noise, it leapt to its paws and paced a few steps one way and then back the other. Head lowered, muscles bunched, it stared at a woman just two down from RyAnne.

RyAnne's heart hammered, and she frantically searched her memory for what Captain Dawson had said about scaring away lions. Face them, he had said. They were much less likely to attack when looking their prey in the face. And make lots of noise. That had been the solution to scaring off a great number of creatures. Loud noise.

Well, there wasn't much danger of any of them turning away from the beast with him looming so close. She certainly didn't want to turn her back on it! But…a terrified silence had now settled over the women, and that simply would not do. "We must all yell! Together!"

"Yes!" Asha took up her instruction and passed it on down the line, adding his own voice to that of the women quickly catching on to his instructions. The other guard seemed to have disappeared altogether.

RyAnne raised her voice like a warrior about to strike his first blow. On top of that she pounded her feet rapidly on the ground to make the chains around her ankles rattle loudly. Women all up and down the line followed her lead even as they used the pounding footsteps to move themselves away from the lion as quickly as a line of people all chained together could move.

Certainly with all this commotion, the lion should have been startled off. But instead it merely lowered its head and curled one lip into a low snarl as it padded after them. And there was a look of intent purpose in its fearsome gleaming eyes.

Asha stepped in front of the women, and now he and his spear were the only line of protection between the women and the beast. But there were too many of them, and too spread out, for one man to protect.

The first rays of the sun lifting above the horizon revealed the flinch of muscles rippling beneath the scruffy golden pelt. And then the lion leapt forward with a feral screech.

Asha and the women lurched back but, hampered by their chains, two of the women fell. They desperately scrabbled to regain their feet.

With the lion's attention on the felled women, Asha leapt forward and thrust his spear into the lion's side.

Yowling a bellow of pain, the lion spun toward him, and since Asha had retained his hold on the spear, perhaps with the hope of withdrawing it for another thrust, the momentum of the creature's spin knocked the shaft of the spear against Asha's still-healing arm. RyAnne heard him gasp in pain just before the creature swiped out with one great paw and sent him literally flying through the air.

The women cried out, and it had all happened so quickly that the two who had fallen were still trying to right themselves.

Bellowing a roar, the lion struck out at the closest one.

The captive screamed as claws tore open flesh along her leg as easily as a letter opener might slit open a letter.

Moyo froze behind RyAnne, and RyAnne was moving so fast when she backed into her that the momentum took them both to the ground. Sensing new prey, the lion turned toward them with another feral roar.

RyAnne jumped to her feet but fell again because Moyo was tangled in her ankle chains.

The creature padded another step toward them, the spear still protruding from its side.

Behind it, Asha climbed to his feet and seemed to assess himself. RyAnne caught a glimpse of red blood against black skin in the morning gleam of the sun before she returned her attention to the lion stalking toward her.

"Jesus! Please, help!"

With a warrior's cry, Asha vaulted over the lion and landed into a crouch before the beast. He took up a stone in one hand and hurled it with all his might at the lion's head. The stone connected with a sharp *crack*.

The beast yelped, shook its great head, and then trotted a few paces away.

Women all up and down the line, seeing that rocks might be their salvation, took up stones and pelted the cat's tawny hide with them.

Giving one last growl that sounded more like the whine of a petulant girl denied the privilege of a year's debutante season, the lion snapped at the spear in its side, succeeding only in bumping the spear and exacerbating the injury. With a mewl of despair, it shook its pelt as if to remove their reproach, and trotted off into the sunrise.

Relief sent a sob shuddering through RyAnne, and all up and down the line other women began to cry too. Moyo was on her feet now and launched herself at RyAnne, burying her face in her neck and sobbing uncontrollably.

"Oh, honey..." RyAnne soothed her hands over the child's back. "Shhhh. I'm alright. We're all alright now. Shhhhh. I've got you."

Asha met her gaze above the child's head, and she took in the angry bleeding scratches across his chest. Thankfully, he must have leapt back far enough to keep the claws from sinking in too deep, for already the blood seemed to be clotting. She would need to clean them later for him, but for now... She angled a glance to the woman the lion had injured. She lay just a few feet away trembling in silent shock as she stared down at a leg so severely lacerated she would likely never have the use of again.

Asha snapped his fingers at the two women on either side of her. "You there. Do your best to stop the bleeding. I will fetch Jabir."

Moyo continued to shudder, and RyAnne continued to sooth her, but all hope began to wane.

Though she had escaped this lion, her future would be full of many more lions, she feared. Oh, they would have a different visage, but they would be lions all the same.

Moyo whimpered again.

RyAnne soothed her once more, but inside she quaked.

For today she had caught a glimpse of her future. Of Moyo's future too. And it was very dark and hideous. Very dark and hideous indeed.

Chapter 25
The Trail of Chains

The morning of the ninth day, much to Trent's relief, they finally caught up to the slave caravan. They had nearly come upon them in the late evening the night before. But Kako had urged caution about proceeding in the dark of night when they had no idea what they might be facing and were weaponless themselves—other than Trent's one small pistol, which was woefully low on bullets since they had been using it to bag small game for eating as they traveled. The only other weapons they had were the two stout clubs Kako had selected from windblown branches beneath a cluster of trees a few days back. And since Trent had been nearly faint with exhaustion after walking five straight hours yesterday—the first time he'd done that much since his recovery—he had agreed, despite everything in him that urged him to rush in to RyAnne's rescue.

Knowing she was so close, even in his exhaustion, he hadn't slept well, but this morning he and Kako had left June and Nyimbo back with the rickshaw and set out to see what they could find.

And when they crested the hill above the encampment just after dawn and crept to the edge to peer into the valley below, his body vibrated with energy that was ready to take on any battle to get to RyAnne this day.

Even though they'd been following the vast swath cut through the grassland by the trampling feet of hundreds of people for more than a week, Trent had not been prepared to discover the sheer number of captives Khalifa had abducted.

His gut curled with a sick feeling as he took in the valley teeming with line after line of captives all chained together. And in that moment he knew that Llewellyn Cornwall had been correct in his assessment that Khalifa had to be working with someone on the island. The only legal thing to do with all these slaves would be to ship them to Zanzibar and sell them to plantation owners. However, there were infinitely more people here than the economy on the island could absorb. They had to be smuggling them, either directly from Bagamoyo, or taking them to the island and then smuggling them on from there. More likely the latter. Too many British ships patrolled the waters near Bagamoyo. Khalifa likely wouldn't want to take that risk when he could move them from a less chancy place. But they wouldn't sail them to the Stone Town harbor, for they wouldn't want to pay the duty required there. So that would limit the number of places they could take them on the island. They would need a harbor deep enough to sail into and a place to house the captives till they could be sorted and shipped off again. Where would that be? He would have to put his mind to work on that.

The encampment seemed to be writhing with a measure of chaos this morning. A man darted through the clusters of chained people calling, loudly enough that Trent could hear it through the dawn stillness, for someone named Jabir. At first, because of the clearly visible blood on the man's chest, Trent thought he was seeking medical attention for himself. But when a second man stumbled from a tent, obviously still half asleep, the injured man directed him with dramatic gestures, and with great verve and insistence back in the direction he'd come running from.

Nausea dropped into the pit of Trent's stomach. Someone had obviously been hurt. What if they had come too late? Had RyAnne suffered injury just minutes before they could rescue her? If only he could hear what was being said!

But from this distance the words were spoken too quietly to be understood. It was only a moment before the one who was apparently Jabir ducked back into his tent and then emerged with a bag in his grasp and ran in the direction the first man had pointed him.

The first man moved more sedately now, but still with quick steps, to a second tent and paused outside it to say a few quiet words.

Trent pressed a fist to his mouth and watched intently. What he wouldn't give right now to have his field glasses. But they had burned along with all his other belongings in the hut he'd been bunking in back at the village.

He didn't need his field glasses, however, to recognize the man who barreled out of the second tent spewing invectives. Khalifa didn't even take time to grab his kofia before he snatched up a rifle from just inside the door of his tent, shoved the messenger of apparent ill tidings out of his way, and dashed off in the direction in which the man named Jabir had gone.

Trent batted Kako with the back of one hand and tipped his head to indicate they should circle around and see if they could discover what had sent Khalifa off in such a dither. Maybe he'd even be able to catch Khalifa all alone. He squinted his eyes at the pleasant thought. He would like that very much.

They slipped quietly away from the lip of the hill and then skirted the perimeter of the encampment at a run. Trent willed his still-weakened lungs to do their duty and not fail him, but he was nonetheless panting for breath when he and Kako pulled up behind a large jacaranda tree and peered around it to see if they could catch a glimpse of whatever Khalifa had rushed off to manage.

It was probably a good thing that Trent was struggling for breath, otherwise the moment his gaze landed on RyAnne kneeling in the dirt, with Moyo clutched to her, he might have done something rash. As it was, the sight of her alive, safe, and whole took the last of the strength from his legs, and he dropped to his knees behind the tree. Whoever was injured, it wasn't her. *Thank you, Father. Thank you.* He knew it was a selfish prayer the minute it entered his thoughts.

The healer, Jabir, was leaning over a woman who writhed and moaned and clutched handfuls of her hair in agony. Through the long grass, Trent couldn't quite make out the extent of her injuries.

But he was close enough to clearly hear Khalifa when he snapped, "Well? Did it kill her, man?"

Jabir offered no response other than to shake his head.

Khalifa cursed and stomped a few paces away, scanning the

horizon as though searching for something.

Trent ducked lower and pressed his face closer to the tree.

Khalifa, however, did not look in his direction. Instead he raised his rifle above his head and yelled across the plains, "I'm coming for you, beast! You aren't going to remain the terror of the savannah for long if I have anything to say about it!" He cursed the lion soundly, stomping and waving his hands in a tirade that could only have been called a temper tantrum in more genteel circles.

Everything in Trent wanted to rush in and get RyAnne and Moyo immediately, but he forced himself to take a breath and wait. He would do no one any good by barreling in and getting shot by the man a second time.

Presently, the injured man who had run to fetch Khalifa returned to the scene. He stopped near RyAnne. And the moment she noticed him, she set Moyo to one side and stood to her feet. The sound of chains rattling around her ankles was like a knife to Trent's heart. Would she ever be able to forgive him for failing her so utterly?

She spoke softly. "Asha, you must let me look at you."

If he hadn't been so distraught at seeing her in chains, Trent might have smiled. The girl's caring heart ran as deep as her marrow. Captive though she was, she remained a nurturer. A healer. A kind person. The sound of her voice was like a soothing balm to dry and brittle skin. Trent's eyes dropped closed at the sweet melody of it. But only for a moment because he could hardly bring himself to remove his gaze from her.

The man, Asha, brushed her away. "Later. For now, we must hunt the lion and finish it. For injured as it is, it will be even more dangerous than before."

Khalifa overheard the words and nodded. "Yes, Asha. Fetch three guards. We are going after this predator and will kill it here and now. I can't afford to lose any more profits to the beast!"

Trent's teeth ground together. *Unbelievable.*

But this was good. Khalifa and three guards. And a fourth who was already injured and, if RyAnne's reaction to him could be read, might be a trustworthy fellow. Those odds weren't great, but if he and Kako could take out Khalifa first, the guards might capitulate to their wishes more easily.

At any rate, taking them while they were away from the camp would be better than trying to take them here. The added worry out there on the plains would be the lion, which had apparently been wounded, likely by the injured guard. But with Bagamoyo only a day or two farther down the trail, it was act now or perhaps lose the chance to rescue RyAnne forever.

Asha was not long in returning with the guards. And Khalifa delineated strict instructions on how he wanted the hunt handled, and then he led his men in the direction Asha indicated the lion had gone.

Trent and Kako crept back from the women who remained under the watchful eye of the healer, until Trent felt sure they were hidden by the still-lengthy shadows of the dawn, and then followed the party at a distance as they set off to hunt the injured lion.

The hardest thing he had ever done was to walk away and leave RyAnne in chains, especially without letting her know he was here. But he prayed this would be the last time he would ever have to walk away from her again.

Trent nudged Kako and pressed his mouth close to his ear. "If they split up, we move in. If we can take out Khalifa, I think the others will surrender. But I need him alive. Do not kill him." Khalifa was still the only one who knew the identity of whomever he was working with.

Kako nodded, and quietly they followed the hunting party.

Khalifa stalked along at the front, his rifle slung over one arm, his boots thudding loudly into the dust of the game trail.

Kako shook his head, and Trent knew he was thinking the party would never catch the lion unawares, with Khalifa walking so loudly.

The injured guard, Asha, was sent out in front of the party to be the tracker. But the animal's path was not hard to follow. Even trailing far back as he and Kako were and seeing the sign after the hunting party had trampled over it, Trent could tell that the creature was bleeding rather badly and wasn't moving any too fast.

The guard Asha suddenly came to a stop.

Trent and Kako crept a little closer through the grass.

Khalifa cursed. "Are you sure it went in there?"

Asha shrugged. "The trail stops here."

Ahead of the hunting party lay the mouth of cave. The opening was low to the ground, and the craggy knoll into which the opening led wasn't much larger than a good-sized beaver dam might have been back in the Americas. To proceed, the hunting party would have to crawl into the cave one person at a time through the narrow opening.

Khalifa shoved one of the guards. "Skirt around and make sure the trail doesn't continue on the other side. This could be its den, but before we go in, I want to be sure."

The guard departed, and Kako looked to Trent with lifted brow.

Trent shook his head and held up a hand, urging him to wait. There were still four men there. He'd rather hold off for a few minutes to see if their odds improved.

Only a moment later, the guard returned to report that the trail did not continue on the other side.

"Is there another exit where the beast could escape us?"

The guard nodded with a shrug. "There are many places the lion could get out. These caves probably extend beneath the land, Master." He tamped the end of the spear he carried into the dust at his feet to emphasize his point.

Khalifa propped his hands on his hips. It was obvious he had no desire to go into the cave after the beast, but at the same time was reluctant to leave before killing it. After a long moment he pointed to the three additional guards. "You three station yourselves around the perimeter in case upon going in we chase the lion out an opening somewhere. Asha will go in first. He is already injured and will be less of a loss to me if the lion is waiting to attack the moment we get inside."

The men trotted off, spears in hand, and Trent gave Kako a nod. Now was as good of an opportunity as they were likely to get to mount their attack. The guards would not be far enough away for his liking, but the element of surprise might provide the benefit they needed.

As he and Kako silently made their way forward, he heard Khalifa say, "Well? What are you waiting for? Get going."

Asha's lips pressed together thinly, but he did lower himself to his stomach and crawl forward into the mouth of the cave.

Khalifa had his back to them as he faced the cave and watched Asha scoot inside.

Trent motioned for Kako to take the flank, and then stood. He cocked his pistol and extended it. "Good morning, Khalifa."

Khalifa jolted and started to spin around to bring his rifle up to bear, but Kako leapt out from beside him and slammed his club down on Khalifa's wrist, sending the rifle clattering to the ground.

Khalifa cursed and gripped his likely-broken wrist, bending over it. He moaned, "Dawson, what are you doing here? I thought I killed you!"

Trent couldn't help the smirk that tipped up one side of his lips. "You tried."

Asha thrust his head back out the entry of the cave, obviously having heard the commotion.

But Kako had by that time appropriated Khalifa's rifle, a knife, and a machete for his own use. He leveled the rifle at the guard.

Asha, still on his belly in the dirt, immediately thrust his hands above his head.

Kicking the knives out of reach, Kako motioned with the gun for him to exit the cave completely, and Asha crawled forward until he could gain his feet, but kept his hands visible at all times.

Kako finished patting Khalifa down for weapons and, finding no others, gave Trent a nod.

Trent kept his distance, afraid of what he might do to the man if he went any nearer. "On your knees, Khalifa. I have some questions for you. And then I'm going to haul you in for the authorities. But first we are going to march back to the encampment and release all those poor wretches."

Glowering with great fervor, Khalifa dropped to his knees. "We could make a lot of money together, you and I. Why not join me instead of fighting me?"

Trent scoffed. "You don't know me at all if you even think that would be a temptation for me."

At that moment a movement from the top of the knoll caught Trent's gaze.

The lion! The beast had not gone into the cave as they'd suspected but had instead jumped from the ground to the peak, likely to lick its wounds in the morning sun.

Khalifa must have seen the look of surprise cross Trent's face, for he partially turned to see what had caught his attention. But the lion had already launched itself at the man kneeling just in front of its den. Khalifa's shriek split the air, but he only had enough time to raise one arm before the creature's enormous fanged teeth sank deeply into his shoulder, and they tumbled together into the grass.

Khalifa screamed and grappled with the animal. Trent tried to set his aim on the lion, but with the two of them tumbling about as they were, he was afraid he would shoot Khalifa. The man had too much information in his head that Trent couldn't afford to lose if he was going to, once and for all, put an end to this smuggling ring.

In addition to that, he wasn't even sure the .36 caliber would faze the beast, but he couldn't just stand by and watch a man get mauled to death by a lion—not even if it was Khalifa.

Maybe if he could get closer. Trent approached cautiously, not wanting the lion to transfer its attention in his direction.

The lion still had its teeth clamped around Khalifa's shoulder, in a grip meant to strangle. Khalifa was also pinned down by the weight of the beast, but he was still fighting. A spear, obviously from the earlier fight back at the encampment, protruded from the lion's side, and blood coated the tawny hide. Even if they could let it live after it had apparently been killing people, the creature would never recover from such an injury. It was mercy to put it out of its misery.

"Help me!" Khalifa screamed.

Trent stepped closer, took careful aim at the lion's head, and squeezed off a shot.

It flinched and loosed its hold on Khalifa, then yowled most piteously.

Trent shot it again.

And this time it went down in a heap on the ground next to the whimpering man.

With his good arm, Khalifa dragged himself away from the carcass, but his shoulder was a mangled mess and badly dislocated. His back also appeared to be broken, because his legs dragged uselessly in the dust behind him.

Trent suddenly realized that Khalifa was desperately trying to reach the knives that Kako had earlier kicked out of reach.

Asha stepped forward and planted one foot on the hilt of the machete Khalifa was closest to. So…Trent had been right to think that the guards might not rush to Khalifa's aid.

Seeing the betrayal of his guard, Khalifa moaned in despair. "Asha!" His fingers scrabbled to try and lift the large blade, but Asha kept it firmly pinned to the ground, and after only a moment Khalifa gave up and collapsed onto his back in the dirt with a growl of pain.

Without a word, Asha snatched up the machete as well as the knife that lay just past it and walked away. He headed around the side of the knoll, presumably to tell the other guards the news of the attack. But Trent didn't think they needed to fear any retaliation.

Trent looked at Kako and tipped a nod in the direction Asha had just gone. "Send one of them to fetch the healer, though I'm not certain there's much he will be able to do."

With that, Trent approached Khalifa and squatted by his side. Seeing blood spurting from a vein in the man's shoulder, he bent closer and pressed the heel of his hand to it.

Khalifa cried out from the pain of it and then squinted one

eye open and scowled at him. "I would have s-sworn I k-killed you."

"As said, you nearly succeeded."

A garbled sound that could only be interpreted as disappointment rattled at the back of Khalifa's throat. The sun was baking down with fervent heat now, and Khalifa licked his lips. "Water."

"I'm sorry. I have none." He really was sorry too. No man deserved to die this way. "You've lived a mean and miserable existence, Khalifa. There's not much in your life to be proud of, I'm thinking."

Khalifa sputtered a derisive laugh. "You might say that."

"Well, here's your chance to do something good with your last minutes. Tell me who your partner is on Zanzibar. I know you are smuggling some of these slaves off the island. Who's helping you?"

Blood coated Khalifa's teeth when he smiled. "W-wouldn't you l-like to know." Pain must have seized him then, for he convulsed, and his eyes widened. A breath wheezed from his throat, and for a moment Trent feared that he had lost the man, but in the next instant Khalifa met his gaze again. "You'll never f-find it."

They were his last words.

The light of life left his gaze, and his head slumped to one side.

Defeat weighted Trent's shoulders. To be this close to learning the identity of the man at the top…and to have failed…

But he couldn't think of that now. Slowly, he wiped Khalifa's blood off his hand onto the man's kanzu.

He lifted his gaze to see Asha standing quietly to one side with two of the other guards. Just to be safe, Trent trained his pistol on the men. A moment later, when the encampment's healer rushed up with the other guard, he included them under the pistol's threat.

Jabir's eyes widened when he took note of the gun trained on him by a stranger and saw Khalifa on the ground next to the dead lion. Flies already crawled over both corpses.

"It is too late for him. But please"—Trent nudged the air with the point of his pistol, directing the man toward Asha—"see to this man's wounds, right away."

With a grateful nod of his head, Asha sank down onto a rock, and the healer set to cleaning the gashes on his chest.

Trent squatted before the men, careful to keep his Colt before him. "My name is Trent Dawson. I need to know how much resistance I might face from the other guards if I go back into the encampment with the intent of setting all those people free."

Asha and Jabir exchanged glances, first with one another and then with the other guards, but it was hard for Trent to assess the emotions contained in the looks.

Finally after a long moment, Asha spoke. "Truly you would set them—us—all free?"

"Indeed. All of you."

The man licked his lips as though savoring the taste of potential freedom, which had likely seemed out of his reach for many years. "There are a few guards who will protest. Those who might want to step in and take Khalifa's place now that he is gone. But most will not fight."

"Do you think we can quietly take these guards? The ones who might fight?"

Asha nodded. "Jabir and I will help you. We can gather all the guards together as though to tell them of Khalifa's death."

Trent looked to Kako. Doubt still lingered at the back of his mind. Should they trust these men?

Kako shrugged, but after a moment dipped his head. What did they have to lose?

Trent concurred. Still…one could never be too cautious. RyAnne had at least seemed to trust Asha to some extent. Had maintained enough compassion for the man to have wanted to help him back there, before Khalifa made him come on the hunt.

Decision made, he stood. "We will have Asha here gather all the guards in the space between Khalifa's and Jabir's tents. That way we can use the tents to shield our approach until we are right upon them." He made sure to look the guards and Jabir in the eyes. "The healer and these other guards will have to remain here tied up until we are sure the encampment is ours."

The guards with Asha immediately started to protest, but Kako leveled Khalifa's rifle on them, and that quieted them down with rather a great amount of haste.

The next problem was what was he going to tie them with?

Khalifa's knife glinted sunlight from where it had fallen in the grass. Trent took it up and used it to cut several strips from the bottom of the hem of Khalifa's kanzu. These strips he used to bind the guards and the doctor. He lashed them all three to the trunk of an acacia tree, where they would at least have some shade. "One of us will be back for you all just as soon as the camp is ours," he promised. And with that, he and Kako followed Asha across the field toward the encampment.

Trent wanted nothing more than to go directly to RyAnne and let her know all was now going to be well, but first he needed to ensure that none of the guards would give him trouble.

Asha glanced over at him. "Your woman saved my life and then saved my arm when the healer meant to cut it off."

Trent once more swallowed down the desire to go straight to her. He smiled. "She talks of me then?"

Asha snorted at the sentiment. "She thinks you are dead. But I have heard her say your name in her sleep."

The thought gave him a little thrill. So she still missed him? Wouldn't be opposed to learning that he'd come back from the dead? He grinned, and Kako chuckled at him. Asha paused behind a patch of bushy palms. "I will send a boy once I have gathered the guards." And with that he slipped from their sight and into the encampment.

Still uneasy about whether they could trust the man fully, Trent wondered how long they would need to wait, but fifteen minutes later a small face appeared through the bushes. The boy could not be more than ten, and when he stepped into full view, Trent could see that his wrists and ankles bore the scars of shackles.

"Asha has sent me to fetch you," he said in a soft voice.

Trent and Kako followed the boy through clusters of apathetic captives to the center of the encampment. Kako approached from one side of the tents with Khalifa's rifle, and Trent approached from the other.

There were nine guards besides the ones he had tied up back there with the healer, but none of them were armed with anything other than a spear. Even so, Trent knew how deadly some of them could be with their spears, so he hung back far enough to give himself a good view of the whole band of them. He held out his pistol and cleared his throat loudly to draw their attention.

"Khalifa has been killed by the lion, and I have taken over this encampment now. If you give me no trouble, you may have your freedom. If you would like your freedom, lay down your spears."

It took a moment, but to a man, one after the other, they all bent and dropped their spears near their feet.

"Good. If you walk straight toward the setting sun, you will exit the encampment. Keep walking and don't come back. If Kako or I see you again, we will shoot you on sight. Understood?" Then, knowing how much of a hardship it would be on them to be left on the plains without their spears, he added. "You may take your weapons with you. Kako and I will escort you to the edge of the encampment."

The men expressed pleased surprise. Several of them bowed their thanks over and over again. Only one man appeared a little disgruntled as they escorted them out of the encampment, but with no one else protesting, Trent didn't think they would have any trouble from him.

Kako hung back, and Trent looked over at him.

He tipped his head toward Asha.

Trent transferred his attention to the man. "Yes?"

Asha kept his head bowed in subservience. "With your permission… Your woman saved my life. It would only be right that I remain with her until I have repaid the debt."

The truth was, Trent was glad for an extra man to help with all the work they would need to do in the hours to come. With a nod, he agreed.

They waited until the guards had all disappeared over the far horizon before they turned back to the encampment.

First things first. He would go see RyAnne, but then they would need to bring water and food to all these starving people before they could in good conscience release them to go back to what might be left of their villages.

Hakim Chadha stepped off the boat in the Stone Town port. He had to admit that as places went, this port was probably the most putrid of harbors he'd ever had the displeasure of sailing into. The stench that hung in the air stung the nostrils and made the eyes water. A corpse bumped against the gangplank as he took the last step, and just up the beach, two Zanzibaris were using a net to drag another corpse onto the shore. It appeared the bodies were gathered and burned.

What a dreadful place this would be to work. But there was nothing for it. He didn't have enough money to make his way to a different port. So until he could save enough to move on, this would be the place he called home.

Best he start asking about for work. The sooner he found some, the sooner he could be shut of this place.

He had only taken two steps up the dock, however, when the first wave of weakness hit him. His stomach rebelled and threatened to cast up its contents. He managed to stumble to the edge of the pier, but once on his knees and finished with the foul task, he found that his muscles refused the order to stand again.

"You there?" A stevedore stepped closer to him. "Be ye in need of 'elp, lad?"

"Aye" was all he managed.

The stevedore carried Hakim to the nearest clinic, but the doctor had been called away to the other side of the island to tend to a birthing.

"I 'ave ta git back ta work, ye see. The doc, he should be 'long, right snappy like. Ye just sit here on the steps, an' he'll 'elp ya soon as he returns."

By the time the doctor returned, Hakim was staring sightlessly toward the sky, and a stiffness had already set into his corpse.

RyAnne fidgeted nervously. She would have given just about anything could she have paced back and forth. Instead she was consigned to being satisfied with merely standing, since her ankles were still chained to those of the women on either side of her.

Khalifa had led Asha and the other guards away to hunt the lion over an hour before. And then one of the guards had rushed back and demanded that Jabir accompany him. Someone had sustained an injury, he'd said, but nothing more than that—not even when she'd prodded for more information.

Her first concern was for Asha. Had he been wounded even worse by the lion? Or was it his initial wounds that were suddenly worsening?

Her second concern was for the children of the camp. Normally they were fed and given water as soon as the sun rose. And since they were given so little fluids, the morning's distribution was an essential necessity for replenishing needed sustenance to small bodies. Yet Khalifa and Asha had not returned, and neither had Jabir.

Moyo had curled up on the ground near her feet and returned to sleep, taking advantage of the rare extra rest she was so in need of. Most of the women had also returned to sleep. Even the woman who had been clawed seemed to have been lulled into a stupor by whatever draught Jabir had given her.

Every once in a while Moyo whimpered, and RyAnne imagined dreams of the lion attack, or perhaps the attack on the village, haunted her.

She stooped down and soothed her hand over the child's forehead. "Shhhh, Moyo. I'm here. All is well now."

She heard footsteps and looked up.

Asha was approaching in the distance with a bearded man she didn't—

She gasped and covered her mouth with one hand.

That oh-so-recognizable casual gait—feet planted wide like a man who'd grown up keeping his balance on sea-tossed ships. His shirt was dirty and torn, but draped over those familiar broad, sturdy shoulders.

Tears filled her eyes as he came closer, making it even more difficult to focus and discern if she was losing her mind.

Yet those wind-whipped curls, though several lengths longer than they had been the last time she'd seen him, could belong to none other.

Still she doubted herself. Surely she was mistaken. Every limb shook with the terror that she was simply seeing the familiar in the form of a stranger.

But his gaze was locked on to hers, and he was heading straight for her, only paces away now. And when he stopped before her, there was no mistaking those gray-green eyes, no matter that most of his face was buried behind a black beard.

"Captain..." The word was barely a breath, and then she lost all the strength in her legs and slipped to her knees as sobs overtook her.

He knelt with her and tugged her firmly into a trembling embrace. "Shhh, RyAnne. I'm here, hmmm? I'm here." He cupped the back of her head and pressed his bristly cheek first against her own, then against her hair, and finally against her shoulder.

His body shuddered, and a gravelly sound, half pain and half joy, slipped from the back of his throat. When she pulled back to take a second, third, and even fourth look, there were tears shimmering on his lower lids. He dashed at them as he gave a gruff bark of self-deprecating laughter and offered a watery smile.

"I can't believe you are here. How..."

He took her face in both his hands and pressed his forehead

to hers. "I have Kako and June to thank for saving me."

A thrill most certain swept through her. "Kako and June? Alive?"

He nodded. "And Nyimbo."

"Father in heaven be praised!" Nyanja came to mind, but she couldn't seem to bring herself to voice the question. Her gaze traveled to Moyo, still sleeping soundly on the ground next to them.

Trent followed her gaze and then when she met his eyes once more, shook his head. "I'm sorry."

Tears spilled anew. Even though it was what she had suspected for weeks. "Moyo has never said, but I think she saw her k-killed."

A muscle bunched in Trent's jaw, and he rubbed one thumb over what she felt sure was the scar left by Khalifa's hand on her cheek.

She held her breath, wondering how terrible it really looked. With no looking glass, she had no way of knowing. The truth be told, she hadn't even thought of it over the past weeks. But now, with Trent looking at her with such pity in his eyes, her heart dropped. "Is it hideous?"

He blinked and met her gaze. "Never could the sight of you be hideous."

As touching as that sentiment might be, she wouldn't let him get away with such a blithe answer. "How bad is it, truly?" She pressed her lips together, almost afraid of what he might say.

He bent forward until she could look nowhere but into the sincerity of his eyes. "The truth is, it is barely noticeable, but my heart breaks at what you must have gone through these past weeks."

The statement should have brought relief, but instead it weighed her down with guilt. She closed her eyes, attempted a steadying breath.

He pulled her head close and pressed a kiss to her forehead. "Don't fret, RyAnne."

RyAnne felt her face crumple. "Oh, Trent, I'm afraid this whole sorry mess is my fault! Khalifa said—"

Trent set her back from him and took her face firmly in his hands. "Never mind what Khalifa said, aye? The man is a liar and the lowliest of villains. This was his doing and none other's. Do you hear me? None other's."

"What happened to him?" She glanced around. The man had been such a part of her life for the past several weeks that she almost expected to see him walk up and with one swipe of his hand dissipate the illusion—Trent here before her, holding her face in his hands, and speaking to her in audible tones.

"Khalifa was attacked by the lion. I'm afraid he met with a very gruesome and painful ending."

At that moment RyAnne realized Asha was unlocking the manacles on all the women up and down the line.

RyAnne closed her eyes. *Please, Father, don't let this all be a dream*. "So what is to happen to all of us?" She swept a gesture to the other women nearby and then to the camp in general.

"Everyone will be freed." He stood, pulling her up with him. He slipped his hands behind her waist, pulling her closer.

She breathed in the earthy scent of him, not even caring that it was hardly the most pleasant of odors at the moment. "Oh, Trent. I can hardly believe my eyes and my ears and my hands." She curled her fingers into the beard along his jaw.

He bent forward and kissed her, lingering over the task. "Believe it. I'm here. Right in front of you. And giddy with the joy of it."

For a long time they simply stared at one another. Touched one another. Breathed the same air as one another.

Trent brushed her hair back from her face. There was a catch in his voice when he spoke. "I feared I wasn't going to make it in time. Forgive me for failing you?"

RyAnne laid one finger over his lips. "You did not fail me. There was naught that you could have done."

"I have rehearsed it a thousand times and think that surely there were a few things I should have done differently. But… What's important is that we've found each other again."

"Indeed."

He swept his hands down her arms. "I could stand here taking in my fill of you all day, but we've much to do. We need to free and feed all these people. And get them water."

"Yes, of course. I will help."

And as she bent to wake Moyo, and watched Trent stride away giving instructions to Asha and Kako, RyAnne couldn't help but turn her thoughts to prayer. *Oh, Father, You promised me Your grace was sufficient for me, and I doubted You. And yet it was. It carried me through until You could bring about the good end that You had planned for us. For this, I thank You. You have taken me from this trail of chains and set my feet on the path of freedom.*

Dear Reader,

Yes, the pinching-ant pinchers really were used to close wounds. In fact this method of suture was used even up into the 1940s and '50s, when my grandparents were missionaries in what was then called the Belgian Congo.

One of the problems that early missionaries faced with bringing the truth of the gospel to Africa was the fact that many African tribes believed that powerful spirits resided everywhere and could be appeased and bargained with, much like powerful human beings. God, being all benevolent and immutable, was an enigma that couldn't quite be grasped. Surely a being so powerful would require remunerations of some sort from anyone who wanted or needed something from Him? Convincing them this was not the case with God, the One True Spirit above all spirits, was not an easy task.

The lion attack in this story is very similar to one described by Dr. David Livingstone in his book *Missionary Travels and Researches in South Africa*. A lion had been plaguing a certain village, killing sheep on several occasions. Dr. Livingstone decided to help them in their attempts to hunt down and kill the lion. The lion was up on a small hill. Dr. Livingstone emptied both barrels of his gun into the lion, but was in the process of reloading when the lion leapt on him. It seized him by the upper arm, and he described what followed as being shaken "as a terrier dog does a rat." He was saved by the fact that another man took up a weapon and shot at the lion. That gun misfired. However, the lion left off attacking Livingstone and turned to attack that second man. Only a moment later it dropped dead from the initial gunshot wounds inflicted by Livingstone. Livingstone's arm was shattered, and he described the teeth marks left by the lion as looking like gunshot wounds.

God bless!

Lynnette Bonner

The Joy of the Morning

…weeping may endure for a night, but joy cometh
in the morning.

Psalm 30:5

Chapter 26

The Joy of the Morning

RyAnne sank to her knees and relaxed back against her ankles. The cook fire she'd been bent over for the past several hours was naught but smoking coals now. She rubbed her fingers into the cramping muscles of her lower back. Despite the pain, she couldn't feel anything but relief to know that all the people of the encampment had now been fed. Several parties had even already departed to return to their villages. As different chieftains located what was left of their people, many hadn't wasted time in taking leave of the white man who, to their way of thinking, might change his mind at any moment and clap them back in irons.

This morning, after Trent rescued the captives, Kako had located the men and women of his tribe and freed them from their shackles. Some of the men he had taken with him on a hunt. The others had been set to releasing the rest of the captives, building up cook fires, and fetching water for those who were too weak to go to the nearby creek themselves.

RyAnne had cleansed and tended, as best she could, more wounds caused by the chafing of manacles than she could stomach. Partway through the day, after she had washed the ankles of a vacant-eyed girl of no more than five years of age, the frustration and heart-wrenching empathy had taken the last of her composure. Trent had discovered her with tears streaming down her face as she cleaned the wounds of the next child, and had made her change jobs with June, whose task it had been to make porridge.

RyAnne couldn't deny that the change of scenery—from blood and blisters and glimpses of white bone through ebony skin, to bubbling porridge with steam wisping from it—had been a most welcome contrast.

With Bagamoyo only a couple days ahead of him, Khalifa had nearly depleted the supplies he had been feeding the captives.

RyAnne hated to think what the meals would have been like over the next few days.

She and Trent *had* found a meager supply of cornmeal, however. The porridge had been thin to make it stretch further, but they had done their best to make sure every person ate a decent meal by including pieces of game from the gazelles Kako and his men had bagged.

Trent had broken up two fights between parties when fear had made them grapple over scraps. The first sight of food on the heels of weeks of near starvation had the tendency to transform people into hoarders. It had taken some convincing on the captain's part for everyone to share equally.

RyAnne knew the portions had been insufficient, yet even at that they were much more plentiful than the people had been fed for the past weeks. Some of the captives had been so hungry that they hadn't even waited for the meat to cook, but had simply devoured their portions raw.

RyAnne shuddered. She was hungry, but she didn't think she would ever be *that* hungry. The thoughts of food penetrated her consciousness, and her stomach loudly protested its emptiness. She had doled out the last of the thin gruel as a second helping to Moyo, and there was nothing left in her pot.

She should go see if any meat was left, but she couldn't seem to work up the energy to rise now that she'd relaxed for a moment.

She glanced over and noticed Moyo and Nyimbo seated together on a rock. Their heads were tipped together, and Moyo was sharing her bowl of porridge.

A smile tugged at RyAnne's lips even as exhaustion draped her shoulders. Though she'd been watching the two of them off and on all day, she could still hardly believe that her long nightmare was over. They were all reunited.

Weeping may last through the night, but joy cometh in the morning. The verse soothed her in that moment. Perhaps her morning had finally dawned.

A bee buzzed around her shoulders, and she swept a hand at it. As she twisted to make sure the bee was flying away and wouldn't get caught in her hair, one of her ankles pressed against a sharp stone. She gasped and shut her eyes at the severity of the pain.

She eased her hip to the ground and carefully lifted the hem of her skirt to examine the ankle. It was red and swollen, and looked like it was getting infected. On the long trek, she'd tried her best to keep the broken skin clean, but it appeared she was losing the battle.

Footsteps sounded, and she quickly tossed the hem back over the injury.

Trent sank down, balancing on the balls of his feet beside her. Resting his forearms against his knees, he clasped one wrist with his other hand. His gaze flicked down to the torn lace edging near her ankle. "Are you okay?" A furrow tucked into his brow.

"It's nothing."

He studied her expression for a moment, and then in one swift move, he reached out and flipped back the hem.

"Captain!" She slapped his hand away and clamped the material firmly in place over her throbbing joint. But she could tell that he had seen all he needed to see.

He pinned her with a stern look. "It's infected."

Another wave of exhaustion swept over her. "I'm well aware of that. Perhaps Jabir will have left something in his tent with which I can treat it."

He reached for her hem again. "Let me get a better look."

She refused to budge. "It would be most improper."

His mouth pressed into a thin line of irritation. "What was it your father used to say? 'Let us leave proper for Stone Town parlors and consider what would be safest and most prudent on the savannah.'"

She could almost hear Papa's voice saying it, and she couldn't help a sad smile as a bittersweet pang of nostalgia gripped her.

Apparently sensing he'd put her in a melancholy mood, Trent lifted one hand and touched her cheek. "You look done in. Did you eat?"

"I will in a moment. My porridge pot is empty. I was just

resting for a bit before I went in search of some food."

Concern crinkled his eyes. "Please tell me you stopped at some point today to eat at least a little something?"

She plucked a pebble from the ground and rolled it between her fingers. "I'll be fine. There were so many hungry people. For weeks I've wanted to feed them. Today I got to see that dream come true. What are a few hunger pangs in the face of that?"

He bent forward and pressed a kiss onto her forehead. "You have one of the most beautiful hearts of any woman I know." He eased back and tipped her a chastising look. "But in order to care for others, you also have to care for yourself. Wait here. I'll bring you a plate, and while I'm gone, I want you to prepare yourself to let me look at that abrasion. I have a feeling it might be worse than you are letting on."

She bit her lip, unable to deny now that she pondered on it, that her ankle had been shooting small pains up her calf all day. "Perhaps a little."

"Ry..." There was despair and displeasure with her all wrapped up together in that one little word.

All the love for this man that had been building inside of her over the past months surged to life in her chest. It was almost too painful to breathe. She reached out and curled her fingers into his beard. "I can't believe you are here. Close enough for me to touch."

He caught hold of her hand and kissed her palm. "I'll only be a moment."

True to his word, he returned with a plate filled with scraps of meat, several loquats that some children had discovered in a nearby grove, and a gourd full of steaming broth.

The broth smelled heavenly, but she wondered where it had come from. At her questioning look, he shrugged. "There was no porridge left, but June had set some of the bones to boiling for a meal later this evening. It likely won't be as tasty now as it will be later, but I figured you needed the nourishment."

The broth tasted like a bit of heaven when she sipped it. And the first morsels of meat... She gobbled much too quickly for propriety. Her hand trembled when she reached for the first golden loquat.

A muscle in Trent's jaw bunched. "I failed you yet again. I did not realize you were so hungry."

She smiled around the bite of luscious plummy fruit. "I didn't realize it either until I started eating. Don't be so hard on yourself."

"But I am." He snatched a blade of grass in disgust. "I should be!" He transferred his troubled gaze toward the horizon.

RyAnne cleaned her plate and then set it aside and reached over to clasp his hand. "I've just been pondering on a verse. 'Weeping may last through the night, but joy cometh in the morning.'" She squeezed his fingers. "Once the dawn arrives, not many look back and consider what they endured during the night hours. They simply move ahead with their day. So let it be with us? We have come through the night, both slightly scathed but whole. And now the day stretches out before us."

Trent stood to his feet and pulled her with him. "Aye, that it does." He scooped her up suddenly.

She gasped and threw her arms about his neck.

He strode toward the tent that the healer Jabir had used on their eastward trek. It was pitched at the center of the encampment, as usual. He ducked through the entryway and then set her on the cot inside. He left the flap of the tent open, but they were mostly concealed from the prying eyes of the few left in the camp. He lit a lantern and then held it high, searching the contents of the tent. "Jabir departed with one of the parties earlier this afternoon. But all of his supplies are still here." There was a leather satchel on a nearby table. He opened it and probed at the contents inside. "You are the nurse. What should I be looking for to sooth that infection?"

Weariness clung heavily to RyAnne's eyes. "Honestly, the best thing I know to do is just what I was doing this morning for the wounded. Clean the area with soap and water. And then it should be wrapped in a clean boiled bandage, but of course we don't have any of those. A light application of carbolic acid would be good if any could be found."

"None of these vials are labeled." Trent slapped the bag closed in frustration.

RyAnne hung her head and worked at the muscles along her neck. She didn't want to have to make a decision right now. Yet if she didn't do something, the infection would only grow worse.

Trent was suddenly back by her side. He squeezed her shoulder. "Rest. I will return in an hour with hot water for a bath."

She eyed the empty space of the cot next to her. Jabir must have taken his bedroll, as there were no blankets, but the cot did look ever so inviting.

Trent slipped out and let the flap of the door fall closed, enveloping her in semidarkness. She slumped onto her side, and let the oblivion of sleep claim her.

Feeling a helpless roil of frustration, Trent stalked across the encampment to put water on to boil. She needed bandages. Where was he going to find something to suffice?

He looked around as he walked. Other than the areas of still-crushed grass littered with a few abandoned ivory tusks and discarded manacles, and the two tents that remained standing, one would never know that just this morning hundreds of poor souls had been chained up in this field. Most of the captives had scattered immediately after receiving their allotment of food, just as he'd suspected they would. His goal had not been to fill them really, but to give them enough sustenance to go on their way with the energy to do their own hunting and picking as they journeyed back to what was left of their homes.

June was still by one of the fires, seated on a rock.

He smiled at her as he approached. "Did you eat?"

She nodded.

He gestured to the fire. "Can you build it up while I go fetch some water from the creek? Miss Hunter will need to bathe."

June nodded.

And once he had the large pot over the fire, he decided that now was as good a time as any to see if Khalifa's tent would reveal any of the man's secrets. Frustration coursed through him as he stomped toward the tent. If only he'd had more time to question the man, he might have learned whom he worked for.

He wasn't sure what he'd expected, but when he flipped back the canvas, he knew he hadn't been expecting the well-supplied, meticulously organized environment that greeted him.

The cot had a feather mattress on it beneath sheets that were still rumpled due to Khalifa's hasty exit this morning. A large silk rug covered most of the floor space inside. An extra pair of boots were tucked neatly beneath the end of the cot. There was a small portable desk with a lantern atop it, a fountain pen lying to one side, and a chair before it that sported a feather cushion. Next to the lantern rested a silver flask. He sniffed the contents—whiskey.

He grunted in satisfaction at that and set the flask back down. RyAnne's wound would have its disinfectant.

The only other thing atop the desk was a shaving kit. Trent scratched at the itch of his beard with another noise of satisfaction. It would be good to rid himself of the annoyance of it.

Beneath the desk and off to one side were two freestanding wooden drawer units stacked one atop the other. Each had a keyhole. And both were locked when he tugged on them. He glanced around. He didn't see any keys. And there was nothing else in the tent.

Taking the knife from his belt, he pried at one of the drawers. The locks were not strong, and it only took him a few moments to open a crack large enough for his fingers to get a good grip, and then he wrenched it open. The drawer had no stop and came completely out of the casement, slipping from his grasp.

Rolled-up pieces of parchment and folded letters tied together with ribbons flew everywhere. Trent growled and set to picking them up. He went to work on the second drawer then, and opened it more carefully. It contained more of the same—letters and parchments.

Lips pinched in curiosity, Trent lit the lamp, sank onto the chair, and started reading. Most of the letters were from a woman—a guess only, since they were written in Arabic that Trent couldn't read. But the script was delicate, and the pages smelled of sandalwood and a sweet citrus-like perfume. *A mother? A wife?* Trent tapped one of the missives against his palm. Keeping correspondence from a woman was a rather sentimental gesture. Not something he would have credited to Khalifa. He studied the stationary again, more carefully this time, yet found nothing out of the ordinary. With a grunt of frustration, Trent stacked the letters together and set them to one side. Several parchments contained drawings of slave ships with instructions for how to best load the ships to ensure maximum capacity of "cargo," depending on the type of vessel. The drawings, depicting people lying side by side on shelves that left not even enough room to sit up all the way, made his stomach curl in disgust. He tossed them down, one after the other.

There was a small stack of blank Harcourt stationary. After those, there were two parchments left. These contained a series of dates and numbers that Trent could only assume were the number of captives seized on each date. Trent tallied the figures. Nine hundred and ninety-seven people. That was the number of captured. How many others had been deemed unfit for transport and left dead and dying in the wake of Khalifa's raids? He closed his eyes at the sick feeling of it.

He massaged his fingers over the headache beginning to build just behind his brow. The evidence of such blatant inhumanity, jotted down so casually and now clasped between his fingers, fluttered in proportion to his rapidly growing outrage. After only a moment, he crumpled the pages into a ball and squeezed tight. His hand trembled.

He tossed the parchment down. No evidence of whom Khalifa was working with…

You'll never find it… Khalifa's last words taunted his memory. He hadn't said, 'You'll never find *him*,' as one might have thought, but *it*. *It*… Evidence?

The fact that Khalifa had mentioned finding something meant there had to be something here to find, didn't it?

He glanced around, then searched carefully inside each of the drawers again.

Nothing.

He overturned the cot, stripped off the sheets and blankets, felt every corner and portion of the feather mattress. He would have torn it open in his frustration, except that he considered it might make RyAnne's next few nights a little more tolerable. The material was thin enough that he would have felt if there were any hidden items, even letters, in it. Next he turned the cot over and searched the underside, running his hands all along each seam to feel for any oddities.

Nothing.

He sank to his haunches and scanned the interior of the tent again. After only a moment of pondering, he strode to the desk and removed everything from it. He examined it from every angle. Turned it upside down. Shook it to hear if anything rattled. The folding legs didn't sound hollow, and there were no hidden compartments that he could find. The chair received his examination next, with the same results.

Nothing.

Trent propped his hands on his hips and studied the walls of the tent. The canvas appeared ordinary in every way.

If he were Khalifa and had important information to hide, what would he do with it?

With that many people set to arrive in Bagamoyo just days hence, Khalifa would surely have ships scheduled to be there, ready to take on the cargo and move it. Khalifa could have planned to sell some captives in Bagamoyo, Trent supposed. But most would likely have been loaded onto ships. Information about that had to be somewhere.

"*Mzee*?" Kako's voice came from outside the tent.

Disgusted with his lack of success, Trent snapped up one of the sheets, strode to the flap, and stepped out onto the grass outside.

Spear in hand, Kako stood waiting for him. "June has asked that I tell you the wash water is ready. All the meat from the ten gazelles we brought in this morning is gone. I'm going out to hunt for our evening meal."

Trent clapped the man on the shoulder. "Thank you, Kako. I know you've had a long day. And I appreciate your help."

Kako shrugged off his thanks. "Legs that will not walk shall later find themselves hungry."

Trent nodded. "Yes indeed." He went to June then and asked her to carry the hot water to RyAnne. And while she did that, he filled the other pot with water and put it over the roaring fire. Using his knife, he cut a strip of material off the end of the sheet, and as soon as the water boiled, he poured off a good measure into a bucket and then dropped the strip of the sheet into the water left in the pot. He set it back over the fire to keep boiling.

The bucket he carried back to Khalifa's tent. He intended to have a bath of his own. If he was going to care for RyAnne, he needed to keep his own wound properly cleaned, and he couldn't wait to rid himself of his beard.

RyAnne couldn't believe how good it felt to sluice warm water over her skin. There was only a razor-thin piece of soap left, and nothing to scrub with, but just the human act of rinsing dust and sweat from her skin made her feel a bit of her old energy returning. After she washed, she even rinsed her hair in what was left of the water and wrung it out as best she could with her hands.

Her dress and petticoats were still rank and dusty, but they were the only garments she had, so she shook them out and slipped them back on. She had just finished that task and turned her attention to Jabir's medical bag to see if she could find something to treat her ankle, when she heard footsteps outside.

"RyAnne?"

"Yes, Captain. Come in." He'd been right in his assessment

earlier. None of the bottles in Jabir's bag were labeled. She couldn't use any of this without knowing what the various powders and potions were. With a sigh, she turned to face the entry.

Trent entered with a still-steaming pot, and she saw him wince as he bent forward to set it down. Concern turned her to fully face him. "Are you well, Captain? In all the hubbub today, I realize I have not asked after your wound. I know Khalifa shot you, as I saw it with my own two eyes."

Trent placed one hand to the opposite shoulder and worked his arm in a circular motion a few times. "He hit me high on the chest in this shoulder. June pried the bullet out, but infection did set in. They said they made a pact with God that if I pulled through, they would serve Him."

RyAnne's joy bloomed on her face. "Truly?"

He nodded. "To be honest, until a week and a half ago, they thought I wasn't going to recover."

All concern for her own ankle and the excitement over his news drained from her, leaving only cold fear in their wake. She strode toward him and snapped her fingers. "Off with that shirt, Captain, and let me see the wound."

He smiled softly, captured her hand, and tugged her closer. His gaze roamed her face. "I've missed your stubborn high handedness."

She pressed her lips together and pinned him with a look. "I am not high handed. Now off with that shirt."

He chuckled. "Nothing high handed about that, now is there? And the answer is no. I just washed and made sure to clean my shoulder carefully. There's no infection in it anymore. Your ankle first."

He dropped a quick kiss against her lips, and that was when she noticed he'd shaved off his beard.

She touched his jaw, relishing the feel of his freshly shaved skin. "We'll make a stubborn pair of old goats, you and I."

A twinkle gleamed in his gray-green gaze. "Mmmm. And one of us is going to have to learn that the other is more stubborn than they are." A quirk of his lips let her know he was teasing her.

And for some crazy reason she was suddenly in a capitulating mood. "Fine." She sank onto the edge of the cot. "But as soon as I clean my ankle, I will feel better if you let me look at your shoulder."

He bowed his agreement and moved the steaming pot closer to her. "Thanks to Khalifa's sheets, you have your boiled wrap." He motioned for her to hike her hem.

Despite her embarrassment at the impropriety of it, she stretched out her leg and tugged the skirts up till he could see her broken skin.

He grunted. "It does look a portion better after being washed." He pressed gently at the area around the wound. "How is your pain?"

She swiveled her foot this way and that. "It's not too bad unless something presses right against it. I think if I keep it clean from here on, it should heal up in the next day or so. Having the bandage will help with that."

His lips twisted. "Thank the Lord for Khalifa's fondness for finer things like sheets, aye? Oh, and I almost forgot—" He pulled a silver flask from his back pocket and held it up, wiggling it for her to see. "And whiskey."

She started to smile at the joke, when she realized what his intentions with the alcohol were.

He held it above her ankle, one eyebrow lifted as though to ask if she was ready.

Gritting her teeth, she nodded for him to get on with it.

Trent drizzled a portion of the whiskey over her wound. Her gasp lifted his concerned gaze to her face. "Sorry."

"It's fine." She took a breath and motioned for him finish.

After another torturous splash of the alcohol, he wrapped the hot bandage around her ankle.

He looked up. "Too hot?"

She shook her head. "No. I actually think the heat might help kill some of the infection also. I'll be fine."

He went back to smoothing the bandage and then tying it off. "You're all set." He tugged the hem of her skirt back into place and then met her gaze. At the loving look in his eyes, RyAnne's heart thudded against her breastbone.

He leaned forward, and his hands were warm when they settled against her cheeks. "Now that we have reached our 'morning,' I'm reminded that I had asked you a rather life-altering question and had not yet received an answer when Khalifa so rudely interrupted us."

"A question?" She pretended forgetfulness and placed one finger over her lips as though deep in thought. "You had asked me a question, Captain?"

His lips curved. "Indeed, and as I recall, I had mangled it rather badly, so let me remedy that now." He moved the pot to one side, took her hand, and settled to one knee before her.

RyAnne covered her mouth with one hand. As tears filled her eyes, Trent's expression blurred, making it nearly impossible to see him. She dashed them away, not wanting to miss a moment of this.

Trent traced his thumb over the back of her knuckles. "I remember the first time I saw you. Did I ever tell you?"

She shook her head and stayed her breath, the better to hear him.

With a faraway look in his eyes, he smiled at the memory. "Father and I had sailed into the Stone Town harbor and made our way to the guesthouse your parents always made available to us. I was probably sixteen that year, and you were no more than eleven or twelve. We had stayed there many times, but I had never seen any member of your family other than your father before. On this day, however, as we wearily strode down the cobbled walk, intent only on a quick meal and then rest, there were two young girls in the front yard. One of them was blond with a laugh that reminded me of church bells, but it was the other, the one sitting primly on a bench, with a violin tucked close to her cheek, who captured my attention."

His gaze shifted to her face, and he traced one finger down her cheek. "She had beautiful tawny skin."

A tingle of desire rippled out from the place of his touch, such that it made its way deep into the depths of her and clenched her stomach tight.

His focus angled to her hair. He wrapped one of her curls around his forefinger and caressed it with his thumb. "And long black curls that shimmered in the sunlight till a lad's hands itched for the feel of them."

RyAnne chuckled in embarrassment at that. If only the man knew how she'd despised her curls all these years.

His gaze returned to hers. "Even at that I might have just passed on by, but then you played the first note. It was as though the melody reached out and took me by the shoulders and said, 'Stand still, lad, and pay attention.'" His eyes crinkled at the corners, as if to admit he knew the sentiment was ridiculous.

He lifted one hand and stroked his thumb down from her forehead to touch the outer corner of her eye. "I don't remember what song you were playing. But I remember the way you closed your eyes. And I remember how you swayed as you poured your whole heart into the melody."

He was once again blurred by her tears. She bit her lip to withhold the sob of sheer happiness welling up inside her.

He shifted slightly. "I had first thought you were playing for your sister, but when the song ended, I realized that she was nowhere to be seen. It was from the gardener tending the nearby rose bushes that you sought your compliments."

RyAnne nodded, capturing the moisture beneath her lashes with her fingertips. "His name was Samir. And he never once criticized my playing. I would mangle a song over and over again as I practiced out on the lawn. And I'm sure his poor ears rebelled many a time, but he always smiled. He would pat me on the head, tuck a rose bud into my hair, and tell me I played as though I were expressing the voice of the angels."

Trent smiled gently and stroked the backs of his fingers across her jaw. "He spoke true." He took a breath. "I think that was the day I fell in love with you."

RyAnne snorted and gave his chest a little shove. "Go on with you. That's not true. You were ever treating me like a bossy big brother. And I should know. I had one. You made it two."

He shook his head. "I tried to act the big brother. I told myself that's who I was to you. But always there was more to it. You made me feel things—*make* me feel things—RyAnne, that none other ever has before or since... Terror when I would find you gallivanting in some neglected corner of the island helping one poor wretch or another, uncaring of the danger you constantly put yourself in. Sheer frustration when you wouldn't capitulate and do as I said. Jealousy when you prattled on incessantly about that fop Brayden."

They both chuckled at that.

He pulled one of her hands to rest it against his face. Kissed the inside of her wrist. Sniffed and blinked dampness from his eyes. "I want to spend my days having the privilege of caressing your curls of a night, kissing your neck of a morning, listening to you pour your heart and soul out through the strings of your violin." He paused to clear his throat, and then he said, "RyAnne Hunter, will you marry me?"

She went down on her knees in order to be face to face with him. She breathed out, "With every beat of my heart, yes."

He kissed her then—long and sure and slow—the silken caress of his lips against hers inducing turmoil at the core of her being like a thousand sunbirds suddenly taking flight.

And she gave of herself as she never had to another, offering her soul to him with every snatched breath, every nip of her teeth, every caress of her tongue.

His hands settled about her waist, and he made a low sound of pleasure as he pulled her nearer. His lips left hers and trailed a hot path across her cheek, to her ear, to her neck, and then back to her lips.

Her heart pounded till she could feel it knocking. She curled her fingers into his hair, relishing the soft feel of it against her palms. Between kisses she whispered, "I…love…you."

He slowed their ardor then, dropping soft kisses against her lips, easing back, and then leaning in again to dole out a few more.

Finally, he pulled back, pressed his forehead to hers, and gripped her face between his palms, holding her back when she would have kissed him again. He shook his head with a self-deprecating smile. "Woman, you can't kiss a man like that and expect him to be able to sleep at night."

She smiled softly and traced the corner of his mouth with one finger. "I believe, sire, that it was you who kissed me. I am completely innocent."

He laughed and leapt up, drawing her to her feet and tugging her toward the flap. "I believe Kako bagged a couple hares. When I came in, June was showing the girls how to spit them over the fire. We should go eat."

RyAnne pulled him to a stop. "Are you trying to get out of letting me examine that shoulder?"

"My shoulder is very much better than your ankle at this point, I assure you. But come out into the light, where you will be able to see it better, and I will show you to allay your worry."

Out on the grass he paused and tugged the collar of his shirt to one side so she could see the wound. She did feel a great deal of relief after seeing it. It was nearly healed over completely with no redness or swelling. She tugged his shirt back into place.

"Thank you for alleviating my concerns."

His lips ticked up at one corner, and he settled his hands at her waist. "Perhaps I just wanted to get you this close."

The thrill of being in his arms swirled through her, but they were standing out in the open for all who were left in the camp to see now. She tilted him as stern a look as she could muster. "I believe dinner is served, Captain." She started off toward the fire.

He fell in beside her, but leaned close to say, "Indeed. And such deplorable timing, that."

Chapter 27
The Joy of the Morning

Jasmine was unsure how cholera had come to Stone Town, but come it had. There had only been a few cases at first, but then suddenly the disease had passed from one to another like flame to dry tinder. For several weeks she'd been helping Dr. Kirk night and day at the clinic. And now not only had it struck her town, but her family as well. She had just found Mother collapsed on the tiles in the entryway.

With Mother's head in her lap, she gently patted her cheeks, willing her tears to remain at bay. Wasn't it enough that first her father had gone off to the Continent to die, and then she'd been forced to watch the relatively quick but excruciating death of several of her students? Was God now asking her to witness the same in her mother?

"Mother, wake up, please. We need to get you to your room. I've not the strength to carry you up the stairs." Even she recognized the desperation in her tone.

Mother didn't stir.

"Sarah!" Jasmine rocked gently, pressing Mother's hair away from her damp face. Where had the maid gone? She'd been fast on Jasmine's heels when they'd walked into the entry and seen Mother, and now she was nowhere to be seen.

With no other recourse, Jasmine turned to prayer. "Oh Father, please don't take her from us."

Lusty birdsong slipped through the open front door.

Jasmine frowned at the square of bright sunlight cast upon the tiles beside her. Had the door been open a moment ago?

"Jasmine!" The call came from outside, and pounding footsteps drew the familiar voice of her brother nearer.

Relief coursed through her, even as the fleeting question over what Rory was doing back in town flitted through her mind. She didn't know why he was here, but perhaps the good Lord had brought him.

He burst through the open door and skidded to a stop by her side. "I just saw Sarah. She's gone on to fetch the doctor. What happened?"

So that was where the maid had disappeared to. Thankfulness for her quick thinking filled Jasmine. She shook her head in answer to Rory's question. "I just walked in and found her collapsed. My guess is cholera."

"Cholera!" Despite his obvious shock, he bent to scoop Mother into his arms. "Here, let me get her. Where do you want me to take her?"

"Take her up to her bedroom. I'll go fetch hot tea. It seems to be something that helps some people recover from the sickness. But we have to spoon it into her every ten minutes round the clock for the next several days." Jasmine bustled toward the kitchen, willing herself to keep her composure, and wishing that Garrett were here. Just his presence somehow had the ability to calm her.

Trent awoke the next morning with the reminder that he still hadn't found any evidence of whom Khalifa might have been working with. His heart was heavy with the failure. Llewellyn—and the queen—were counting on him to get the job done.

The savannah trilled with its typical morning serenade of warbled birdsong and wind-swept grasses, interrupted by the occasional bark of a gazelle or the braying of a zebra. Already he could feel the oppressive heat that was slinking over the horizon to scorch everyone and everything with its hot, fetid breath.

He sighed and sat up on the edge of his pallet and studied the side of the tent across the way.

He had given the feather tick to RyAnne the evening before, but she had declared that she could not sleep on anything so befouled by Khalifa.

"More than once I witnessed him take women in there and—" Her words had cut off, and she had looked out toward the setting sun, its golden light glinting off the tears shimmering in her eyes.

Fear threaded through him as surely as though a needle were drawing it. He stepped around to ensure he had a good look at her face. "Did he…touch…you?" Everything in him seemed to still as he waited for her answer.

She gave a derisive snort and shook her head. The tears spilled over. "No. Never me or any of the other women who were chained with me. We were *worth more*, you see." Self-derision hung in her tone. "To get one of us with child would have cost him money. And he was ever about his profits." She looked at him then with a world of hurt dulling the green of her eyes. "I despise myself for being glad that I was deemed too costly to touch."

He had pulled her into his arms, his soul quaking with thankfulness that she had been spared, and yet aching with her at all the evil she had been witness to.

Trent's jaw bunched now as he shook out his boots to ensure no scorpions had taken refuge in them during the night, and then he tugged them on.

The feather mattress had been given to Moyo and Nyimbo, who had in turn insisted that June sleep on one end of such a luxurious anomaly of bedding. Trent had worked with Kako and Asha to transport those who were wounded, or too weak from sickness and malnutrition, into the larger tent that had been Khalifa's. RyAnne had also wanted to give up Jabir's tent, but he had convinced her to take June, Moyo, and Nyimbo into the shelter and stay with them. And he was glad she had capitulated, for he knew he would not have slept a wink had she insisted on sleeping under the stars last night. Sometimes one rogue lion followed another. Thankfully there had been no incidents in the night hours.

He rolled wearily to one side. Today his task would be to convince RyAnne that they should leave for Bagamoyo, post haste. He knew she would want to stay and help care for the sick. But Kako and June had confided in him the evening before that they would not be traveling farther with them. They had no desire to go anywhere near the fateful city called Lay Down Your Heart. They would stay here and care for the invalids, they had said, but he should take Miss RyAnne back to her people, where she would no longer be in danger.

And that was the very thing he planned to convince her of today.

After that he would have to face his failure and decide how he was going to reveal the disappointment to Commodore Cornwall.

Last night before they had moved the captives into the tent, he had torn the place apart again. Even going so far as to flip back the rug and check the ground beneath it. But the lantern light had revealed nothing out of place. No buried safety boxes. No parchment secured to the underside of the rug. Nothing.

In disgust he looked over at the two wooden drawers that he had lugged out and set by his pallet. He wasn't sure why he had decided to take them, but if nothing else he could hand them over to Llewellyn to show him they contained no proof of illegal activity, nor revealed whom Khalifa's contact on the island might be. And he would like to have the Arabic letters translated by a trustworthy source just to be sure they contained nothing revealing.

The morning sun spilled across the drawers as though to mock him with his lack of evidence. But then something caught his eye. He sat up. There was a crack along the base of the top drawer that he hadn't noticed in the dim interior of the tent the evening before. At first glance it could have been a seam in the wood, but it was in an odd place.

Trent dragged the drawer closer and held it to the light to study it from all angles. The seam continued around the entire circumference of the bottom side of the drawer. It had a false bottom! He pressed on it from several angles, to no avail. Then he removed the drawer casing and peered inside the cavern left by its absence. There! A small round piece of bronze protruded from the front lip on the inside. He pressed it with one finger and heard a satisfying click.

The bottom of the drawer tilted open. The inside was lined with thick felt and contained four things. A small ink pot. A sharpened quill. A small pouch filled with coins that would come in handy once they arrived in Bagamoyo and needed to book passage. And a scrap of red silk wrapped around a thin rectangular object at the back of the space. Trent tugged it free and unwrapped the silk, his heart rate matching the tympani of village drums in the distance. The silk fell away to reveal a small leather-bound journal. And Trent's brows shot up.

The journal's cover was embossed with a golden insignia of Harcourt Shipping. That in itself was not too surprising since Khalifa was commodore of their fleet. But every page of the book was blank, so why had Khalifa kept it hidden in the secret compartment?

One other thing struck him as odd… The same citrus scent he'd smelled upon the letters infused the pages of the journal. Perhaps it had seeped through the box? Yet it seemed too strong for that to be the case. With a disheartened huff, he closed the book and ran one finger over the gilt-foil ship on the front. Could Llewellyn have been right all along? Perhaps Khalifa was indeed working for Brayden.

But of course this was not proof. Khalifa could have any number of reasons for having a blank Harcourt logbook in his possession. If not for the fact that he'd found it concealed in the false bottom of the drawer, he likely would have passed it over as something of little consequence. Yet…how could a blank book be evidence of anything?

The question remained… Why had Khalifa kept it hidden?

Trent gnawed on his lower lip for a moment before stuffing everything back into the compartment and clicking it closed again.

He sighed and clambered to his feet. For now he needed to see what he could do about convincing his stubborn wife-to-be that they should head down the road while the morning was still relatively cool. They would need to stop through midday and find some shade, on a day shaping up to be as hot as this one.

He found her just emerging from Jabir's tent. Her dress was stained and torn, and it was quite obvious that her hair hadn't seen the use of a brush for quite some time, yet his heart lurched in his chest at the joy of simply being near her. And her beauty shone through even in these lowliest of circumstances. How had he garnered enough luck to have her agree to be his wife?

He took her hands in his and leaned close to drop a quick kiss against her lips. "And how are you this morning? Sleep well?"

She nodded. "I did. It's amazing how well one can sleep when they don't have an iron manacle clanking against a chain or gouging into their ankle every time they move."

Trent tucked his fingers into his armpits and plunged ahead with what he'd come to talk to her about. "I've something to say, and I'm going to ask that you hear me out before you decline me."

She smiled. "If you are so sure of my answer, then why ask at all?"

"Because I hope that in this instance you will see sense and do as I ask."

She dipped her chin and gave him her signature look. "It's how you sell it, Captain."

He grinned at that. "Perhaps. But I'm a seaman, not a salesman."

Taking his hand, she tugged him toward the fire. "Well then, let us break our fast, and you can try to convince me to see things your way."

He strolled with her to the fire, relishing the feel of her soft fingers intertwined with his.

The fish traps Asha had hastily woven using grass and twigs the night before, and set in the creek overnight, must have done their job, because several fish roasted on the spit above the flames. He slipped one off and took half for himself and gave the other half to RyAnne. There were more loquats too, and he put several of those on his plate while he decided the best way to sell the subject to her.

When they had sat down together and blessed their food, he launched in. "I know you probably want to stay here to continue helping to tend the wounded, but as I told you just before you were captured, I've been under a commission from Commodore Cornwall to discover whether Khalifa was up to some illegal activities, and if so, to bring him proof of who the man worked for. Despite my lack of evidence here, I can't help but think that Khalifa would have ships waiting for his arrival in Bagamoyo, and perhaps I can learn something more from those captains or crews."

She opened her mouth to respond, but he wasn't done stating his case yet, so he held up one hand. "Please let me finish. I promised your father before he passed that I would care for you, and I'm begging you to make that job easier for me by agreeing to accompany me."

She leaned toward him. "Captain?"

He barged ahead. "I can conclude my business for Llewellyn, and we can visit your family in Stone Town and have Bishop Tozer perform the wedding ceremony for us. Then if you like, we can return, but for now—"

"Captain!" RyAnne laughed.

Irritation furrowed his brow. But at the humor dancing in her eyes, he offered a begrudging "What?"

"I've been trying to tell you that we can leave as soon as you deem it necessary."

"We can?"

Humor lifted one corner of her mouth. "Indeed."

Relief eased through him. "I see. I thought you would want to stay and help nurse the sick."

RyAnne glanced toward the newly christened sick-tent, and an emotion he couldn't quite define crossed her features. "Papa trained June quite well in the weeks that she traveled with us and worked with us in the clinic at the village. I think she will do just as well as I can. Besides..."

When she didn't go on, he prompted, "Yes?"

She flicked her hand as though to bat away a pesky idea. "I can't really say for sure, but I think...well..." A hint of embarrassment crossed her face. "Do you think the Lord can speak to us, Captain? Really speak to us?"

Trent tossed the bones of his fish into the fire and licked the grease from his fingers. "I don't see why not. What is it you feel He is speaking to you?" A leery foreboding gripped his middle. With RyAnne, one never knew what the next words out of her mouth might be. Life with this woman would certainly keep him in the thick of the dance.

"That's just it. I'm not exactly sure. But ever since I walked the gangplank up to *The Wasp* that first dawn and saw the horrors of the harbor, I keep hearing a question." She pressed her lips together and met his gaze.

"And it is…"

"'Whom shall I send, child?'"

Trent lifted his brows, his curiosity piqued. "Send where?"

RyAnne shrugged. "I don't know. I first thought it might have meant I was to go to the village with Papa. Which I did. But then, just a couple weeks back, I heard the question again." She laughed derisively. "I thought I might be going crazy, because of course at that point I thought you were dead and my future would be as the slave to some palace in the East, and I knew I would have no say in where I would go. But then you came and…" She waved her hand again. "I'm once more trying to discern what it means and why God would want to use someone as lacking in faith as I."

Trent reached over and squeezed her wrist. "Even the prophet Elijah struggled with faith at times, did he not? Immediately after the victory over the prophets of Baal, where God proved beyond a shadow of a doubt that He was in control, Elijah feared for his life and ran from Queen Jezebel."

RyAnne pondered that. "I suppose he did."

Trent nodded. "Our human frailty is no excuse for not following God's leading. I'm sure it will all become clear in time."

She sighed. "I suppose so."

"For now, let's say our good-byes and get on our way as quickly as possible? I'm still hoping to find some information in Bagamoyo about who Khalifa might have been working with." He debated the merits of his next words but decided it might be best to prepare her for the bad news now. "I have a strong suspicion he might have been working for Brayden."

Her eyes widened, and her jaw slacked. "What evidence have you?"

His lips twisted into a grimace of frustration. "Not much, I admit." He couldn't bring himself to tell her that it was only a blank logbook with the Harcourt Shipping insignia that had given resurgence to his suspicions.

RyAnne's chin tipped up, and her jaw took on that oh-so-familiar stubborn jut. "You must be mistaken. Brayden could never do something as despicable as this."

Trent might have known she would take up for young Harcourt. And he was man enough to admit to the sheer jealousy roiling through him—if only to himself. He stood. "I pray you are right. Be ready to go within the hour?"

She nodded.

And with that he walked away and left her there, hopefully to adjust to the idea that her former beau might be the one behind her kidnapping.

RyAnne watched Trent stride away, her eyes narrowing with each step he took, until they finally fell closed with dread and exasperation. What if he was right? Could Brayden really be responsible for all of this? On the other hand, could the captain simply be jealous of her past association with Brayden and trying to pin this on him?

She shook her head. If there was one thing she knew about Trent, it was that he'd never do something like that.

She sighed and stood to her feet. She had better get on with her good-byes. She had nothing to pack of course, so his hour long deadline would be easily met.

She searched out June who was in the loquat grove. June stood on the ground catching the clusters of fruit that Moyo and Nyimbo, who were aloft in the trees, tossed to her. It looked like they were scavenging the last of the fruits to feed to the sick with the noon meal. "June…" Emotion clogged her throat. Instead of facing her task, she asked instead, "What will you do to supplement meals when this grove is picked clean?"

June caught another cluster lobbed by Nyimbo and then called to the girls that they had enough for now. Lifting the basket and tucking it against her hip, she faced RyAnne. "There are enough loquats here for two more days. Most should be rested and much recovered by that time. Only half a day's journey from here we passed a guava grove. Kako plans for us to travel there and rest again if all are not well enough to keep traveling." She dipped her knees and offered a shy smile. "Captain Dawson has assured us that the God we now serve will provide for us."

RyAnne smiled and clutched her hand. "He will indeed. You've been a good friend to me these past months, June. I've come to say my good-byes. The captain and I must be off within the hour." She pulled the startled woman into an embrace, basket of fruit and all.

June laughed nervously. "Go well, my lady." She turned then and called the girls to come and say farewell. RyAnne had thought she might escape without shedding any tears, but when Moyo wrapped her skinny little arms about RyAnne's waist and squeezed with all her might, her vision blurred before she could take command of herself. She embraced the girl in return, holding her in silence for a long moment because she had no words to express all that she was feeling. Finally she set Moyo back and knelt before her. She took the little shoulders into her hands and ensured she had Moyo's attention before she spoke. "You are very special and precious to God, Moyo. Never let the actions of anyone, future or past, make you doubt that, aye?"

Moyo nodded.

"And Nyimbo." RyAnne tugged the other little girl close. "You were spared for a reason. You and Moyo will be sisters now. And you must help each other remember to serve the One True God, yes?"

Nyimbo nodded, her eyes sparkling. "Captain Dawson told me many stories from God's book. I will tell them to Moyo."

"That's good. Very good. Come here." She pulled both the girls against her, one in each arm. She reveled for a moment in the feel of precious little ones tucked close, and then she kissed their cheeks. "I must be off." And with that she left them there quickly, before she might change her mind and refuse to return to Zanzibar with Captain Dawson.

She found Yani next. The poor woman looked listless. RyAnne had no word of comfort for a woman whose child had been taken from her in such a senseless way, so she simply pulled her in tight for a long moment.

She was ready and waiting when Trent and Asha found her not too long later. The captain was pushing a two-wheeled cart. The rickety cart looked like it might cause more trouble than it was worth.

Trent took one look at her and tipped his head to urge her to fall into step beside him. "Let us be on our way, before the emotions I see swimming so close to your surface cause you to change your mind." He smiled softly, even if he didn't stop walking.

With a sigh and a bit of a grouse that he seemed to know her so well, she hoisted her violin and her skirts, and strode out in his wake. The savannah grasses were thin here, and it gave her no comfort to realize that so many slaves had passed this way that a veritable trail had been worn into the plains.

The cart Trent pushed was covered with what was left of the sheet he had used to wrap her ankle the evening before. She reached out and tugged at one corner to see what the bulges beneath it were. Two wooden drawers with locks in the front face sat to one side. The rest of the cart had been stacked with a few ivory tusks. She dropped the corner of the sheet, her lips thinning at the sight of the ivory.

She glowered at the man beside her.

Trent swiped a trickle of sweat from his temple with his shoulder and didn't even pause his trek down the path. "Lest you forget, my intentions when coming to the Interior were never to get rich on ivory, as I first told you. So don't look at me as though

I were something to be scraped from the bottom of your little boots. We are going to need the money I'll get from selling this ivory to reserve passage aboard a ship for Zanzibar."

RyAnne only sighed as she settled her violin into one corner of the cart.

Chapter 28
The Joy of the Morning

It took them two days to reach the port town of Bagamoyo, and RyAnne's revulsion as she walked the streets of the city was just as great, if not greater, than it had been the first time she'd been exposed to Bagamoyo from the deck of *The Wasp* in the harbor.

Trent led the way down a dusty street. Asha, bringing up the rear, pushed the rickety cart that had somehow miraculously made it this far. Row upon row of chained captives slumped against buildings on either side, awaiting their fate with vacant stares and glum expressions.

The sun baked down with merciless heat, yet none of the captives had any water.

RyAnne's steps faltered. Slowed. Stilled. "Captain, surely there is something we can do?" A well sat in the middle of the next intersection. She lifted her skirts and started toward it, but Trent took her elbow and urged her down a side street in the direction of the harbor.

"We can't just leave them!" She tugged away from him and started to go back, only to find Asha, arms folded, blocking her path.

Trent sighed. "RyAnne, there are slaves there who would not hesitate to attack you and use you as a hostage to try and negotiate their freedom."

RyAnne felt tears sting her eyes. "But surely there are many more who would be appreciative of just a drink of water."

Trent crossed his arms and kicked at the dust for a moment. He looked up and studied her face, then reached out to cup her cheek and thumb away a tear that slipped loose. "Aye. And well I know how your soft heart leads you into danger time and again."

Asha spoke up from behind her. "Water will be given to them at noon." When she glanced back at him, still unsure whether she could walk away without at least trying to offer some help, he gestured to the sun hanging just below its zenith. It would be noon within the next quarter of an hour.

"You're certain?"

Asha nodded. "Many times I have…walked this city with Khalifa. Always water is given at noon."

Trent took her hand and urged her to follow him. "Let us find a room, and then I will go to the docks to see if I can book us passage for Stone Town."

And see if he can't find more evidence to convict Brayden of slave smuggling. The thought washed a wave of despair through RyAnne. The world was a bad enough place without finding out that your childhood friends might be slave runners.

Reluctantly, she gave in and let him pull her down the alley. Asha took up pushing the cart behind them.

They had only gone about a few blocks when Trent came to a stop. RyAnne glanced up and realized they stood before an Arabic bookshop. Trent strode to the cart and opened one of the two drawers. He withdrew several missives, all of a similar size, and motioned with them toward the interior of the shop. "Care to join me?"

Asha folded his arms and stoically stood guard over the cart.

RyAnne, anxious for her first glimpse of civility in months, hurried to follow Trent inside.

A hunched elderly man with round spectacles perched on the end of his nose and a white kufi upon his head smiled from behind the counter.

Trent touched his forehead in greeting. "*Unazungumza Kiswahili?*"

The man nodded that he did indeed speak Swahili, and then his smile broadened. "But I also speak English, my friend."

Trent chuckled. "Then I'm doubly blessed to have stumbled upon your shop." He laid the packet of letters on the counter. "I wonder if you have a moment to read a few letters?"

The shopkeeper tugged his spectacles up to his eyes and nodded.

Trent pulled one of the pages from its envelope and slid it across the counter. "Can you read that language?"

RyAnne felt a tingle of anticipation rush through her. If Khalifa had been hiding information in plain sight, the next few minutes might reveal it to them!

The old man's eyes lit up. "Yes. Yes."

Trent and RyAnne looked at each other exultantly.

Wizened hands drew the paper closer, and RyAnne held her breath.

After only a moment the old man set the letter back on the counter. He tugged his spectacles free and polished them with a cloth. "This letter is written to a man named Ali, yes?"

Trent nodded.

RyAnne stepped closer, not wanting to miss a word of what was about to be said.

The shopkeeper tapped the missive. "This is from his wife back in Oman. She writes of their two daughters, and Ali's"—he paused for a quick chuckle—"wretched mother, who apparently lives with them in Oman."

RyAnne glanced at Trent, her shoulders slumping. There didn't seem to be any hidden information in that…did there?

Trent too looked disappointed. He handed the other letters to the man, who read each one to them word for word. All were similar correspondence from Khalifa's wife. And none contained anything important.

Trent scrubbed one hand over his face, thanked the man, and paid him the few coins he requested.

Back out at the cart, Trent thrust the envelopes into the top box, and they continued on their way in silence.

RyAnne angled a look upward. *Have you seen our suffering, Father? Where is the justice?*

Silence was her only answer.

RyAnne sighed. And yet… Wasn't that partly what faith was about? Trusting that God was good and His Word was true, even when things didn't turn out exactly as hoped for?

Just before the wharf, Trent parked the cart outside an alehouse. The Sanskrit and English sign above the door read *Rooms for Let*. Trent paid a lad a few coins to guard the cart, and then he hoisted the two wooden drawers to his hip and handed RyAnne her violin. He led the way inside. Near a set of stairs off to the left, two turbaned men played a sitar and a tanpura. The room was dim and hardly appeared like a place to frequent. However, many tables were full, and the luscious scents emanating from the kitchen made RyAnne's stomach grumble embarrassingly.

The proprietress, a stooped old woman with only one front tooth, who was barely visible above the back counter, informed them that she only had one room left for the evening.

"We'll take it," Trent said. "Please send up water for a bath." He held out the required payment.

The woman snatched the shillings from Trent's outstretched fingers and then tipped her head toward the north. "Baths two house that way. Big sign."

It would be a public bathhouse then, and now that she was in the sheltered interior away from the grit and noise and anguishing sights of the city, RyAnne had no desire to go back out again. Besides, she'd gone for weeks on end without so much as warm water to wash with, so any water at all would be a luxury. "Just a bucket of warm water will do. Can we at least have that?" She offered the old woman a pleading smile.

The woman sniffed, but snapped her fingers at a girl hovering in the shadows just behind her. The girl scrambled off to presumably fetch a bucket of warm water.

Trent gave Asha the bag of coins. "Get us some food?"

Asha sank down at one of the empty tables in the corner of the room.

Trent then touched a hand to RyAnne's lower back and nudged her up the stairs. "I'll bring you up a plate. I'm sure you are exhausted and would like to rest."

RyAnne's heart dropped. She was exhausted, but the truth was she'd only just gotten used to having the captain around again, and the thought of being without him, even for a little while, filled her with trepidation. "You aren't going to leave me, are you?" The moment the words left her mouth, her face heated. She didn't want to turn into a clingy woman who never wanted to let her man out of her sights. "I'm sorry. I shouldn't…I'll be fine. It's just that I've only just gotten you back and—"

Trent stepped through the door to her room and set the two drawers on a table. He took her violin and laid it next to them. Then, stepping back into the entry, he settled both hands on her shoulders and bent to meet her gaze. "I won't be far. I need you to promise me you'll stay in the room? I have to head to the docks and see if I can get a good price for that ivory and book us passage to Stone Town. But I'll return just as quickly as I can, and tonight I'll sleep right here"—he tapped one toe on the stone tiles beneath their feet—"just outside your door."

RyAnne wrapped her hands around his forearms. "Hurry back. And please be careful."

He pressed his forehead to hers. "Khalifa is gone. There's no need to worry about me. I'll be fine. I promise you."

Reluctantly, RyAnne let him go.

Hot water came, and she washed. Her ankle was much improved with the constant cleaning she'd been giving it, for which she was thankful.

A plate of curry and rice arrived, and she devoured it, not recalling the last time she'd eaten something so delicious.

And then she waited.

Garrett took the stairs to the upper floor of the Hunters' home two at a time. Jasmine would be up in her mother's room, just as she had been the past several times he'd visited. Each of those times he'd tried to coax her into resting herself, but she'd insisted that her mother's recovery was too delicate to leave in the hands of someone else. She'd been sleeping in ten-minute snatches for the last two days. This time he was going to insist that she let the maid, Sarah, handle some of the care so Jasmine could get some proper sleep herself. Provided her mother was still fighting. He prayed she would pull through. Jasmine's tender heart could not take another loss.

He knocked softly on the door. "Jas?"

A flurry of soft footsteps gave him a picture of her running on tiptoe to the door, and then it opened. Her eyes were bright and filled with a joy that gave him immediate relief.

"Is she better then?"

She nodded, excitement fairly vibrating from every pore in her body. "She's finally able to hold down some broth. And kept a whole cup of tea down for the past twenty minutes!"

"Heaven be praised." He could see the utter weariness clinging to her beneath the excitement.

She glanced over her shoulder to where her mother slept on the bed. "Yes. Indeed."

Garrett reached out and took her hand.

She swung back to face him.

"I hope you'll allow me to convince you to get some rest of your own now?"

She tilted her head as though considering that for the first time since her mother had improved. "Yes," she responded slowly. "I think I might." Even as she said the words, a large yawn stretched her jaw. She flushed. "Forgive me. I'll just get Rory to take a turn watching her. We must keep fluids—"

Garrett lifted a hand to interrupt her, his relief over her agreement making him hasty. "I'll get Rory after I escort you to your room. And I promise to instruct him to keep giving your mother fluids every…"

"Thirty minutes should be sufficient now that she's on her way to recovery."

Garrett nodded. "I'll tell him." He stepped back so that she could leave if she was ready. "Is there anything you need to retrieve?" He motioned behind her into the room.

She lifted her skirts and stepped past him. "No. Thank you." She started down the hall with another yawn, but stumbled a bit and paused to lean one hand against the wall.

Garrett didn't hesitate. "You've exhausted yourself beyond your strength." He scooped her into his arms.

Jasmine didn't even fight him. She nestled her head against

his shoulder and mumbled, "I believe I have."

She was asleep before he'd taken more than three steps toward her room.

Trent easily found a vendor near the docks who paid him top price for the ivory. He wasn't sure what he'd expected to find upon reaching the harbor, but certainly seeing Brayden Harcourt's *Indigo Fields* floating placidly in the bay had not been on his list of possibilities. What were the odds that a Harcourt ship would happen to be in this harbor at the exact time Khalifa was set to arrive? *Brayden Harcourt's* ship.

Trent snorted. Could Brayden truly be so arrogant as to be here himself?

He glanced over at Asha. "Did you ever see the man Khalifa worked for?"

Asha leaned into his heels and folded his arms dispassionately. "Two times each year for the past three years."

Trent spun to face the man fully. "I say, what?" Surely he hadn't heard correctly. Could his answers really be that simple?

"Hair the color of savannah grass. Eyes the color of the cloudless sky."

The very picture of Brayden.

Trent tapped a fist to his lips. He had to think. "Would he recognize you, do you think? This man?"

Asha shrugged. "To most Anglos, one native looks much like another."

That was true enough and could work in his favor. "Asha, you understand that freedom is yours, correct? So nothing I ask of you is required?"

Asha gave a curt nod.

"Very well. Then we wait."

"He will come," Asha asserted. "Always he comes near two hours before the setting of the sun."

Trent glanced at the sun. It was still early afternoon. So they were in for a long wait, then. He scrubbed his hands over his face and sauntered to a slab bench against the shake siding of an alehouse. The deep canvas awning overhead would ensure that, come late afternoon, he and Asha would be cloaked in shadows.

As they settled in to wait, Trent willed away the trembling in his limbs. Why did he suddenly feel as though he had stepped onto a thin ledge that jutted out over a canyon with hundreds of hungry lions below?

He'd been more than disappointed to learn that Khalifa's letters really were nothing more than communications from back home. But the answers he'd been hunting could be within his grasp by this evening.

In that same amount of time, things could also turn terribly wrong.

A metallic tingle spread across his tongue.

Things had definitely been going more wrong than right lately.

RyAnne paced the small room, hating being separated from the captain only days after their reunion.

And it was stifling! Sweat trickled in a rivulet down her back, and her neck was damp and sticky.

She paused at the built-in window bench, hoping for a breeze, or at least something beautiful to look at. But the only view was of the stone wall of the next building across the back alley, and despite the fact that her window was pushed wide open, no breeze even stirred the gauzy drapes.

RyAnne fanned her face with her hand, trying to be grateful as she recalled that only a few days ago she had been chained to several other women and bound for slavery. She oughtn't be so disgruntled.

Flapping her hand only made her hotter, so she gave up and glanced around the room, hoping for something to use as a fan. Her search landed on the two wooden drawers.

Quickly, she crossed the room and opened the first drawer.

RyAnne hastily extracted one of the envelopes and put it to use. Her eyes dropped closed in satisfaction at the first few puffs of stirred air that cooled her neck. She moseyed back to the window again. If she couldn't see anything, she might at least be able to hear the sounds of the city. She sank onto the pillowed window seat and, since there were no windows in the building across the way, audaciously propped her feet against the casement on the other side and pulled her skirts up nearly to her knees.

"Sweet relief!" Mother would flay her for such unladylike conduct were she here, but Bagamoyo was even hotter than RyAnne ever remembered Stone Town being.

She sat fanning for a long time, and then as she cooled, the soft lull of gull-song and the plush comfort of the pillows at her back lured her into a hazy world halfway between wake and sleep. She settled the envelope onto the cushion at her side, snuggled deeper into the soft seat, and gave in to the luxury of a nap.

When she woke, she could not have said how long she had slept, but it had been long enough that the sun had sought out her resting place, and she was once again dripping with perspiration. Tongue thick with thirst, she rolled from the cushion and padded her way over to the pitcher and glass on the table near the door.

She downed a full glass of water and another half before her thirst was quenched. Drizzling some of what remained in the cup into one hand, she then set the cup down, rubbed both hands together, and then patted the water droplets across her face and neck. She doused her arms next, stopping herself short of soaking her entire head with the water that remained in the pitcher. Now to get a breeze working with the water. She moved back to the window seat and took up the envelope to once again fan herself. The air moving against her damp skin felt like a little bit of heaven.

Something caught her eye. She paused for a moment and frowned at the envelope. There was a round brown dot just to the right of the address that she would have sworn wasn't there when she first took the letter from the box. She examined the seat cushion to see if something had been spilled on it that could have transferred to the envelope. The captain likely wouldn't take kindly to her getting anything on any of them before he could turn them over to Commodore Cornwall.

Nothing sticky or damp seemed to be on the cushion.

Frowning, she studied the envelope again, turning it this way and that. There was certainly a spill of some sort there. She slipped one finger under the flap and withdrew the paper from within to examine the inside of the envelope. The stain was visible there but not as distinctly. And yet several blotches seemed to have transferred to the pages of the letter it contained.

"Oh, dash it all, how do I seem to do these things?"

She strode over to the window seat again and smoothed open the letter in the sunlight so that she might get a good look at the damage she'd somehow done.

The letter was written in a delicate hand on a fine creamy parchment. The black, carefully scripted Arabic was intricately penned and so straight as to perhaps have been written with a ruler. But it was in each space above and below the lines of black lettering that the damage seemed to have been done.

Something made her still, and she held the letter away from her, studying it more carefully. The brown splotches were just as neatly lined up as the black ink! She glanced at the sunlight beating down on the cushion where she'd napped and then back to the paper in her hands. The paper had rested in the direct sun for probably quite some time before the sun had sunk far enough to reach her and wake her with its heat. The hand holding the letter trembled, and she could feel her heart thumping against her breastbone.

There was hidden writing on the parchment!

It wasn't clear enough to make out yet, but with a little more heat carefully applied... Her gaze flew to the two wooden drawers on the desk across the room.

She had to tell Trent about this now! There could be information written here that he needed to know!

Quickly closing the window, she laid the two sheets of paper from the letter into patches of sunlight. With any luck, by the time they returned to the room, the heat would have done its work to reveal the hidden text on the pages. With that, she lifted her skirts, carefully locked the door of her room, dropped the key into her reticule, and then hastened down the stairs and out onto the street.

Trent and Asha had been headed to the docks. She would start her search there.

Just as Asha had predicted, a longboat lowered from the side of the Harcourt ship as the sun dropped into the four o'clock hour. The ship was too far out, and the day too drained of light, to identify the people who descended the ladder and set to rowing toward the shore, but Trent felt a curl of anticipation even so.

He stepped over to a market vendor selling keffiyehs and purchased two. Quickly wrapping one around his head and lower face in the fashion of many of the vendors and traders already walking the street near the harbor, he returned to his position on the bench under the awning.

He thrust the second keffiyeh at Asha. There was no point in tempting fate. Unlikely as it was, Harcourt just might recognize him.

While Asha wrapped the headscarf around his face, Trent pondered. If only he had more proof. Even if they came ashore, and upon discovering that Khalifa was not here, purchased a shipload of slaves, he needed more than the simple purchase of slaves to convict them. Since he had no written proof, he would have to catch them sailing slaves beyond the island of Zanzibar.

He shrank farther into the shadows cast by the awning and continued to watch as the longboat drew nearer.

Too bad Brayden knew him, otherwise he could pose as a slave trader and try to trap him into agreeing to sail the cargo to Shanghai. But that particular option was out, considering he'd known the Harcourts for almost his entire life.

The longboat tied up at the dock, and the men climbed out. When Harcourt turned toward them and started down the pier,

Trent felt everything inside him tighten up.

The man walking toward them was indeed a Harcourt, but it wasn't Brayden, as Trent had supposed, but his father, William. Could the corruption run all the way through the family? How much did Brayden truly know about his family business? Trent clamped his teeth together in irritation. He didn't like to be wrong. And he'd been so certain that it would be Brayden he would find here. So certain that Brayden was working with Khalifa quietly, and right beneath his father's nose.

But now… Obviously, he had to rethink that assumption.

Harcourt stepped past him and headed into the heart of the city. But Trent needed to be cautious. Despite his head covering, Harcourt had known him for years and would recognize him in only a moment's time should his gaze land upon him.

Trent thumped Asha on one shoulder. "Follow him. I need a full report of his actions. I'm returning to the inn and Miss Hunter."

Asha nodded and faded into the wharf crowd. Trent waited a moment more before heading down the alley to take the back way to the inn.

RyAnne hustled toward the wharf with her skirts lifted to aid her speed. The answers Trent had been investigating for months might at this very moment be revealing themselves on the parchment back in her room. Her heart pounded at the mere thought!

When she and the captain returned to the inn, she would ask the old woman at the front desk for a flatiron, and she and Trent would work together to reveal the dark secrets that Khalifa had been hiding.

She skirted around a hawker selling dried fish, and then angled the other way to avoid a woman who thrust fresh fruit into her face with the demand that she buy. "No thank you. Not right now."

An old man with a white-faced monkey on his shoulder ambled along in front of her. The walk was too narrow and crowded with wares here for her to get around him.

His arthritic shuffle filled her with frustration. She walked on her tiptoes, trying to see if she could spot Trent ahead somewhere. Nothing.

The black monkey clambered atop the old man's turban and studied her with a curious tilt to its white head. Its white-tipped tail curled around its feet, and it stretched its lips wide in a grin that only served to heighten RyAnne's impatience. An opening between vendors' carts finally presented itself, and RyAnne made haste to dart around man and monkey. The colobus reached out and swatted at her hair as she went past. RyAnne ducked away and gave the little beast a glower that made the toothless old man chuckle.

When she reached the street in front of the wharf, she paused and looked both directions. Where exactly would the captain have gone? She shaded her eyes. She didn't see him to the south. She swung around and stepped out of the path of a trundling cart to look the other way.

"I beg your pardon, lady." A British man walking down the street almost barreled into her. He tugged on the brim of his hat and grumbled in a tone that indicated he would much prefer she simply remove herself from his presence. What she could see of the lower half of his face was set in stone, and he looked none too happy to be here in Bagamoyo.

"I'm sor—"

The man dropped his hand back to his side and lifted his gaze to hers.

RyAnne's mouth fell open. "Mr. Harcourt, sir! What a pleasant surprise, this!"

He'd been set to move past her, but upon hearing her use of his name, or perhaps it was on seeing her, he jolted to a stop. He scanned her up and down, blinking rather dazedly for a moment, and if she wasn't mistaken, his face paled a few shades. He gave a quick assessment of the street, both up and down, and then stepped back and took a moment to look at her again. "Miss Hunter... What a...surprise...to see you here."

RyAnne blushed as she remembered the state of her dress. She must present quite a shocking appearance, judging by his expression. And yet she couldn't help the grin that stretched her face from ear to ear. She reached out her arms and pulled him down to kiss both his cheeks. This was perfect! "Oh, it's really rather fortuitous, me bumping into you like this! Providence, really! Is Brayden with you?"

"Ah..." He hesitated briefly. "Not here, no, lass."

"Well"—RyAnne waved away that line of the conversation—"that's not really important. But, you see, the captain and I have need of a ship to sail us to Zanzibar. The captain is here at the wharf, in point of fact. I was just looking for him. I don't suppose we could prevail upon you to give us a lift?"

William Harcourt's brow bunched. "The captain?" he asked.

"Captain Trent Dawson. I'm sure you'll remember him. He and his father have sailed in and out of Stone Town since I was just a girl in braids."

"Indeed, I remember." He dragged out the words and once again searched the area.

And there was something in his expression that made a chill seep down her spine. She suddenly remembered Trent's suspicions of Brayden. But Brayden wasn't here. His father was. And Mr. Harcourt was acting quite strangely—fidgety and testy. Not at all like the man whom she'd thought of more like an uncle all her growing up years.

He'd seemed surprised to see her, yes. But not in a joyous way that someone might feel upon meeting an old acquaintance in the street. It was in a...different sort of way that she couldn't quite place her finger on. She thought of Khalifa's letters. And she remembered that routinely Khalifa had sent runners off on errands while they'd been marching across the plains. Had he sent communications to his partners? If so, what information had he included? Could he have informed them that he had captured one Miss RyAnne Hunter and that her lineage wasn't quite as impeccable as everyone back on the island thought?

RyAnne suddenly felt a great need to put as much distance between herself and William Harcourt as possible.

She lifted her skirts and stepped back. "Well, it's been lovely to see you again. I'll just continue on and find the captain, and then perhaps you and he can negotiate our passage back home?" The truth was, she suddenly felt sure that the last ships they would seek passage aboard would be Harcourt ships.

A smile bloomed on William's face, as though he wanted to put her at ease, but it had quite the opposite effect. "Nonsense!" He moved closer, and she had the distinct impression that were she to try and dart away, he would have her arm in his grasp before she even took two steps. His smile widened, if that was possible. "I'll come with you. Heading this way, were you?" He put one hand to her back and snapped his fingers at the men who accompanied him. They fell into step behind them.

RyAnne swallowed. Her apprehension was foolish, wasn't it? She'd known William Harcourt for even longer than she'd known the captain, after all. Yet… She couldn't shake off the remembrance of the stationary baking in the sun back at the inn. She pulled in a steadying breath. *Be calm.* He might have a perfectly legitimate reason for being here. "So, what brings you to Bagamoyo, Mr. Harcourt?"

William flapped a hand as if to make light of his reasons for being in a thriving slave entrepôt. "Business. Just business. I'm meeting an associate of mine. But I fear he is late to arrive. I was just going to look for him. But it will wait. I couldn't live with myself if I left you wandering the harbor alone and something happened to you. Your father, God rest him, would never forgive me."

Another chill rippled down RyAnne's back. This one so strong that it stopped her in her tracks. Her hands tightened about fistfuls of her skirts. She hoped the voluminous material would hide her trembling. "How did you know? About Papa?"

William turned to face her. He lifted a hand to rub the back of his neck. "Forgive me. I assumed… He was very unwell the last time I saw him, and you mentioned you were here with the captain, but said nothing of your father."

A little relief swept in at that. His explanation was quite logical. Perhaps she was seeing shadows in a field of sunshine. Her hands loosed their hold. "Yes. Well… You are correct. Papa has…passed on. The captain is escorting me back home to bring the news to my family."

She realized then that they had walked nearly the full length of the street and were almost to the water. "Oh, look at me. I've been talking so much that I must have passed the captain right by."

She started to turn back.

A black cloth fell over her head, and a firm hand clamped over her mouth. Terror washed through her as she kicked and clawed to fight her way free. All to no avail. A painful blow to the side of her head stunned her to stillness.

"Hurry! Get her on the ship!" Mr. Harcourt's voice.

She felt sticky warm blood seeping through her hair. Two men lifted her, and with the hand clamped over her mouth making breathing difficult, it was taking all her concentration just to find her next breath.

"How did she even escape from him?"

"I know not, Cap'n."

Harcourt cursed. "My cargo better be intact!"

There was a thump and a clatter, and then she landed in a puddle of rank water—likely in the bottom of a row boat. A boot pressed into her chest, keeping her pinned down, and the sound of oars dipping into the waves left her weakened by hopelessness.

Chapter 29
The Joy of the Morning

Praying that Asha would not come back to him empty of helpful information, Trent wearily climbed the stairs to RyAnne's room at the inn. He rolled his shoulder in a circular motion, trying to work out some of the knots that had built up in it. His body begged for a few hours of sleep, but he didn't have time to rest, nor would he be able to with Harcourt roaming the streets.

He leaned his shoulder into the wall next to RyAnne's door and knocked softly in case she might be sleeping. When there was no answer, he tried again, just a little louder. Still she did not come to the door. An eerie foreboding filled him. Should he burst in to make sure she was all right? And if he did and she was simply sleeping soundly, he didn't want to disturb her, especially when he didn't have much of an update to give her.

He was still deliberating over what to do when pounding footsteps drew his gaze to the stairs.

Asha burst into sight. "Miss Hunter!" Asha was panting so hard he could not get any other words past his throat, but he was gesturing wildly to RyAnne's door and then toward the wharf.

A sick feeling wrapped a fist around Trent's stomach as he scrambled back from the door and prepared to breach it.

Asha bent double, hands propped on his knees, but he waved toward RyAnne's door again, his eyes wide. "Captured!"

"She can't have—" But his concerns had just been validated.

Dear Father above, when was the woman going to learn to consider her own safety! His chest constricted till the beat of his heart thumped against his rib cage. Uncaring of the damage he would do, Trent slammed his boot into the door.

Splinters flew as the old wood gave way to his assault, but he was left gasping in pain and holding his shoulder. The impact had vibrated through him and found his weakness.

Quickly he assessed the room, his frail hopes flagging. Empty.

Just as he'd feared. "Talk, Asha! What happened?"

Asha swept a hand down his face. "I followed this Harcourt, just as you asked." He paused to gulp another couple of breaths.

And it was all Trent could do not to step forward and pummel the man for more information. "And?"

"In the street, there was Miss Hunter." He made a gesture like she had just suddenly appeared from thin air. "They spoke. But I was too far away to hear these words. Then Miss Hunter seemed to try and leave him, but he walked with her. They walked to the wharf, and then…" He lowered his eyes. "They thrust a gunny sack over her and took her to Harcourt's ship."

Trent lost the strength to stand and sank onto the window-seat cushion. "Did the ship sail?"

Asha shook his head firmly. "No. The men left the ship again and came ashore. I have a boy following them. He is to meet me here as soon as they start back to the wharf."

Trent dabbed at his forehead. It was hot as blazes in here, and he needed to think. He stood and turned to open the window behind him. His gaze landed on the paper even as he twisted open the latch and shoved the casement open.

RyAnne must have been looking at Khalifa's letters. But what was this?

He picked up the parchment and bent closer.

His breaths started to come in earnest then, for clearly revealed between the womanly black scrawl were words written in Swahili, a language he very much understood. The more he read, the faster his breaths came. Never taking his eyes off the paper, he spoke. "Asha, light the lantern."

"Much light still comes through the window."

"Just do it please." Trent strode across the room to fetch the two wooden drawers that contained Khalifa's correspondence. "You're sure that the ship had not sailed?"

"Yes."

"And they didn't look like they were leaving soon?"

"Harcourt still walked deeper into the city when I came here. And the boy is to come to me here as soon as they start back to the harbor."

Trent realized Asha had already said as much, and eased out a breath. The ship wouldn't sail without its captain. He had a few minutes then to see what the rest of these letters contained.

Pray to God all the letters in the drawer contained as much information as the one in his hand. For it seemed that Khalifa hadn't trusted the people he was working with and had kept detailed information about all their interactions. And quite cleverly he'd put it down onto correspondence that wouldn't be suspicious for him to keep in his possession at all times. Perhaps he had written it down as a means for blackmail later down the road? Would it be enough proof for a court though?

Asha was still frowning in puzzlement, but he had lit the lantern, and the moment Trent held a new letter above the chimney and the brown letters of the hidden words began to appear, he gasped in amazement.

Parchment after parchment detailed the plans and how they were smuggling the slaves beyond the island of Zanzibar from a series of underground caves on the north end of the island. This was exactly the kind of information that Cornwall needed!

It was also the exact kind of evidence he might be able to trade for RyAnne's freedom. His heart constricted at the dilemma. And yet… He glanced back toward the wooden boxes. Perhaps…

He took up the "blank" logbook and carefully held the first page over the heat from the lamp. Just as he'd suspected, the blank logbook was not blank at all. And the information it contained was precisely the kind of proof a court would need. It revealed a list of Khalifa's contacts off the island. Merchants—if such men deserved such a benign term—living in India and the Far East. And then finally the last lines contained the names of Khalifa's partners on the island. Trent whistled low at the number of names on the list and their various positions on Zanzibar. But of course they would have needed men in their pay who could look the other way at key moments. Trent scanned the names again. The name Harcourt was there right at the top of the first column, and with a line beneath it. But it only appeared once and with no other initials or names to indicate if the whole family was involved or just the head. Could Brayden be totally innocent of his father's operations?

Trent closed the logbook. He quickly gathered Khalifa's letters from his wife and folded them together, then thrust them and the logbook into RyAnne's violin case.

He sank down at the writing desk and quickly opened the secret compartment at the base of Khalifa's wooden box and withdrew the small bottle of ink. He sniffed it and was satisfied to detect the distinct citrus scent he'd expected. Taking up the quill and several of the blank sheets of Khalifa's Harcourt letterhead, he set to hastily scrawling words across the pages. When he finished the first one, he pushed it toward Asha. "Heat that." He scrawled information on several more sheets, having Asha heat the pages as they went. For the ruse to work, there should be more pages, but he was out of time. Hastily gathering up his handiwork, he tucked the newly minted letters into the wooden drawers. These he put into a haversack, which he slung over his shoulder.

He shoved RyAnne's violin against Asha's chest. "Let's go and save Miss Hunter and put a stop to a slave smuggling ring, shall we?"

When they arrived at the harbor, Trent was relieved to see that indeed Harcourt's ship still remained in the bay. He realized he'd halfway been afraid Asha might be wrong about that. His plan was really quite simple.

William Harcourt was about to experience a mutiny on his ship. Trent's only concern was whether he and Asha could pull it off, just the two of them. He was thankful for the guns he'd taken off Khalifa. He checked the rounds on the revolver and then held it out to Asha. "Can you shoot?"

Asha gave a single dip of his chin, flipped open the cylinder to check the rounds for himself, and then slammed it home again. His face was set, and he gave Trent another brief nod.

Good. The man at least looked like he was telling the truth. Trent turned to double-check his rifle and tuck extra ammunition into his pocket.

There was a lad with a rowboat waiting for a fare at the end of the dock. Trent slung his haversack aboard and climbed in after it. Asha sank down on the seat just behind Trent, propping RyAnne's violin across his knees.

Trent motioned to the boy. "To the *Indigo Fields* there."

The boy didn't move. "One shilling."

Despite his tension, Trent grinned at the lad's savvy. He reached in his pocket and pulled out the required payment, handing it over.

The boy nodded and dug his oars into the water without so much as a word after that.

Trent turned on his seat to face Asha. "The crew will be light at this time because many will be on shore enjoying some leave." He tipped his head toward the *Indigo Fields*. "A ship this size… I'm guessing there will be five men on board, at the most. We take them, and the rest will be easy to take as they come aboard."

Asha nodded. "I am not afraid."

Trent held out his palm for a handshake. "Glad to have you with me, friend."

The row boat bumped up against the side of the ship then, and a sailor peered over the side at them. "You lot! What you want?"

Trent stood and smiled up at him, giving a gesture back to the pier. "I'm an old friend of Captain Harcourt's. I bumped into him on shore, and he has offered me passage back to Zanzibar with my slave here."

He heard Asha give a little snort, but it was soft enough that the sailor above wouldn't have heard it.

"Cap'n Harcourt, you say?"

Trent nodded. "Indeed. I'm actually a closer friend of his son, Brayden. But Captain Harcourt's known me since I was a boy."

The sailor still didn't look convinced that he should let them aboard.

"Look." Trent dug into the boxes at his feet. "I've got this letter here. Giving me permission to come aboard." He held a page of Harcourt stationary aloft for the sailor to see. Of course from this distance Trent knew the sailor couldn't read the writing, but hopefully he could make out the Harcourt letterhead at the top.

Trent's hopes were satisfied a moment later when the man's countenance relaxed. "Right then. Gi' me a moment." The sailor disappeared, and a few seconds later the rope ladder fell over the side of the ship.

Trent looked at Asha and said quietly, "Ready?"

Asha nodded. "Indeed."

"Fast on my heels now. We'll only have a moment before he'll be demanding to see my reference clearly." Trent took to the ladder, relishing the familiar feel of the buoyant vessel and swaying rungs testing the agility of his feet. The moment his boots landed on the deck above, he dropped his haversack to one side and stretched his arms languidly over his head. He made a show of bringing relief to an achy back, giving Asha time to join him, and himself time to evaluate the other topside occupants.

He'd been right in his assessment. For there was only one other up top, and he was preoccupied with the nets he was mending.

"I'll see that letter of introduction now." The sailor reached out a hand for it.

But Asha was over the gunwale now, so Trent leveled his rifle on the man instead.

"I say what—"

"Hush now, lad, for if you make a fuss, I might just have to shoot you so I can deal with the others who'll come to your aid." He motioned with the muzzle of his rifle for the man to lie down on the deck.

Asha had wasted no time in depositing RyAnne's violin near the haversack and cat-footing it over to the man repairing the nets, and now he prodded him into a sprawl next to the first man. Trent covered them while Asha bound and gagged them. The moment the two men were secured to the mizzenmast, Trent motioned for Asha to follow him below.

Why was it that now when he was close to rescuing RyAnne, his heart started hammering like a bosun repairing a loose deck railing? His mouth felt filled with cotton.

Please, Father, don't let me be too late this time.

In the darkness of her cell, RyAnne felt her way to the bulkhead and put her back to it. She tipped her head against the wood and eased out a sigh. She'd really done it this time. No one on the docks would have even known who she was—even if they'd seen her kidnapped. Trent was going to return to the room and find her missing. But by the time he figured out where she was, it would likely be too late. She would be sold to some palace in the East before he could discover what had happened to her.

Normally that thought would have sent her into a snit of despair, and yet she found herself feeling rather peaceful. She couldn't quite put her finger on the reason, except that she'd already been through so much and knew all her trials had only made her stronger. They'd made her lean more heavily on her heavenly Father. And so she would in this instance too.

If only she didn't have to leave behind the captain. But even in that she had at least known love. It would give her a reason to keep on living in the years ahead. And perhaps one day the captain would find her.

RyAnne huffed out a disparaging sigh. Now she really was in danger of putting a damper on her determination to hang on to her joy.

From behind her there came the *snick* of a match flaring to life, and warm illumination spilled through a square above her head, growing brighter as the match was apparently used to light a lantern.

RyAnne scrambled to her feet and took hold of the bars in the doorway, standing on her tiptoes to peer out and see if she could catch a glimpse of who might be in the passageway.

A figure stood outside her cell. The person was obviously studying her, but she could only make out a shadowy form, for they held the bright lantern high and in front of them.

RyAnne squinted and shaded her eyes. "Who's there? Can you please help me? I've been taken against my will. I'm the daughter of Doctor Ryan Hunter from Zanzibar. There is a man in Bagamoyo, Captain Trent Dawson, who will gladly pay you for my release."

A low snort preceded the lantern moving a little closer, but just then there was a sound in the passageway. Quiet voices. Stealthy steps.

The lantern light snuffed out, and the quick sound of retreating footsteps was the only evidence that someone had indeed been there.

Hinges squeaked. "RyAnne?"

"Captain!" She could hardly believe her ears. "Is that you? I'm here!"

"Asha, here!" Trent called. "The light."

A thrill of joy had RyAnne jumping up and down in her cell. "Be careful! Someone was just here!"

A soft light grew stronger as Asha's footsteps grew louder, and then he stepped into the room with a lantern held off to one side. It was truly them!

RyAnne stretched her hands through the bars.

But Trent was all business. "Someone was here? Which way did they go?"

Her joy deflated somewhat. He was quite put out with her this time. "I d-don't know exactly. They blew out the lantern before they retreated. But it had to be that way because you would have run into them if they'd come past you."

The captain moved beyond her cell door without so much as a glance her way. He held a rifle in his hands, its barrel glinting light from the lantern Asha held.

Asha at least smiled at her. "You are well, Miss Hunter?"

"I am. Thank you, Asha."

The captain and Asha searched the remainder of the compartment.

Aided by the lamplight, RyAnne made out one other cell, which was empty, and an assortment of barrels and foodstuffs stacked along the bulkheads and hull, and hanging from overhead beams. But none of them concealed a person, neither behind nor within. Trent growled. "We look again, Asha." They commenced their very thorough search a second time, but still not a soul was found hiding in the room.

Trent returned to stand before her cell, hands hooked on his hips. He glanced around, then strode over and took down a ring of keys from near the main entrance. His boots clomped loudly as they returned to her cell. As he thrust the key into the lock, he met her gaze through the bars. "Are you sure you saw someone? It couldn't have been your imagination?"

RyAnne lifted her chin. "Someone was there!"

Trent's mouth quirked, and when he swung the door open, he took her hand and yanked her into a fierce embrace.

She nestled her head beneath his chin, relishing the feel of his arms around her when only moments earlier she'd been certain she'd never experience this again. She felt a tremor work through him. So he truly was glad to find her safe. "I thought you seemed angry with me."

A sound rumbled in his chest. "Oh, I am. But we can talk about that later. For now, I need to get you to safety." He took her hand and firmly drew her out into the passageway. When Asha followed them, Trent turned and locked the door shut behind them. "Wherever they are hiding, that ought to hold them." He gave the stout oak door a slap with his palm. "Now come. Harcourt should be returning within the hour. We've a lot to accomplish before then." Trent led them all up to the quarterdeck.

RyAnne heard moaning and glanced up. Her brows rose. For there on the sterncastle stood four sailors all bound to the mizzenmast. One more had been bound to the deck's rail. Trent pointed her into the captain's cabin and thoroughly searched it.

The room was lavishly appointed with a red velvet settee and silk curtains cordoning off the feather-ticked bunk against the bulkhead. The desk was a golden-red hardwood with gorgeous dark grains and intricately etched leaves around the lip. Clawed feet were hewn with the same delicate leaves. A large mahogany statue, crudely carved to look like a giraffe, stood to one side of the door. It was lashed to the bulkhead with a couple loops of rope, presumably to keep it from rolling around in case of a storm.

RyAnne ran her hands over the smooth wood and then sank wearily onto the plush settee. "I suppose dealing in slaves must pay quite well." The thought made her feel rather ill. She rubbed the toe of her boot over the place on her ankle that was still healing from the manacles she'd worn for weeks on end.

Trent squatted before her and squeezed her shoulder. "We are going to put a stop to at least this ring. You have my word."

She pressed her lips together and nodded silently.

Trent angled his head. "I need your word that you'll stay in here. There's about to be some nasty business outside, and I can't do what I'll need to do while I'm worrying about your safety."

RyAnne didn't have the energy to even be offended that he didn't trust her to stay put. She only dipped her chin. "You have my word."

Trent started away, but a thought occurred to her. "Trent?"

He paused and looked at her.

"How did you know I was here?"

"Asha saw you kidnapped." He tilted his head. "I found the letters."

Her heart pounded. "That's why I was coming to find you. They have hidden words on them. I think heat—"

"Yes. I know." He seemed restless—in a hurry to return to the deck.

"Did you…heat them all?"

He nodded. "And they contain all the information we need to hand these scallywags over to Cornwall."

He left her then, and RyAnne paced the interior of the cabin. Surely her ordeal was almost over? All that remained was for Trent to capture William Harcourt, and then they would sail him and his crew to Commodore Cornwall and turn them over to him. Then she could go home and see Jasmine and Rory. And Mother. Her fingers clenched together in dread at the prospect of giving them all the bad news. But there was anticipation too. It would be good to see them again.

She paced past the desk again, trailing her hand across the top. Her fingers bumped over a silver letter opener, and she paused to pick it up. The handle was a carved indigo flower, and the sharp blade gleamed in the light from the porthole.

Beyond the cabin door, she heard raised voices. She dropped the letter opener back onto the desk and hurried to press her ear to the door. She didn't want to miss a word of what was being said out there.

Trent and Asha noticed the longboat leaving the docks at the same moment. Five men were aboard. A quick glance with a glass revealed that Harcourt was indeed among them. Trent strode over and made sure the rope ladder still hung to the waterline and then moved to stand behind a capstan. Asha had already taken his own shelter, out of sight.

To ensure that all of the men came aboard and none escaped, they would need to let them all board the ship before attempting to take them. This was likely the most dangerous part of this whole mission, for it would quickly become obvious that something was amiss when none of their crew met them on the foredeck.

He took a calming breath and studied the placid sky above. This was it. For RyAnne. And all those like her who hadn't been given a choice as their freedoms were snatched away.

One set of boots thumped to the deck. Followed by another.

"I say," one exclaimed. "Where is everyone?"

"Likely in their cups w' the cap'n's best ale." The other laughed.

Two more sets of boots landed on the deck before the first voice spoke again. "I'm not liking the feeling of this, Captain."

"Aye," Harcourt responded. "Spread out and see if you can discover what's amiss."

"Asha, now!" Trent yelled as he swung out from behind the capstan and leveled his rifle on the five men, one of whom was still straddled over the gunwale. Trent adjusted his aim so that it rested pointedly on Harcourt. "Tell your men to lay down their arms."

Asha cocked his pistol meaningfully from where he'd appeared on the other side of the group.

Flanked on both sides, the men who had automatically reached for their weapons hesitated and looked to their captain.

Harcourt was no fool. He slowly lifted his hands into the air. "Lay down your weapons, men." As his men complied and Asha set to tying them up, one by one, William glowered passionately at Trent. "What is this all about?"

Trent almost laughed. "Oh, I think you know."

"Actually, I have no idea," Harcourt retorted, but there was a tremor in his voice that gave away the lie.

Trent delayed his response until Asha had finished tying each of Harcourt's four men and had tugged Harcourt's hands behind his back. Then Trent tilted his head to assess the impact of his next words. "I have letters written by the late Ali Khalifa that say otherwise." He motioned to the gunnysack he'd left near the gunwale.

"Late?" Harcourt broke off and glanced down to study the sack, his features paling slightly.

So perhaps he hadn't been aware that his lackey had been killed. "I'm afraid he was attacked by a lion that had been stalking the slave caravan he was driving across the continent. It only happened a couple days ago. It's no wonder you hadn't heard yet."

Harcourt's face twisted into dismay.

"I can see the question on your face. You are wondering what happened to all the slaves. I'm afraid I took the liberty of freeing all of them." Trent felt great satisfaction upon delivering that bit of news.

William's face was now nearly as pale as his white shirt.

"It's a nasty business… Making profit off the lives of others. So much can go wrong, aye? Including letters left behind that reveal far more than you are likely to be comfortable with. Names… places…past interactions." Since Asha had resumed his vigil over the men with his pistol, Trent took the opportunity to lower his rifle and rub at the skin of his neck dramatically. "Smuggling slaves is a hanging offense, isn't it, Asha?"

Asha nodded with a smile.

William shuffled his feet uneasily and swallowed visibly. "Nonsense. What could Ali have to say about me that would result in such impertinent actions on your part?"

Trent couldn't help the smile that tilted his lips. "He said plenty. And we'll let Commodore Llewellyn Cornwall determine whether my actions are impertinent or justified." He motioned toward the aft ladder. "For now we should get you and your men settled into your quarters belowdecks." He tilted Asha a look. "Asha, I'm thinking that they should make the trip to Cornwall's estate in the same manner that any slaves might have been asked to travel, don't you? Perhaps that will help them to have a little more compassion the next time, should they somehow weasel their way out of this?"

"Ye cain't put us down there!" One of the crew protested. "There only be a meter between decks, and I get sick in tight spaces."

"Awe! Don't worry lad. You'll be fine." Trent took his arm in one hand and the nearest sailor's in the other. "The trip to Llewellyn's will only take a few days from here. What say you, Asha? A week?"

Asha nodded, even though Trent felt quite certain he had no idea how long the trip would actually take.

Trent continued making his point by offering the sailor a large grin. "There. You see? Certainly nothing like a cross-Pacific trip to India or China."

Chapter 30
The Joy of the Morning

RyAnne covered her mouth and chuckled.

The sailor protested loudly. "But some of the slaves don't survive such crossings!"

Trent's rejoinder was almost glib. "Since you are apparently of such better lineage than the people you seem happy to sell, I'm certain your hearty qualities will see you in good stead and bring you alive and well to the end of our sail. Surviving Newgate, now that's going to be the trick."

RyAnne was about to start laughing again, when she heard a floorboard squeak behind her. Her heart lurched, and she spun around.

Brayden stood there.

And he had a pistol in his hand.

"Hello, RyAnne." His boyish smile tilted his lips, but there was something hard about his eyes. She'd known him long enough to recognize that.

"Brayden." RyAnne touched her fingers to her throat, her eyes dropping to the pistol. "How did you get in here?"

His smile slanted into a look of consternation. He ignored her question, but he stepped to one side, and she could see that behind him a panel in one wall had come open. Brayden must have been the one in the storeroom below, and he'd somehow escaped into a passageway that led from that room to this.

Brayden hooked one thumb into his belt loop and kept the gun trained on her in a lazy fashion. "I heard that Anne isn't really your mother. That the woman who bore you was a slave of your father's. Is that true?"

RyAnne spread her hands. "'Tis as you say."

A muscle pulsed in his jaw. "How long have you known?"

"All my life." She laced her fingers before her.

"All your life… And yet you let me make a fool of myself over you? As though you were not tainted? Not someone on whom I would be ashamed to waste my attentions?"

The words were like a slap in RyAnne's face. She took a step back and came up against the cool wood of the cabin door. "I'm still me, Brayden. Still the friend you played with in the indigo fields for all those years."

"I never would have been permitted to associate with you had your true lineage been known!" He shook his head, and his lips twisted into a sneer now. "No. You are nothing like the woman I thought you to be."

"Simply because of a few drops of blood that flow through my veins that you didn't know about before?"

"*Cursed* blood."

RyAnne's anger spilled over before she could think better of it. "If we are cursed, it is because of trifling-minded men like you who feel empowered to abuse simply because the color of our skin is a little different." She stretched out one arm and yanked up her sleeve until her wrist was revealed. "Look here! What do you see that gives you so much cause to feel superior?!"

Brayden's face transformed into a hard mask of anger. "Impertinence!" He stepped forward and grabbed her by one arm, thrusting his gun into her ribs. His fingers dug so painfully into her arm that she clenched her teeth to hold back a whimper.

But there was something she had to know. "So all those times when you spoke out against slavery? Like at the ball that night? What was that?"

Brayden leaned in and spoke close to her ear. "Appearances, dear RyAnne. Appearances. We can't hardly be suspected of smuggling when we are so outspoken against the mean practices of slavery, now can we?"

"Why would you even resort to smuggling? You certainly aren't in need of the money!"

A look crossed his face that filled her with realization.

"That's it, isn't it? Something happened, and you needed the money. What was it?"

Brayden shrugged. "It wasn't so much the need as the want. Father realized there was much greater profit in shipping slaves than indigo, yet the plantation was the perfect cover. We already had the fleet of ships so..." He shrugged again, as if to say *why not?*

RyAnne felt a swirl of nausea.

Brayden took in her face and chuckled, but there was no humor in the sound. "Now open the door and stay quiet. Your pretty little hide is worth quite a lot, and I'd hate to have to mar it with a bullet."

A shiver of revulsion slipped down RyAnne's back. How could she have been so deceived by this man? She slowly reached out and unlatched the door.

Brayden thrust her out into the sunlight, sticking fast to her side.

Trent stood several paces away, set to descend the aft ladder with two of his prisoners, William Harcourt and a sailor RyAnne didn't recognize. Several others must have already been taken belowdecks, for RyAnne only saw two other sailors left topside, and they were both still tied to the mizzenmast. Asha also was nowhere to be seen. He had probably taken a couple of the smugglers down ahead of Trent.

"Dawson!" Brayden bellowed.

Trent jolted and spun around, his prisoners still clasped in each hand. RyAnne noted that he and Asha had taken time to gag each of the captives with a strip of sheeting. Probably to prevent them from conspiring with each other once in the hold.

Brayden waved his pistol in a quick flash before pressing it back to RyAnne's ribs again. "I'd seriously consider letting my father and his men go. I hear you have quite a fondness for Miss Hunter here."

Even from this distance RyAnne could see the telltale bunching of Trent's jaw that indicated his irritation. He pinned her with a look that narrowed his gray-green eyes and demanded to know if she'd left the captain's cabin.

She supposed she deserved his suspicion after the many times she'd disregarded his requests. Swallowing, she gave a little shake of her head. "He came through a passage in the wall."

Trent transferred his gaze back to Brayden. Deliberately, he released the two men on either side of him. He bent forward slowly and laid his rifle on the deck and then raised his hands almost languidly.

William's and the soldier's hands were still bound, but they both quick-stepped several paces away from Trent. The sailor turned to watch the confrontation unfold. But William darted over to a gunnysack by the rail and kicked it forward, drawing Brayden's attention to it with a couple grunts.

"What have we here?" Keeping his gun trained on them, Brayden took up one corner of the sack and dumped out the contents.

The two wooden boxes that RyAnne knew would be full of Khalifa's letters tumbled out. Brayden opened the box closest to him and pulled out one of the parchments.

RyAnne gasped, and her gaze darted to Trent. Those weren't the hidden messages!

He nodded subtly, his face calm.

RyAnne glanced back toward the rail and saw her violin case there. And from the narrowing of Trent's eyes, she knew all the letters must be in with her violin.

She looked down to find Brayden's attention on her. He glanced back and forth from her to Trent and then to the violin.

RyAnne's heart pounded. *Please don't—*

Brayden strode to the violin and hefted it, still keeping them under the eye of his pistol. "Let's see what we have in here, shall we?" He flipped the latches and dumped the contents of the case, violin and all, onto the deck.

RyAnne's eyes fell closed as her violin, the silk cover, a bundle of letters, and a leather journal with the Harcourt insignia all tumbled to the boards.

A muscle bunched in Trent's jaw, and he looked out toward the horizon for a moment. RyAnne saw him take a slow breath.

She had done this. It was her reaction to the fake letters that had clued Brayden in to the ruse.

RyAnne returned her focus to Brayden. He had tucked the packet of letters beneath his arm and was flipping through the logbook. What would he do with them? All their evidence against the Harcourts resided in those! Could she distract him?

She stepped toward him. "Brayden, please! You must reconsider what you are doing here."

"RyAnne! Stay back!" Trent's voice held real fear that made her heed his command.

"Not another step, nor another word!" A hard edge had crept into Brayden's words that made RyAnne's heart stutter in fear. His hand trembled, and if she had kept moving toward him, there was no telling what he might have done. He looked at his father, lifting the book. "That weasel Khalifa has written down everything!" He dropped the journal and the packet of letters into a nearby cauldron and withdrew a match from his front pocket.

RyAnne's eyes dropped closed. Of course he had matches on his person. He'd just been down in the hold and had lit the lantern. Despair threatened to be her undoing. Tears pricked at the corners of her eyes. After all their heartache and loss, was it going to come down to this moment? Surely they weren't just going to stand here and watch Brayden burn up all their evidence?

Brayden struck the match against the deck, and it flared to life.

RyAnne looked to Trent. What should they do? What *could* they do with Brayden—especially in his current state of mind—training a gun on them?

Trent shook his head at her, commanding her without a word to remain still.

Brayden dropped the match onto the pile of papers, and RyAnne felt all her hopes flag as the flame quickly spread to devour the evidence.

Next Brayden picked up both wooden drawers and dropped them on top of the fire. The flames licked greedily at the wood. When the fire had completely consumed the contents of the cauldron, Brayden resumed his position by RyAnne, with his pistol gouging into her ribs.

"There, now that is taken care of, and we can pick up where we left off."

William was grinning from ear to ear behind his gag and looked quite pleased.

RyAnne recalled that when she'd met him on shore, he'd hesitated before he said Brayden was "not here, no." She realized now that he meant that Brayden was aboard the ship. Why hadn't she thought of it and warned Trent? But none of them could have known that the ship held secret passages! Another thought struck… Was Brayden even the same man that she'd seen with the lantern when she was locked up below?

"So that was you that we couldn't find in the storeroom?" Trent's question was the epitome of calm and proved that his thoughts were traveling the same channels as hers.

"It was." Brayden sounded quite proud of himself.

With a jolt of admiration, RyAnne realized what Trent was doing. They'd just discovered that Brayden was working alone.

"I should have thought there might be a secret passage. Quite clever of you."

Brayden gave a little half bow, keeping his pistol pressed firmly to her side. "Thank you!"

"Just to satisfy my curiosity… Where was the entrance to your passageway?" Trent's voice was rather loud for the distance that stretched between them, and RyAnne realized he must be speaking for Asha's benefit. Thank heavens he had been out of sight when she and Brayden had stepped out of the captain's cabin.

William leaned forward and tried to say something, but his gag was doing its job quite effectively.

And Brayden grinned languidly. "Don't worry, Father. I've no intention of telling him the location of the secret passage."

William's shoulders slumped in relief, and he grumbled something else indiscernible, but Brayden didn't seem to notice.

RyAnne's heart pounded with despair! If only he had told them the location, Asha might have been able to use it to help them. Now he would be no use to them, for there was no way for him to come on deck without Brayden seeing him.

Brayden was caught up in his own cleverness. "So, Dawson.

It appears you are at a disadvantage. First you are going to untie my father and his crew, and then we are going to sail out of this harbor, and when we get far enough out, we are going to dump you overboard." He laughed. "I hope you can swim?"

"And if I refuse?" Trent's voice remained calm. He folded his arms and stuffed his fists into his armpits, looking for all the world like he planned to remain that way for quite some time.

RyAnne realized he was doing all he could to delay.

Brayden's laugh was almost hysterical now. "You may refuse to swim, if you like."

Trent only looked at him, allowing the moments to stretch.

Brayden stopped his cackling as suddenly as he'd begun. "Get on with untying them!"

RyAnne took a breath as Trent slowly started toward William. Trent seemed set on delay! And delaying was something she could help with. She only prayed Brayden's gun wouldn't go off by accident.

She felt her hands grow clammy at just the thought.

Trent would likely instruct her to keep out of it. But she could do this! And hopefully it would give Trent or Asha the time to do something.

Giving a little whimper, she pressed the back of one hand to her forehead, rolled her eyes up, and slumped into the best faint she could conjure. She'd never actually fainted herself. But she'd seen Mother do it a time or two.

"What the devil?!" Brayden exclaimed, clutching at her as she collapsed.

RyAnne was thankful for the resistance of his arm that had somewhat broken her fall, and also thankful to note that her person was still intact without any bullet holes.

She heard Trent's boots thumping across the deck. He was probably set on taking advantage of Brayden while he was distracted, but in the next moment Brayden exclaimed, "Stop right there, Dawson, before I put a shot through her pretty skull!"

RyAnne felt the cold press of a muzzle against her forehead, and it was all she could do to keep herself from flinching.

"I've stopped! I've stopped. Please, just help her." Trent's voice sounded distraught.

A trace of guilt washed through RyAnne. Did Trent know she was pretending? She dared not open her eyes to offer him assurances. She lay as still as possible, hardly even daring to inhale.

"Is she breathing?" Trent persisted. "Please, you have to check to see if she is breathing!"

RyAnne shallowed her breaths as much as she could and forced herself to remain limp.

She felt Brayden lean over her at the same moment she heard William grunt out an exclamation.

Brayden started to pull away. "Wha—"

There was a loud hollow *thunk*, and then Brayden's dead weight collapsed atop her.

RyAnne's eyes flew open. Trent and Asha both leaned over her, peering concernedly into her face. Asha held the large wooden giraffe from the captain's cabin in his hands.

William's cry of anguished frustration was loud despite the cloth stuck in his mouth, and RyAnne heard his footsteps slapping the deck.

Trent must have heard them too, because he stood, spun around, and, in one smooth motion, brought his fist into Harcourt's midsection.

William squawked and bent double, coughing and wheezing through the cloth.

Trent guided the man to his knees and then eased him over till he was on his side. "Lay here and catch your breath while I tie up your son."

William's shoulders slumped in defeat. RyAnne could tell from his expression that he knew he'd been beaten. With his hands tied securely behind him the way they were, there wasn't much resistance he could offer. RyAnne almost felt sorry for the man.

Trent stood and came back to her. There was a glimmer of admiration in his eyes when they met hers. "Asha, help me get Harcourt off of her, would you? Nice hit, by the way. Remind me never to come up behind you in a dark corridor."

Asha chuckled. "Long time coming."

Each man took one of Brayden's arms and hauled him up and off of her. He hung limply between them, and when she sat up, she could see a large lump forming on the back of his head.

The men laid him out facedown on the deck, and while Asha set about tying him up, Trent turned back to her. He helped her sit up and then took her shoulders and peered into her face. "Trouble, RyAnne, simply has a way of sniffing you out. Are you all right?"

She nodded, even though a tremble was starting in the vicinity of her knees now that the danger was past.

Trent pulled her into a firm embrace that revealed all the fear untethering from inside him. She felt his arms shaking.

She eased back until she could look him in the eye. "I'm fine, Trent. I'm fine. But we lost all our evidence! I'm so sorry! I drew his attention to the violin."

He shook his head and tapped his temple. "If there is one thing managing a fleet of ships with my father all my life has taught me, it's to never put all your eggs in one basket." He glanced over at William, who glowered back passionately. Trent lifted his shirt slowly and pulled a parchment from beneath his belt. "You see, RyAnne, it's not really written evidence we need to convict the Harcourts in a court of law. It's the testimony of people. And"—he flicked the paper with a smile of satisfaction—"I have all the names Khalifa mentioned written out right here! All we have to do is offer a few of them deals, and I'm sure we'll have all the testimonial corroboration that we'll need." Trent stood and hauled William to his feet. "Because, you see, if there's one thing I've learned over the years about those who live on the wrong side of the law, it's that no one trusts each other. If all of them kept quiet… Well, then we'd have a problem. But I'm guessing tongues will be wagging before a fortnight has past."

William glanced out over the water and uttered a sound that could only be interpreted as a curse.

"For shame, William! A lady is present," Trent admonished

him with a grin in RyAnne's direction. Holding on to William's arm with one hand, he squeezed her shoulder with the other. "Why don't you go on into the cabin? Asha and I will get these gentlemen settled in the hold, and then we'll be on our way to Cornwall's."

RyAnne retrieved her violin and tucked it carefully back into its case. She was relieved to see that it didn't seem to have suffered any damage. As she once more sank onto the settee in the captain's cabin, she noticed the silver letter opener that had been on the desk lying on the floor near where the wooden giraffe had once been lashed to the wall. Asha had obviously found the hidden passageway and then, upon arriving in the captain's cabin, used the sharp blade to slice through the thin ropes lashing the giraffe to the bulkhead.

RyAnne could hardly believe that their search might have finally come to an end. There was only one additional thing that could make her feel more complete than she felt right now, and that was to see her family again.

Trent had been correct about the wagging tongues. Commodore Cornwall had immediately sent fast ships to Zanzibar to round up the people on Trent's list, and he hadn't encountered any trouble getting most of them to talk. Their testimony would be the nail that sealed the lid of the Harcourts' coffins.

Trent and RyAnne now stood on the shore below Commodore Llewellyn Cornwall's estate. The commodore was about to board his ship to take the captives to England for a trial, and there was a great deal of glee glimmering in his gaze. He stretched his hand out to Trent. "Once again, I thank you, Captain, for a job well done. Her Majesty will be most pleased that we have shut down this ring. I've already sent ships to the smuggling locations you remembered from Khalifa's correspondence. I'm sure we will have it wrapped up within a fortnight."

"Good. I hope so."

"Before I go…" He held out a hefty bag. "Your promised payment."

Trent accepted the bag with a nod of thanks.

RyAnne was surprised when Commodore Cornwall turned to her next. "Young lady, I'm sure you've had quite an ordeal, but I wonder if you might consider sailing to England and sharing your story before Parliament? It is stories such as yours that help in the forming of new and better laws."

Whom shall I send, child?

RyAnne felt a chill pebble her skin as an answer formed almost immediately in her spirit. *Here I am, Father. Send me.* To the commodore she responded, "I think I would be very happy to do that. If you set it up, I will go, providing"—she turned a look on Trent—"that my soon-to-be husband agrees to sail me there?"

Trent laughed. "I'm beginning to realize that there won't be much I can deny you."

The commodore's chuckle was hearty. He slapped Trent on the back. "That's as it should be, lad. As it should be!" To RyAnne he said, with a bow over her hand, "I will arrange for you to stand before Parliament next session, if that is suitable to you?"

RyAnne lifted a brow to Trent.

He nodded.

She turned back to the commodore. "Next session will be most suitable. Thank you for asking me."

The Commodore waved away RyAnne's thanks. "'Tis I who should be thanking you. After all, you are a beautiful and well-educated young woman who according to the laws of the land ought to be stripped of all your rights and left to the whims of others. But thoughts on that are changing, and you've been through so much! You will be the perfect one to speak directly to the heart of the matter. Sometimes it takes the humanizing of an ethereal conceptualization to open people's eyes to truth. Perhaps all the severe hardships you've encountered will aid the politicians in opening their eyes to change, eh?" He patted her hand. "Well… I'd best be off before the tide leaves without me." With a hearty wave over his shoulder, he climbed aboard the dingy that would row him out to his ship, which was anchored in the deeper waters farther out.

But the moment he walked away, RyAnne dropped to her knees with a gasp.

"What is it?" Trent sank to his haunches before her. "Are you hurt?"

RyAnne shook her head but placed one hand over her heart. "No, I'm just so overwhelmed with all the answers God just heaped upon me. Things I've been praying about for so long. Do you remember me telling you earlier that I felt the Lord was asking me to go somewhere, but I wasn't sure where that was?"

Trent nodded.

"The moment Commodore Cornwall asked me to go to England, I had my answer."

Trent smiled with understanding.

"And do you remember when I asked you how a good God could be defended in the face of such misery as I had witnessed?"

Again he nodded.

RyAnne threw up her hands. "I've been in such turmoil. Trying to understand how a good and loving God could allow such terrible things to happen. I understand man's free will plays into it. As well as people who may be called to do good things but choose not to respond. But for my part, I can honestly say that it was all for this moment." She gestured to where the commodore was just ascending the ladder to the deck of his ship. "If I hadn't followed Papa from Zanzibar to here, and if I hadn't been captured and hadn't gone through all those hardships, then I wouldn't have a story to tell to Parliament. But because of my hardships, laws might be changed! Others' lives might be bettered." She could no longer hold the tears at bay. "And for that to happen I would go through these last torturous months all over again."

"Come here." Trent stood and pulled her to him, tucking her against his chest. He rested his chin atop her head. "Months ago when I had first taken on the task of escorting your father to the village, I questioned the veracity of his call. I wondered if God really called people to go to specific places. And figured your father ought to be content to go to the places that were easier for him to reach. But he insisted that it was to that exact village he must go. I think looking back now we can see how the Lord wove all those varied colored threads to the accomplishing of His good purpose. Meeting Kako here at Cornwall's… Kako's father being the chief of the exact village your father was called to… You saving Nyanja's life and us learning that she was from that very same tribe also… The confrontation with Wankulu on our way to the village that eventually led to your capture… All of those strands came together and brought us to this place of answers."

RyAnne sighed. "But there were so many tragedies that happened along the way that are still unexplained."

Trent rumbled a sound of agreement. "But the Lord is a master artist, aye? And He's weaving so many stories other than just our own together. Just because we can't see where the threads of trials or tragedies lead for someone else, it doesn't mean that God isn't using them to perfect his tapestry."

RyAnne felt a pure wave of peace for the first time in many months. She wasn't guaranteed a life of no trials. But she was guaranteed that she served a God who loved all of mankind beyond measure and that He was trustworthy and loving.

He did indeed work all things for the good of those who loved Him.

RyAnne sighed in near perfect contentment. "Trent?"

"Hmmm?"

"Take me home?"

Trent eased her back and pressed his forehead to hers. "On one condition…"

Her lips tilted up at the gleam of mischief in his eyes. "What's that?"

"Marry me right now," he said. "Before you decide to run off to a cockfight, or a crocodile tries to attack you, or another slave driver captures you, or you simply change your mind."

RyAnne laughed. She knew he was teasing, but she played along. She gave him a *be serious* look. "There is not a chance of me changing my mind, Captain. But I can't marry you right this moment. Who would perform the ceremony?"

He grunted. "As a captain I'm qualified, but I don't suppose I can officiate my own wedding. As soon as we land on Zanzibar, then?" He pumped his brows hopefully.

This time RyAnne batted his arm. "I need time to sew a wedding dress. And it might be nice to invite our families?"

"You could wear a gunny sack for all I care," he grumbled. He looked at her intently. "How fast do you think you can get your family to the beach after we dock? Garrett has a fast horse and is used to taking my orders, so I can get him there right snappy."

RyAnne laughed at his antics. "The beach is it?"

"Mmm." He slid his fingers down her arms until they intertwined with her own. "Looking over the Indian ocean where I first realized I wanted to marry you."

RyAnne's brows lifted. "When was that?"

"After I'd found you nearly dead in my longboat and took you into the ocean to cool you off. You woke up in my arms, and I knew right then that I would do anything to keep you safe." His thumbs grazed the sides of her hands, and he pulled her closer.

Her heart was so full of joy it was near to bursting. She reveled in the feel of his arms around her, curling her fingers to intertwine with his at the small of her back. "I'm quite content right here, Captain. Mayhap there is no need for a wedding at all." She grinned at him cheekily.

He growled. But a good-natured smile tipped up the corners of his lips and crinkled the corners of his eyes. "Perhaps I'll have to kidnap you myself." He scooped her up and started down the beach.

RyAnne laughed. "Let's have none of that. I've experienced quite enough of kidnappings for a lifetime, thank you very much. How about Saturday next?"

"Now you're talking sense," he said.

And then he kissed her.

Exactly one week after *The Wasp* docked in the Stone Town harbor, RyAnne sat aboard a topless carriage with her wedding dress tucked in about her as they headed toward the white-sanded beach Trent had chosen for their special day. Valah and Halame, her friends the princesses of Zanzibar, sat across from her on the bench next to Jasmine, and Rory sat next to her, plastered to his side of the carriage on instructions from Jasmine that he not crumple even a frill of her lace.

The driver pulled the carriage to a stop at the head of the path, and Rory helped the girls climb down. A small stone wall separated the road from the beach below and prevented RyAnne from seeing the seats they'd carefully arranged in the sand the evening before. Seats that were at this very moment filled with guests who were here to celebrate with them.

As RyAnne waited for her turn to alight, she took in her surroundings. She wanted to savor every moment of this day.

The day couldn't have been more beautiful. She closed her eyes and memorized the sounds all around her. The shushing of the waves against the shore. The birdsong warbling through the air. The wind whispering secrets to the palm leaves overhead.

Thank you, Father, for Your many blessings.

"If I don't get you down there soon, it is reported that Trent is going to wear a trench in the sand," Rory chuckled.

RyAnne opened her eyes to see him stretching out one hand to help her down. The moment her feet were on the ground, Jasmine swooped in, brushed Rory aside, and set to adjusting ribbons and straightening lace. She gave one last glance and then stepped back with a satisfied nod.

Valah and Halame opened the boot of the carriage and pulled out the bouquets they had carefully laid out before leaving the house thirty minutes ago.

RyAnne suddenly felt all atremble with nervousness like she hadn't felt since she'd been chained to a tree while thinking Trent was dead. "You're sure I look okay?" She bent and fussed with the hem of the dress even as Jasmine thrust into her hands her bouquet of bougainvillea and bird of paradise they'd cut from Mother's garden just this morning.

"You couldn't be more beautiful," Jasmine reassured. "Now come along. The girls and I will walk down ahead of you. Bishop Tozer is already waiting at the front. And the last time I checked, there was a very handsome groom waiting rather impatiently at the end of the aisle."

RyAnne smiled at that.

Jasmine led Valah and Halame off, and RyAnne knew they would be headed to the seats that had been saved for them next to Mother.

Taking a deep breath, she stepped forward onto the stone pathway that led down to the beach.

Rory smiled at her and stretched out his arm. "One look at you, and Captain Trent Dawson will be lucky if he can keep breathing."

"Let's just hope I don't lose the breakfast Mother forced me to eat, while we're walking down the aisle." RyAnne shook out her hands nervously.

Rory laughed. He gave Bishop Tozer a signal then, and the orchestra struck up the music.

RyAnne hadn't been joking about losing her breakfast, but the moment they stepped past the wall and her eyes landed on Trent, all of her nervousness washed away. He was dressed in the same ballroom finery that he'd worn on that long-ago night of the Harcourts' ball. So much had grown between them from that moment to this.

Mother was the first one to stand as Rory started them down the aisle, and as RyAnne met her gaze, a bubble of thankfulness swelled in her chest. The day she and Trent had arrived back in Stone Town, Mother had still been abed recovering from cholera. But RyAnne had gone to her immediately and apologized for her part in the pain Mother must have been feeling for all these years. Mother had apologized for her own prickliness, and they had shared tears over the loss of Papa. Mother had seemed to be much softer after that. And RyAnne couldn't be more thankful than to see her smiling from the front row. Though she knew she would likely never share the same relationship with Mother that Jasmine did, she was thankful to at least have taken a step in a positive direction.

Asha was there toward the back, and even though he did not smile, there was a softness about his expression that she didn't remember seeing before. Trent had hired him as one of the crewmen on the newest ship he'd purchased from his father, who was hoping to turn his entire fleet over to Trent soon.

John Knight, Trent's bosun, was there, with Dabu, Trent's youngest crewman, squirming by his side. Two weeks after the village was sacked, John had received word that his captain had been killed and RyAnne captured. He and the crew of *The Bee* had sadly made their way back to Stone Town to collect Garrett, and had arrived only hours after Trent had docked. RyAnne almost giggled now as she remembered how gleeful the padded bosun had been to find them both alive and well. He'd quite nearly danced an entire jig.

Valah's attention upon them was rapt, but RyAnne wasn't fooled. Her friend was looking at Rory, not her. And from his seat in the front row on Trent's side of the assemblage, Garrett wasn't even pretending to look at her. His gaze had moved across the aisle, where it rested upon her sister. Jasmine was trying valiantly to keep her focus on RyAnne, but her gaze kept slipping back to the man across the way. And when Garrett winked quite boldly, RyAnne giggled to see Jasmine's face match the bougainvillea of her bouquet with such perfection.

Her gaze returned to Trent then, and she couldn't remember the last time she had felt this much happiness. Rory handed her off, and she slipped her fingers into the warm, strong grasp of the man who would always hold her heart. His gray-green eyes crinkled at the corners, and she heard his soft sigh of contentment as he tugged her closer and tucked her hand into the crook of his arm.

The details of the ceremony were fuzzy. She must have mumbled her lines in all the right places however, for suddenly

Bishop Tozer was pronouncing them husband and wife. Trent turned her to face him. He swept a quick, appreciative glance down the length of her before he drew her into his arms with a pump of his brows. And RyAnne knew she would always remember the first kiss they shared as husband and wife, standing on the white-sanded beach with their dearest friends and family cheering wildly behind them.

Dear Reader,

Yes, lemon juice has been used for thousands of years as an invisible ink. The acidity in the juice weakens the fibers of the paper slightly so that when heated, that portion of the paper darkens sooner than the rest. African heat in this portion of the country can often climb to 120 degrees in the shade. Even up into WW I and WW II methods such as these were being used to smuggle secrets. A little Googling on "invisible inks" will reveal some fascinating stories for those who might be interested in learning more. For this story, I needed something simple that would have been readily available in Africa during that time and that could be developed with a very simple method. The lemon juice ink was the perfect solution. No pun intended!

I hope you have enjoyed this conclusion to the Sonnets of the Spice Isle series. If you would like to find more of my historical fiction, please check out my website at www.lynnettebonner.com. I also have a very simple request… Please take a moment to leave an honest review on Amazon or Goodreads. These don't have to be wordy, but each review helps others know whether this is a story they might enjoy and gives the series more visibility on Amazon.

Thanks for reading, dear friends. I couldn't do what I love to do without you!

Blessings to one and all,

Lynnette

If you enjoyed On the Wings of a Whisper, you might also enjoy…

THE SHEPHERD'S HEART - BOOK 1

ROCKY MOUNTAIN Oasis

He's different from any man she's ever known.
However, she's sworn never to risk her heart again.

Brooke Baker, sold as a mail-order bride, looks to her future with dread but firm resolve. If she survived Uncle Jackson, she can survive anyone.

When Sky Jordan hears that his nefarious cousin has sent for a mail-order bride, he knows he has to prevent the marriage. No woman deserves to be left to that fate. Still, he's as surprised as anyone to find himself standing next to her before the minister.

Brooke's new husband turns out to be kinder than any man has ever been. But then the unthinkable happens and she holds the key that might save innocent lives but destroy Sky all in one fell swoop. It's a choice too unbearable to contemplate…but a choice that must be made.

A thirsty soul. Alluring hope. An Oasis of love.
Step into a day when outlaws ran free, the land was wild, and guns blazed at the drop of a hat.

Find out more here: www.lynnettebonner.com